THE ULTIMATE HIJACK

Six hundred miles east of Moscow, the deadliest aeroplane in the world is being made ready for its final weapon trials. It is the Mig-31 – NATO codename 'Firefox' – and with its 4,000-plus m.p.h. speeds, impenetrable anti-radar screen and thought-controlled weapons-system it poses the greatest threat to the global balance of military power since the atomic bomb. There is no way that the West's technology can catch up with the Firefox in time. Unless . . .

In desperation, a joint British Intelligence/ CIA team devises the most daring undercover operation since the Second World War. The best military pilot in the West must be smuggled into the Soviet Union and on to the closely guarded base where the ultimate warplane awaits its final proving tests. His mission: hijack the Firefox . . .

FIREFOX is one of the most gripping aviation thrillers ever written. Taut, compelling and brilliantly researched, it moves at trans-sonic speed to a climax of explosive, nerve-shredding intensity.

Firefox

CRAIG THOMAS

THE CRAIG THOMAS LIBRARY

SPHERE BOOKS LIMITED
London and Sydney

First published in Great Britain by
Michael Joseph Ltd 1977
Copyright © 1977 by Craig Thomas
Published by Sphere Books Ltd 1978
30–32 Gray's Inn Road, London WC1X 8JL
Reprinted 1978 (three times), 1979 (three times),
1980 (twice), 1981, 1982 (five times), 1983 (three times)
1984 (twice), 1985 (twice)

Printed and bound in Great Britain by
Collins, Glasgow

for TERRY
who built the Firefox, and made her fly

ACKNOWLEDGEMENTS

I wish to acknowledge the invaluable help given to me, in time and expertise, by T. R. Jones, with all the technical matters connected with the experimental aircraft that features so prominently in the book.

I am indebted also for their assistance with matters geographical to Miss Audrey Simmonds and Mr Graham Simms; I would also like to thank Mr Peter Payne, whose enthusiastic scepticism kept me alert, but hopeful, during the writing of the book.

I am indebted finally to various publications, particularly to John Barron's highly informative and invaluable book, *KGB*, and to the admirable series of Jane's publications – particularly to current editions of *All the World's Aircraft*, *Fighting Ships*, and *Weapons Systems*, from each of which I gleaned much valuable technical information.

Craig Thomas
Lichfield

Nor law, nor duty bade me fight,
Nor public men nor cheering crowds,
A lonely impulse of delight
Drove to this tumult in the clouds;
I balanced all, brought all to mind,
The years to come seemed waste of breath,
A waste of breath the years behind
In balance with this life, this death.

W. B. Yeats

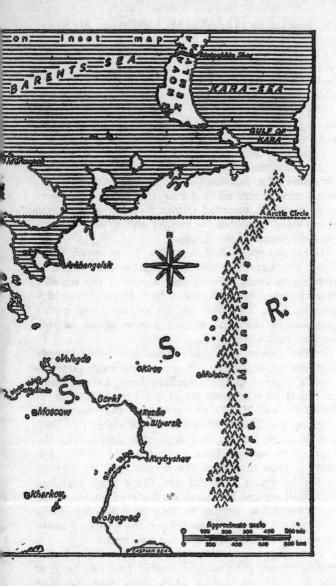

BARENTS SEA

KARA-SEA

GULF OF KARA

Murmansk

Arctic Circle

Arkhangelsk

S. S. R.

Vologda

Kirov

Molotov

River Volga
Rybinsk

S.
S.
R.
Moscow

Gorki

Kazan

Ural

Bljarsk

River Volga

Kuybyshev

Orsk

Kharkov

Volgograd

Approximate scale

```
100    200    300    400    500 mls
   200    400    600    800 km
```

CASPIAN SEA

The man lay on the bed in his hotel room, his hands raised like claws above his chest, as if reaching for his eyes. His body was stretched out, rigid with tension. A heavy perspiration shone on his brow and darkened the shirt beneath his arms. His eyes were wide open, and he was dreaming.

The nightmare did not come often now; it was like a fading malaria. He had made it that way—he had, not Buckholz or the psychiatrists at Langley. He despised them. He had done it himself. Yet, when the dream did come, it returned with all its old force, the fossilization of all memory and all conscience. It was all that was left of Vietnam. Even as he suffered, sweated within its toils, a cold part of his mind observed its images and effects—charting the ravages of the disease.

In his dream he had become a Vietnamese, Viet-Cong or peasant it did not matter—and he was burning to death, slowly and horribly; the napalm that the searching Phantom had dropped was devouring him. The roar of the retreating jets was drowned in the roar of the flames as he singed, burned, began to melt. . . .

In the flames, too, other times and other images flickered; flying sparks. Even as his muscles withered, shriveled in the appalling heat, he saw himself, as if from a point far at the back of his brain, flying the old Mig-21 and frozen in the moment of catching the USAF Phantom in his sights . . . then the drugs in Saigon, the dope that had led to the time when he had been caught in the sights of a Mig . . . then there was the breakdown, the months in the Veterans' Hospital and the crying, bleeding minds all around him until he teetered on the verge of madness and wanted to sink into the new darkness where he would not hear the cries of other minds or the new shrieks of his own brain.

Then there was the work in the hospital, the classic atonement that had turned to a vile taste at the back of his throat. Then there was the Mig, and learning to fly Russian, think Russian, be Russian ... Lebedev, the defector with the Georgian accent, they had brought in to coach him, thoroughly—because he had to be fluent. . . .

Then the training on the American-copied Mig-25, and the study of Belenko's debriefing, Belenko who had flown a Foxbat to Japan years before . . . and the days and weeks in the simulator, flying a plane he had never seen, that did not exist.

The napalm and the flames and Saigon. . . .

The smell of his own burning was heavy in his nostrils, vividly clear, the bluish flame from the melting fat . . . Mitchell Gant, in his hotel room, burned to death in agony.

LUNCH WITH SAMMY?
— THURS. 1245

Call H.S. 2136/EXT 74.

ESTIMATES 76/77
Check with Godfrey

KNOWN FACTS 22 AUG 75

① The A/c 10-16 years ahead of M.R.C.A and USAF's Y16.

② It will be flying by 1980 - Operational by ?

③ Performance — projected Mach 5 plus etc!

④ Designed around Adv. Tech. Engines and possesses Thought Guided Weapons System.
— Nato does not. — NOR IS IT LIKELY !

⑤ Nato codenamed - without euphemism —
"FIREFOX"

⑥ We do not have —— a) the budget b) technology.
.... so — we must have the Firefox !

SOLUTION ?   ← Simple 'really

STEAL ONE

Talk to Plessey
Ferranti
etc.

Dear Prime Minister,
    You asked for fuller information concerning
the Mikoyan project at Bilyarsk. I therefore enclose
the report I received last Autumn from Aubrey,
who is controller of the espionage effort there. You
will see he has a rather radical suggestion to make!
Your comments would be illuminating.

                              Sincerely,
                              Richard Cunningham

          ☆   ☆   ☆   ☆

My dear Cunningham,
    You have received the usual digests of my full
reports with regard to the espionage effort being
made against the secret Mikoyan project at Bilyarsk,
which has received the NATO codename "Firefox."
In asking for my recommendations, I wonder whether you are sufficiently prepared for what I propose.
    You do not need me to outline Soviet hopes of
this new aircraft. Something amounting to a defense contingency fund has been set aside, we believe, to cope with eventual mass-production of this
aircraft. Work on the two scheduled successors to
the current Mig-25, the "Foxbat," has or is being
run down; the Foxbat will remain the principal
strike plane of the Soviet Air Force until that service
is re-equipped with the Mig-31, the "Firefox." At
least three new factory-complexes are planned or
under construction in European Russia solely, one
suspects, to facilitate the production of the Mig-
31.
    As to the aircraft itself, I do not need to reiter-
ate its potency. If it fulfills Soviet hopes, then we
will have nothing like it before the end of the eigh-
ties, if at all. Air supremacy will pass entirely to the

Soviet Union. We all know the reasons for SALT talks and defense cuts, and it is too late for recriminations. Suffice it to say that an unacceptable balance of power would result from Russian possession of the production interceptor and strike versions of this aircraft.

With regard to our own espionage effort, we are fortunate in having acquired the services of Pyotr Baranovich, who is engaged on the design and development of the weapons-system itself. He has recruited, as you are aware, two other highly-qualified technicians, and David Edgecliffe has supplied the Moscow end of the pipeline—Pavel Upenskoy, his best native Russian agent. However impressive it all sounds—and we both know that it is—it is not sufficient! What we have learned, or are likely to learn will be insufficient to reproduce or neutralize the threat of the Mig-31. Baranovich and his team know little of the aircraft outside their own specializations, so compartmented is the secrecy of the research.

Therefore, we must mount, or be preparing to mount within the next five years, an operation against the Bilyarsk project. I am suggesting nothing less than that we should *steal* one of the aircraft, preferably a full production prototype around the time of its final trials.

I can conceive your surprise! However, I think it feasible, providing a pilot can be found. I would think it necessary to employ an American, since our own RAF pilots no longer train in aerial combat (I am considering *all* the possibilities), and an American with combat experience in Vietnam might be best of all. We have the network in Moscow and Bilyarsk which could place pilot and plane in successful proximity.

Your thoughts on the above should prove enlightening. I look forward to receiving them.

Sincerely,
Kenneth Aubrey

My dear Sir Richard,

I am grateful for your prompt reply to my request. I really wished to know more about the aircraft itself—perhaps you could forward a digest of Aubrey's reports over the past three years? As to his suggestion—I presume he is not in earnest? It is, of course, ridiculous to talk of piracy against the Soviet Union!

My regards to your wife.

Sincerely,
Andrew Gresham

☆   ☆   ☆   ☆

Kenneth—

I enclose a copy of the P.M.'s letter of yesterday. You will see what he thinks of your budding criminality! At least as far as aircraft are concerned. His opinion is also mine—officially. Privately, I'll admit this Bilyarsk thing is scaring the pants off me! Therefore, do what you can to find a pilot, and work up a scenario for this proposed operation —just in case! You might try making inquiries of our friend Buckholz in the CIA, who has just got himself promoted Head of the Covert Action Staff —or is his title Director over there? Anyway, the Americans have as much to lose as Europe in this, and are just as interested in Bilyarsk.

Good hunting. On this, don't call me, I'll call you—if and when!

Sincerely,
Richard

☆   ☆   ☆   ☆

My dear Prime Minister,

You requested Sir Richard Cunningham to supply you with clarification of certain technical matters arising in connection with the aircraft we have codenamed the "Firefox" (Mikoyan Mig-31). I suppose that this letter is an opportunity to further plead my cause, but I think it important that you understand the gravity of Russian development in certain fields of military aviation, all of which are to meet in the focal point of this aircraft.

Our information comes principally from the man Baranovich, who has been responsible for the electronics that make practical the theoretical work of others on a thought-guided weapons system for use in high-technology aircraft. Baranovich cannot supply us with all the information we require even on this area of the Bilyarsk project, and we would be unlikely to successfully remove him from Russia, guarded as they all are in Bilyarsk. Hence my suggestion that we steal one of the later series of production prototypes, which will contain everything the Russians intend to put in the front-line versions.

Perhaps I should cite at this point an interesting civil development of the idea of thought-guidance—the latest type of invalid chair being studied in the United States. This is intended to enable a completely paralyzed and/or immobilized person to control the movements of an invalid carriage by positive thought activity. The chair would be electronically rigged so that sensors attached to the brain (via a "cap" or headrest of some kind) would transmit the commands of the brain, as electronic impulses, to the mechanics of the wheelchair or invalid carriage. A mental command to move ahead, turn round, to move left or right, shall we say, would come direct from the brain—instead of the command being transmitted to wasted or useless muscles, it would go into the artificial "limbs" of the wheelchair. There is no projected military development of any such system; whereas the Soviets, it would appear, are close to perfecting just such a system for military use. (And the West has not yet built the wheelchair.)

The system which we are convinced Baranovich is developing seems designed to couple radar and infra-red, those two standard forms of detection and guidance in modern aircraft—with a thought-guided and -controlled arsenal aboard the plane. Radar, as you are aware, bounces a signal off a solid object, and a screen reveals what is actually there: infra-red reveals on a screen what heat-sources are in the vicinity of the detection equipment. For guidance purposes, either or both these methods can be used to direct missiles and to aim them. The missiles themselves contain one or both of these systems themselves. However, the principal advantage of the thought-guided system is that the pilot retains command of his missiles after firing, as well as having a speeded-up command of their actual release, because his mental commands become translated directly to the firing-system, without his physical interference.

It must be said that we do not have, nor do the Russians we understand, weapons that will exploit such a sophisticated system—such as new kinds of missile or cannon. However, unless we quickly nullify the time advantage of the Russian program, we will be left too far behind by the undoubted acceleration of missile and cannon technology ever to catch up.

Therefore, we must possess this system. We must steal a Mig-31, at some time.

Sincerely,
Kenneth Aubrey

☆   ☆   ☆   ☆

My dear Aubrey,

My thanks for your communication. I appreciate your anxiety, though I reject your solution. And, in view of the recent "present" brought to the West by Lt. Belenko, namely the "Foxbat," are you not perhaps worrying unduly? It will take the Russians years, surely, to recover from the loss of the Foxbat's secrets?

Sincerely,
Andrew Gresham

☆   ☆   ☆   ☆

My dear Prime Minister,

In reply to your query, I am convinced that the Foxbat, the Mig-25, is little more than a toy compared with the projected aircraft which NATO has codenamed the Firefox. We must not be lulled into a false sense of security by the recent accident in Japan—a piece of good fortune we hardly deserve, and which may not prove to our final advantage.

I should also add that information coming back to our technical experts here from Japan suggests that the Mig-25 is not all that it might be. It is constructed in large part of steel rather than titanium, it has difficulty in obtaining its maximum speed and holding it, and its electronics are by no means as sophisticated as we were led to believe.

However, we have the opinion of Baranovich in Bilyarsk that the proposed Mig-31 *will* live up to even extravagant expectations. He is aware of the shortcomings of the Mig-25, by means of scientific gossip—but no one is carping at Bilyarsk about the Firefox.

Sincerely,
Kenneth Aubrey

160843 TUESDAY.

Richard,

Have you seen the S.A.C. Radar reports on the initial trials of FIREFOX?

The Americans had everything, including the Breakfast bar in the air, monitoring the performance trials, based on Baranovichs Info. ref times, flight path etc.

— she flew and — NOTHING. !

② If it's what I think it is — then the Soviets have developed Anti-Radar for FIREFOX and the DEW-Line can be put away along with the longbow and cutlass!

③ Advise the P.M. — NOW.

In haste

Kenneth

My dear Prime Minister,

I do not know what anti-radar is, nor how it works, in the case of the Russian system. Reports from Bilyarsk, from our sources who are not privy to its secrets, indicate that it is not mechanical or electronic at all—and therefore cannot be adversely affected by any counter measures. It is therefore totally unlike our own "Chaff," which is used to confuse radars, or any American developments in terms of electronic confusion of radar. Neither the USAF nor the RAF have anything in mind such as the Russian system would appear to be.

It is evident now that the Firefox is the most serious threat to the security of the West since the development of nuclear weapons by the Soviet Union and China.

Sincerely,
Kenneth Aubrey

☆   ☆   ☆   ☆

'C'/KA   30/7/79

Kenneth—

You have the go-ahead from the P.M. and from Washington. You will liaise with Buckholz. Your scenario, including pilot (an odd bird, wouldn't you say?), refueling point, and method of getting pilot to Bilyarsk, are approved. It is understood that the pilot should have some kind of homing-device which he can use to find the refueling point—one which the Russians will not be aware of, and will therefore be unable to trace. The P.M. realizes the urgency, and Farnborough have started work. See a man there called Davies.

Good luck to you. The ball is now firmly in your court.

Richard

Alone in his office, the smell of fresh paint still strong in his nostrils, KGB Colonel Mihail Yurievich Kontarsky, Head of the "M" Department assigned to security of the Mikoyan project at Bilyarsk, was again a prey to lurid doubts. He had been left alone by his assistant, Dmitri Priabin, and the sense of reassurance he had drawn from the work they had done that afternoon had dissipated in the large room. He sat behind the big, new desk, and willed himself to remain calm.

It had been going on too long, he realized—this need for the sedative of work. He had lost, he knew, the sense of perspective, now that the date for the final weapons trials on the Mig-31 was so close. It was nothing, it seemed, but a last-minute panic —grabbing up the bits and pieces of his job like scattered luggage. All the time afraid that he had forgotten something.

He was afraid to leave his office at that moment, because he knew his body could not yet assume its characteristic arrogance of posture. He would be recognized in the corridors of the Center as a worried man; and that might prove an irretrievable error on his part.

He had known about the security leaks at Bilyarsk for years—about Baranovich, Kreshin and Semelovsky—and their courier, Dherkov the grocer. Over such a period of time as the Mig had taken to be developed and built, it was impossible that he should not have known.

But, he and his department had done nothing about them, nothing more than reduce the flow of information to a trickle by tightening surveillance, preventing meetings, drops, and the like. Because —he suddenly dropped his head into his hands, pressing his palms against his closed eyelids—he had gambled, out of fear. He had been afraid to recommend the removal of vital human components from the project, and afraid that even if he did then the British or the CIA would suborn others whose existence would be unknown to him, or put in new agents and contacts he did not know. Better the devil you know, he had told Priabin when he made the decision, trying to smile; and the young man had gone along with him. Now it seemed an eminently foolish remark.

The price of failure had been absolute, even then. Disgrace, even execution. He tried to comfort himself by thinking that whatever the British and Americans knew, it was far less than they might have known. . . .

His narrow, dark features were wan and tired, his gray eyes fearful. He had had to let them continue working, even if they were spies. The words sounded hollowly, as if he were already reciting them to an unbelieving audience, even to Andropov himself . . .

THE THEFT

1
THE
MURDER

The walk from the British Airways BAC-111 across the tarmac of Cheremetievo Airport seemed interminable to the slightly-built man at the end of the file of passengers. The wind whipped at his trilby, which he held in place, jamming it firmly down with one hand while in the other he held a travel bag bearing the legend of the airline. He was an undistinguished individual—he wore spectacles, heavy-rimmed, and his top lip was decorated with a feeble growth of moustache. His nose was reddened, and his cheeks blanched, by the chill wind. He wore a dark topcoat and dark trousers, and anonymous shoes. Only the churning of his stomach, the bilious fear, placed and defined him.

It was only because it was the express practice of the KGB to photograph all passengers arriving on foreign flights at Moscow's principal airport that he, too, was photographed with a camera equipped with a telephoto lens. He guessed that it had happened, though he could not have said at what point in his walk across the tarmac, his head bent in an attempt to keep the flying dust from his face and eyes.

The sudden warmth of the disembarkation lounge struck him, tempted him to turn down the collar of his coat, remove his hat, and brush at the brown hair. He slicked it away from his forehead, so that with its evident white seam of a parting it belonged to a man unconscious of fashion. At that point, he was photographed again. In fact, it was as if he had posed for such a study. He looked about him, and then moved towards the customs desk. Around him, the human tide of any international terminal flowed, attracted his attention. Delegations filed through, and his eyes picked out the flamingo colors of African national costume. There were others—Orientals, Europeans. He became an item in that vast congress, and the cosmopolitan familiarity of an airport lounge settled his stomach. If anything, he appeared very cold, and more than a little airsick.

He knew that the men who stood behind the customs officials were probably security men—KGB. He placed his airline bag between the screens of the detector, and his other luggage came sliding towards him on the conveyor belt. The man did not move—he had already anticipated what would happen next. One of the two men standing with apparent indifference behind the customs men, stepped forward and lifted the two suitcases clear of the belt.

The man watched the customs officer fixedly, seeming to ignore the security man as he opened each of the suitcases, and urgently, thoroughly, ruffled through the clothing they contained. The customs official checked his papers, and then passed them to the controller at the end of the long counter. The ruffling of the clothes became more urgent, and the smile on the face of the KGB man disappeared, replaced by an intent, baffled stare into the well of each suitcase.

The official said: "Mr. Alexander Thomas Orton? What is your business in Moscow?"

The man coughed, and replied: "As you can see

from my papers, I am an export agent of the Excelsior Plastics Company, of Welwyn Garden City."

"Yes, indeed." The man's eyes kept flickering to the frustrated mime of the security officer. "You —have been to the Soviet Union several times during the past two years, Mr. Orton?"

"Again, yes—and nothing like this has happened to me before!" The man was not annoyed, merely surprised. He seemed determined to be pleasant, a seasoned, knowledgeable visitor to Russia, and not to regard the insults being levied at his possessions.

"I apologize," the official said. The KGB man was now in muttered conversation with the customs officer. The remainder of the passengers had already passed through the gate, and spilled into the concourse of the passenger lounge. They were gone, and Mr. Alexander Thomas Orton was feeling rather alone.

"I have all the correct papers, you know," he said. "Signed by your Trade Attaché at the Soviet Embassy in London." There was a trace of nervousness in his voice, as if some practical joke which he did not understand were being perpetrated against him. "As you say, I've been here a number of times—there's never been any trouble of this kind before. Does he really have to make such a mess of my belongings—what is he looking for?"

The KGB man approached. Alexander Thomas Orton brushed a hand across his oiled hair, and tried to smile. The Russian was a big man, with flattened Mongol features and an unpleasant aura of minor, frustrated, power about him. He took the passport and the visas from the official, and made a business of their scrutiny.

When he appeared satisfied, he stared hard into Orton's face and said: "Why do you come to Moscow, Mr.—Orton?"

"Orton—yes. I am a businessman, an exporter, to be exact."

"What do you hope to export to the Soviet Union, from your country?" There was a sneer in the Russian's voice, a curl of the lip to emphasize it. There was something unreal about the whole business. The man brushed his oiled hair again, and seemed more nervous than previously, as if caught out in some prank.

"Plastic goods—toys, games, that sort of thing."

"Where are your samples—the rubbish you sell, Mr. Orton?"

"Rubbish? Look here!"

"You are English, Mr. Orton? Your voice . . . it does not sound very English."

"I am Canadian by birth."

"You do not look Canadian, Mr. Orton."

"I—try to appear as English as possible. It helps, in sales abroad, you understand?" Suddenly, he remembered the vocal training, with a flick of irritation like the sting of a wet towel; it had seemed amidst his other tasks absurd in its slightness. Now, he was thankful for it.

"I do not understand."

"Why did you search my luggage?"

The KGB man was baffled for a moment. "There —is no need for you to know that. You are a visitor to the Soviet Union. Remember that, Mr. Orton!" As if to express his anger, he held up the small transistor radio as a last resort, looked into Orton's face, then tugged open the back of the set. Orton clenched his hands in his pockets, and waited.

The Russian, evidently disappointed, closed the back and said: "Why do you bring this? You cannot receive your ridiculous programs in Moscow!" The man shrugged, and the set and the passport were thrust at him. He took them, trying to control the shaking of his hands.

Then he stooped, picked up his hand grip, and waited as the KGB man closed his suitcases, and then dropped them at his feet. The lock of one burst, and shirts and socks brimmed over. The KGB man

laughed as Orton scrabbled after two pairs of rolling gray socks, on his knees. When he finally closed
the lid, his hair was hanging limply over his brow,
interfering with his vision. He flicked the lock
away, adjusted his spectacles, and hoisted his cases
at his sides. Then, mustering as much offended dig-
nity as he could, he walked slowly away, into the
concourse, toward the huge glass doors which would
let him into the air, and relief. He did not need to
look behind him to understand that the KGB man
was already consulting with his colleague who had
not moved from his slouched, assured stance against
the wall behind the customs desk, and who had obviously been the superior in rank. That second man
had watched him intently throughout his time at the
desk—customs, passport and KGB.

Gant knew that they would be 2nd Chief Directorate personnel—probably from the 1st section, 7th
department, which directed security with regard to
American, British, and Canadian tourists. And,
Gant reflected, his stomach relaxing for the first
time since he had left the aircraft, in a way he was
all three, and therefore, very properly, their concern.

He called for a taxi from the rank outside the
main doors of the passenger lounge, setting down
his suitcases, and cramming his trilby on his head
once more against the fierce wind, little abated by
the shelter of the terminal building.

A black taxi drew up, and he said: "Hotel Moskva, please," in as pleasant, innocuous a voice as he
could muster.

The driver opened the door for him, loaded his
suitcases, jumped back in the cab, and then waited,
engine idling. Gant knew he was waiting for the
KGB tail-car to collect him. Gant had seen the signal from the KGB man who had bullied him, a
shadowy, bulking figure. He took off his hat and
leaned sideways, so that he saw the long, sleek,
vividly-chromed sedan in the driver's mirror. Then

the driver of the taxi engaged the gears and they pulled out of the airport, onto the motorway that would take him south-east into the center of Moscow—the wide, prestigious Leningrad Avenue. He settled back in his seat, being careful not to glance behind him through the tinted rear window. The black sedan would be behind him, he knew.

So, he thought, feeling the tension drift down and vanish, Alexander Thomas Orton had passed his first inspection. He was not sweating—the taxi had an inefficient heater, and the temperature inside was low. Yet, he admitted, he had been nervous. It had been a test he had had to pass. He had had to play a part already familiar to his audience, so familiar that they would have noticed any false note. He had had to become totally self-effacing, not merely behind the mask of Orton's greasy hair, spectacles, and weak jaw, but in his movements, his voice. At the same time, he had had to carry with him, like the scent of a distinctive after-shave, an air of suspicion, of seediness. Thirdly, and perhaps most difficult for him, he had had to possess a certain, ill-fitting, acquired Englishness of manner and accent.

As he considered his success, and was thankful for the solid lack of imagination and insight of his interrogator, he acknowledged the brilliance of Aubrey's mind. The little plump Englishman had been developing Gant's cover as Orton, a cover merely to get him unobtrusively into Russia, for a long time. For almost two years, a man looking very much as Gant did now, had been passing through customs at Cheremetievo. An exporter, touting with some success a range of plastic toys. Apparently, they sold rather well in GUM, in Red Square. A fact that had amused Aubrey a great deal.

There was, naturally, more; Alexander Thomas Orton was a smuggler. The KGB's suspicions had been carefully aroused concerning Orton's possible activities in the drug-smuggling line a little more than a year before. Orton had been watched carefully, closely—yet never harried so openly before. Gant wondered whether Aubrey had not turned the screw on him. The big, dumb KGB man had expected to find something in his luggage, that was certain. And, now that his suspicions, aroused and then frustrated, had remained unfulfilled, Gant was being tailed to his hotel.

The taxi passed the Khimky Reservoir on the right, the expanse of gray water looking cold and final under the cloudy, rushing sky. Soon, they were into the built-up, urban mass of the city, and Gant watched the Dynamo Stadium sliding past the window to his left.

Aubrey, Gant knew, had been unimpressed by him. Not that he cared. Gant, for all his involvement in the part he was playing, had never intended to impress. He was at the beginning of his journey and, if he felt any emotion at all, it was one of impatience. Only one thing had mattered to him, ever since Buckholz had found him, in that deadbeat pizza palace in Los Angeles during his lunch-break, when he had been working as a garage-hand —it had been the first, and only time, he had left the Apache group, the tame Mig-squadron belonging to the USAF, and only one thing had ever mattered. He would get to fly the greatest airplane in history. If Gant possessed a soul any longer, which he doubted, it would be in that idea, enshrined perhaps, even embalmed therein. Buckholz had got him to fly again, on the Mig-21, and then the Foxbat; then he had left, tried to run away. Then Buckholz had found him again, and the idea had been broached . . . the Firefox.

His playing at being Orton amused Aubrey—was necessary. With true and utter single-mindedness, however, Gant viewed it merely as a prelude. It got him nearer to the Firefox.

Gant had always possessed a self-belief that amounted almost to illness. He had never lost that belief. Not in the nightmares, in the drugs, in the hospital, in the breakdown, in the attempted atonement. He had never ceased to think of himself in any other way than as a flyer—and as the best. Buckholz had known that, the bastard, Gant reflected—and he had used that because it was the lever that would work, the only one. . . . He couldn't run away. The job in Los Angeles—that had been a fake, a drop-out as real as putting on a disguise. Before that, the hospital, and the white uniform he had adopted—they had been disguises, too. He had tried to hide from the truth, the truth that the best could be afraid, that he could overtax himself, that he could, might fail.

That had been the real nightmare. Gant's precarious world, the whole person that he was, was threatened, by stretched nerves, by too many missions, by too much danger and tension.

Gant rubbed a hand across his brow, and looked down at his damp fingertips. He wore an expression of distaste, almost disgust, on his face. He was sweating now. It was not reaction from the goddamn stupid games he was beginning to have to play with the KGB, on their home field—not that; rather the memory of his attempts to escape.

Gant came from a family of nonentities. By the time he entered his teens, he despised his parents, and his brother, the insurance salesman who was a conspicuous failure. He despised, though he could not help loving, the elder sister who was an untidy slut with four kids, and a drunk for a husband. He had come from a dirt town in the vast, featureless expanse of the Mid-West—Clarkville, pop. 2763, the signposts had read—together with the legend "A Great Little Town." Gant had hated Clarkville. Every moment he spent within its confines, or locked within the rolling, flat corn-belt that buried it, he had been nothing, had felt himself nothing. He had left Clarkville behind him long ago, and he had never been back, not even for the funeral of his mother, or the comfort of his aging father. His

sister had written to him, once, berating and plead-
ing in turns. He had not replied. The letter had
reached him in Saigon. Gant had never escaped
from Clarkville. He carried it with him, wherever
he went. It had shaped him.

He wiped the sweat from his forehead on the leg
of his dark trousers. He closed his eyes, and tried not
to think about the past. It had been the dream, he
thought. That damned dream had started this. That,
and his nettled, irritated pride because smug, pa-
tronizing Aubrey had looked down his nose at him.
Gant's hands bunched into fists on the plastic seat.
Like a child, all he wanted to do now was to show
them, show them all, just as he had wanted to show
them in Clarkville, that dead town of dead people.
There was only one way to show Aubrey. He had
to bring back his airplane—the Firefox.

Kontarsky was on the telephone, the extension that
linked him with his superior officer within the In-
dustrial Security Section of the 2nd Chief Directorate, of which the "M" department formed a
small, but vital, part. Dmitri Priabin watched his
chief carefully, almost like a prompter following an
actor, script open on his knees. Kontarsky seemed
much more at ease than during their interview the
previous day, as if action had soothed him during
the last twenty-four hours.

During that elapsed period, Kontarsky had received an up-to-date report from the KGB unit at
Bilyarsk, and surveillance of the underground cell
had been increased. There had been no unaccount-
able arrivals in Bilyarsk during the past forty-eight
hours, and only the courier, Dherkov, had left the
small town. His grocery van had been thoroughly
searched on his return from Moscow. Kontarsky had
ordered searches of all vehicles arriving in the town,
and a thorough scrutiny of all personnel passing
inside the security fence of the factory. Dog patrols
had been intensified around the perimeter fence,

and the number of armed guards in the hangars had been trebled.

Once those things had been done, Kontarsky and Priabin had both begun to feel more at ease. Priabin himself was to leave for Bilyarsk that night by KGB helicopter, and take over effective command of the security forces from the officer on the spot. Effectively, within hours, he could seal Bilyarsk tight. Kontarsky had decided not to travel with the First Secretary and his party, but to impress by being on the spot himself twenty-four hours before the test-flight. They would arrest the members of the underground only a matter of hours before the flight, and at the time of arrival of the First Secretary, they would already be undergoing interrogation. It would, he calculated, be sure to impress the First Secretary and Andropov who would be part of the entourage. Both Priabin and Kontarsky anticipated extracting the maximum satisfaction from the interrogations. Baranovich, Kreshin, Semelovsky, Dherkov and his wife, would be snatched out of their false sense of security in a theatrical and impressive display of ruthless KGB efficiency.

Kontarsky put down the telephone receiver. He smiled broadly at his aide, and at the third person in his office—Viktor Lanyev, assistant KGB security chief at Bilyarsk. Lanyev had been flown to Moscow to make a report, thereby doubling Kontarsky's sense of security after having received a written report from Tsernik, the chief security officer at Bilyarsk. After listening to Lanyev's meticulous diary of the movements and contacts of the three men under observation, Kontarsky had been relieved, had set himself on a course of optimism, at the end of which journey he could already envisage a successful conclusion.

The security arrangements at Bilyarsk were a minor classic, entirely orthodox, without imagination—a policy of overkill. There were the resident, declared hierarchy of KGB officers, and their select squad from the 2nd Directorate; as a support group, there were personnel of the GRU, Soviet Military Intelligence, who performed as guards and patrols both at the airstrip and in the town; thirdly, there were the "unofficial" members of the KGB, the informants and civilian spies closest to the research and development teams. All three groups were focusing their attention on four men and a woman. They watched everything, saw and knew everything.

Kontarsky, prematurely luxuriating in the congratulations of his superior, said, after a while, steepling his fingers as he leaned back in his chair: "We will make doubly-sure, my friends. We must take no risks at this point—this late point in time. Therefore, I suggest we commandeer a special detachment from the 5th Chief Directorate, one of their Security Support Units. You agree?"

Lanyev, the man on the spot, seemed somewhat insulted. "There is no need, Comrade Colonel."

"I say there is—*every* need!" Kontarsky's eyes were angry, commanding. "I must have the most complete assurances that nothing will, or can, go wrong at Bilyarsk. Are you prepared to guarantee —in the most definite, unequivocal way—that nothing can go wrong?"

Kontarsky was smiling at Lanyev. The middleaged man, who had risen as high in the ranks of the KGB as he would ever achieve, looked down, and shook his head.

"No, Comrade Colonel, I would not wish to do that," he said quietly.

"Naturally—and we are not asking that you should, Viktor Alexeivich, no." He beamed at his two subordinates. Priabin sensed the swing of Kontarsky's mood. At times, his chief struck him as portraying many of the symptoms of the manic-depressive in miniature. Now the doubts of the previous day were deeply buried. Kontarsky would, almost, not have recognized himself had he confronted the frightened man of yesterday.

"How many men, Colonel?" he asked.

"Perhaps a hundred—discreetly, of course—but a hundred. We may run the risk of frightening them off, but that will be better than failing to catch them at whatever they have planned."

"Comrade Tsernik does not believe that anything is planned, Comrade Colonel," Lanyev interpolated.

"Mm. Perhaps not. But we must act as if they intend to sabotage the test-flight—something wrong with one of the missiles, or with the cannon . . . a mid-air explosion, I do not have to draw pictures for either of you. Production of the Mig-31 would be put back, perhaps reconsidered. Either that, or we should all, *all* of us, be—heavily disgraced?" Kontarsky was still smiling. For a moment, there was a worried drawing together of the eyebrows, and then he shook off the doubts. He could face his fear now, because he could not see or envisage how he might fail. Mere multiplication gave him confidence. Almost two hundred men at Bilyarsk—not to mention the informers. . . .

"I must check with the Political Security Service as to which of the informers we have been—*loaned* —are most reliable," Kontarsky went on briskly. "We should not need them—but they will be inside the factory complex, and therefore closest to the dissidents. They will be armed, under your direction, Viktor Alexeivich." Lanyev nodded. "And issued with communicators. Now, where will our three traitors be in the hours before the flight, when the aircraft is being armed?"

Lanyev consulted his notes.

"All three of them will be inside the hangar itself, Comrade Colonel—unfortunately."

"Yes, indeed. Three times as dangerous as they might otherwise be. Give me details."

"Baranovich has worked on the weapons system itself, Comrade Colonel—as you know."

"He will be working on the aircraft during the night, until it takes off?"

"Yes, Comrade Colonel."

"He cannot be replaced?"

"Not possibly."

"Very well! What of the others?"

"Kreshin and Semelovsky are both little more than highly-favored mechanics, Comrade Colonel," Lanyev supplied. "They will be concerned with the fueling, and the loading of the missiles and the other weapons. Also, the Rearward Defense Pod. But they are most familiar with the systems, and not easy to replace."

"They can be watched?"

"Very closely. Our informers will be shoulder-to-shoulder with them throughout the night."

"As long as our informers know enough to recognize attempted sabotage when they see it!"

"They do, Comrade Colonel."

"Good. For that, I can take your word. Dherkov, naturally, will be at home, sleeping with that fat wife of his." Kontarsky smiled. His mood was being sustained by what he was hearing, by the action he appeared to be taking, the decisiveness of his manner, his voice. . . . "Yes. May I sum up, gentlemen? Our GRU colleagues will throw a ring around Bilyarsk that will be impregnable; our borrowed Security Support Unit will arrive tomorrow, and will assist the guards on the perimeter fence, the hangars, the factory, and the boundaries of the town itself. Our three dissidents will be very closely watched—especially Baranovich. Have I left anything out, Dmitri?"

"I have everything here, in my notes," Priabin said.

Kontarsky stretched behind his desk, arms above his head. The smile that was beginning to irritate Priabin was fixed on his thin, dark features. His uniform collar was open at the neck, showing his prominent Adam's apple, and the thin, bird-like throat, the skin stretched, yet loose, like a turkey . . . Priabin dismissed the irritation from his mind.

"I think, as a further precaution, we will go and collect the Moscow end of the chain. No, not tonight. If they disappear with almost forty-eight hours to go, then Lansing may discover that fact, and warn off our friends at Bilyarsk. No! Tomorrow will do, giving us perhaps twenty-four hours to find out what they know! You will take care of that, Dmitri?"

"Yes, Colonel. I shall have the warehouse they use as a cover watched from tonight—and move in on your orders."

"Good. I would like to see them before—before I myself fly down to Bilyarsk tomorrow. Yes. Ask for surveillance by the 7th Directorate, Dmitri, on the warehouse. We—need not spare too many of our own men, and they are in business to watch people. They can be replaced by our team when I give the word."

"Very well, Colonel."

"Very well? Yes, Dmitri—I begin to feel that it may indeed be very well!" Kontarsky laughed. Priabin watched the Adam's apple bob up and down in the turkey-throat, hating his superior's overconfidence more than he feared his lapses of nerve.

The black sedan had eased itself into a convenient parking-place opposite the portico of the Moskva Hotel. As Gant had passed into the hotel foyer, and had patted his pockets as if to insure he still had his papers, he had observed that the two men inside the sedan had made no move to follow him. One was already reading a newspaper, while the other, the driver, had just lit a cigarette. Warned by their inactivity, Gant surveyed the foyer from the vantage point of the hotel desk, and picked out the man who was waiting to identify him. His picture must have been transmitted via wireprint from Cheremetievo to Dzerzhinsky Street.

Had he not been thoroughly briefed by Aubrey as to what to expect, Gant might have been left breathless by such efficiency; the intrusive, dogged pursuit of himself. As it was, the realization of the degree and intensity of the security with regard to himself, merely as a suspected "economic criminal," though deadened, still caused him a momentary feeling of wateriness in the pit of his stomach.

The man watching for him, masked by his copy of *Pravda*, showed no sign of interest. He was seated in one of the many alcoves off the central foyer, overcoat thrown over a chair, apparently at his ease. If, and when, Gant left the Moskva, that man would follow him. Probably already, the car outside had been relieved by another, operating under the auspices of the same Directorate of the KGB as the man behind the newspaper.

Once in his room, Gant removed the clear-glass spectacles, ruffled his hair deliberately, and pulled off his tie. It was as if he had released himself from a strait-jacket. He opened his suitcases, then slipped off his shoes. The room was a small suite, with the tall windows looking out over the windswept expanse of Red Square. Gant ignored the window, and helped himself to a Scotch from the drinks trolley placed in one corner of the room. He seated himself on a low sofa, put his feet up, and tried to relax. He had begun to realize that his attempted indifference would not work, not even in the apparent, luxurious safety of his centrally-heated, double-glazed hotel room. He had been instructed not to look for bugs, since he couldn't be sure that he was not being observed through some two-way mirror device.

He glanced in the direction of the huge mirror on one wall, and then dragged his eyes away from it. He began to experience the hypnotic effect of KGB surveillance. It was so easy—it required a real effort of mind to avoid doing so—to imagine himself pinned on a card, naked and exposed, with a bright white light beating down upon him. He shivered involuntarily, and swallowed at the Scotch. The li-

quor, to which he had become used merely as a part
of his general training to assume the mask of Orton,
warmed his throat and stomach. He inhabited a landscape of eyes.

It was difficult to consider, coldly, objectively, the
Russian defense system, the hours of the flight in
the Firefox, the training on the Foxbat and the
simulator constructed from the photographs and descriptions supplied by the man at Bilyarsk—Baranovich. With an effort, he decided to postpone such
considerations.

He lapsed into thoughtless inactivity. Getting up,
he moved to the window and looked down from the
twelfth floor over Red Square. He had no interest
in the rank of cars parked directly below. Under
the lowering sky, in the gathering gloom of the late
afternoon, he stared, for a long time, down the vast
length of the square, over the roof of the History
Museum, towards the towers and domes of the
Kremlin. He could just pick out the guards before
the bronze doors of the Lenin Mausoleum, and the
tiny figures moving in and out of the glass doors of
the gray edifice of GUM. At the far end of the
square, huge, incredible, was St. Basil's Cathedral
—garish, irreligious. His eyes continued to rove over
the desert of Red Square, barely focused.

The Scotch, as he swallowed another mouthful,
no longer warmed him. Already his thoughts were
reaching into the immediate future, toward the
meeting with three men he did not know on the embankment of the Moskva, near the Krasnokholmskiy
Bridge. He was to leave the hotel after dinner, and
behave as a tourist, no matter who tailed him. All
he had to do was to be certain to arrive at ten-
thirty. He was to be sure to take his hat and overcoat—no, to wear them—and he had to take the
transistor radio. That told him that he would not be
returning to the hotel; it would be the beginning of
his journey to Bilyarsk.

Alexander Thomas Orton left the bar of the Moskva Hotel a little before ten that evening, having taken dinner in the hotel dining-room. Throughout his meal he had been observed by a KGB man from the Surveillance Directorate—a short, obese man who had dined at a single table placed advantageously so that he could observe everyone in the huge room. The man had followed him into the bar, and had sat blatantly watching him, a large vodka before him on the table. Gant suspected that his room would be thoroughly searched during the meal, which was why the small transistor radio sat in the pocket of his overcoat, as it had done throughout dinner—he had hung the coat where he could see it, and where he could be seen to be able to see it. The pockets had not been searched.

Throughout dinner, he had studied his *Nagel Guide to Moscow*, following the text on a large map which he folded ostentatiously out over the table cloth during his dessert. He had continued to study map and text during the hour he had spent in the bar. When he left, he was followed almost immediately.

As he went down the steps of the hotel, into Red Square, the short fat man paused, and overtly lit a cigarette, the gas lighter flaring in the darkness. Gant did not see the signal, but he saw the dark figure detach itself from a large car parked near the spot where the tail-car had pulled in that afternoon. Only one man there, he thought—and the short fat man coming down the steps behind him. Two.

The headlights of the car flared in the darkness, flickered in time with the coughing engine, then blazed as the engine roared. It had seemed quiet until that moment, that the noise of the engine was exaggerated. Gant had a momentary fear that he was about to be arrested, prevented from leaving the vicinity of the hotel—but there was no attempt to overhaul him, even though he paused to check, turning up his collar against the wind that was blowing down the square into his face. He had to hold the unfamiliar, irritating trilby on his head, and bend forward into the wind.

He chose the left-hand pavement as he came out of Manezhnaya Square and into the Red Square proper. This would take him past the façade of GUM. There were many Muscovites in the square —the queue outside the Lenin Mausoleum had dispersed, but many people window-shopped in the glass of the great store, cold faces lit by the white lighting. Gant did not bother to check his tail—its distance, or persistence. He knew they would stay with him, and that some kind of general alert would go out the moment they lost him, and he would be hunted. Which was precisely what he did not want. These men had to stay close to him. Hence, he spent some time looking at the fashion displays, the often inadequate replicas of Western fashions that GUM offered, the gray monster that was the largest department store in the world, before he passed out of Red Square, again taking his time, strolling, staring across the windy space at the towers of the Kremlin.

By the time he reached the Moskva river, and the Moskvoretski Bridge, he was thoroughly cold. His hat was jammed on his head, and his hands thrust in his pockets. He did not appear to be a man going anywhere in particular, but he could no longer be taken for a sightseer, enjoying Moscow by lamplight. The wind coming off the river seemed icy, and he now reluctantly held on to his hat, because it was a signpost, it informed the man tailing him where he was, even though he would have rather kept his numb, white hand in his overcoat pocket. He bent over the parapet of the road bridge, looking down into the black, lamp-flecked water, its surface rippled by the wind. Someone paused further back down the bridge, immediately highlighted by his lack of movement since all the other figures on the bridge moved swiftly, tugged and pushed by the wind. Gant smiled to himself.

He turned his back to the river, and pulled his collar tight about his neck. Casually, he inspected the road across the bridge. The car had stopped, headlights switched off, seemingly empty, parked well away from the street lamps. And there was a second pedestrian, leaning with his back against the bridge, on the other side of the road, slightly ahead of him.

Gant began to walk again. Despite what he had been told, despite the tail-spotting in which he had engaged in New York and Washington as part of his training under Buckholz, a small knot of tension had begun to form in his stomach. He did not know what would happen when he reached the Krasnokholmskiy Bridge, downriver of where he was now, but he had been instructed not to lose his tail. Aubrey had made that clear in the smoke-filled room of his hotel in London the previous night. The KGB was to be kept with him.

As he crossed the Drainage Canal that ran beside the Moskva and turned onto the Ozerkovskaia Quay, descending a flight of stone steps down to the embankment, he wanted to stop and be violently sick. He realized that the artificial calm he had felt until that moment had deserted him finally. He could no longer pretend to himself that this was only a tiresome preliminary, to be gone through before he came face-to-face with his part in the total proceedings. *This was real.* The cold and the wind had now been abated slightly by the level of the bridge; the men on his tail—he could hear them now, footsteps softly clattering, unhurried and assured, down the flight of steps to the embankment, forty or so yards behind him. He was frightened. One hand came out of his pocket and he gripped his coat where it sat across his stomach, twisting the material in his hand.

He wondered about the car and its occupants. He could not turn round now, to count heads. He knew, with a sickening certainty, that there were three, perhaps four men behind him now, and that the car would be driving along the Ozerkovskaia Quay above him, waiting for him to regain the street.

He passed the Oustinski Bridge, and glanced at his watch. Ten-twenty. It would take him no more than another ten minutes to reach the next bridge, where he was to make his rendezvous with . . . with whom? In the shadow of the bridge there was a strange silence. The Sadovisheskaya Embankment, where he stood, was empty except for one or two couples strolling towards him, arm-in-arm, idling by the canal as if miles from the center of the city.

He breathed deeply three or four times, in the way he had done when settling his flying-helmet on his head, and glancing, for the first time, across the instrument panel of the aircraft he was about to fly. The memory, inspired by the physical control he asserted, seemed to calm him. He had to think that he was doing something of which he was a master—flying. If he could think that, then he could go on. The footsteps had stopped behind him, like patient guardians, waiting until he might be strong enough to continue.

He walked on, passed a young couple absorbed in each other without even a glance in their direction, and measured the pace of his footsteps. He could hear footsteps behind him, a little clatter rebounding from the embankment wall, then the stronger, overlapping signals from the following KGB men. The footsteps of the couple, slower it seemed and less purposeful, faded away behind him. He wanted to run—he could not believe that they would let him reach the bridge. He wanted to run . . . It was a question of easing back the speed, not to overfly: he imagined the aerial situation, of having overflown a target, pulling back, waiting patiently, even though he had lost sight of the Mig, lost sight of the Phantom, when he himself had been flying the Foxbat . . . the terrible moments before recontact. He calmed himself. It wasn't the same, this situation, it was *less* dangerous.

He walked on, having regained an hallucinatory equilibrium. He *was* the best there was . . . he was flying.

He climbed up the steps of the embankment to the Krasnokholmskiy Bridge, crossed the canal without seeming to hurry, and descended the flight of steps down to the narrow embankment of the Moskva, on the south side of the river. The black water stretched away to the line of yellow lights along the Kotelnitcheskaia Quay on the other bank. There were no footsteps behind him for seconds after he ended his descent, yet his refined, nervous hearing picked up the muffled sound of the engine from the bridge above. The car had rejoined the tail. Now, the KGB would be predicting his movements and purposes. He looked at his watch. Ten-thirty. They, too, would probably see some significance in the exactitude of the time. He heard footsteps come cautiously down the stone steps, as he stared out into the river. Two pairs. Then only one. One of the KGB men had paused half-way down the steps.

He stared into the darkness under the bridge. No figures detached themselves from the shadows. He turned his back, and began to walk along the embankment.

It was only a few hundred yards to the first flight of steps down from the Gorovskaia Quay and, as he approached, three shadows appeared on the steps and moved towards him. For a moment, he wondered whether they were not KGB men—then one of the men spoke softly in English.

"Mr. Orton?" the voice said.

"Yes." There had been no trace of a foreign accent.

The three men joined him swiftly, and a torch

flared in his face. The English voice said: "Yes, it's him."

The tallest of the three men, young, square-featured, blond, took up the dialogue.

"How many followed you?" His accent was Russian, though he spoke in English.

Gant replied in Russian, testing his pronunciation: "Three on foot, I think—and a car. It's up on the bridge."

"Good," the Russian replied. Gant was watching the first man, the Englishman he assumed was from the Embassy security staff. He was the same build as Gant, and his hair was brushed back from his forehead. He smiled at Gant, as if in encouragement, or conspiracy. Gant returned the smile.

"What are they doing, Pavel?" the Englishman asked, keeping his eyes on Gant.

"The one on the steps has returned to the car —the short fat one is wondering what to do, since there are four of us here now." The Russian laughed softly. "I think he is frightened!"

"Then help is on the way—we'd better get Mr. Orton away from here right away, while they're still in two minds."

Gant was on edge, ready for sudden movement, for flight . . . They had been standing in a tight group and the material of the Englishman's coat, so like Gant's own, was pressed against him. The big Russian, Pavel, drew a heavy wooden truncheon from beneath his own dark coat. They were a circle of dark coats, Gant thought irrelevantly, and the Englishman was wearing his hair in the same out-of-date style as he was. . . .

Fenton, the Englishman who had played the part of Orton many times in the last two years cried out in surprise—then the surprise became pain. Pavel brought the heavy club down across the Englishman's forehead—once, twice. Then the Englishman was on the ground, moaning, and the club descended another three sickening times. Even as his stomach revolted, as his mind screamed that he was in a pit of snakes, like the Veterans' Hospital, Gant realized that the big Russian was rendering the Englishman's face unrecognizable.

The police whistle scratched across his awareness, then seemed to accelerate and to slide up the scale, as if it were on record and the turntable had speeded up to make the sound recognizable. The KGB man was calling for reinforcements.

"Your papers—quickly!" Pavel snapped, bending over the battered features of the Englishman. The sight of the face seemed to hypnotize Gant. "Your papers!"

He reached into his breast pocket and handed over his passport, his movement visas, his identification from the Soviet Embassy, in a trance-like state. They were stuffed into Fenton's pockets, and the Englishman's own papers removed. The third man snatched the trilby from Gant's head, and then helped the big Russian to lift the body and roll it the few yards to the edge of the embankment. They released it and it slid into the black ruffled waters of the Moskva. The dark topcoat billowed, and the man's arms became the arms of a crucifix—he floated slowly away, drawn by the current.

"Quickly! Follow us—to the Pavolets Station, the Metro," Pavel growled in his ear, shaking him out of immobility. Other whistles were answering the summons from the KGB man fifty yards away.

Gant's feet began to move, a hundred miles away beneath him. He stumbled up the steps onto the Gorovskaia Quay, following Pavel and the other Russian. Whistles shrilled behind him, and feet galloped echoingly along the embankment. Pavel and the other man were running ahead of him, drawing away. He saw the flash of white as Pavel turned his face to him.

"Quickly!" he yelled.

Gant began to run, faster, faster, leaving the whistles behind, leaving the floating body . . .

The short, fat man, and the taller figure who had detached himself from the car in front of the Moskva Hotel, were up to their waists in the chill waters of the Moskva, dragging the body to the embankment. The fat man was grunting and cursing with the effort.

When they had tugged the corpse up onto the flagstones, the fat man bent over it, wracked by coughing, fishing in the breast pocket as he did so. He pulled out a British passport, soggily closed around other papers. The taller man flashed a torch onto the picture of the man with the greasy hair, then at the ruined face at the edge of the circle of torchlight.

"Mm," the fat man said after a while. "I warned them at the Center about this." There was a note of self-satisfaction in his voice. "He didn't have any drugs on him at Cheremetievo. It was obvious that he was unable to meet demands. They have killed him, Stechko. His smuggling friends have killed Mr. Alexander Thomas Orton."

2

THE
JOURNEY

Gant had a hurried impression of a huge façade, ornamental, almost oriental, that was the main-line railway station, and then their pace slowed, they were descending the elevator to the level of the Pavolets Metro station. Gant tried to disguise his breathing from those few incurious Russians and his eyes wandered over the brightly lit, somber marble walls of the descent. Nothing he had seen in New York, or London, or Paris, was like this. The Pavolets Station was like the grandiose architecture of a museum in which the actual vehicles that rushed with a sigh of air from the dark tunnel holes seemed almost out of place.

The platform was uncrowded, but they remained apart so as to be inconspicuous as they waited for the train. Pavel stood next to Gant for no more than a moment and deftly slipped a bundle of documents, inside a blue British passport, into Gant's hands.

He murmured, "Study these before you leave the train. Your name is Michael Grant, almost your own name. You are a tourist staying at the Warsaw Hotel. They are not looking for an Englishman, remember. Just stay calm."

Pavel wandered further along the platform. Gant glanced at the passport photograph, registered the image of himself there, and took off the trilby and the spectacles and shoved them into the pockets of the overcoat. Then he removed the overcoat, and held it casually over his arm. His dark, formal suit still seemed to betray him; its cut was so obviously foreign. One or two Russians appeared to stare at him.

The train swooped into the bright strip of station and he moved forward, tugging his overcoat back onto his shoulders. He knew he had made a mistake, that the overcoat was more anonymous. He turned in his seat as the train pulled out, and saw Pavel unconcernedly reading a newspaper, his long legs stretched out into the aisle. The other man was not in the same compartment.

Gant began to scrutinize the faces in the compartment. There were only faces of travelers—tired, bored, introverted, eyes avoiding contact with fellow passengers. The faces of the world's subways, he thought. He had seen them a million times before. Yet the feeling of nakedness would not go away. The train sighed into another brightly lit strip of platform, and he saw the name slide past his gaze—Taganskaia. They were heading north-east, away from the center of Moscow. The doors of the compartment whispered open, and Gant watched those who left, and stared at those who came. No one even so much as glanced in his direction. He felt sweat beading on his forehead, and glanced once more in the direction of Pavel. The big Russian glared silently at him, his whole manner of body and the force of his expression displaying a command to behave normally.

Gant nodded, and attempted to relax. He was moving, but it appeared too much like drifting to comfort him. He did not know where he was going, and he had no idea how far he could trust his companions—except that he had Aubrey's assurance. But Gant could not relax. A man had been murdered in the center of Moscow, and they were making their getaway on public transport. The whole thing had a faint atmosphere of the ridiculous about it—and, Gant acknowledged, anonymity. Aubrey again.

Aubrey had told him nothing about the manner of his disappearance from Moscow, nor of the manner of his transportation to Bilyarsk. He was luggage, freight, until they reached the factory and the hangar. And that was how, he admitted, he had tried to regard the whole operation—yet, the shock to his system, to his reserves of calm and indifference, administered by the death on the embankment, made it increasingly difficult to remain freight, or luggage. He was scared.

When the train stopped briefly in the Kourskaia Station, he managed not to look out of the window, except in the most bored manner, and he managed not to inspect the passengers boarding the train. When he looked back at Pavel, however, as the doors sighed shut and the train surged forward, the big Russian was looking back down the platform. Gant followed the direction of his gaze. At the gateway to the moving-staircase passengers who had just descended from the train were being questioned by two men in overcoats and hats.

Gant, fear dry in his throat, waited for Pavel to turn his gaze back into the carriage. When he did so, and saw Gant staring at him, he merely nodded, once. Gant understood him. KGB. They were covering their bets. Even if they had not yet begun the massive operation of boarding every metro train, they were already sealing up the bolt-holes. They knew how good an escape route the metro was—they had a map of the system and a timetable, just as Aubrey had done when he planned the escape route. And the murder had been done conveniently near the Pavolets station.

Swiftly, almost as a distraction, he studied the papers Pavel had given him. When he had finished, he put them away, and his eyes were drawn hypnotically to the window again.

The dark tunnel rushed past the window, and Gant felt the knot of tension harden in his stomach, and tasted the bile at the back of his throat. He stared, helplessly, at the door connecting his carriage with the one ahead, waiting for it to open, to admit an overcoated figure whose manner would betray his authority, whose eyes would scorch across his features.

The train slowed, the darkness beyond the grimy windows becoming the harsh lighting of the Komsomolskaia Station. Involuntarily, he looked at Pavel. The big man had got casually to his feet, and was hanging idly onto a handrail near the sliding doors. Gant got up unsteadily—he knew that his face must be pale and sweating—and stood squarely at the second set of doors in the carriage.

As the train stopped and the doors slid open, he realized that he knew nothing of what the papers in his pocket contained. In sudden panic, he had forgotten. He stepped shakily down onto the platform, was pushed from behind by another passenger and the movement was a grateful trigger. Grant . . . like his own name. He remembered. His eyes sought the exit flight. Yes, there were two KGB men there.

Pavel pushed close to him, as if as a reassuring presence. A small crowd of people seemed to have left the train at that station, and he and the big man were at its heart. It moved slowly, as if with communal wariness, towards the exit. The station's opulence glanced across his awareness. Even here there were no hoardings, no advertisements of women in underclothes or huge bottles of scotch or cinema posters—only frescoes of the great and praiseworthy victories of the Russian people since 1917, in the bold, awkward, cartoon style of Soviet realism.

He sensed Pavel fade back into the crowd again, but did not turn his head. The crocodile drifted toward the waiting men at the foot of the exit stairs. They were inspecting papers, and he reached into his pocket for Michael Grant's documents. He pulled them from his pocket and re-inspected them as swiftly as he could. Michael Grant—passport, entry visa, hotel reservation, Intourist information brochure.

The KGB man's face loomed in front of him, a white, high-boned, thin face, with a large, aquiline nose, and sharp, powerful eyes. He was inspecting Gant's papers thoroughly, and glancing from photograph to face, and back again. Then he looked at the documents issued to Michael Grant since his arrival in Moscow, three days before. Gant wondered whether such a man had booked into the Warsaw Hotel on that day—and he knew it wouldn't have been overlooked Michael Grant would be a bona-fide tourist, whose papers had been borrowed and duplicated.

"You do not appear to be in the best of health, Mr.—Grant?" the KGB man said in English. He was smiling, and seemed without suspicion.

"No." Gant faltered. "I—a little tummy trouble. The food, you know . . ." He smiled weakly.

"In your photograph you are wearing glasses, Mr. Grant?"

Gant patted his pockets, and continued to smile, a smile that was wan, and remarkably stupid. "In my pocket . . ."

"The food at the Warsaw—it is not good?"

"Yes, fine—just a little too rich for me."

"Ah. Thank you, Mr. Grant."

The man had taken the number of the passport, and the numbers of the documents that he had handed back. Gant had walked a dozen steps before he realized that he had bluffed his way through, that his feet had automatically stepped onto the ascending flight of stairs, and he was being moved up and out of sight of the two KGB officers. His stomach felt watery, and he belched. He wanted to be sick with relief. He forced himself not to turn round to look for Pavel and the other man, to stifle the growing panic of the thought that they might have been picked up, and he was now alone . . .

He stepped off the staircase, and moved over to study a large map of the Moscow metro system. He did not dare to turn his attention from the map, his hands thrust deep into the pockets of the topcoat, his shoulders slightly bowed, as he fought against the tide of nausea. He told himself, over and over, that this tension was the same as flying, the sudden, violent twists of time which moved from calm and boredom, to terror, were things that he had experienced many times before. But it did not seem to work, the sedative of familiarity. Perhaps, in the huge, ornate foyer of the metro station, with its gigantic statuary, marbles and bronzes, and the mosaic floor and frescoed walls—perhaps he was unable to transpose himself to the cockpit, and calm his growing panic. All he knew that moment was that he was alone, stranded—they would have picked up Pavel, and the other man. What could he do?

A hand fell on his shoulder, and he jumped away as if stung by some electric charge within him. He turned round, and Pavel saw the damp, frightened face, and doubt flickered in his eyes.

"Thank God," Gant breathed.

"You look terrible," Pavel said, without humor. "Mr. Grant—I watched your performance . . . it was not very convincing."

"Jesus! I was shit-scared, man!" Gant burst out.

Pavel looked at him, towering over him. Gant seemed smaller, slighter, less impressive than even his disguise would normally have made him. Pavel, remembering what Edgecliffe, the SIS Head of Sta-

tion in Moscow, had said of the American, agreed.
This man was a risk. Edgecliffe had said—if he
causes serious trouble on the journey, get rid of him
—don't risk the whole network, just for him. And
Gant looked as if he might be big trouble.

"Go and make yourself sick," Pavel said, with
distaste in his voice. "Go, and hide yourself in the
toilets. There will be more KGB men on the way.
We shall leave the station *after* they feel they are
sufficiently reinforced—when they are confident
that, if we reach the main entrance, then we must
have been searched at least three or four times. Go!"
He spat out the last word and Gant, after staring at
him for a long moment, turned his back and walked
away. Pavel watched him go, shook his head, and
then set himself to watch, from the cover of his
newspaper, the arrivals at the Komsomolskaia Metro Station.

David Edgecliffe, ostensibly Trade Attaché to the
British Embassy, was in the bar of the Moskva Hotel. From his position near the door, he could look
out into the foyer of the hotel. He saw the KGB men
arrive, together with at least two people from the
Political Security Service. If his diagnosis was correct, then Fenton, poor lad, had not died in vain.
He shook his head, sadly, over his Scotch, and swallowed the last of it. The appearance of those particular KGB officers would mean that the bluff of
Orton's murder at the hands of his supposed Moscow pushers because of the failure of supplies to
reach them, would have been swallowed. Orton was
dead—long live Gant.

He smiled sadly to himself and a waiter, at his
signal, came over with another Scotch on a tray, together with a small jug of water. He paid for his
drink, and appeared to return to his book. Covertly,
he watched the KGB men as they carried away
Gant's luggage. They would have searched the
room, he knew, and would have removed every-

thing. Orton, the mysterious Englishman who looked so harmless, but who had infected the youth of Moscow with the terrible affliction of heroin, would be thoroughly investigated. Edgecliffe was smiling. In his signal to Aubrey, that night at least, he could report a state of satisfactory progress.

Besides the false papers he had shown to the KGB searching the metro, to protect himself from identification as a suspected drug-trafficker, Pavel had in his pocket, among other things, something that would have caused Gant to become far more ill than he had thus far seemed to be: it was a red card, such as was only carried by members of the KGB. It was a card which he sincerely hoped not to have to use since it was a fake, but which he knew he might have to employ if there was no other way out of the station.

He had watched them arrive. As yet there were few, but they were thorough. He had already shifted his ground a dozen times in less than fifteen minutes, straining his nerve and patience to make his movements appear casual, unobtrusive. There were KGB men at the main entrance, where a hastily erected barrier had been thrown across the gap into the square and the night, and all departing and arriving passengers were having their papers inspected. They were a motley collection of duty and off-duty personnel from the various departments of the 2nd Chief Directorate, and some faces he knew from Edgecliffe's files on the Political Security Service. They were looking for the murderers of Orton, the "economic criminals" that formed one of their main interests in life.

He had seen Vassily, the third man on the embankment, only once, sitting in a station restaurant, eating a huge, doughy cake, and sipping coffee. The coffee was good, and the pastries and cakes cheap and filling for a man like Vassily, whose papers proclaimed him to be a nightwatchman. Vassily could

stay in the restaurant for a couple of hours yet, and
be searched and questioned, without arousing suspicion. So might he—but not Gant.

The remainder of the KGB personnel, who had
not dropped out of sight to the lower levels and plat-
forms of the metro station, were engaged in searching all possible places of concealment in the station
foyer. A small team was busy opening all the left-
luggage boxes, set against the far wall. Others
checked papers, questioned ascending passengers,
bullied and threatened. Pavel watched, with a degree of fascination, a typical and very thorough
KGB operation against the citizens of Moscow.

He tried to keep in his line of sight the entrance to
the gents' where Gant had retreated. The man was
having a bad time. He could not comprehend how
Gant had ever been selected for this mission. Pavel
himself was only a link in the chain, one of Edgecliffe's small Russian force in Moscow, but he knew
more than perhaps he should have done, since Edgecliffe respected all those native Russians who
worked for him, Jew, or non-Jew, with a more than
ordinary respect. He, unlike Aubrey, appreciated the
risk they took—and, if he could avoid it, he wouldn't
let them walk in the dark: in the case of Pavel, not
even for the Firefox.

Pavel almost missed the KGB man heading down
the steps to the gents', because he was watching the
furor as some one was arrested at the entrance to
the station. Some irregularity in the man's papers,
in his travel visas or work permit, perhaps—it
had been sufficient. As soon as he saw the KGB man,
head bobbingly descending the steps, he moved
away from his position near the restaurant, coming
casually off the wall like a hoarding unstuck by the
weather. It still wasn't sufficient to prevent another
KGB man coming from the restaurant, wiping his
lips with a dark blue handkerchief, from asking him
for his papers. For a moment, but only for a moment,
Pavel considered ignoring the order. Then, he turned

his head and tried to smile nervously, reaching slowly, innocently, into his breast-pocket.

Gant was still in one of the closets, seated on the lavatory, his coat pulled around him, one hand gripping the lapels tightly across his throat, the other clenched in a pocket in an attempt to disguise its shaking. He knew he was close to the condition he had found himself in in Saigon. He was close to having the dream again.

He hadn't needed to make himself sick. He had only just made it to the sanctuary of the closet before he had heaved up his dinner. The bout of nausea, continuing until he was retching drily and gathering bile at the back of his throat to make the retching less painful, had left him weak and unable to move. He had settled wearily, agedly, onto the seat, trying to control his racing heartbeat, and the flickering, fearful images in his head. He listened to the footsteps, the muttered talk, the whistling, the splashing of water and the tugged clicks of roller-towels. A dozen times, the washroom had been empty, but he had not moved. He did not think he could.

He felt like a man beginning a ten thousand mile journey who breaks his leg, slipping on his own doorstep. The cold part of his mind which continued to function, though merely as an impotent observer, found his situation ridiculous, and shameful. He could not explain why he should feel so shot to hell, but he suspected that he simply had not prepared himself for what he had encountered. Gant had no resistance to fear. His brittle, overwhelming arrogance left him vulnerable to situations he could not control—and, however much he tried to persuade himself that his situation was controllable, the fiction would not take root in his imagination, calm him.

He heard footsteps on the tiled floor outside the cubicle. He promised himself he would leave as soon

as the washroom was empty again. Then a fist banged
on the door.

"In there," he heard, in Russian. "Your papers.
Quickly."

"I—I . . ." he forced the words out. "I'm on the
loo," he said, recollecting the English vernacular
that had been drummed into him.

"English?" the man called out, in a thick accent.
"State Security," he added. "Your papers, please."

"Can you—wait a minute?"

"Very well," the man replied in irritation.

Gant tore paper from the roll, crushed it noisily,
the flushed the lavatory. He undid and rattled the
buckle on his belt, and the loose change in his pocket, and then slid back the bolt and stepped out of the
cubicle.

The KGB man was thick-waisted but heavily-
muscled, and displeased. He was, Gant guessed, low
in status within the service, but did not intend to let
an English tourist see that. He puffed his chest, and
glared theatrically.

"Your papers—please." He held out his hand, staring at Gant's face. "You are ill—or, maybe, frightened?"

"No—stomach," Gant said weakly, patting his
overcoat.

The KGB man went through the papers carefully,
without imagination or haste. Then he looked up. He
offered them to Gant, and said: "Your papers are
not in order!"

Buckholz had told Gant repeatedly that such a
trick was a stock tactic in preliminary investigation.
The accusation, of something, anything—just to
gauge the reaction. Yet he was unable to respond innocently. He panicked. Fear showed in his eyes, in
the furtive darting of his gaze—the animal seeking a
bolt-hole. The KGB man reached for his pocket, and
Gant knew the man was about the draw a gun. Re-
acting instinctively, he bulled against the man, hand

reaching for the hand in the Russian's pocket, driving him off balance, even as he sought the gun.

The KGB man was driven up against the roller-towel cabinet before he could regain his balance. He was still trying to reach the gun in his pocket, the one reassuring factor, as Gant tugged frantically at the towel. The hand that had closed upon the gun wriggled in his grasp—he found it difficult to hold the thick wrist. He brought his knee up into the Russian's groin, and the man's breath exploded and he groaned, sagging against the wall. Then Gant had a huge loop of towel free and he wound the loop around the man's head. Then he pulled. The Russian's free hand struggled with the tightening folds —his eyes seemed to enlarge, become totally bulbous. Gant's own vision clouded, and he continued twisting and tugging the towel. He seemed to hear a voice, distant and high, and feel a hand on his shoulder, pulling at him . . . he held on. Then, he was turned bodily, and something exploded across his face.

He was staring at Pavel, his hand raised to slap him a second time. His face expressed a cold, ruthless fury.

"You—stupid animal! He was KGB—don't you understand what that means? And—you've killed him!" Gant turned to stare dumbly at the pop-eyed, discolored features of the Russian on the floor. The man's tongue was hanging out fatly. He turned back to Pavel.

"I—I thought he'd—guessed who I was . . ." he said in a feeble voice.

"You're a menace, Gant!" Pavel said. "You could get us all killed, do you realize that?" He stared at the body for a moment, as if mesmerized, then he bent swiftly, galvanized by a cold fear, and unwound the towel. Taking the body under the armpits, he dragged it across the floor of the washroom and into an empty cubicle. He tucked the legs inside

the door, rummaged in the pockets, and then locked
himself in the cubicle.

"Is it clear?" Gant heard him ask.

"Yes," Gant replied in the voice of a zombie.

He looked up, and watched as the big man
climbed over the door of the cubicle and dropped beside him. He was wiping his hands which were dusty
from the top of the door. He patted a pocket. "I have
tried to—disguise your stupidity by making it appear that the man was robbed." He sniffed at Gant.
"Now," he added, "quickly go up the stairs, and make
your way slowly to the entrance. If anyone—*anyone*
—calls on you to stop, obey them. Show your papers,
and pretend you're ill, as before—understand?"

"Yes. He—he said my papers were not in order."

"You damned fool—you killed him for that? They
are in order. He was only trying to put you up."

"I—didn't know where you were . . ."

"I was stopped, by the KGB. But my papers also
were in order." He pushed Gant ahead of him. "Now
—quickly, up to the entrance. This fat officer could
become the object of a search at any moment, and
then no one would be allowed to leave this station!"

Gant was stopped twice crossing the station concourse by minor KGB officers who glanced at his
papers, asked after his health and his movements,
and then let him go. Slowly he approached the temporary barrier thrown across the entrance of the
station.

He had no idea how far behind him Pavel was.
He would have to wait for him—if he got through
the barrier.

The men at the barrier, at least a tall, gray-haired
figure with the side of the face that had, at some
time, received very poor plastic surgery—Gant assumed it to have been a war-wound—appeared to
possess more authority than the big man he had
strangled. Gant passed his papers across to a younger man standing in front of the gray-haired expres-

sionless senior officer, and waited. He tried not to
look at the scarred, half-repaired face, but found his
gaze drawn to it. The tall man smiled thinly, and
rubbed his artificially smooth cheek with one long-
fingered hand.

"English?" the younger man asked.

"Uh—oh, yes."

"Mm. Mr. Grant—we must ask you to wait at one
of the tables here for a moment, until we check
with your hotel."

"I have the papers . . ."

"Yes, and your passport and papers have received
a security service stamp—nevertheless, we must ask
you to wait."

The young man lifted up the barrier, so that a
hinged section stood on end, and Gant was ushered
through. Other tables besides the one at which he
was directed to sit, were occupied. About half-a-doz-
en people in all. Not all of them Russians. He heard
an American voice, belonging to an elderly man,
saying:

"There's no right on earth makes you question
that passport and those papers, sonny!" A young
KGB man, crop-haired, waved the remark aside, and
continued with a telephone conversation.

Gant sat down, heavily, at the table. It was a rickety affair, erected for the express purpose of providing a semblance of the KGB's normal interrogation
facilities. He swallowed hard. He turned his eyes
to the barrier, and saw Pavel repossessing his papers
and passing out of the entrance to the station, without a backward glance. Suddenly, he felt deserted,
alone. He was once more no longer in control of the
situation. He stared at the black telephone isolated
on the table.

Then the young man slid into the chair opposite
him, and smiled. "This won't take very long, let us
hope, Mr. Grant," he said.

As he dialed the number of the Warsaw Hotel,
Gant saw, clearly, and for the first time, the odds

against him. He was taking on the largest, the most ruthless, the most thorough security service the world had ever seen. It was small comfort to recollect that Aubrey had described the KGB as notoriously inefficient because of its very size. To Gant, sitting at that table, in the cold foyer of the metro station, it was no comfort at all, the smooth platitudes of a man in an hotel room in the middle of London.

"Hotel Warsaw?" the young man asked in Russian. Gant kept his eyes on the table, so that he did not betray any sign that he followed the conversation. "Ah—State Security here. Let me talk to Prodkov, please." Prodkov would be the name of the KGB man who worked on the staff of the hotel—he might have been a waiter, desk-clerk, dishwasher, but he possessed far more power than the hotel manager.

There was a considerable wait, then: "Prodkov—I have a tourist here, Michael Grant. He is registered in room 308. . . . Yes, you know him. Tell me, what does he look like? Would you look at me for a moment, Mr. Grant, please? Thank you—go ahead, Prodkov. . . . Mm. Yes . . . yes—I see. And he is not there now?" There was another, longer pause. Gant waited, in disbelief. Aubrey could never have anticipated what was happening to him now—now it would emerge that Grant looked different, or was already tucked up in his bed. "Good. Thank you, Prodkov. Goodbye."

The young man was smiling affably to deny what had just occurred. There had been no suspicion, no force—merely a very ordinary, routine check on a tourist's papers. He handed back the sheaf of papers, tucked neatly into the cover of the passport bearing the name of Michael Grant.

"Thank you, Mr. Grant—I apologize for any delay. We—are engaged in a search for—criminals, shall we say? Of course, we wished merely to eliminate you from our inquiries. You are now free to resume

your nocturnal sightseeing tour of our city." The
young man was obviously proud of his English. He
stood up, gravely shook hands with Gant, and then
waved him through the barrier. The gray-haired
man smiled crookedly as Gant passed him, only one
side of his face wrinkling with the expression.

Gant nodded to him, and then he was outside the
barrier and walking as steadily as he could towards
the entrance. Outside the ornate entrance, beneath
its elaborate, decorated portico, the wind was suddenly cold. Gant realized that his body was bathed
in a sweat of relief. He looked around him and saw
Pavel detach himself from the shadows.

"Good," he said. "Now, we have wasted far too
much time already. Soon, it will be dangerous to be
on the streets, impeccable papers or otherwise.
Come—we have a short distance to walk. You go
ahead of me, down the Kirov Street. When we are
away from the station, I will catch you up, and
show where we are heading. Good? Very well, begin
walking."

They picked up two of the known associates of
Pavel Upenskoy and Vassily Levin just before six in
the morning. Both were family men, living in the
same tower block of Soviet Workers' flats on the
wide Mira Prospekt, overlooking the vast permanent
site of the Exhibition of Economic Achievements in
the northern suburbs of Moscow. The black sedans
of Kontarsky's team parked in the forecourt of the
block, while it was hardly light, and the men moved
in swiftly. The whole operation took hardly more
than three minutes, including the ascent of the lift
to the fourteenth and sixteenth floors. When the
team returned, the two additional human beings appearing satisfactorily disturbed, barely awake, and
deeply frightened, Priabin knew that his chief would
be satisfied.

Priabin grinned into the frightened, wan faces of
the two men taken from their beds as they passed

him with nervous sideglances. They knew, he
sensed, why he had come for them—and they knew
what to expect when they were returned to the Center, to Dzerzhinsky Street. He watched them being
loaded into two of the black cars, and then glanced
up at the block of flats. On the sixteenth floor, he
could make out the smudge of a white face at a dark
window—the wife, or perhaps a child. It did not
matter.

His breath smoked round him in the cold dawn air
as he returned to his car. Dipping his head at the
passenger window, he said to the driver: "Very
well—give the order for the surveillance-team to
move in on the warehouse. Let's get Upenskoy as
well, while we're about it!"

Gant woke from a fitful, dream-filled sleep as the
doors of the removal van were opened noisily by
Pavel Upenskoy. Shaking his head, muttering, he
pulled himself into a sitting position on the mattress
which had been laid just behind the driver's cab.
Gant had boarded it in the warehouse of the Sanitary Manufacturing Company of Moscow.

The light of cold, high bulbs filtered into the interior of the truck, but Upenskoy was hidden from
Gant's view by the stacked lavatory bowls and cis-
terns that he was to drive that day to Kuybyshev, a
town lying more than a hundred miles south of
Bilyarsk, and more than seven hundred road miles
from Moscow. A new hotel being constructed in
Kuybyshev awaited the toilet fittings.

"Gant—are you awake?"

"Yes," Gant replied sullenly, trying to moisten
his dry, stale mouth with saliva. "What time is it?"

"Nearly five-thirty. We leave for Bilyarsk just before six. If you want, the old man has made some
coffee—come and get it."

Gant heard the heavy footsteps retreat across the
concrete floor of the warehouse, and ascend some
steps. A flimsy door banged shut. Then, the only

sounds were those of his hands rubbing at the stubble on his chin, and the sucking of his lips as he tried to rid himself of the dry, evil taste in his mouth. He brushed a hand across his forehead and examined the thin film of sweat on his fingertips carefully, as if it were something alien, or something familiar the appearance and nature of which he had long forgotten. Then he wiped his hand on the trouser leg of his faded blue overalls into which he had changed when he arrived at the warehouse.

He had not slept well. He had not been allowed to sleep for more than two hours after being brought by Pavel to the warehouse, in a narrow commercial street that ran off the Kirov Street. They were only a quarter of a mile from the Komsomolskaia Metro Station. Pavel had not allowed him to sleep as he had hammered home to him the facts and nuances of his new, and third, identity—that of Boris Glazunov, driver's mate, who lived in a block of flats on the Mira Prospekt, who was married with two children and who, in reality, Pavel had explained, would be staying home and out of sight, while Gant accompanied him in the delivery truck as far as Bilyarsk. The briefing had been conducted entirely in Russian—Gant had been forcibly reminded more than once of his language training with the defector, Lebedev, at Langley, Virginia.

At last, after a recital of his assumed life history, and a repeated account of what papers he carried, and what they represented, he had been allowed to sleep—to sleep as soundly as his own mind would allow him. He had relived the strangulation of the KGB man in the washroom, in a grotesque, balletic slow-motion in endless repetition—to relive the reaction that had caused him to sag against a shop window in the Kirov Street, so that Pavel had hurried to catch him up, and hold his shaking body until the epilepsy of reaction passed.

Gant climbed to his feet, and tried to put the vivid

images from his mind. As he clambered and squeezed
his way out of the back of the truck, he tried to consider the future, the hours ahead, to help drive away
the past. He knew now that he could rely completely
on Pavel Upenskoy.

In any and every word that the big man had spok-
en, Gant had sensed the contempt in which he was
held by the Russian. It was as if, Gant admitted, he
had been insulted with the company of a weekend
flyer in the cockpit of the Firefox, Pavel having to
tag him along until he could dump him outside Bilyarsk. Gant understood the ruthless professionalism
of the big Russian. Where and how British Intelligence had recruited him, he did not know, but the
old man, the nightwatchman at the warehouse, had
muttered through his gums something about Pavel
having had a Jewish wife, who was still in prison or
labor camp for having demonstrated against the Russian invasion of Czechoslovakia, twelve years before.
That had been when Pavel had left him briefly alone
with the old man who had tried to soften Pavel's
harsh treatment of the American. Apart from that
fact, Gant knew nothing about Pavel Upenskoy. Yet,
strangely, he accepted the big man's contempt and
brusque manner with equanimity. The man was
good.

Pavel and the old man were sitting at a small,
bare table in the dispatch-office of the warehouse. As
yet, none of the daystaff had reported for work. Pavel intended to be long gone before they arrived. He
looked up as Gant shut the flimsy door behind him,
as if inspecting the American critically in the light
of the naked bulb suspended from the ceiling. The
room, like the warehouse, was cold and Gant rubbed
his hands together for warmth. Pavel indicated the
coffee pot on the ancient electric ring plugged into
the wall, and Gant collected a chipped mug from the
table and poured himself some black coffee. Without
sugar, the drink was bitter, but it was hot. Un-

easily, as if uninvited, he settled himself at the table. The old man, as if at a signal, finished his coffee, and left the room.

"He goes to see if we are under surveillance here," Pavel explained without looking at Gant.

"You mean they. . . ?" Gant began quickly.

"No—I do not mean they know where you are," the Russian replied. "These will not be the men who followed you last night, or that gang at the station —but the department of the KGB that is concerned with the security of the airplane knows who I am, and who the others are—they will be watching, no doubt, since the weapons-trials are in," he looked at his watch, "less than thirty hours' time!"

"Then—they'll know I'm on my way?"

"Not necessarily. They will merely be watching us."

"If they stop us?" Gant persisted. "It'll all be blown to hell, before I can leave Moscow!"

"No! If we are stopped, there are other arrangements." Pavel seemed to be battling with some doubt in himself.

"What other arrangements?" Gant said scornfully. "I've got to get six hundred miles today, man! How do I do it—*fly*?" Gant laughed, a high-pitched sound. Pavel looked at him in contempt.

"I am ordered to—die, if necessary, to insure that you get away free," Pavel said softly. "It is not what I would consider a willing or worthwhile sacrifice . . . However, if we get out of here safely, then we shall not be stopped again until we reach the circular motorway, where another vehicle will be waiting, in the event of trouble, to collect you. If there is no trouble, then you continue with me. Understood?"

Gant was silent for a time, then he said: "Yes."

"Good. Now, go and shave, in the next room— clean yourself up, a little, yes?" Gant nodded, and crossed the room. Just as he was about to close the door behind him, he heard Pavel say: "Gant—can you fly that plane—really fly it?"

Gant poked his head back round the door. Pavel was staring into the bottom of his mug, hands clasped round it, elbows on the bare wooden table. His big frame seemed somehow shrunken in the blue overalls.

"Yes," Gant said. "I can fly it. I'm the best there is."

Pavel looked up into Gant's eyes, stared at him for a long moment in silence, then nodded, and said: "Good. I would not want to die to deliver faulty goods to Bilyarsk."

He returned his gaze to the coffee mug, and Gant closed the door behind him. He switched on the weak, naked bulb, ran the water until it was luke-warm, and inspected himself in the speckled mirror. Pavel had cut his hair the previous night, and then he had washed it. It was short now, flat on his head, without hair oil. He looked younger, perhaps a little like he had done as a teenager in Clarkville—except for the ridiculous moustache that survived from his personae as Orton and then as Grant. He soaped his face with a stubby brush and tugged at the bristles of the moustache until it had become hairs floating in the gray shaving water. Then he began, methodi-cally, to shave the rest of his face.

When he returned to the office, Pavel was obvi-ously ready to leave. The old man had returned, and vanished again, presumably to keep watch.

"They are here," Pavel said softly. Gant sensed a new tension about the man, his ordinariness showing through.

"How many?" Gant asked, keeping his voice steady with an effort.

"Three—in one car. The old man has seen them before. They are part of the team appointed to the security of the Bilyarsk project. They follow Mr. Lansing about Moscow, and Dherkov, the courier

who comes from Bilyarsk. The old man thinks they
are only watching—if they had come to make ar-
rests, there would be more of them."

Gant nodded when the Russian had finished.
Then, his expression turned to one of surprise when
Pavel drew an automatic from his overall pocket.

"What—?"

"You can use this?"

Gant took the gun, and turned it over in his hand.
It was a type he had not met before, a Makarov, but
it seemed close enough to the Walther P-38 that he
had used more than once, if only on the range. He
nodded.

"Good. *Don't*—unless it's absolutely necessary!"

"Yes."

"Are you ready?"

"Yes."

"Then let us be gone from here. It is a little before
six—soon it will be light, and we have six hundred
miles to go." He opened the door, and followed Gant
through.

Once they were in the big cab of the truck, whose
nose pointed at the double-doors of the warehouse,
Pavel started the engine and flickered the headlights. Gant spotted the old nightwatchman by the
doors, then they began to swing open; Pavel eased
the truck into gear and they rolled forward towards
the widening gap of gray light. He caught a glimpse
of the old man's face, smiling grimly, and then they
were out into the side street, with Pavel heaving on
the wheel of the truck to straighten it. Gant caught a
glimpse of a black sedan further down the street,
in the opposite direction to the one they had taken,
and then they were turning into the Kirov Street,
sodium-lit, gray, and deserted.

Behind them, the KGB car was quiet. No one
had panicked, started the engine. Instead, one of the
three men, the oldest and largest, had picked up the
car telephone, and was in direct contact with KGB
Colonel Mihail Kontarsky within seconds.

"They have just left—two of them, in the sanitary ware delivery truck. What do you wish us to do, Colonel?"

There was a pause, then: "I will check with Priabin at the Mira Prospekt. For the moment, you may follow them—but do *not* close up!"

"Yes, Colonel." He nodded to the driver, who fired the engine. The car pulled out from the curb, past the now-closed doors of the warehouse, and stopped at the junction with the Kirov Street. The truck was a distant black lump on the road, heading north-east towards the Sadovaya, the inner ring road around the city.

"Close up," the man in charge said to the driver. "But not too close. Just enough not to lose him on the Sadovaya."

"Right!" The driver pressed his foot on the accelerator, and the sedan shot forward, narrowing the distance between itself and the truck. By the time they were a hundred meters in the rear, the truck was slowing at the junction of the Kirov Street and the Sadovaya. The sedan idled into the curb, waiting until the truck pulled out into the heavier traffic of the ring road. The indicator showed that the driver, the man Upenskoy, intended to turn right, to the south-east.

The truck pulled out, then the man in the passenger seat said: "Colonel—Colonel, they're on the Sadovaya now, heading south-east. We're pulling out—now." The car skittered across the road, and was hooted at by an oncoming lorry, straightened, and the truck was more than five hundred meters away. "Close up again," the man said, and the driver nodded. He skipped the sedan out into the outside lane, and accelerated. Kontarsky's voice came over the radio receiver.

"Priabin has just requested you pick up the man Upenskoy—he has the other two, Glazunov and Riassin. Who is that in the truck with him, Borkh?"

"I do not know, Colonel—it should be—"

"Exactly! It should be Glazunov, should it not, if Upenskoy is making a real delivery somewhere . . . should it not?"

"Yes, Colonel. The truck has turned onto Karl Marx Street now, Colonel—it looks as if they're heading out of the city, all right."

"Where is Upenskoy scheduled to deliver?"

"I don't know, Colonel—we can find out."

"He will have to report to the travel control on the motorway, Borkh, we can find out then. You follow them until they reach the checkpoint, then we shall decide what to do. Priabin is bringing in Glazunov and Riassin—perhaps they will be able to tell us?"

The men in the car heard Kontarsky's laughter, and then the click of the receiver. Borkh replaced the telephone, and studied the truck, now only a hundred meters ahead of them on Bakouninskaia Street, headed like an arrow north-east out of the city, towards the Gorky road.

"Our Colonel seems to be in a merry mood this morning," the driver observed. "Then, he hasn't spent the night in a freezing car!"

"Disrespect, Ilya?" Borkh said with a smile.

"Who—me? No chance! Hello, our friend is taking a left turn," he added. The car was crossing the Yaouza, the tributary of the Moskva, flowing south at that point to join the river at the Oustinski Bridge. The truck ahead of them had turned left directly after the bridge over the sluggish tributary. The car followed, keeping its required distance. "Think he's spotted us?"

"Not necessarily—he's picking up the Gorky road, maybe—see, I thought so—right onto the Chtcholkovskoie Way, and heading east," Borkh said. "He's on his way to Gorky, all right."

"And to Kazan—and then to . . . ?" the driver asked, smiling.

"Maybe—maybe. That's for our Colonel to worry about."

"And worry he will," the third man added from beneath his hat in the back seat, where he was stretched out comfortably.

"Oh, you're awake then, are you?" Borkh asked with heavy sarcasm.

"Just about—it must be the boring life I lead, and the boring company," the man replied, settling himself back again,

"You will have your photograph taken at this checkpoint," Pavel was saying as he pulled the truck into the side of the road, along the narrowing line of posts that signified the lane for heavy goods vehicles. Gant, looking ahead, saw that they were approaching what, to all intents and purposes, was a customs post, as if the motorway ringing the outskirts of Moscow marked some kind of territorial boundary.

"Are they KGB on guard here?" he asked, as the face of a soldier in drab brown uniform slid past the cab window.

"No—Red Army. But they're commanded by a KGB man—he'll be sitting in that hut over there." Gant followed the nod of Pavel's head, and observed a young man in civilian clothes lounging in the doorway of a wooden hut, smoking a long cigarette. Gant could not see through the window into the interior —the newly-risen sun reflected in a sheet of yellow-orange from the glass.

"What happens—just a check on papers?" he asked.

"Usually, and your photograph is taken, from the smaller hut next to the office, but don't smile— they'll wonder what you're trying to hide!" Pavel smiled grimly, and tugged on the handbrake loudly. "Now, get out," he said.

Gant opened the door, and climbed down. The tension in his stomach was returning, but not se-verely—it seemed just to be moving up a gear from the slightly unsettled feeling that had been with him ever since Pavel had told him that the sedan had

followed them all the way from the Kirov Street out
to the motorway. He resisted an itching desire to
look behind, to see the faces behind the windscreen
of the KGB car.

Pavel stood beside him, casually smoking a cigarette. Gant tried not to look about him with too obvious an interest. His cover presumed him to have
undergone this formality a number of times before.

A military guard collected their papers, and took
them away and into the office. Gant idly watched
the cars and trucks that drew up in the three lanes
that were used by outbound traffic. The circular motorway swept above them on huge concrete piles,
and he could hear the thrumming of the traffic from
overhead.

"One of the men from the car has just gone into
the office," Pavel said levelly. "You know where the
car is, if you have to run for it . . ."

"You think it might come . . . ?"

"No. At the moment, you are unremarkable as far
as they are concerned. Ah, here come our papers."

The same guard crossed from the office, his boots
clattering distinctly on the concrete, and handed
them their papers, which had been stamped with
the necessary permit for travel as far as Gorky on
the main road. At Gorky, they would need another
permit to travel as far east as Kazan, and then another from Kazan to Kuybyshev. Pavel nodded,
stubbed out the remainder of his cigarette, and
climbed back aboard the truck. Gant, careful not to
watch the door of the office, rounded the front of the
truck and regained his seat.

Pavel switched on, slid the engine into gear, and
drew away. A red and white barrier slid up in front
of them, to allow them to pass beneath the motorway out onto the Gorky road.

Pavel looked across at Gant, and said, "Gorky by
lunchtime, and Kazan in time for tea—or don't you
Americans take tea?" He laughed, encouraging
Gant to smile.

Gant said, "Are they tailing us?"

Pavel looked into the wing-mirror, and said: "No, not yet—but they'll have someone pick us up later on. Don't worry! The KGB aren't worried—just curious. They want to know who you are!"

"You mean they don't believe I'm this guy Glazunov?"

"If they do now, they won't before long. Your picture will be at the records office of the State Highway Militia by this afternoon, and checked against existing photographs of Glazunov, then they'll *really* want to know who you are!"

"And they'll stop us, and ask me?" Gant persisted.

"Perhaps. But—they are very confident, at Bilyarsk. Let us hope they want to play a waiting game. There are alternatives for you at each of our scheduled stops, so don't worry. If they stopped us on the road, they would be asking for trouble, wouldn't they?" He smiled. "We shall hope that they leave us alone, until they come to be just a little bit afraid —and that takes a long time for the KGB!"

It was early in the afternoon when David Edgecliffe, looking immensely regretful, grave and dignified, identified the body of his agent, Fenton, as the mortal remains of Alexander Thomas Orton. He stood with Inspector Tortyev of the Moscow Police in the mortuary, a cold and depressing room, and gazed down at the battered, barely recognizable face and nodded after a suitable pause and catch in the throat. The wounds did not take him by surprise. Fenton looked now as Gant might have looked, in his persona as Orton. There was not sufficient left of the features for anyone to be able to distinguish between the American and the Englishman—especially since Gant had gone through two further transformations since he left the Moskva the previous night.

"Yes," he said softly. "Insofar as I can judge, that is the body of Mr. Orton." He looked up at Tortyev, who dropped the cloth back over Fenton's ruined features.

"You could not be mistaken, Mr. Edgecliffe?" he asked.

"I—don't think so, Inspector," Edgecliffe said levelly, with a tiny shrug. "There was a—lot of damage, of course."

"Yes, indeed. Almost as if his former associates did not want him to be recognized?"

"Quite. Why, though?"

Edgecliffe's eyes appeared a little baffled, but he was watching Tortyev keenly. He did not know the man, but he was aware that, though he posed as an ordinary civil policeman, Tortyev was KGB.

"I don't know, Mr. Edgecliffe—nor do you know, I suppose?" Tortyev was smiling. He was young, ruthless, charming, and tough. His gray eyes were piercing and intelligent. He was one of the university graduates increasingly appearing in the frontline of the KGB, Edgecliffe reflected. A man to be watched.

"Mm. Wish I could help you, Inspector—devil of a fuss, this'll cause at home."

"It will cause a devil of a fuss, Mr. Edgecliffe, here in Moscow," Tortyev snapped, "until we find the men who killed him!" Then he relaxed, and he said: "But come, Mr. Edgecliffe, I am sure you could do with a drink. This is not a pleasant task. Shall we go?"

He ushered Edgecliffe from the room with a winning smile.

"Then who is this man?" Kontarsky was saying, holding the photograph of Gant standing by the truck at the checkpoint under the noses of Borkh and Priabin. "Have either of you any idea?"

The light was on in his office as the day outside the window darkened. It had been a fine April day. Kontarsky had walked in the Alexandrovski Gardens after lunch and the air had been mild. Now, with something of a satisfied mood about him still, he looked at his two subordinates. He was hardly worried, merely concerned that the driver's mate with Upenskoy had not yet been identified. He was unknown to the "M" Department. The truck, naturally, was being tailed, always in sight of the tail-car. Lanyev had returned alone to Bilyarsk, with new orders for Tsernik, and advance information concerning the movements of Upenskoy and the truck.

"We do not know, Colonel," Priabin said.

Kontarsky, despite his confidence, was adroit at displaying anger with his subordinates. He said: "Do not know—we have had this photograph for hours!"

"We are checking, Colonel. The Computer and Records Directorate is giving it priority, sir," Borkh felt called upon to say.

"Is it? Is it, indeed? And why them?"

"We are assuming that this man is a foreign agent, sir," Priabin said. "British, perhaps?"

"Mm. Is that likely?"

"Why don't we stop the truck and ask him, Colonel?" Borkh blurted out.

Kontarsky turned his angry stare upon him. "Idiot!" was all he said.

Priabin understood. Kontarsky was looking for a spectacular triumph. He sensed that the man in the truck with Upenskoy was important, but he reacted by assuming that Bilyarsk was impregnable—which it was, Priabin had to admit—and that he therefore had leisure to play this man on a line, hoping that he would lead him to others, tie in with some big SIS or CIA operation. Priabin was irritated—but he, too, could not consider the threat of a single individual, even if he was traveling towards Bilyarsk, as anything to be taken seriously.

Kontarsky, seeing the keenness of his assistant's study of him, said:

"What of your interrogation?"

"Nothing—so far. They're holding out, so far."

"Holding out, Dmitri?"

"Yes, sir."

"You showed the man Glazunov this photograph of someone who was pretending to be him—was he not outraged?"

Priabin did not feel called upon to smile. He said: "Colonel—I don't think he knows who is in the truck with Upenskoy."

"But—you and I agree the truck is heading for Bilyarsk?"

"Yes, Colonel—it must be."

"Then this man, whoever he is, and from wherever he comes—must be a saboteur?"

"Probably, Colonel."

"Undoubtedly, Dmitri." Kontarsky rubbed his blue jowl. "But, what can one man do to the Mig-31 that cannot be done by Baranovich and the others already on the spot—eh?" He was thoughtful for a moment, then he added: "What kind of operation could it be? If we knew *who* he was, then we might net ourselves something very useful." He smiled, and Priabin wondered again at his motives. Kontarsky was enjoying himself, of that there was no doubt. He expected some kind of additional success, connected with this man—but what? Priabin would have stopped the truck by now.

Kontarsky went on: "I shall delay my flight to Bilyarsk by a few hours. Meanwhile, alert the security there concerning this truck . . . Borkh, get me Colonel Leprov in Records—I want this man identified as soon as possible. Meanwhile, Dmitri, get back to our friends and ask them once more who he is!"

Kontarsky's finger tapped the photograph of Gant as Borkh dialed the number and Priabin left the room.

Gant was tired, cramped with travel, his mind numbed by the endlessness of the Russian steppe, that great sweep of plain stretching as far as the

Urals, two hundred miles beyond Bilyarsk. His mind
had plumbed his own past, prompted by the similarity of the country to his own Mid-West. It had not
been a pleasant experience, and he was sick with
the memories and the gasoline fumes that seeped
into the cab.

It was dark now, and Upenskoy had switched on
the headlights. The tail-car was a steady five hundred meters behind. It had picked them up on the
outskirts of Kazan, taking over from its predecessor
as they had crossed the vast new Lenin Bridge over
the Volga which had replaced the ferry. The tail-car
was not using its lights—but both he and Pavel
knew it was there.

"How far now?" he asked, breaking a long silence.

"The turn-off is about four miles further on—then
Bilyarsk is fourteen miles up that road."

"And I have to meet the pick-up on that road—at
the point you showed me on the map?"

"Yes."

"Then it's time for me to leave you . . ." Gant said.

"Not yet."

"Yes. The first copse up ahead, and I'm going to
jump for it," Gant said decisively.

Pavel looked across at him, then said, "Very
well. I will try not to let them overtake me for as
long past the guard-post as possible. Then, with
luck, I shall leave them behind when I abandon my
trusty vehicle, which is bringing the benefits of
modern plumbing to the Volga Hotel at Kuybyshev!" Pavel, curiously to Gant, roared with laughter.

Gant said, "Don't get yourself caught."

"Not if I can help it," Pavel replied. "Semelovsky
will have passed through the guard-post less than
fifteen minutes ago."

"How do you know?"

"He was at the gasoline station in Kazan. I didn't
speak to him, but he was there."

"How—did he get out of Bilyarsk? I thought it

was sealed up tight until after tomorrow's show."

"It is. He's from Kazan—his mother is dying, so they let him out—in company with a KGB man, of course. No, don't worry. The KGB man saw him on his way. They're not worried about him. They know he's one of us, and they expect him to return to Bilyarsk."

"His mother is—really dying?"

"It would appear so—to the doctor, that is. However, she is a very tough old lady . . ." He smiled. "Semelovsky will be waiting for you on the road."

It seemed to Gant that every man he had come into contact with was under sentence of death. A sentence they all accepted as their lot. He wanted to say something to Pavel, in the selflessness of the moment.

Pavel's voice cut across his mood. "Trees coming up, and a few bends in the road, just to keep truck drivers from falling asleep!" He looked at Gant, and added: "Don't say anything—your words would be useless, maybe even insulting. Just fly that damn airplane out of Russia!"

3

THE SUSPICIONS

A pair of men's shoes were placed on Police Inspector Tortyev's desk, under the hard strip-lighting, and the young man's attention seemed to be riveted upon them. He leaned back in his chair, one foot pushing against the desk, steepled fingers tapping insistently at his pursed lips. At that moment, he was alone in his office and had been for half-an-hour, because he had wanted to think. He had still not decided what to do about the shoes.

The chair creaked as he regained an upright position, and reached out a hand. He picked up the white label tied to one of the shoes, and read again that it was the property of Alexander Thomas Orton. Shaking his head. as if in puzzled amusement, he shunted the left and right shoes, which were not a pair—one being black, the other brown—together. One shoe was a size-and-a-half bigger than the other. The black shoe from Orton's body was still damp from its ducking in the Moskva. The other shoe, still shining and barely worn, though the heel was showing signs of wear already—the other shoe had been taken from Orton's room at the Moskva Hotel.

He shunted the shoes apart, then together again, his lips pursing as he did so. He whistled softly, tunelessly, his eyes staring at the shoes, as if willing them to inform him of the cause of their discrepancy in size. The hat size had been the same, the collar size the same, the overcoat at the hotel had fitted the dead man, the suits had fitted, the socks . . . but not the shoes. Why not? Did any man have shoes that varied so much in size? Why?

He pushed back his chair again, assuming his former position. It was, indeed, mysterious. The answer, of course, forming itself in his mind all the time he had been alone in his office, was that the man in the river was not the man who had booked into the Moskva Hotel, the man who had passed through security at Cheremetievo, who had taken that walk from the hotel along the embankment, only to be murdered.

Why was it not the same man? The question was more important than the discovery, the solution to the problem of the shoes. One of the three men who had met Mr. Orton had—taken his place in the river? Why?

The question might not have interested an ordinary policeman, not as directly, or as insistently as it interested Tortyev. But then, Tortyev was not an ordinary member of the Moscow police. He held a police rank, and his offices were situated in the Police Headquarters but, like many of his colleagues, he was a member of the KGB 2nd Chief Directorate. His only superiors, the only people to whom he was answerable, were KGB officers in the Political Security Service.

Tortyev had been in charge of the Orton case since the first addiction cases had come to the attention of the Moscow police and, naturally and inevitably, to the attention of his section of the KGB.

His rank in the police had been made up to Inspector, at thirty-three, and he was given authority to co-opt suitable resources in order to unearth, and smash, the ring creating the addiction.

Tortyev had a hatred of drugs, and of pushers. It was as burning a hatred as belonged to any member of any drugs squad anywhere in the world. Tortyev would have done equally valuable work in New York, or London, or Amsterdam. He hated Orton. When Holokov, fat, efficient Holokov, had informed him of the Englishman's death, he had been pleased, though, in another way, frustrated. He had wanted to confront Orton, see him sentenced. Yet his death had not mattered—they knew the others, the ones Orton had supplied.

Yet now, Orton was not dead at all, he admitted. His teeth ground together audibly in the silence of the room. He picked up the telephone. An operator at a special switchboard divorced from the switchboard that served the rest of the police building, answered.

"Get me the Seventh Directorate—the office of Colonel Ossipov," he said, and waited for his call to be answered. When it was, he swiftly requested assistance, in the form of men and time, from the KGB Colonel responsible for the surveillance of English tourists. The call took less than a minute. Tortyev had priority with the Seventh Directorate.

When he had put the telephone down again, he went back to studying the shoes, pushing them together, pulling them apart, as if making them perform some simple dance. Now that he had requested more men, to begin checking on Orton's movements, he would need Stechko, Holokov, and possibly the sergeant, Filipov, even if the man was a Jew, to begin checking through their records of the previous visits of Orton to Moscow, their records of his contacts, behavior-pattern, habits. . . .

As he pressed the intercom switch to summon

his subordinates, he was still staring at the odd shoes.
He was smiling, as if they represented a challenge
to him.

At the moment he was about to speak, he suddenly wondered what had become of the transistor-ra-
dio that had been itemized at the airport—and had
been inspected for drugs. It had not been in his hotel
room, not on the body. Of course, it might be at the
bottom of the river.

"Stechko—get Holokov and Filipov right away——
I've got some important paperwork for you," he said ,
his smile becoming puzzlement once more. Where ·
was that radio?

*   *   *

Semelovsky was waiting for him, the small Moskvitch sedan pulled into the side of the narrow road
leading to Bilyarsk, the hood open. Gant could
see the faint outline of Semelovsky hunched into the
open jaws of the car, as if in the process of being
swallowed. He settled down at the peak of the bank
which bordered the road, and waited. The man went
on working, or appearing to work, on the engine of
the small car. Gant spent ten minutes checking that
the figure was alone, and that the road was empty.
When the man stood up, stretched his back, and
cursed in Russian, Gant ducked back out of sight.
Semelovsky was small—Gant saw light glint from
the two moons of his spectacles. The man looked
around him, and up and down the road, then returned his head beneath the hood. Gant heard muffled tinkering, and a tuneless whistle, then slowly got
to his feet, and eased himself down the slope of the
bank. The man's back was to him, and if he were not
Semelovsky, then . . .

"How long have you been watching me?" the little man asked in Russian, in an irritated voice, without lifting his head from beneath the hood. Gant

stopped in his tracks, one foot raised from the ground in a half-made step.

"Semelovsky?" he asked as the shock dissipated in his system.

The man emerged from beneath the hood, ~~wiping~~ his hands on an oily rag. He studied Gant by the light of the moon, low on the horizon still, nodded to himself as if in satisfaction, and closed the hood loudly. Gant moved closer to him. The man was in his late forties, possibly fifties. The remainder of his frizzy gray hair clung to his ears, but the top of his head was bald. He was dressed in a drab suit, and wore a raincoat. He was barely more than five feet in height. He looked up at Gant, the light glinting from his spectacles as he studied the American.

"You're late," he said at last.

"I'm sorry," Gant snapped back, irritated by the man.

"It's a question of the guards," Semelovsky explained, as if to a child. "A little longer, and one of the guard-posts, either at the junction or the other end of the road, would have sent someone to discover where I was. It is almost an hour since I checked through the first guard-post—which is why my car has, to all intents and purposes, broken down."

Gant nodded, and then said: "How do I get into Bilyarsk?"

"A good question. In the trunk of the car, of course."

"Won't they search it?"

"Probably not. It was searched at the other end. Thoroughly. The KGB work very mindlessly, most of the time," he added, as if lecturing on the subject of an inefficient mechanism. "If the one guard-post is detailed to search all incoming vehicles, and the other all outgoing traffic, then they do not, as a rule, change functions—despite the recent draft of extra guards into the town. Do you know, there were more than a dozen jammed into the guard-post at the highway junction." Semelovsky smiled suddenly, brilliantly. "They must be expecting trouble, of one kind or another!"

He walked around Gant to the rear of the car, and opened the trunk. He gestured to the American, sharply, as if accusing himself of having wasted valuable time, and Gant joined him. The trunk was empty, and small. Pocketing the gun he had held all the time in his right hand, Gant climbed into the small space, hunched himself into a fetal position, and nodded. The Russian stood watching him for a moment, and then nodded back. The light disappeared, and Gant was in a confined, cramped darkness. He accepted that Semelovsky would have prepared the trunk so that he would not asphyxiate. The darkness held no terrors for him. The trunk was not as cramped as his own thoughts had proved, those months in the hospital. He heard the tinny roar of the engine, realized that Semelovsky, with careful attention to detail, was firing on only three cylinders, and then was heaved against the cold metal of the trunk-door as the Russian pulled onto the road.

Semelovsky gave little thought to his passenger as he negotiated the remaining miles to the outskirts of Bilyarsk, where the quarters for the technical and scientific staff had been constructed. The road was narrow and deeply rutted by the passage of numerous heavy vehicles, bringing equipment to the project site. Semolovsky thought only of his function within the total operation that was intended to bring Gant and the Mig-31 into successful proximity. He had been recruited into the underground cell by Baranovich, for whom, and for whose sufferings at the hands of the NKVD and later the KGB, he had an almost religious respect. Semelovsky was himself a Jew, but had spent most of his adult life working successfully on various technical and military projects for the regime that despised and harried in large numbers the people of his race. But, Baranovich was sufficiently his hero to shake him out of the political cowardice of years; like all converts, he was zealous to an extreme.

The second guard-post lay in a gap in the high wire fence that surrounded the whole project area, including the airstrip. The original farming village of Bilyarsk lay outside the wire, a separate, and separated, community of wooden houses, communal agriculture, and poverty. The project-town had been grafted on to it, a hybrid growth surrounded by trees, ordered, secret.

Semelovsky slowed the car as he approached the gates in the wire, and he saw the increased size of the guard, a pattern he already expected from the junction guard-post fourteen miles down the road. Two guards, rather than the usual one, approached the vehicle, and he was almost blinded by the new, powerful searchlight mounted on the back of a truck. The beam of a searchlight mounted on one of the guard-towers, fifty yards away, swung to pick him up, and he was bathed in cold, white light. He wound down the window, and stuck out his head. He recognized the guard.

"Ah, Feodor—I see you have some new toys to play with, eh?" He laughed naturally, smiling inwardly at his own bravado.

"Dr. Semelovsky—where have you been? You were checked through the guard-post more than an hour ago." The guard was frowning, more, Semelovsky suspected, because an officer he did not recognize was watching the little scene, than because he was suspicious, or angry.

Semelovsky held out his hands, and the oily stains were clearly visible in the searchlight's glare.

"Damn car broke down!" he said. "Much as the latest Five-Year Plan has achieved, it has not solved the problem of the Moskvitch—eh?" He laughed again, inviting the guard to join him. The guard smiled.

The second guard joined him, and said: "Turn

on the engine, please." Semelovsky did not recognize
this guard, looked at Feodor for a time, then
shrugged and did as he was ordered. He revved loudly, and the missing cylinder could be plainly detected. The guard motioned him to release the hood-
catch, and lifted the hood, his head disappearing.
Semelovsky spared a momentary glance at the officer, who appeared to be persuaded of the normali-
ty of the situation. He was smoking, and appeared
bored.

Leaning out of the window, he called: "Any idea
what it is?"

The second guard slammed down the hood suddenly, as if caught at some forbidden prank, and replied gruffly: "That engine's filthy. You're a scientist
—you should take more care." Then he seemed to
realize that his mask of deference had slipped.
Semelovsky, surprised by his unguarded tone, realized that the man had to be KGB or GRU, whatever
his uniform said. He nodded in reply.

"They keep us too busy . . ." he began.

The second guard turned away, and shook his
head in the direction of the officer lounging against
the wall of the guard-hut. The officer waved a hand
nonchalantly, and the gates swung apart. The guard
Feodor waved Semelovsky through.

He eased the car into gear, and pulled forward.
He passed through the gates, and they closed behind
him. At that point, and at that point only, a wave of
fear swept over him. The incident was more fraught
in retrospect than it had been as he experienced it.
He had smuggled Gant into the complex, and his
job was done.

He steered the car through the straight streets of
the living quarters. Each *dacha*-like dwelling, wood-
en and one-storied, was identical, set back from the
road behind a strip of lawn. It was, he thought, more
of a camp than a town. Not a camp like the ones
Baranovich knew from personal experience, on what
they called the Gulag Archipelago, but it was a

camp, nevertheless. It did not have walls like Mavrino, where Baranovich had spent years of his cre-
ative adult life—but there were electric fences, and
guard-towers, and the KGB.

He turned the wheel of the car, and drove it up
the slightly-sloping drive and into the opened garage
of a house half-way down Tupolev Avenue. It was
near the middle of the fenced-in township identical to almost every other street, except those which
contained the shops, the bars, and the cinema and
dance-hall.

Semelovsky glimpsed the watcher in the black
car parked across the street from the house. He was
suddenly afraid again. It did not matter that Baranovich had told him, and that he knew himself perfectly well, that they would not arrest them until
after the weapons-trials—otherwise, who would
complete the arming of the plane, the rest of the
work. . . ? It was only by recalling Baranovich's face,
and by hearing his voice, that he was able to calm
himself. Then the bumper of the car bounced gently
away from the car-tire at the end of the garage, and
he tugged on the handbrake and switched off the engine. As if forgetting Gant, locked in the trunk,
he sat for some moments, breathing regularly and
deeply. He had seen too much, too quickly.

Then he opened the door, took the key from the
ignition, and closed the garage door before he
opened the trunk.

"And you have learned nothing from either of them,
Dmitri—*still* nothing?" The silkiness that had earlier invested it was gone from Kontarsky's voice. Instead, it was querulous, impatient. He was pacing his
office, while Priabin sat in a chair before his desk,
maintaining a ceaseless patrol. It was ten past seven.
Priabin had left the cellar-room in Dzerzhinsky
Street only minutes earlier, after Riassin, the
man who seemed most likely to break of the two
they had collected from the Mira Prospekt flats that

morning, had slipped again into unconsciousness.
Priabin tasted the ashes of an unsuccessful interrogation. There had been no time for the more refined,
slower processes he preferred—this had been a bru-
tal softening-up, and the massive misuse of pentathol
on both men. Yet, they had learned nothing. Priabin
was of the opinion that there was nothing to learn,
other than the fact that the two men knew Pavel
Upenskoy, and that one of them, Glazunov, worked
with him, as driver's mate on his delivery truck.
Glazunov had been instructed to remain at home
that day, despite the fact that Upenskoy was leaving
for a delivery to Kuybyshev, a long trip but, so he
claimed under drugs, he had not been told why.

However, Kontarsky was in no mood to believe
that Priabin had tried as hard as he could, pushed
as hard as he dare, without killing Glazunov and
the other man—he was prepared to believe only
that his aide had failed. Kontarsky, it was obvious,
still believed that the two men possessed the information.

Priabin's eyes followed Kontarsky as he paced the
carpet. He, like his chief, had a sense that there was
a mounting urgency about the circumstances of the
second man in the truck. The problem was the inability to understand what these agents of British
and American intelligence could hope to gain by
smuggling one man into Bilyarsk . . . for that must
be where the impostor was heading. What could he
do, that one man, that could not be done by Baranovich, the brilliant original mind, or Semelovsky, or
even Kreshin—all of whom would be working on
the actual aircraft during the night? A stranger
would not be able to get anywhere near the Mig.
And to consider that he had come merely to spy,
to photograph, was ridiculous, Priabin concluded
once more.

He realized that Kontarsky had halted in front
of him. He looked up into the colonel's strained face.

The man was already hours late in departing for Bilyarsk, since he wanted to go with positive information concerning the man traveling in the same direction in Upenskoy's truck. A KGB helicopter had been waiting for him on the outskirts of the city since early afternoon.

"Very well," Kontarsky said, appearing to have come to some decision. "Pick up the phone, Dmitri. Get in touch with the tail-car, and have Upenskoy and the other man pulled in—at once!"

"Sir."

Priabin picked up the telephone. A simple instruction would be relayed via radio to the KGB office in Kazan, whence it would be passed on to the tail-car.

"Tell them to request what help they need from the guardpost at the Bilyarsk junction," Kontarsky added. "How many men in that car?"

"Three," Priabin replied. Then he said: "The last position of the truck showed it to have passed the junction to Bilyarsk—it didn't slow down, and it didn't stop . . ." He held the phone loosely in his hand.

Kontarsky whirled round, and snapped: "Then they must stop it now—I want to know if that second man is still aboard!"

As soon as he passed the Bilyarsk junction, glancing at the guard-post as he did so in the deepening dusk, Pavel Upenskoy knew that his time was limited. Without slowing, taking one hand from the wheel, he unzipped his jacket, and tugged an old service automatic from his waistband. He laid it gently on the passenger seat which Gant had occupied.

The tail-car had abandoned the idea of following him without lights. He could see the spreading stains of its headlights on the road behind. He wondered whether it would stop to consult the guards on the road to Bilyarsk, but it did not—probably, they were in conversation with them by radio. They would learn that he had not stopped, or slowed—and they would wonder why.

Upenskoy reckoned on having perhaps ten miles of road before they would become suspicious, or whoever they were answerable to ordered them to investigate his mysterious passenger. Then they would overtake, and order him to slow down. He knew the road between Kazan and Kuybyshev fairly well. It was farming country, isolated villages miles apart, some farms, but no town on the road before Krasny Yar, itself only ten or fifteen miles from Kuybyshev. He would not be allowed to get that far.

He had accepted the risks. He knew how important the Bilyarsk project was to the Soviets, how vital it was to NATO. He understood the desperation behind the plan to steal the aircraft. And the desperation that had induced Edgecliffe to sacrifice himself, and poor Fenton, and the others. He prided himself that Edgecliffe knew his worth, and would not lightly throw him away. Now, however, he was on his own, expendable—he was to avoid capture, if possible, for at least twelve hours, until Gant . . . There was no time to wonder about Gant, or to retrace the uncomfortable, depressing feeling the man exuded, like body odor.

He decided that he would run for it—there would be no road-blocks, in all probability, before Krasny Yar. He had to make sure he could get close enough to stand a chance of hiding there. He knew no one in the town, but that thought didn't worry him. He needed only shelter which he could find, and food which he could steal—then. . . . He sensed that it did not do to consider the future. No, he would not think about it, merely react when the car behind him made its move.

He thought about Marya, his wife. It was time, he considered, to allow himself that luxury. How old was she now? Thirty-seven, three years older than himself. Twelve years in prison—for demonstrating against the invasion of Czechoslovakia in 1968. Her original sentence had been for three years, but she had smuggled out pamphlets and writings describing her treatment in prison, had been discovered, and her sentence had been increased by ten years. Pavel knew, with a sick certainty, that she would never be released—that she would not take that much favor from a regime she hated and despised.

Marya was Jewish, and highly educated. She had once been a school-teacher, before her political activities had got her dismissed, then locked away. He had never understood how she came to marry him, simple, uneducated as he was. Yet he worshipped her for having done so, and he had spent the last twelve years trying to be worthy of her. Whatever had been asked of him by Edgecliffe and Lansing, and those who had preceded them at the British Embassy, he had done.

He was not sure, because one could never be sure of such things, but he thought it probable that his wife had been given forcible mental treatment, such as was concomitant with Kremlin and KGB thinking. Anyone who dissented must be a lunatic, thus ran the official line. Yet the worst thought of all was not that, but the fact that, because of the way the years in prison would have aged her, he might have passed her in the street without recognizing her. He was almost afraid, should that impossibility ever come to pass.

He checked the driving-mirror, and saw that the car had pulled up on him. He glanced to his side, checking that the gun had not shifted. The butt still lay towards him so that he could snatch it up. He checked the mirror again. The car was flashing its lights now, as if to overtake. Pavel smiled grimly. They knew that he knew who they were, and they assumed, in semi-divine arrogance, that now they had decided the little game was played out, he would fold like a house of cards. He pressed his foot

down on the accelerator, and the lights of the car
dropped away behind, then spurted nearer as the car
realized he was attempting to escape.

They were on a straight stretch of road, but a
stretch that had not yet been converted and widened
to dual carriageway. To overtake him, the car
would have to pass close to him, in the northbound
lane. It was that for which he hoped. If he attempted
to outrun the car for long enough, he reckoned on
insulted KGB arrogance to make that attempt to pass
him. He watched, the smile set on his features,
as the car attempted to stop him by flashing its
lights. He accelerated up to seventy miles an hour.

Again, the lights fell away behind, and then
neared suddenly. Pavel knew that the men in the
car would be angry by this time—they were unused
to being defied, in any way at all. He tensed himself,
and studied the road ahead. There were no trees on
this stretch, merely the road itself bordered by low
banks which separated it from the wheat-growing
countryside through which it passed. The bank
would have to do, would do for his purposes.

The car began to nose out into the other lane,
cautiously, as if suspecting some trick. The driver
was hanging back, still flashing his lights. Then
the car seemed to leap forward, as the driver's foot
went hard down and, almost taking Pavel by surprise, was all but level with his cab before he reacted. Viciously he swung the wheel, and the truck
swerved across the road. He heard, and felt, the tearing impact as the two vehicles collided, then he
straightened the wheel, and the lights of the car
wavered crazily before ploughing into the bank. He
took his foot from the accelerator, and braked sharply. The truck screeched to a halt. He rolled down
the window and listened. There was silence. The
engine of the car had stalled as it collided with the
bank. He picked up the gun and climbed down
from the cab. The car was more than a hundred
yards away, its nose buried in the bank. As he

walked toward it, he could see the body of the
front-seat passenger lying across the hood, thrown
at seventy miles an hour through the windscreen.

He was surprised when the rear door fell open
and a dark shape slumped onto the road. He stopped,
tense for movement. The flash from the gun and the
noise of the shots, two sharp, flat cracks shocked
him as if they were entirely out of place in the
scene. One bullet missed him, the other tore
through his shoulder. Raising the gun, as if oblivious
of his wound, he fired twice in return. The dark
figure slowly, balletically, extended itself on the
road.

He did not have to inspect his wound to know that
it would make steering the heavy truck almost impossible. Holding the wounded arm at his side, he
turned back to the truck and, with great difficulty, a
mist of pain before his eyes, sweat cold on his brow,
he hauled himself aboard. With a supreme effort, his
whole frame shaking, he shoved the truck into gear
and pulled away from the scene of the accident, his
body leaning heavily on the steering wheel, his eyes
clouded with the pain and the loss of blood. He had
only two thoughts in his mind—to get to Krasny Yar
before he passed out, and the face of his wife, Marya,
as he remembered her. . . .

Pavel Upenskoy died when the truck failed to
negotiate a bend in the road ten miles from the
scene of the accident with the KGB car, overturned,
and he was flung unconscious from the cab onto the
road. The truck half-mounted the bank, then fell
back on top of his body.

Pyotr Vassilyeivich Baranovich was no longer puzzled by the American, Gant. At first, and during the
first hour or more of his presence in the house in
Tupolev Avenue, he had been increasingly puzzled
by his behavior. He had watched the man eat his
meal, served by the woman who lived with Kreshin,
a secretary from the finance office of the Bilyarsk

project. He had watched the American, and had not understood him. He had studied him while they talked of his journey, and of Pavel—who was God knew where by now on the road to Kuybyshev, or in the hands of the KGB—and still been puzzled. Then they had begun to talk of the Mikoyan Mig-31, the Firefox as NATO called it, and he had seen the eager, dry hunger, like lust, in the man's eyes and he no longer was dubious about Buckholz's choice of pilot.

Gant, he understood, *needed* for some deep reason of his own, to fly the airplane. This man seated before him had been bundled from America to England, then to Russia, from Moscow to Bilyarsk, like so much washing—and he had allowed it to happen to him because at the end of the journey, like a monstrous child's prize for good behavior, was the shiny toy of the Mig.

Semelovsky had left them almost as soon as he had delivered the American, to return to his own quarters. They would not meet again until they reported to the hangar to prepare the aircraft for the weapons trials the following day. Kreshin and he, on the other hand, would pass through the security net into the factory complex together at two in the morning.

Baranovich was aware that the KGB would keep a careful watch upon himself and Kreshin and Semelovsky throughout the night. Without doubt, they would have orders to arrest them hours before the flight. That was only to be expected. But, until the work was done on the weapons-system they would not touch him. All they could do was watch from a car across the street. This was why Gant's presence in the house, so apparent a security risk, was in reality a safety precaution. It was safer than trying to hide him anywhere else in Bilyarsk. It was the last place they would look.

Baranovich had no intention of dwelling on his personal future. Like Gant himself, and like Aubrey in London, Baranovich accepted the slivers of time that were given to him, and did not seek to understand what might occur in the future hours and days. He had learned to live like that in Mavrino, and before that in the labor camps. He had known what he was doing when he had accepted the order to work at Bilyarsk, to develop the purely theoretical work that had already been done on a thought-controlled weapons-system, by a man now dead. The KGB had been aware of what they were doing when they released him to take up the appointment. Baranovich had lived on borrowed time for many years, almost since the end of the war—no, before that, he corrected himself, since a soldier lives on borrowed time, especially on the Russian front in winter. Because he had done so for the greater part of his life, it came as no special occasion now to understand that he was living on borrowed time.

"How well have you been briefed?" he asked, settling himself to throw off the useless speculations about himself and the character of the American.

They were seated in Kreshin's living-room, small, warm and comfortable. The younger man had left them alone—Baranovich suspected that he and the woman were making love in the next room, perhaps with the desperation of the young to whom time, borrowed or otherwise, is precious. Kreshin would, perhaps, be trying to forget the hours ahead in the illusion of passion. Baranovich had told Gant that he could speak without being overheard. The house was indeed bugged—but for that evening the electronics expert had rigged pre-recorded tapes to supply innocuous talk and the noise of the television a background mutter, for the KGB listeners.

"I told you—I flew some of the Mig-25 copies we built in the States for a couple of years, then I spent months on the simulator flying the Mig-31," Gant replied. In his turn, he was impressed by Baranovich. The man's patriarchal appearance,

white hair and goatee beard, clear blue eyes, and
unlined brow, demanded respect.

"No doubt your training, then, was thorough,"
Baranovich said, smiling, puffing at his pipe, seemingly relaxed as if he and Gant were happily theoriz-
ing in a university common-room. It had been a
very long time, perhaps forty years, since Baranovich had been in such a room.

"It was," Gant agreed. He paused, then said: "The
weapons-system . . . you need to tell me about that."

Baranovich seemed unaffected by Gant's directness. In fact, he respected it. This was the time and
place for such directness.

"Yes. It is not, I must say, my own development,
though I have done most of the work on the electronics involved, the miniaturization, and so forth."
He puffed at his pipe. "You are literally plugged
into the weapons-system. The sensors which respond to your thought-processes and your eye
movements are built into the helmet you wear, into
the shell and the visor. A single lead carries the
brain-impulses to the firing mechanisms, which you
manually plug into the console—you know where
that is located on the panel?" Gant nodded. "Good.
What happens is not important as a process, only,
for you, as an end product, a result. The radar system in the aircraft is specially developed to work
in conjunction with the weapons-control—basically,
it speeds up the firing-time. You receive an impulse
quicker than the eye can respond, from the radar,
which causes a reaction in your brain to which the
weapons-system reacts. It makes the launching of
air-to-air missiles, or the firing of the cannons, that
much quicker . . . and, of course, for visual contact
as opposed to radar contact, it places you seconds
ahead of any other airplane or pilot. When your eyes
see the target, the impulse is transmitted from the
brain to the weapons-control—and whatever weapon you *decide* to launch, *is* launched and it allows

your brain to guide the missile in flight to its target."

Baranovich smiled at Gant's staring eyes. "Don't worry, my friend—some of our Red Air Force pilots are very unintelligent. This system works only as long as you are wearing the helmet, and are plugged in. Besides," he added with a smile, "I cannot tell you more—it is top-secret, eh?" Baranovich took his pipe from his mouth, and roared with laughter. Still smiling, he added: "There *is* a master lockout switch, by the way, which prevents you from blowing friends out of the sky with evil thoughts!"

After a pause, Baranovich sighed. His eyes seemed to be directed inwards, and when he spoke next, it was as if he were summarizing a problem for his own satisfaction alone.

"Your government realizes the importance of the weapons-system. It is the logical next step, and it has endless possibilities. I could tell them much, of course, except that they know they can never get me out of the Soviet Union. To steal the Mig is easier . . ." He sucked at the dead pipe, and continued, "The United States has hardly begun to develop such a system. If it does not have one soon, then it will never be able to catch up with the flood of refinements and applications that will follow from what is, at present, still a crude electronic implement. So, they have to have the Mig, since they cannot have me. The applications could be endless, infinite as the system is refined. You, naturally, are interested only as a pilot, not as a scientist. At the moment, it employs conventional weaponry—who knows? Soon, the weaponry may leap ahead to match the thought-guided system . . ."

He looked sharply at Gant, who wiped the lack of interest from his face. There was a look sharp with pain in Baranovich's eyes as he said: "Of course, I bore you. Perhaps it is self-pity. I would like to go on living, perhaps in the United States . . ."

Gant said gently: "The—anti-radar . . . ?"

"Ah." Baranovich shook his head. "About that, I know nothing. It is the most secret aspect of the whole project—a Jew with a long record of dissidence would not be allowed to become familiar with it." Gant nodded.

"I have to know," he said, "whether the Russians can switch it off by remote control when I'm airborne—or if I could switch it off by accident?"

Baranovich looked thoughtful for a moment, puffing stolidly at his pipe. Once again, Gant was forcibly reminded of a university seminar, rather than a vital intelligence briefing.

"No," the Russian said, shaking his head, then rubbing his nose with thumb and forefinger. "As far as I have heard from rumors—and those rumors have been few and uncertain—I understand that the anti-radar capacity is not mechanical at all."

"What in the hell . . .?"

"As far as I understand it, that is so," Baranovich repeated levelly. "It is something—perhaps a skin, even a paint, of some kind, like the low-friction finish developed for certain American airplane projects?" Gant's eyes widened. "Mm. Even we know of it—American security is not as good as the Pentagon would like to think. . . . However, as I was saying, it would appear that the anti-radar stems from some such system, so that the radar-beam flows over the surface of the aircraft, and passes on, nothing having registered on the screens. I do know that the system can be neutralized for safety requirements, such as landing at your own airfield in the worst weather, by the pilot, but I can't tell you how it is done." His face darkened. "You won't be able to use it." He shook his head. "I am dubious myself, Mr. Gant. I only repeat what I have heard. And we both know it works. That part of the project has been developed elsewhere, not in Bilyarsk."

There was a silence, then Gant said, "How long can you give me inside the cockpit?"

"No time at all, I think. The security is tighter than ever. You know that the First Secretary is flying down here tomorrow to witness this triumph of Soviet technology? Accompanied by Andropov, the Chairman of the KGB, and other Party notables, of course. Well, because of that—or, even, because of us, Semelovsky, Kreshin and myself—the security is massive, more than ever before." He paused and puffed at his pipe in silence. Then he added: "A special detachment of GRU troopers was flown in yesterday. They will be under the command of the KGB, of course, but there are more than one hundred of them, in addition to the considerable garrison already here." He spread his hands in front of him. "Which is why we have been forced to the extremity we have in order to get you into the hangar area . . ." Baranovich's eyes twinkled, and he smiled. "You will need to have your hair cut even shorter, of course, so that the helmet and sensors can work efficiently, and your photograph taken for a very special set of papers—but nothing more will need to be done to you."

Gant shrugged. There was no resistance whatever to the idea of disguise, of assumed identity. His indifference to his own identity, a quality that Buckholz had understood from the first, made him successful as a chameleon. Most agents attempt, subconsciously, to retain something of themselves—an item of clothing, a mannerism, an inflection—as if they were swimmers, fearing to leave their personalities heaped like clothes until they should come back, fearing they might not be there when they returned. Gant had no such qualms, conscious or subconscious. Orton, Grant, Glazunov—and the man he was shortly to portray, whoever he was—they were shadows, as he was.

"What about my route—what's the lay-out of the hangar area?" he said bluntly.

Baranovich watched the American's face for a moment with keen eyes, then nodded as if satisfied, and stood up, gesturing Gant to where a large-scale drawing hung like the edge of a white tablecloth from the small dining-table. Kreshin had left it there after Gant had finished eating.

Baranovich fussily straightened and smoothed the pencil-drawn map of the huge compound, and began to point out its features to Gant.

"We are here," he said, "almost in the center of the living-area—and all technical and scientific staff enter the hangar and factory complex through this gate . . ." His finger traced a route along the streets until it stopped at a line marked in red, further marked by red crosses at intervals. "Yes," Baranovich continued, "there is another fence, electric, and guarded by these watch-towers . . ." his finger tapped at the red crosses, "inside the perimeter fence, which keeps us and the project divided from the village. There is only one other gate in this fence—over here, on the other side of the airstrip." Again his finger tapped at the stiff paper. "That is used only by security personnel—it is the one *you* will use."

"How, for God's sake?"

Baranovich smiled.

"With bravado, naturally—and a little help from myself and the others. Don't worry about it." The Russian returned to his pipe, sucked at it energetically, and spilled a thick cloud of smoke from his lips. Gant wrinkled his nose, as if in disapproval. "Do you smoke?" Baranovich asked.

"No. Not any more,"

Nodding, Baranovich reached into a pocket of his worn, leather-elbowed jacket, and pulled out a packet of American cigarettes.

"Learn again—now," he said simply.

"Uh?"

"Learn to smoke in the next hour, before you rest."

Gant pulled a face. "They're not Russian," he said.

"A status-symbol? Foreign cigarettes, in the

mouth of the person you will be, will prove as convincing as anything else—even your papers." Baranovich smiled, then returned his attention to the map. Gant picked up the pack of cigarettes from the map, and slipped it into the breast-pocket of his overalls. "From this gate, you will make your way to this area here, on the far side of the runway." The long finger tapped. Gant watched, as if fascinated, the mottled, thick-veined hand as it lay on the white background of the map. "This building is the main hangar, where both prototypes are stored. We will be working here through the night, preparing the airplane that is to take part in the trials. Attached to the hangar are the security offices, right on the spot, and also the pilots' rooms. You see that?" Gant nodded. "Good. You have to go upstairs, and along this corridor . . ." Baranovich's finger was now tracing the direction on a second-storey plan of the buildings attached to the huge main hangar. "The other buildings—they are merely the laboratories, wind-tunnels, test-houses, and the like. Waste no time with them. Get yourself to the pilots' dressing-room as soon as you can. Red Air Force Lieutenant-Colonel Yuri Voskov will arrive some hours before the flight. You must be ready for him."

"What about visitors?" Gant asked. "I could be there for three, four hours."

Baranovich explained patiently, as if to a child: "Conceal the body—there are a number of lockers, metal ones, all with good locks." He smiled. "The pilots complained of a great deal of pilfering of the Western luxury items supplied them for being well-behaved and well-adjusted . . . the locks are good. As for yourself, since you do not appear to be very much like Voskov, except in general build—you will be taking a shower."

"For three hours?"

"You will appear to be taking a shower. Once it nears the time for our little—*diversion* to occur, you will dress and the visor of the helmet will conceal

your features. We on the weapons-guidance system
request the pilots to wear the helmets until removed
in the laboratory. It will not seem strange that you
are wearing it even an hour or more before the
flight."

Gant nodded. "What about this diversion?"

"You need not worry. I have a very small radio
device which will tell you when to come down from
your room to the hangar-area. What you will see
there will enable you to enter the cockpit and roll
the aircraft out of the hangar, without anyone being
in the least suspicious."

Gant's eyes widened again. He was thoughtful for
a moment, and then he said: "What happens to you
guys, after I lift out of there?" His voice was quiet,
breathy, as if he already knew the answer.

"It does not matter," Baranovich said softly. His
expression betrayed a sympathy for his visitor that
the American could not comprehend.

"The hell it doesn't!" Gant said, stepping back, his
arms raised at his sides. "Hell!" He turned away
from the Russian, his shoulders hunched, then
turned back and said, waving his arm before him:
"You guys, all of you—you're so damn *willing* to
die, I don't understand! Don't you resent those guys
in London, ordering your deaths?"

Baranovich was silent for a long time, then he
said: "It is easy for you to feel indignant, Mr. Gant.
You are an American. *Any* order that you are given
is a source of resentment, is that not so? You are
a free man . . ." Gant smiled cynically, and Baranovich seemed angered by his expression. "You *are*
free! I am not. There is a difference. If I resent the
men in London who are ordering me to die, then it
is a small thing when compared with my—*resentment* of the KGB!" Baranovich was staring down at
the map with unseeing eyes, his features strained,
his hands knuckled on the table, so that the heavy
blue veins stood out like ropes. It was a long time

before he straightened, and was able to smile at
Gant.

"I'm sorry . . ." Gant began.

"Nonsense. Why should you be aware of—our little problems? Now, shall we go over the armament
of the plane again. Luckily, for your purposes at
least, they will be concerned to use air-to-air missiles in the first trial, not ground-attack weapons."

He waved Gant back to his chair. "Please smoke,"
he said. "We don't want you coughing amateurishly
at the gate, do we?" His eyes had recovered their
smile.

The beat of the rotors over his head had become
almost inaudible to Kontarsky during the flight
from Moscow. Now, at ten o'clock, they were more
than half way to Bilyarsk, flowing over the moonlit,
silvered country below, marked by the lights of the
scattered villages and collective farms, sliced by the
beams of the occasional truck or car on the road
between Gorky and Kazan, which they were, at
that point, paralleling. The helicopter seat was comfortable in the interior of the MIL MI-8. Behind
Kontarsky as he sat behind the pilot and co-pilot,
were seats for twenty-eight more passengers. Only
four of the seats were occupied, by Kontarsky's personal guard, a male secretary and a classified radio
operator—all of them were KGB staff.

Kontarsky was sleepy, despite the tension within
him. He had delayed leaving for as long as possible,
in order that he could arrive in Bilyarsk with at
least some information concerning the identity, and
therefore the mission, of the man who had passed
through traffic controls at Moscow, Gorky, and
Kazan as Glazunov. The result of Priabin's investigations was—nothing. True, they had found the tail-
car, a few miles beyond the turn-off to Bilyarsk;
true, also, that they had found the overturned truck
and the crushed body of Pavel Upenskoy ten miles

further down the road to Kuybyshev. There was no
sign of the second man. Therefore, with a nauseous,
logical certainty, Kontarsky and Priabin had been
faced with the knowledge that the second man was
on his way, on foot, or by some alternative transport, to Bilyarsk. The old man at the warehouse had
died almost as soon as they began to beat his knowledge out of him. Frail, weak heart. Kontarsky was
still angry at such unfastidious waste.

The man's photograph had been transmitted to
Bilyarsk, and the security-guard alerted. Kontarsky
had panicked himself into flying at once to Bilyarsk, to take personal charge of the counter-measures.

He lit yet another cigarette, having glanced over
his shoulder at the radio-operator sitting before his
console. The man, as if telepathically aware that his
chief's eyes were on him, shook his head mournfully.
Kontarsky turned back, facing forward in the helicopter again, staring at the helmeted heads in front
of him, as if they might provide some inspiration.
There was the taste of fear in the back of his throat.
He brushed a hand across his eyebrows nervously.
He knew there would be no sleep for him until the
trials were successfully completed. He felt the common KGB impotence of having to rely upon computers, upon the whole huge unwieldy apparatus
of the security service for results.

At that moment, Priabin was gaining access to the
central records computer in Dzerzhinsky Street, a
priority request for computer time. He was searching for a man, British or American without doubt,
who had entered the Soviet Union recently, under
a false name and passport, who could be identified
as an intelligence agent. He was using the electronic mind of a huge machine to run to earth the
second man in the truck. An electronic hunt, he
summarized bitterly. Like Priabin, Kontarsky's
faith lay in what people could tell him, what they
could extract from individual minds and tongues.

Yet the two they had picked up knew nothing, that much was obvious, except their own speculations that the man was an intelligence agent whose destination was Bilyarsk and the Mikoyan project; and Upenskoy, who would have known for certain, was dead, crushed to pulp beneath the weight of the truck.

Kontarsky's thought processes were defensive, even at the moment when he most needed daring, and imagination. Mentally, he was already preparing a defense for the officers of the Special Investigations Department who would be calling on him in the event of his failure. He writhed at the thought of having to depend upon a computer's master index of files in the Registry and Archives Department of the KGB. Yet, rely upon that machine he had to. There was no other alternative now. There was no one living to ask.

There was a further problem, of course. Unless he allowed the three dissident agents of the CIA and the British SIS to complete their vital work on the aircraft, there would be no trial the following day.

He cleared his throat, cleared his mind. He was terrified of espionage, of an attempt to sabotage the trial in front of Andropov and the First Secretary . . .

He would, he decided, allow himself at least two hours before the arrival of the official aircraft, to question the dissidents. He looked at his watch. Ten-fifteen. He was anxious now, to arrive, to be on the spot, to become active.

Police Inspector Tortyev was scrutinizing a dossier of photographs of Alexander Thomas Orton. He had spread the snapshots across his desk regardless of date or place, and picked up samples at random. For half an hour, he had been picking up and discarding, and comparing samples from the heap. It had taken his small team three hours to collect the full dossier, from various sources within the KGB 2nd Chief Directorate. He had been denied computer time,

which would have immensely simplified and
speeded-up his inquiries. He gathered there was
some kind of priority-search being mounted, and his
team had been lucky to obtain the number of photographs they had done by manual extraction from
the files, to supplement his own dossier on Orton.

Again, as with the man's shoes, Tortyev recognized the significance of the photographs. Almost
casually, he selected two, one of Orton taken at
Cheremetievo two days ago, and one of the man
taken eighteen months before, in a Moscow street,
just leaving a tourist shop. It had been taken as part
of a routine surveillance, before Tortyev had become interested in the activities of the businessman
from England. Holding them together between
thumb and forefinger, he passed them across his
desk to Holokov and Filipov, who had sat silently
awaiting the outcome of his deliberations.

"What do you think?" he said, offering the two
pictures to Holokov. Filipov leaned across, almost
touching Holokov's shoulder.

The fat man studied the pictures for some time,
then shook his head. "What is it you want me to say,
Inspector?" he asked.

Tortyev smiled. "What you *really* think—even if
that is a rather unusual request for me to make."

"Mm." Holokov glanced at Filipov, flashed the
pictures at him, and then added: "It's not the same
man."

"Good, Holokov—good." Without interest, he
added: "You agree, Filipov?"

Filipov looked dubious, and then said: "I—I'm not
sure, Inspector."

"Naturally. *I* am—you, too, Holokov?" The fat
man nodded. "Which poses a question—eh? Which
of these two is the dead man?"

"How can we tell? They're very alike," Filipov
said.

"Their common disguise makes them alike, Filipov!" Tortyev snapped. "The face was ruined so that

we would not discover that there were two men involved in this deception. Why were there two of them?

Holokov looked bemused, and Filipov remained silent. Tortyev left his desk and began to pace the room. Suddenly, a sense of urgency had come over him, though he could not explain its origin. He felt a nervous energy, a sense of being trapped by the walls of his office. He looked up at the clock. It was ten-thirty. He turned to Holokov.

"What of that KGB man killed at the Komsomolskaia Metro Station yesterday evening—who killed him?"

"One of Orton's associates?" It was Filipov who spoke.

"Why not Orton—he's not dead, after all!" Tortyev replied, bending over Filipov as he sat in his hard upright chair before the desk. "Why not Orton himself?" Filipov shrugged, as if he had no answer to the question. "*Who* are Orton's associates? We have men you have pulled in, the usual crowd, the ones in Orton's file—you have searched their homes, their storeplaces. What have you found—eh? Nothing—nothing at all!"

He moved away from Filipov and Holokov, and began to reason aloud. "Where is Orton—where have they hidden him? Why did he want it to appear that he had been killed? To throw us off the scent? Why not die in London, if that was the case, where we could not check so thoroughly, where we would not have the evidence of the body itself?" He paused, turned, paced the length of the room once in silence, and then continued. Holokov and Filipov sat mutely, digesting their inspector's ruminations. "No. The answer does not lie there. Orton had to disappear here, inside the Soviet Union, inside Moscow. Why?"

He paused again in his stride, in the middle of his office, and said, calmly, but with a catch of excitement in his voice that both his subordinates felt: "If we had not been persuaded that Mr. Alexander

Thomas Orton was a drug-smuggler, what would we think he was? Eh? Based on what has happened—including the killing of a KGB man, which must have had something to do with this, and which shows the desperate extent of what has been happening—two deaths, a fake Orton and one of ourselves ... based on that, what would we think?"

He stood staring at them, willing them to arrive at his own conclusion, nervous of the leap his mind had made, hoping that theirs would leap in the same way.

Holokov cleared his throat, fussily, apologetically, infuriatingly, and said: "He is an agent?"

"Exactly!" Tortyev was smiling. "He is an espionage agent, of the British, or the Americans—the drugs blinded us to the truth! Now, now he has disappeared—for what reason? Where is he—what is he up to—eh?"

Neither of his subordinates appeared to be possessed of further ideas. Gathering up the sheaf of photographs, Tortyev bundled them into his arms, and made for the door.

"Holokov—come with me. I want this face processed by the central computer—now! This man is dangerous, and I want to know who he is. The central registry of known or suspected agents may give us some clue as to his real identity." He turned to Filipov. "Get in touch with our people in the British Embassy, Filipov. Give them my authority for your inquiries, and tell them it's urgent. I want to know who Orton's contact is—and I want to know now!"

Filipov nodded, but the door had already closed behind the inspector and his fat assistant trailing in his wake. Filipov picked up one photograph that Tortyev's sweeping arms had failed to gather, and looked down at it. By chance, it was a photograph of Gant in the persona of Orton, rather than Fenton. He seemed to study it for a moment, turning it in his fingers, letting the face catch the light from the strip-light overhead. Filipov's dark, swarthy features were harassed, his shoulders bowed with concern.

Filipov knew that it would take only a little time if Tortyev began to ask questions of the KGB informants who worked in the kitchens, the corridors and the typing-pool of the British Embassy, a little time before he began to realize that there were a multitude of connections between Edgecliff and Lansing at the Embassy and the man Fenton in his persona as Orton. Fenton was SIS, based in London. He had come to Moscow this time undisguised, an ordinary tourist with a package holiday, and had gone to ground in the Embassy only an hour or so before his death—re-emerging briefly as Orton. Someone might have seen him, made the connection. They might even discover that the substitute for Fenton on the package holiday, now moved on to Leningrad, was not the man who arrived at Cheremetievo from London.

He realized that Edgecliffe had to be told, and quickly. He got up from the chair, in a quick, nervous bound. He could not call from Tortyev's office, the line would be monitored. Yet he could not leave the building—Tortyev would be back within ten minutes, perhaps a little more. As far as he knew, the telephones—the "social lines," as they were called—in the off-duty rest-rooms on the second floor would not be monitored at that time of night. He would have to risk it. He had to call Edgecliffe, before Tortyev received any information from the informants in the British Embassy. He closed the door of the office noiselessly behind him.

At the direct order of the Head of Intelligence, "C," Kenneth de Vere Aubrey had condescended to temporarily vacate the usual offices of SO-4, his own section of the SIS's Special Operations Function, and to take up residence in a specially prepared and utterly secure room within the complex of the Ministry of Defense. Aubrey did not like M.O.D. He and his number two, Shelley, had occupied the room

with its wireprint and secure telephones for most of
the day and evening, preparing it with the maps
that now covered the walls—European Russia, the
Barents Sea and north into the Arctic Ocean, the
Moscow Metro system, a Moscow street plan. All the
necessary landscapes and seascapes of his operation.
Now the room had acquired two other occupants,
the Americans Buckholz and Anders, his aide. They
had commandeered two of the small desks that had
been moved in, scorning, apparently, the trestle-ta-
bles that Aubrey had drafted in with the original
furniture. Shelley, returning to the room from a
journey to the kitchens, saw Buckholz talking on
one red telephone, and Anders up the step-ladder,
pinning a satellite weather photograph of the Arctic
region on the wall, next to the map of the same region. That map, like the others of European Russia
and the North Sea, was ringed by satellite weather-
pictures. It was not those, however, that especially
caught Shelley's eye. His gaze was drawn to the
map of European Russia that Buckholz had begun
working on when he had left with the supper dishes
for the kitchens. Aubrey had allowed no one inside
the room except himself, Shelley, and the two
Americans who had arrived a little after eight. It
was now one o'clock in the morning in London,
two hours ahead of Moscow time.

Shelley walked over to Aubrey and stood beneath
the huge map, looking up. Facing him now, instead
of the clean unmarked map, was something that
made him, thousands of miles away, frightened and
dubious. He had a sudden image of Gant standing
belligerently before him in his hotel room—and he
regretted his stupid, petty dislike of the American.
What Shelley was staring at was Buckholz's breakdown, in graphic form, of the Russian defense system
which Gant would have to penetrate, even if he got
the Firefox off the ground at Bilyarsk. Much of what
was on the map Shelley already knew, but to see

it, indicated in colored pins and ribbons, shocked him thoroughly.

Near the top of the map, extending deep into the polar pack at the neck of the conical orthomorphic projection map, was a yellow ribbon, in great loops reaching upwards. This signified the effective extent of the Russian DEW-line, the least of Gant's worries. What really attracted his gaze, riveted his attention, were the sweeps of small pins that marked the fighter bases, those known or guessed, and the missile sites. The fighter stations, all of which would be manned in a twenty-four-hour readiness manner, would possess at least a dozen aircraft that could be scrambled within minutes. These bases were marked in blue and extended along the northern coast of the Soviet Union from Murmansk and Archangelsk in the west to the Taimyr Peninsula fifteen hundred miles to the east. The bases were a little more than one hundred miles apart.

Below these pins were two sweeps of red circles, showing the missile sites. These were slightly less than a hundred miles apart, and extended over the same area of the map, its total east-west projection. Each missile site was semi-fixed, and possessed perhaps a dozen or more surface-to-air proximity and infra-red missiles, launched from concrete pads. Between each pair in both chains, though unmarked, Shelley nevertheless knew there would be mobile, truck-borne missiles, perhaps half-a-dozen to each convoy. The radar system would be located at each of the missile bases, linked to the central radar-control which processed the information supplied by the DEW-line.

Shelley felt mesmerized by the two sweeps of red circles, one along the coast, the second another three hundred miles or more inland, following the same path. It looked like a plan of a classic battle, an army drawn up in two parallel lines—an army of missiles, in this case, linked to radar that scanned every cubic

foot of air over the Soviet Union. Gant would have
to cross each line, and avoid the fighter-scramble
that would follow hard upon his theft of the Firefox.

And, thought Shelley, Buckholz hasn't yet filled
in the positions of Soviet spy trawlers, missile cruisers of the Red Banner Northern Fleet, and submarine activity in the Arctic Ocean and the Barents
Sea.

He saw that Aubrey was looking at him, quizzi-
cally, perhaps even vulnerably. "There are a lot of
them—eh, Shelley?" he said softly.

"Too many," Shelley blurted out. "Too bloody
many by half! He hasn't got a chance!" He dropped
his eyes, seeing Aubrey's anger at his impolitic display of emotion. "Poor sod," he muttered.

4
THE CONCEALMENT

Gant was tired, yet his mind refused to stop racing. Baranovich and the woman, Kreshin's mistress, fussed around him fitting his disguise. Kreskin himself sat in one of the room's low, inexpensive armchairs, watching intently, as if studying the American, expecting to learn something from the way he moved, the way he stood still.

Gant despised the building tension and excitement within himself. It was the wrong way to be, he knew. Yet however he strove to control his feelings, he could not avoid hanging over the edge, staring into the abyss of the hours ahead.

The disguise was, when he considered it, inevitable. There was only one way to walk through a tight security net which was on the look-out for the least unfamiliar thing—to be a part of that net. Baranovich got up from his knees and stood back, hands on hips, in the posture of a couturier inspecting his creation. Gant self-consciously pulled the uniform jacket straight at the hips, adjusted the belt, and looked across at himself in the mirror. The cap he now wore hid his newly-cropped hair, cut close to his head, so that the contacts inside his flying helmet that would control the weapons-system would function, picking up his brain patterns, transmitting them to radar, missiles, or cannon.

Underneath the dark peak, the face that stared at him was cold, narrow, lined and tired. It was the face of a stranger, despite the fact that nothing in the way of disguise had been done to it. In the wall mirror, all he could see of himself besides was the collar of the brown shirt, the dark uniform tie, and the bright tabs on the laps of his uniform jacket.

"That is—good," Baranovich pronounced at last. "It is a good fit now that Natalia has made the little alterations." He smiled over Gant's shoulder at the woman, who was sitting on the arm of Kreshin's chair, her arm about his neck, as if seeking warmth. Something about the uniform seemed to disturb her, make her seek physical contact with her lover.

"Captain Grigory Chekhov, attached to the Security Support Unit of the GRU, at present assigned under the command of . . ."

"Major Tsernik, KGB officer responsible for security of the Mikoyan project, Bilyarsk." Gant finished for Baranovich, a slight smile at the corner of his mouth.

Baranovich nodded. "What do you think of him, Ilya?"

"Very—convincing," Ilya Kreshin offered, holding the girl's hand at his shoulder. "At least, he frightens Natalia—doesn't he?" He was smiling at the girl as he looked into her face, and she tried to smile back. "You see?" he added, turning back to Gant and Baranovich. "She takes you for the real thing, and she helped you into the disguise!" He laughed loudly, reassuringly, patting the girl's hand as he did so.

"You recall the rest of your operational background?" Baranovich asked. Gant nodded. "Good. Now, sit down, or walk about—let that uniform be-

come comfortable—strut a little!" There was an almost malicious humor in Baranovich's blue eyes.
Gant smiled, and began to walk up and down the
room. Baranovich watched him, and then said: "No
—with the thumbs tucked into the belt—so . . ." He
demonstrated by hooking his thumbs into his trousers. Gant copied him. "That is good. You must always remember—you will only give yourself away
if you fail to be what the guards at the gate expect.
And they will expect to see a captain who is arro-
gant, detached—who means business. If you get the
chance, reprimand at least one or two of them, for
minor things—their uniform, for example, or anyone who is smoking." Again Gant nodded. This was
an expert talking, one who knew the *look* of the
KGB, or the GRU, intimately, through long and bitter experience. Gant surrendered his own ego, accepted the expertise he was being offered. "Now
—sit down. You stand rather well, eh, Ilya?"

Gant sat down, first wiping the seat of the vacant
armchair, and inspecting his fingertips for dust.
Then he sat in the chair, completely relaxed, one
booted leg crossed over the other. Without looking
at them, he drew a silver cigarette case from his
pocket, and a rolled-gold lighter—items he could
only have purchased in the KGB luxury shop across
the square from the Center itself in Dzerzhinsky
Street—extracted an American cigarette, lit it, exhaled noisily, picked tobacco from the tip of his
tongue, and then turned his head and looked stonily
towards Kreshin in the armchair. The young man
clapped loudly.

"It is amazing," Baranovich observed. "How melo-
dramatic it all was—and how *correct!*" His face
clouded, as if he were assailed at that moment by a
bad memory, then he smiled, his eyes clearing, and
added: "That was very good—you have the gift, Mr.
Gant. You can be, without trying, someone else . . ."

Gant nodded his head politely, frostily.

"Tell me about the observations you made on your lovers' walk earlier," he said to Kreshin, his eyes hard. It was not a request, but an order. Gant had found that he could channel the useless, wasted adrenalin pumping in his system into his characterization of Chekhov, whose fictitious papers he had in his pocket, complete with the all-important yellow GRU ID card, transit papers, and the rest. His fake dog-tags were on a thin chain around his neck. He had not asked how the forgery, the disguise, had been accomplished. Baranovich was an expert, driven by hate, and by ego. The results were good.

Kreshin smiled, and said: "The guard on that gate has been reinforced—there are troops of the usual KGB guard, but more of them. The Security Support Group has not been used there—probably because Tsernik feels insulted that the GRU have been called in . . . it's always happening."

"What about the perimeter fence?"

"The watch-towers are full to overflowing—and there are dog patrols inside the fence, every ten minutes or so. It's a double fence, by the way, and the dogs will be loose by the time you arrive—no one in their right mind would try cutting the wire. The watch-towers are a hundred yards apart—you'll have to pass at least four of them."

"You must look as if you are inspecting the wire itself—don't forget to challenge the guards in the towers, wake them up," Baranovich interrupted. "Go on, Ilya."

"There is a lot of light at the gate itself—you will be seen from some distance as you approach. The outer gate is merely a barrier with its accompanying guard-post. You will be required to show your papers here. The guards will be curious, because they will not recognize you, but the GRU tabs on your uniform will allay any suspicions they might have. When you are allowed to pass inside the outer barrier, you will encounter a mesh-gate, which will be locked. The guard will be *inside* this gate, and they will require you to show your papers again before they will open up."

"They will open up?" Gant asked softly.

"There is no need to worry—we have checked the current papers and identification of GRU officers of the Special Groups, and yours are in order," Baranovich explained. Gant merely nodded. Baranovich took up the narrative, Kreshin returning to an idle, thoughtful patting of Natalia's hand as it lay on his shoulder. "Once inside, you should make as directly as possible across the airfield. You may ignore any helicopter activity overhead—the uniform will be enough to satisfy them. When you arrive at the security guard outside the administrative building which, as I mentioned earlier, is physically linked to the hangar containing the Firefox, you will need to show your papers but, since you will be walking into the KGB headquarters at Bilyarsk, no one is likely to assume that you do not, in fact, belong there!" Baranovich smiled. "Once inside, make for the pilots' rest-room on the floor above. It will not be occupied at that time."

"Where is the pilot—Voskov?" Gant asked sharply.

"At this moment?" Kreshin asked, exaggeratedly looking at his watch. "He will be in bed."

"He has quarters in a special compound—where the KGB and other *reliable* members of the team here are housed." Baranovich's contempt showed for a moment, as if he had lifted a veil and shown a corner of his soul. "It is where they keep those who work on the anti-radar, which is why we have picked up nothing in scientists' gossip during the last months."

"But, he *will* come to the rest-room?" Gant persisted.

"Yes. He will change there, and perhaps have a meal—though Voskov is not a good eater before one of these flights. . . . Are you, Mr. Gant?" Baranovich's eyes twinkled.

"No, but I can usually sleep," Gant replied.

"Yes, of course. We will be leaving at two-thirty. You will have perhaps only a couple of hours."

"Never mind," Gant said, stifling a yawn and forcing himself into wakefulness. "I want to go over it all again."

"The security?"

"No. The airplane. The weapons-system, the Rearward Defense Pod. Tell me again—everything."

Gant felt himself as two layers of response, suddenly. At the surface of his mind was the growing excitement, now that he had put aside his masquerade as a GRU officer, the tension connected with the Firefox, burning hot as a lust in him; he had a curious reluctance to stay awake, an unformed desire to be in darkness, with an empty mind. It was the first time he had ever wished back the void of the Veterans' Hospital, since the day he had left it. It was a feeling he avoided examining.

*   *   *

Dmitri Priabin and Alexei Tortyev knew each other —not as close friends, but as graduates of the KGB training school. They had been contemporaries, and as junior officers had worked within the same department. This was before Priabin, who was regarded as the more promising, was promoted as aide to Kontarsky in department "M," and Tortyev, whose brilliant mind was officially mistrusted by such a degree which would insure his rotting at his present rank until he retired, had moved into the KGB section of the Moscow Police, into the Political Security Service.

It was not unnatural, then, that having met in the cold, metallic room which housed the programmers for the central records computer, below ground level in Dzerzhinsky Street, and having inquired after each other's recent careers, and complained about their own and each other's superior officers, that they began to discuss the cases on which they were working.

It was a remarkable coincidence that had brought them to the central computer at the same time. Such discussion was the privilege of young officers, safe from their superiors, each alive to the possibilities of their separate cases. The senior echelons of the KGB, like its predecessors, have always discouraged the professional gossip associated with police forces in other countries, other societies, in a further attempt to enforce the absolute security seemingly demanded by a secret police force. However, the present generation of KGB officers, among whom were Tortyev and Priabin, both highly intelligent graduates of the Lenin University of Moscow, possessed, in the eyes of many of their seniors, a remarkable degree of scepticism toward some of the cherished aims of the service—notably in the matter of gossip. They realized, unlike their hidebound seniors, that the cross-fertilization of such gossip more than outweighs its detraction from absolute security. Priabin, seated in one of the armchairs in the waiting-room next to the metallic, sterile room with its banks of lights and spools and controls, was saying as much to Tortyev.

"They don't realize, Alexei, how much they lose by being so rigidly compartmentalized. One hand never knows what the other is doing."

Tortyev, who had shoved his file of photographs into the hands of one of the white-coated operators, and was merely waiting for an estimate of how long the computer-run would take after the features of the man Orton had been broken down into computer-language, nodded his head sagely, a smile of complicity playing around his mouth.

"Quite true," he replied. "Take us, for instance."

"True—we are, after all, both looking for foreign agents, are we not?"

There was a silence. Priabin lit a long cigarette of British manufacture, while Tortyev was content

to pick at his fingernails. Priabin had revisited the
computer room throughout the afternoon and evening, almost as a kind of obsessive, childhood habit,
as if he could, by appearing before the officers with
irritation plainly written on his features, prompt the
operators into jogging the computer into more rapid
activity. Thus far, the computer had failed to answer
his question—who was the man in the truck with
Upenskoy. This was despite the fact that it had at its
disposal the files, descriptions, possible disguises—
a whole identifit library of each face in every file,
and suggestions as to how those faces might be disguised successfully—and present whereabouts, if
known, of thousands of known or suspected agents
—American, European, Israeli; even Warsaw Pact
countries and developing African nations had their
places in the computer-banks as possible enemies of
the KGB.

Priabin was angry with the computer—he had
presented the machine with a simple problem, the
sort of problem it would take a large team of men a
week to complete, and he wondered what machines
were for if they couldn't come up with the answers
he required. He puffed angrily at his cigarette now
that the conversation had idled, and wished that,
indeed, Tortyev could help with his problem—what
was it he was worrying about, some body in the
Moskva, with its face beaten in?

"Who is this man you're after?" he asked, as much
for the sake of distracting himself as for the sake of
conversation, or interest in what Tortyev was doing. Kontarsky would already be at Bilyarsk, strut-
ting like a turkey-cock, attempting to drive doubt
from his mind by an over-zealous inspection of security there. While he left his assistant holding the
damned baby! Priabin concluded. What was it Kontarsky had said to him, just before leaving, and for
perhaps the twentieth time since he had seen that
bloody photograph of the man who called himself
Glazunov, and who had popped up out of nowhere

like the devil himself. What was it? Find out, Dmitri
—for your sake, and for mine. Find out tonight. Yes
—that was it.

Priabin grimaced at his thoughts. Dmitri Priabin
was doing it for Dmitri Priabin's sake—he would find
out, if that damned computer didn't break down—for
his own sake.

"Ah," said Tortyev meditatively in reply. "That is
what I want our noble machine to discover—I
know him as Orton . . ."

Priabin creased his brow in thought, and said:
"What's he supposed to have done?"

Tortyev looked slighted for a moment, and then
replied: "He came to my attention as a drug-smuggler." Priabin nodded, and appeared to lose interest.
Tortyev continued, nettled that a man with whom
he was at training school should regard his problems as unimportant: "But, the strange thing is—this
Orton, who died by the hand of one of his associates
—or so we believed—is not the man who arrived at
Cheremetievo two days ago."

Priabin sat bolt upright in the comfortable armchair. "When?" he snapped.

"Two days ago . . ."

"When did he—die?" Priabin asked, his voice
shaky with excitement. Even as the surface of his
thoughts leapt at the impossible proximity, he was
telling himself that he was being merely foolish.

"The same night."

"You—caught the men?"

"We rounded up all of Orton's known associates
—and found nothing to connect his death with
them," Tortyev explained, gratified that he seemed
to have stung Priabin into interest, though he was
puzzled at the man's upright, attentive posture.

"Who killed him, Alexei?"

"We—don't know, in fact, we don't even know
who died."

"What?"

"As I said—the man who died was not the Orton

who arrived at the airport, complete with passport
and papers from the London Embassy . . ."

"Then who the hell was he—who were they
both?"

Tortyev spread his hands in a gesture of ignorance.
"I have enlisted the aid of our glorious revolutionary
computer to discover that very fact."

Priabin nodded, then said, a tone of suppressed
excitement in his voice: "All right—you think
there was a substitution—yes?"

Tortyev nodded. "Why?" asked Priabin.

"One reason only—the one who arrived two days
ago—is an agent, covering his tracks with this dead
body."

Priabin slapped his forehead. His face was flushed
with excitement—then paled, momentarily with
doubt, then he smiled at Tortyev.

"What—happened to the men who—left the body?"

"They ran off."

"Where?"

"To the nearest metro station—the Pavolets."

"And then?"

"Nowhere. They were lost—by the people from
here, and the police—they weren't looking out for
Orton then."

Priabin said, "We're looking for a man—an agent,
we are sure—who appeared suddenly driving out of
Moscow in a truck early yesterday morning. . . ." His
face drained of all color. "Stop . . ." he breathed, as if
realizing for the first time with the whole of his
mind what he had stumbled upon. "Stop . . ."

Tortyev leapt in the same direction as Priabin,
a fact which pleased, and comforted, Kontarsky's
lieutenant.

"You think—?"

"There's no record of a man of his appearance arriving in the Soviet Union during the past two
weeks. He could have been here longer but, even
then, how did he get in? I'm having the computer

run down all known or suspected American or British agents, trying to match the photograph."

"And I'm looking for Orton . . ." Tortyev added. "Where is this agent of yours now?"

"In Bilyarsk."

"God! You mean he's . . ."

"Probably he's inside the complex by now—in another disguise."

"To do what?"

"Who knows? Anything—blow up the bloody plane, perhaps?"

Tortyev stared at Priabin, seeing the fear, the recurrent fear, that had replaced the earlier fiery enthusiasm.

There was a knock at the door. "Come in," Priabin said abstractedly.

A young, crumpled individual in a dirty white coat entered, a sheaf of photographs in his hands. He stood before Priabin, evidently pleased with his work, but nervous of its reception by the KGB lieutenant.

"We haven't run down your man . . ." he began.

"You haven't?"

"No. Nothing in the files on him, under American or British."

"Then start with the . . ." Priabin began.

"What we've done meanwhile," the young man pressed on, keeping his eyes behind their horn-rimmed spectacles on the sheaf of photographs, "is to draw up for you a series of identifit pictures of what he might look like in various disguises—without detectable make-up or surgery. We're running these through the computer, to see whether he appears in any guise. It'll be a long job, I'm afraid."

Priabin looked up at the young man, scowled, and said: "You'd better bloody get on with it, then—hadn't you?"

The young man, considering himself let off lightly, turned on his heel and scuttled from the room, leaving the sheaf of pictures in Priabin's lap. Priabin glanced down at them, shuffled them disconsolately.

"Well?" Tortyev asked, on the edge of his chair.

"Well what?"

"Look at the bloody pictures, man!" Tortyev said angrily.

"What's the point?"

Tortyev crossed the space of dark carpet that separated them, snatched up the sheaf and flipped through them. Once or twice, he stopped, or looked back at a previous identifit mock-up, then he threw the sheaf away from him. Priabin smiled at his irritation, until he saw his face and the fact that he retained one picture still in his hand.

"It's him—Orton," he said softly, turning the picture of a seedy, tired, moustached individual with spectacles in Priabin's direction. "It's him. . . ."

Priabin stared at him. The knock on the door caused him to leap to his feet, as if guiltily surprised. The door opened to reveal Holokov, out of breath, his overcoat badly tugged on, collar up, his face red with exertion. Tortyev had left him in the restaurant at the Center, upstairs, where the food was as good as any of Moscow's principal hotels, and cheaper. Holokov had spilled tea on his tie, which was askew, Tortyev noticed.

"What is it?" he said sharply, rising to his feet.

"Stechko . . ." Holokov said wheezingly. "Phone call from headquarters—that bloody little Jew, Filipov, has been in contact with the British Embassy."

"What?"

"True. They were monitoring the phones in the rest-room, and he placed a call from there. Stechko's got him in your office now."

Tortyev continued staring at Holokov for a moment, digesting his information. Then he turned to Priabin, and said: "All our problems solved in one fell swoop, Dmitri—eh? This bloody little traitor must know who Orton is, and why he's gone to Bilyarsk! He's warned the British that we're close to finding out who he is—we have the answer in the palm of our hands."

Priabin's face broke into a slow smile. "Come on," he said. "Your car still waiting for you?" Tortyev nodded. "Then I'll come, too—with your permission?"

Tortyev smiled. "Naturally, Dmitri."

As they passed through the door, and fat Holokov closed it behind them, Priabin said: "The value of gossip, eh, Alexei—the value of gossip!" He slapped Tortyev on the shoulder, and he and the detective laughed loudly in unison.

Priabin stood at Tortyev's desk, the telephone receiver in his hand, waiting for the Center's code-room to answer him. He looked across the room, to where the unconscious, bloody form of Filipov was collapsed into a chair, held there only by the straps on his wrists. The man's dark, ascetic features were bruised and swollen. Blood had run over his chin from broken teeth and a damaged lip, and the skin was split and discolored around his closed eyes. His nose had bled freely when Holokov's huge fist had broken it. Stechko and Holokov hovered in that same corner of the room, silenced machines awaiting fresh commands, while Tortyev paced the room. The time was after one in the morning.

Priabin was indifferent to the damage done by Tortyev's apes. They had had to work swiftly—too crudely for his taste but, surprisingly, not for Tortyev. Perhaps Alexei Tortyev was angry with Filipov, especially angry because he had trusted him—or merely because he was a Jew. Such anti-semitism was by no means unusual in the KGB.

Priabin had communicated with Kontarsky, as his first priority, reporting that the man in the truck was obviously an agent, and that he expected swift results from the interrogation of the traitor, Filipov. At twelve-fifty, he had to call his chief again, to

report that Filipov had not talked, even though he
had confessed himself an agent of the British, had
spilled the whole story of his recruitment by the
Cultural Attaché, Lansing. Filipov had talked, but
he had not told them what he ought to have been
able to tell them.

Kontarsky was thus left suddenly in the dark as to
the present appearance of the man known to Filipov
as Orton, despite the fact that Priabin had wire-
printed the pictures of Orton. Kontarsky already
had with him the photographs of Upenskoy's com-
panion from the security checks at Moscow, Gorky
and Kazan, wire-printed to him from the local
KGB offices as a matter of urgency.

Kontarsky, Priabin now had to admit to himself,
was panicky. He knew that a human bomb was in
Bilyarsk, somewhere, but he had no idea of the time-
mechanism, the extent, the force. . . . He was ham-
strung. He had requested all the identifit pictures of
Orton supplied by the computer to be wire-printed,
a task which had just been completed.

What concerned him now, as the code-room answered Priabin's call, was sending coded instructions to the Russian Embassies in London and
Washington, in order to request the senior KGB
Resident at each of them to supply information, descriptions, and whereabouts of all recent arrivals
at the CIA headquarters in Langley, Virginia, or at
the Ministry of Defence in London, or any of the
various SIS offices in the city. It might be, he knew,
a forlorn gamble, but it was one he had to take. At
best, such records of arrivals and departures at the
security headquarters of the two organizations were
patchy and incomplete, nevertheless, unlike Tortyev, who seemed unable to ignore, or leave alone,
the beaten, bloody policeman in the chair, he had
doubts that Filipov even knew the real identity of
the man who had been Orton, and then had posed as
Glazunov. His only real hope was to obtain a lead

which would enable them to discover just what kind of agent the man was, and thereby to forestall his purpose at Bilyarsk.

"Hello—Priabin, Department 'M,' 2nd Directorate here," he said into the mouthpiece. Tortyev looked up at him for a moment, and then looked away. "I want the following coded messages transmitted, on the authority of Colonel Kontarsky, to the Washington and London Residents, as soon as possible . . ."

The call took only a couple of minutes. When he had finished, he put down the telephone thoughtfully. He looked in the direction of Filipov, and saw Tortyev attempting to revive the man for further questioning.

"Not for the moment, Alexei," he said. "I've an idea—I may want to make another call."

Tortyev turned away from Filipov, as if with reluctance, and said: "What is it?"

"Let's review what's been done thus far," he said. "We've checked on known or suspected agents of most of the Western intelligence services, who might be interested in the Bilyarsk project, and capable of mounting this sort of operation." Tortyev nodded. "Because the man's been clever, we've assumed that he's a very good agent, one of their top men—which means we ought to have found him by now—eh?"

"Agreed. He's obviously new, or been kept back for this one job—it's big enough to warrant that."

"Too bloody true," Priabin commented gruffly.

"Exactly. So—why haven't we found him—and where do we look?"

"Just my own thought. As I was saying—he's either a top agent or, he's not an agent at all."

"He *has* to be—with this kind of cover-operation going on." Tortyev nodded over his shoulder at the slumped form of the Jew. "They've used Filipov knowing they might be expending him. They expended another top man, the truck-driver. That's

two down. The British are always careful of their
operatives, Dmitri, they don't throw them away!"

"No—I don't mean he's not working for the British, or the Americans . . . just that he's been recruited from some other field. Look at it this way.
What if he's not there to damage the project? After
all, what would be the point? As far as we know,
the Americans are so far behind, they'd need ten
years to catch up with the Mig-31 despite being
handed a Mig-25 by Belenko four years ago." Priabin's voice had sunk to a confidential whisper, and
he glanced sideways at Stechko and Holokov who,
politically, seemed to be occupied with the limp form
of Filipov, minutely inspecting him in a grotesque
form of damage-report.

"I agree—from what you've told me."

"So—our security has been able to intercept most
of what has been passed to London and Washington
by the underground at Bilyarsk, via the Embassy
here. Therefore, the Americans and British want to
know more. They want a first-hand report of what's
going on, perhaps even photographs, and an eye-
witness account . . . ?"

"You mean—an expert?"

"Yes!" Priabin's voice was suddenly louder. "What
if they've sent an aeronautics expert, who knows
what to look for, what questions to ask?"

"God—it could be anyone—someone we don't
even know!"

There was a silence.

"I don't think he knows," Priabin said, nodding
towards Filipov, who groaned with returning consciousness as he did so.

"He *could*," Tortyev replied. "Besides," he added
in a menacing tone, "I haven't finished with him
yet, the little Jewish shit!"

Priabin shrugged. "Suit yourself," he said. "But
don't start on him again until I've made another
call. I want a check run through the computer on the

entire American and British aerospace indus-
tries."

"It'll take hours . . .!" Tortyev protested.

"No longer than it will take your gorillas to beat
it out of Filipov. There won't be many names—not
capable of making the most of this elaborate sub-
terfuge to smuggle him into Bilyarsk. Let me make
the call—then you can resort to the physical stuff!"

Tortyev hesitated for a moment, shrugged in his
turn, and Priabin picked up the receiver.

The searchlight picked him up early, with fifty yards
still to go, fixed on him, and he walked into the tunnel of its white, blinding light. He tried to appear
casual, yet irritated, and shaded his eyes studiously.
Each footstep threatened to become reluctant, to
stutter to a halt, his frame and motive power running down, like a machine dying. He forced his legs
to work. The cramp was coming back to his stomach.
He knew the sweat was standing out on his forehead,
and his hands were shaking. Gant was suddenly
threatened. It was as if his ego had been stripped
and he knew he could not carry it through. This was
worse than the flying—this was the struggle of the
stranded fish.

"Identify yourself," the voice said and he realized,
with a shock, that he was close to the gate. A guard
was pointing a rifle in his direction. "Identify yourself."

His voice sounded old and weak, winding up
hoarsely like an ancient clock to strike. "Identify
yourself—*sir!*" he snapped. "Soldier!"

The guard reacted. It was what he expected from a
GRU officer, even though he did not know the face,
and he replied as expected.

"Identity, please—sir."

Gant fished in his papers and passed them across,
the yellow ID card on the top. The guard took it,
and inspected it. Gant knew he had to light a

cigarette now, to calm himself, to occupy the hands that threatened to betray him. He reached as casually as he could into the hip-pocket of his jacket, and pulled out the cigarette case. He lit the cigarette and inhaled, almost choking on the raw smoke. He exhaled thankfully, stifling a cough. He began to inspect the arrangements at the gate.

There were six guards, frozen into unreal postures in the harsh light that bathed the wire and the open space before it. The red-and-white barrier remained firmly lowered, and two uniformed KGB guards stood woodenly behind it, rifles casually pointed in his direction. There was a guard-hut at either side of the barrier, giving it the appearance of a customs-post, and in the doorway of each another soldier was visible. The sixth man stood behind the guard inspecting his papers. Gant checked the piping and the tabs on each of the uniforms. Each guard was KGB, not part of the GRU Security Support Group to which he was supposed to belong. That, at least, would explain his unfamiliar face.

"Why were you outside the wire—sir?"

There was a silence, and then Gant said: "You have your orders, soldier—I have mine. You *know* that a suspected agent is in the vicinity." He leaned forward, staring into the soldier's face, and smiled. "Or perhaps you don't?"

The soldier was silent for a moment, then he said: "Yes, sir—we've been alerted."

"Good. Then I suggest you get a dog out here, and look at that clump of trees regularly during the next few hours."

Gant watched the soldier's eyes. His whole consciousness focused on them. Slowly, infinitely slowly, he watched the moment turn over, like a world orbiting. It retreated. The soldier snapped to attention, and nodded.

"Yes, sir. Good idea, sir."

Gant touched his cap ironically, still smiling. The barrier swung up at a signal from the guard, and

Gant saw one of the figures in a hut-doorway turn inside, presumably to inform the guards at the second gate that the officer had been cleared for entry. Nodding, he stepped forward, feeling the sudden weakness of his legs, as if they were somewhere far away from the rest of his body.

The rotors of a chopper buzzed suddenly loud, as if his hearing had become suddenly acute. He looked up, forcing himself to act casually; then he had reached the gate, which remained closed against him. He saw the guard, gun at the ready, then saw a second guard emerge from the guard-hut, and signal that the gate could be safely opened. Gant drew his ID card from his pocket, dropped his cigarette in the dirt and ground his heel on it. He appeared irritated at the delay, standing with his hands on his hips, his lips pursed. He saw, comfortingly, that the guard was beginning to fall back into his routine pattern of behavior. He had been confronted with a uniform, superior in rank to his own, and he had accepted it.

The gate opened, not the huge double gate but a small personnel door set into the gates. Gant, nodding irritatedly, stepped through, and it clattered shut behind him. He didn't bother to study the guards, but headed down the track which skirted the runway, towards the hangar. It was all he could do to prevent the surge of adrenalin through his system from driving his body at a run. Probably, the guards at the gate had already forgotten him. Yet, their eyes bored into his back. His shirt was sticky with sweat across the small of his back. His heart pumped loudly in his ears, drumming him into activity, into a run ...

He stepped across the runway, turning off the road. He glanced swiftly along its length, then gazed ahead of him. The hangar was nearer now. He followed the taxi-way that led to it from the runway proper.

A chopper buzzed overhead, the downdraught

plucking at his cap and jacket, flapping his trousers. He held onto his cap, and looked up. He saw a face at the open door of the chopper and he waved, the abrupt wave of an officer with every right to be where he was. The chopper pulled round in a tight circle, and the face grinned at him, a hand waved, and the chopper pulled away. Settling his cap firmly on his head, Gant walked on.

It was less than a hundred yards now, he estimated. He could see the guards stationed at the hangar doors, see the spillage of warm light on the concrete, hear the sounds of echoed metal dimly. The hangar door, as the taxi-way curved and straightened, opened before him, and he felt a quickening of his pulse, the surge of adrenalin in his system—but not as before, not because fear was gripping his stomach, crawling up his spine. This was an elation, an excitement. He could not pause, to stare open-mouthed into the hangar, but he possessed all the sudden wonder and response of the child at an exhibition. Gant was a single-minded individual. There was no real complexity to his character. The only thing he had been able to do supremely well, ever, was to fly airplanes. Now, in the hangar spilling its raw, warm light, echoing with voices and noise, he glimpsed the Firefox. Its elongated nose was tilted up and towards him, and he saw the attendant, insect figures busy about the gleaming silver fuselage. Two huge intakes glared blackly at him, and there was the fleeting impression of wings edge-on . . . Then he had turned aside. His momentary pause would not have been out of character for a man new to the project and who had flown in the previous night.

There was activity of a different kind at the door of the KGB building, the security headquarters attached to the hangar. It was, Gant reflected, with an unusual poetry, a symbol—wherever Soviet achievements went, the KGB was sure to go, linked

by an umbilical cord. As he approached, guards on
the door snapped to attention, and for a moment he
wondered whether he had not attracted this respect
—then the door opened, held by a guard from inside, and he was face to face with KGB Colonel
Mihail Kontarsky, head of security for the Mikoyan
Project. He snapped to attention, fingers at his peak,
as he confronted the short, slim, busy-looking man,
and noticed the edge of worry in the eyes, the
nervous movement they possessed.

Kontarsky stared at Gant. "Yes, Captain?" he
snapped nervously.

Gant realized his mistake. He had made it appear
that he wished to report to Kontarsky. Behind Kontarsky was Tsernik, looking at him in puzzlement.
He was a strange face, and Gant knew that to Tsernik he should not have been a strange face. Tsernik
would have met him, had he really arrived with the
GRU detachment the previous day, or would have
seen his file and photograph.

The moment hit him in the stomach, bunching it,
twisting it in its grip. He was less than a hundred
yards from his objective, the airplane, and he had
walked straight into the arms of the security chief.

"Sir—I have, without your permission, ordered a
dog for the guards on the security entrance . . . to
search the belt of trees, thoroughly," Gant said, his
voice level, controlled by a supreme effort. His mind
screaming at him to break and run.

Kontarsky seemed to take a moment to realize
what was being said to him, as if he were concentrat-
ing on something else, then he nodded.

"Good thinking, Captain—my thanks." Kontarsky
touched the peak of his cap with his glove and passed
on. Gant dropped his hand, then raised it again to
salute as Tsernik passed him. With a sweeping relief, Gant realized that his report had been accepted
by the second-in-command. He merely nodded, no
longer looking puzzled, and passed on behind Gant.

As they moved away, he heard Kontarsky say: "Now is the time to pick up Dherkov—now that the others are safely inside. You agree, Tsernik?"

"Yes, Colonel, of course. I will get onto that right away—and his wife."

Gant heard no more. He passed inside the door, the guards remaining at attention until he was inside. Once there, he leaned against the wall in a narrow corridor, hardly noticing the guard posted there in his sudden, overwhelming relief, until the guard said: "Are you all right, Captain?"

Gant looked at him, startled. The guard saw a white face, sweaty and strained, and a hand gripping the stomach—and the uniform.

"I—just indigestion. Think I've got an ulcer," he added, for the sake of veracity.

"Would you like a drink, Captain?" the guard was solicitous.

Gant shook his head. He had to move away now. The incident was already becoming too memorable, his face too familiar; the story would be recounted in the other ranks' mess when the guard went off-duty. He smiled, a poor imitation of the real thing, and straightened himself.

"No—thanks, soldier. No. Just comes in spasms . . ." Then he realized he was being far too human, he was responding as if he did have an ulcer. He brushed his jacket straight, and jammed his cap on his head. He glared at the soldier, as if he had in some way offended rank by noticing his officer's difficulties, then strode off down the corridor, his boots clicking loudly along the linoleum. In front of him were the stairs up to the officers' mess, and to the pilots' rest-room.

As he mounted the stairs, the images of the last minutes dying in his mind, the feverish pulse slowing, he hoped to his God that Dherkov, the courier, did not know what he looked like. He glanced at his watch. Still not three o'clock. More than three hours. He wondered how brave a man the grocer was.

There were five of them now in Aubrey's secluded operations room: the two CIA men and the two representatives of the SIS had been joined by a man wearing the uniform of a Captain in the U.S. Navy —Captain Eugene Curtin, from the office of the Chief of Naval Operations, USN. Curtin it was who had been responsible for the arrangements for the refueling of the Firefox, presuming Gant to be able to steal it on schedule, and head in the right direction—north, towards the Barents Sea.

Curtin was in his forties, square-built, the uniform stretched across his broad shoulders and back. His hair was clipped so short it seemed he had recently survived an internment in some POW camp. His face was large, square, chiseled, and his eyes were piercingly blue. He had just completed some amendments to the huge projection of the Arctic seas, marking the latest reported positions of Russian surface and sub-surface vessels. To Aubrey's eye, there appeared a great many of them—too bloody many, he reflected wryly, as Shelley might have said. Also, Curtin had brought with him a new set of satellite weather photographs, as well as sheets of more local weather reports, and some of the numerous SAC radar and weather planes flying over the seas to the north of Soviet Russia.

Curtin saw Aubrey regarding his amendments to the wall-map, and grinned at him.

"Looks bad—uh?" he said.

Aubrey said nothing, but continued to regard the wall. He disliked the disconcerting honesty that Curtin shared with Buckholz, and other Americans he had encountered in the field of intelligence, whether operational, or merely analytical. The Americans, he considered, had a penchant for being disconcertingly blunt about things. It simply did not do to assume that Gant had no chance of success—the only way to prevent such gloomy reflections was not to think too far ahead—one step at a time.

Aubrey sipped at the cup of tea that Shelley had

poured for him, and continued to study the map without any apparent reaction on his features.

Curtin joined Buckholz and his aide, Anders, at their desk where they were analyzing the weather reports linking them with the latest positions of the Soviet trawler fleets supplied by the office of Rear-Admiral Philipson over the telephone.

"Well?" Curtin asked softly, his eye on Aubrey.

Buckholz looked up at him. "It looks good," he said adopting the same conspiratorial whisper. He picked up his coffee and swallowed the last of it. He pulled a face. He had let the coffee get cold in the bottom of the cup. He handed the empty cup to Anders, who went away to refill it.

"The weather up there can change like—that," Curtin said amiably, clicking his thumb and forefinger.

"It's been good for the last four days," Buckholz pointed out.

"Means nothing," Curtin observed unhelpfully. "That means there's four days less of good weather left to play with."

Buckholz scowled at him. "How bad can it get?" he said.

"Too bad for Hotshot ever to find the fuel he's going to need," Curtin replied, "*if* he ever gets off the ground at Bilyarsk. What about that information Aubrey received?"

"I don't know. Our British friend plays it very close to his chest."

Curtin nodded. "Yeah. I don't understand why. But, if they're onto Hotshot—what chance has he got?"

"Some," Buckholz admitted reluctantly, "These guys at Bilyarsk on Aubrey's payroll are no fools, Curtin."

"I never said they were. But I heard the KGB were pretty good at their job, too. If they find out we sent a flyer to Bilyarsk, Hotshot will never get near that damn plane."

"I know that." Buckholz appeared suddenly irritated with Curtin. He was being too honest, too objective—breezing in late, like a cold wind, disrupting the close, confined, suppressed subjectivity of the mood of the four intelligence operatives. Sometimes, Buckholz considered, there was a right time for a little deceptive hope. And now was the right time.

"Sorry," Curtain said with a shrug. "I'm only the Navy's messenger boy—I just bring you the facts."

"Yeah, I know that, too."

Curtin looked down at the mass of papers on Buckholz's desk, and observed: "Jesus, but this is a half-cock operation."

"Yeah?"

"Uh-huh. I wonder why you let the British do all the planning, Buckholz. I really do."

"They had the men on the ground, brother—that's why."

"But—so much depends on—so many people."

"It's called the element of surprise, Curtin."

"You mean—it's a surprise if it works?" Curtin said, his eyebrow raised ironically.

"Maybe—maybe." Buckholz looked down at the papers before him, as if to signal the end of the conversation. Curtin continued to regard him curiously.

Buckholz, he knew, had survived, even benefited from, the purges which had followed the Congressional inquiry into the activities of the CIA, following Watergate. In fact, it had placed him as Head of the Covert Action Staff within the coterie of top advisers that surrounded the Director himself. It was he, seemingly fired by Aubrey's crack-brained scheme to steal the new Mig, who had pushed through the arrangements for the theft, laid on, in his own bulldozing, dogged fashion, the refueling arrangements, the radar-watch, the coordination of SAC and USN assistance he required. He had persuaded the Chief of Naval Operations to second Curtin to his staff until the completion of "Operation

Rip-Off," a fact for which Curtin was only dubiously grateful. It had handed him immense, if temporary, power, but it was an operation that could write *finis* to Curtin's naval career. And that was something he did not like to contemplate.

The details of Russian surface and sub-surface strength in the Barents Sea and the Arctic Ocean that he had transferred to the wall-map filled Curtin with doubt. He, better than anyone there, knew the current strength of the Red Banner Northern Fleet of the Red Navy, and how swiftly and thoroughly it could be brought to operate against any discovered intruder into what were considered by the Kremlin to be Soviet waters. So far, the refueling vessel had not been detected—at least, no moves had been made against her, which ought to have meant the same thing. But, in the upheaval which would follow the theft of the aircraft, in the comprehensive radar and sonar searches by missile cruisers, spy trawlers and submarines—who could say?

As he headed for the coffee percolator on a trolley in one corner of the room, he said to Buckholz, who continued studiously to ignore him: "He hasn't got a hope in hell, brother—not a hope in hell!"

It was after three-thirty when Lieutenant-Colonel Yuri Voskov arrived in the pilots' rest-room on the second floor of the security building attached to the Firefox's hangar at Bilyarsk. He paused inside the door, and his hand reached for the light switch. When that hand encountered another guarding the light switch, his surprise had insufficient time to become shock and alarm before he was struck behind the ear by a terrible, killing blow. He never saw the face of his assassin—the floor rushed up, unseen, as he keeled over from the force of the blow which flung him half-way across the room.

Gant flicked on the light, and crossed to the inert body, rubbing the fist that had delivered the blow. Then, like some great exhalation, the nerves ex-

ploded in him, shaking his body like a wind. He had
been able to kill Voskov, coldly and mechanically
and with his hands, when even Buckholz had sometimes wondered about it. But the reaction continued
to shake him, and it was what seemed like minutes
before he could kneel steadily by the dead man.
Then, gently, as if a medical expert, he felt for the
pulse he knew would not be evident. Voskov was
dead.

Gant rolled the body onto its back and looked
down at the dead face of Voskov. The man was
older than Gant, in his early forties, perhaps. He
felt no remorse. He had removed a necessary piece
from the board, that was all. He merely wondered
how good Voskov had been.

Suddenly galvanized into action, he tugged the
body across the carpet towards the tall steep lockers
ranged against one wall. Dumping Voskov in a heap,
he fished in his jacket pocket for the master key that
Baranovich had supplied, and opened one of the
lockers. It was, as he had expected, and had been
told to expect, empty. Holding the door ajar with his
foot, he pushed the head and shoulders of the body
into the locker. Then, as if engaged in some grotesque, energetic dance in slow-motion, he heaved
at the body, until it stood as if alive, upright in the
locker. Swiftly, he closed the door and locked it,
hearing the soft concussion of Voskov's body as it
leaned forward against the door. Then he pocketed
the key.

Opening another of the lockers, he inspected the
pressure-suit that hung there—Voskov's. Voskov
was about his own build. At least, they were sufficiently alike for Gant to be able to use the Russian's
pressure-suit. Fortunately, it was merely an adapta-
tion of the normal aircraft pressure-suit, not something tailor-made like a NASA space-suit. Had that
been the case, the slightest difference in form,
height, build, would have made the wearing of Voskov's suit impossible.

Having completed his inspection, Gant began to remove his GRU uniform. It was three-forty-six in the morning. Gant felt his nerves beating his stomach, a fist. As he removed his shirt, he looked at the bleeper device taped beneath his arm that would summon him to the hangar.

He had two-and-a-half hours to go.

5

THE
RIP-OFF

Kontarsky glanced at his gold wrist-watch. It was four o'clock. From where he was standing in the open doorway of the main hangar, he could survey the scene of quiet, intense activity within. He had seen the guards become aware of him, not only those on the doors, but those at their stations close to the aircraft became suddenly more aware, more intent in their scrutiny. Many of the scientists and technicians took no notice of him—though he had seen Kreshin look up and then mutter something to Semelovsky, who stood next to him. Baranovich he could see as a hunched figure, swallowed to the waist by the open cockpit, giving instructions to the technician seated in the pilot's couch of the Mig-31.

Kontarsky had no aesthetic or military feelings concerning the aircraft. Its aerodynamic lines, its potency, the huge gaping mouths of its air intakes, were nothing to him but a problem in security. And with that problem, he had taken every precaution he possibly could.

He ought to have felt a comfortable self-pride,

he realized. Such a feeling, however, eluded him. The night had remained mild, but he felt cold. He was chewing on an indigestion tablet now as he stood outside the hangar. It seemed to be having no effect whatsoever.

The Production Prototype One was less than a hundred feet from him; behind it, ignored by the team of patient, hardly moving technicians, a second aircraft—the PP Two—stood near the rear of the giant hangar.

Kontarsky wondered whether to speak to the guards near the aircraft, but decided against it. They were all picked men, and he had briefed them thoroughly before they went on duty. To have inspected them now at close quarters would have been an error of leadership, a sign of absent confidence, and he knew it. Reluctantly, he crossed the strip of light spilling from the open doors, and rejoined his personal bodyguard who was in conversation with one of the door-guards. Nodding to him to fall in behind him, he headed for the second hangar, the one in which the Mig-31 had been built—it was locked and in darkness, but it would not hurt to have the guards who ringed it make one more interior search.

Priabin was, at that moment, he knew, running the agent to earth. As the hours of the night had limped by, he had become more and more open to his aide's suggestion that the man must be some kind of technical expert, sent to talk to Baranovich and the others before they were arrested, as would be inevitable as soon as the trials were successfully completed, and to observe as much as he could of the trials themselves. What kind of equipment, other than his eyes, he had brought with him, Kontarsky had no idea. As he crossed the bright, stark space between the hangars, he looked out beyond the fence, seeking some vantage-point from which such an observer might consider he had a good view of the runway. There was no hillock, no rising ground.

When he had completed his inspection of the production hangar, he told himself, it would be as well to send out dog patrols beyond the fence—just in case.

Despite his decision, he still felt that the man was inside the fence, a part of the complex, in some disguise or other. He would have the whole area searched again.

Baranovich watched the form that he recognized as belonging to Kontarsky as it crossed the black hole of the night, and vanished in the direction of the production hangar. When he looked down again from his perch on top of a pilot's ladder wheeled against the fuselage of the Firefox, he saw the squat, flattened features of the mechanic in the pilot's couch looking up at him, grinning. Baranovich, with as much aplomb as he could muster, smiled back and the mechanic, who had expected and wished to see fear, or unsettlement at the least, on Baranovich's face, scowled and turned back to his work. He was in the process of checking the circuits within the weapons-guidance system. Part of the instrument panel on the left-hand side was removed, and the intricate wiring and miniature circuits of the system were exposed. Under Baranovich's direction, the final check proceeded slowly.

Baranovich knew that the mechanic was KGB. For months now, as he had installed and perfected the system on which he had been forced to work originally while still in the scientific prison of Mavrino, he had had assigned to his technical team this man, Grosch, an electronics technician of high capability. Grosch was the child of a German scientist captured by the Red Army early in 1945; there was no more loyal member of the Party.

Baranovich felt no anger at the man—not because his father was a Nazi, or because he himself was a secret policeman. If Gant had been able to see the look on his face as he gazed down at the top of Grosch's cropped head, he would have recognized that look of painful wisdom, of detached pity, which

he had seen at Kreshin's quarters. Baranovich
looked unobtrusively at his watch. Four minutes after four. He looked round him at the security within
the hangar as Grosch absorbed himself in checking
a printed circuit. He had decided already on the
method of diversion he would use.

He looked back over the tail-unit of the Firefox,
to where the second production prototype stood,
rather shunted into a corner. The aircraft, seemingly
in shadow, unglamorous, lacking the pristine deadli-
ness of the model atop which he stood, was fully
fueled, in a state of readiness for take-off against
some kind, any kind, of airborne attack upon the
factory. All Soviet aircraft, whether prototype, production model, or service aircraft, as long as they
were military, remained in a maximum twenty-
four-hour condition of readiness while on the
ground.

Therefore, Baranovich concluded, there was only
one thing that could be done when Gant escaped
at the controls of the first aircraft. They would send
the second one after him. There would be a delay, of
course, while it was fully-weaponed—perhaps an
hour, including a quickest possible check of systems
and controls. And the second aircraft would be refueled in mid-air, unlike Gant, who would have to
refuel on the ground, wherever that ground was.
Unless he, Kreshin and Semelovsky could put that
second aircraft out of action, Gant could be caught,
and destroyed, by the only plane capable of doing
both to him—PP Two.

Fire: he knew the answer. A hangar fire would
create a panic, and allow Gant to climb aboard as
the pilot, and taxi the aircraft onto the taxi-way outside without suspicion. Two birds with one stone,
he remarked to himself. Gant away, and the pursuit
of him prevented at the same time. There was so
much fuel, oil, timber and other inflammables in the
hangar that causing the fire would be no problem.
Fire was one of the plans he had outlined to the

others—now he would tell them of his final decision in its favor.

Baranovich spent no time wondering whether Gant would survive the flight. He would show up on no radar, which meant the Russians would need a visual sighting before they could loose off infra-red or proximity missiles, or send aircraft after him. He glanced towards the tail where Semelovsky was supervising the fitting of the special tail-unit, his own project from first to last, on which Kreshin had worked as his assistant—the tail-assembly that provided Gant's most effective anti-missile system and ECM gear. Semelovsky said it would work, but it had only been tried on an RPV—that day, it would be a part of the weapons-trials and a man would have to use it. Gant would need it, he knew.

It was all a question of timing, he decided. The First Secretary's aircraft was scheduled to arrive at nine. Before that, he knew, he and the others would be placed under arrest. Their work would be completed by six-thirty at the latest. This meant that six-thirty was the latest time for the diversion, and the take-off. He would have to arrange the time-table with the others at their next coffee-break, which was at five.

The security was so tight that when he had visited the toilets at the other end of the hangar an hour earlier, a guard had detached himself from the wall, and followed him inside, making no effort to relieve himself, but merely contenting himself with observing Baranovich. Grosch should find that damaged power transistor within the next few minutes, he thought, which would helpfully lengthen the final checks.

He was suddenly, oddly, assailed by memory, a memory that was akin to his present situation, but removed from self-concern. He was in the same overalls as now, but those in his memory were oil-stained, uncleaned. The temperature was well below zero, and his hands were numb. He was bending forward into the cockpit of a Mig, an old, wartime Mig. He was in a hangar at the Red Army air base outside Stalingrad. Because he was a Jew, he was an army mechanic, nothing more glorified than that.

He shrugged off the memory. The past was an intrusion, an interference in what he had to do, had to plan. He thought of the gun beneath his armpit. He had not been searched on entering the gates. The gun, he realized, with the kind of shock of cold water on the drowsy skin, meant that he had accepted that this was the end. He did not expect to live through the day.

Baranovich smiled as Grosch found the malfunctioning circuit-board, and looked up into his face. Grosch held up the extracted plastic square, with its thirty-seven gold-plated tags, into his face.

"Looks like the power transistor, Comrade Director Baranovich," he said. Baranovich smiled. Grosch was being obsequiously civil. He, too, then understood that it was the end.

"Mm." Baranovich turned the square of plastic over in his hand, nodding. Then he handed it back to Grosch. "Scrap it, then. I'll get another."

"From the experimental technical stores, Director?" Grosch queried with a smile.

"Yes, Grosch. But you won't have to get out of that comfortable seat to accompany me. The guard will take me."

Before Grosch could reply, he began to descend the ladder, with a light, youthful, untroubled step.

"You incompetent bloody fool, Stechko—he's dead! You've killed him!" Tortyev exploded. He rounded on Stechko, and the big man stepped back, a look of confused, abashed defeat on his face. Tortyev rose from his haunches where he had squatted before the sagging, lifeless form of Filipov, and glared at his subordinate. The beatings had been too regular, too vicious, too hurried—he knew that now. In his desperate effort to make the man talk, he had allowed

Stechko and Holokov to kill him. He ground his teeth and clenched and unclenched his fists in the fury of impotence.

When he turned to Priabin, the KGB lieutenant was already on the telephone. His indifference seemed to anger Tortyev further. He crossed the room to confront Holokov who was sitting on a hard chair, astride it, watching the body intently as if for some sign of life. Tortyev stood before him, and Holokov's intensity of expression became transformed to doubt.

"You stupid fat shit," Tortyev breathed, his eyes blazing. "You incompetent lump of dogshit!"

"You pressed us . . ." Holokov began, and then recoiled as Tortyev slapped him across the cheek with the back of his hand. He reached for his cut lip, in surprise, inspected his fingers, and the smear of blood on them in some state of shock.

"He knew nothing." Tortyev heard Priabin speak quietly, and turned on him. Priabin was holding one hand over the receiver, and smiling. His smile irritated Tortyev.

"What the hell do you mean by that?" he said.

"He knew nothing—hell, he'd have told you long ago if he had anything to tell."

"You clever bastard—what's the answer, then? Your precious bloody aircraft is still in danger, or had you forgotten that?" Tortyev wiped the saliva from his lip.

Priabin continued to smile irritatingly, and waggled the receiver in Tortyev's direction.

"Why do you think I want to talk to the computer?" he said mildly.

Tortyev looked at the clock, and said: "You'd better get a bloody move-on! It's four-thirty, or hadn't you noticed?" There was a sneer in his voice, a returning self-confidence. He had done his part. Now it was up to Priabin.

"Hello?" Priabin said into the receiver. "Priabin. What news?" He listened for a while, and then said:

"How quickly are you checking out the whereabouts of these people?" Irritation crossed his face. "I don't care—the information's in that machine's guts somewhere, and I want it!" He slammed the telephone down, and saw Tortyev smiling at him.

"What's the matter—less than miraculous, is it, that machine?" he said.

Priabin ignored him, thought for a moment, and then said: "We couldn't do it any faster—a lot slower, in fact." He looked across at the body and said: "Get that out of here, you two—now." Holokov looked at Tortyev, and the policeman nodded. The two detectives hoisted the body to its dragging feet, and took it through the door.

The break seemed to calm both men. When they were alone, Tortyev said: "What are they checking out?"

"They've got a list of less than a dozen top aeronautics experts in America and Europe, young enough and fit enough to be our man. But they're checking current whereabouts of all of them, and it's taking time . . . too much time," he added quietly, his voice strained. "They've linked into the First Directorate's computer, whose banks have constant monitor-records, as you know, on thousands of useful or important public and scientific figures in the West. The answers are coming. . . ."

"But they might be too late."

"Too true."

Priabin left his desk and began to pace the room, his hand cupping his chin, or pulling at his lower lip. It was minutes before he spoke again. Then he said: "I can't speed up the process. We'll either get the information in time, or we won't. In which case, I prefer not to think about it. But, what *else* can I do—what else can I ask that bloody machine to do at the same time as it's processing these people?" He was standing before Tortyev, a look of appeal on his face.

Tortyev was silent for a moment, then he said:

"Anything to do with aircraft. Check everyone and everything, Dmitri."

"How?"

"Check on every file of every person we know to be connected with the American or European aerospace programs, or who ever has been connected . . ." Tortyev's face seemed to illuminate from within. "They sent a young, fit man—with brains. Why not an astronaut? One of our own cosmonauts would know what to look for, know how to analyze information received from someone like this Baranovich, wouldn't he?"

Priabin was silent for a moment. "It seems unlikely, doesn't it?" he said, wanting to be convinced.

"Well—is it, though? Think of it. You're looking for a man in his thirties, fit, intelligent, elusive . . . you thought he was an agent, at first. He has to possess some of the qualities of a commando, and of a scientist. The NASA astronauts are the most highly-trained people in the world. Why not?"

Priabin seemed still reluctant. "Mm. I wonder."

"You don't have too much time in which to wonder, Dmitri," Tortyev reminded him.

"I know! Let me think . . . I wonder how many files there are relating to astronauts and to air force pilots, and the like?"

"Hundreds—perhaps thousands. Why?"

"In that case, because our service collects anything and everything and, like the careful housewife, never throws anything away, we have to have an order of preference. We'll have to look at the computer-index."

"Very well," said Tortyev, seemingly glad of action. "I'll help you."

"Thanks."

"Besides which—this place is beginning to smell of Jews—and death," Tortyev added.

"Very well, then—I'll ring for a car."

"Don't bother—at this time in the morning, it'll be quicker to walk."

It was four-forty when the two men left the room together.

Gant had moved a chair into the shower-cubicle and arranged a fold of the shower-curtain to shield him from the spray. The cubicle was full of steam.

He was in no doubt that Pavel was dead by now, or in some local KGB cellar, having his name and mission beaten out of him. It troubled Gant to know for certain that Pavel would take a lot of punishment before he would tell, if he ever told. Again, he was forced to feel responsible.

More than Pavel, however, who might well have died neatly and quickly in a gunfight of some kind, he was troubled by Baranovich and the others. He had never encountered dumb, accepting courage such as that before, and it puzzled him.

Gant had removed his uniform, and was sitting in the cubicle in his shorts. The GRU uniform, now an encumbrance, had gone into the same locker as Voskov. He had had to hold the body with one hand, to stop it toppling outwards, while he flung the creased bundle that had been Captain Chekhov into the corner of the locker. He had not looked into Voskov's face and thankfully he had locked the body out of sight once more. Then he had turned on the shower. The steam, though it made his breathing unpleasant, kept him warm. He sat astride the chair, his arms folded across the back, chin resting on his arms, letting the constant stream of the hot water lull him, closing his eyes. He could not sleep, and knew he must not, but he tried to reduce the activity of his thoughts by the semblance of sleep.

At first he didn't hear the voice from the room beyond, from the rest-room. The second call alerted him and he sprang to his feet, unconsciously being careful not to scrape the chair on the floor of the shower.

"Yes?" he called.

"Security check, Colonel—important."

It had to be the KGB—it had to be Kontarsky's last fling, his final attempt to trace the agent he must suspect was already inside Bilyarsk.

"What do you want?"

"Your identification."

Gant panicked. He had left Voskov's papers in his pockets, bundling the body quickly and thankfully into the locker. Now they wanted to see his papers —if they didn't see them, then they would want to see him . . .

He wondered how he might bluff his way out. The nervous reaction had jolted him awake, and his pulse was hammering in his head, and he found it hard to catch his breath. Though he only half-suspected it, this latest, unexpected jolt was drawing vastly on his reserves of control. Clearly, above the levels of the blood's panic, he thought that Voskov would be a pampered individual, one likely to take unkindly to such an intrusion.

Loudly, irritatedly, he called out: "I am having a shower, whoever you are. What do you mean by disturbing me with your stupid questions?" To him, his voice sounded, in the steam-filled curtained hole, to be weak, high-pitched, unconvincing. He heard a cough, deferential, abashed, from the man in the rest-room. He peered through the steam and the shower-curtain. There was a shadow, against the light from the door into the bathroom. It was two or three steps across the space of tiles between himself and that shadow.

"Sorry, Colonel, but . . ."

"This is your idea, of course—soldier? It is not Colonel Kontarsky's direct order that the rest-room should be searched, and myself questioned?" He felt his voice gaining power, arrogance. He could play the part of Voskov—it was a part close to his own professional arrogance, expressing his own contempt.

"I—orders, sir," he heard, and knew that the man was lying.

Gant hesitated, until he thought the moment was

almost past and he was too late, then he barked:
"Get out, before you find yourself reported!"

He waited. No doubt the man could see his shadow, as the shower-curtain wafted against his skin,
drawn in by the heat. He wondered whether the
man would dare cross that space of cold tiles, just to
be sure. He had left the gun, Chekhov's regulation
Makarov automatic, in the pocket of Voskov's bathrobe, hanging behind the bathroom door. He cursed
himself for that lapse, and wondered, at the same
moment whether he could kill the man with his
hands before a shot was fired.

The moment passed. Again, Gant had the sense of
something massive, a whole world in orbit, turning
over, leaving him spent, tired, drained.

"Sorry, sir—of course. But—be careful, sir. The
Colonel issued us with instructions to kill—the man's
dangerous. Good luck with the flight, sir," he added
ingratiatingly. Gant felt his blood pumping like a
migraine in his temples.

He hardly heard the bathroom door close behind
the man who had been only a voice, and a shadow
against the light. When he realized that the patch of
light which had outlined the KGB man was no longer there, he stepped from behind the shower-curtain,
and fumbled in the pocket of Voskov's bathrobe. He
clutched the gun in both hands, then pressed the
cold metal of the barrel against his temple. Then he
held his left hand in front of his face. He saw the
tremor, faint, but increasing. His face registered the
fear, as if he were looking at something outside himself, something inevitable that he could not prevent.
He sagged, dripping wet, onto the seat of the lavatory, head hanging, gun held limply between his
knees.

Gant was terrified. He knew he was about to have
the dream again, that the last minutes had drained
him of his last reserves of bravado, self-deception,
and nerve. He was a limp rag, an empty vessel into

which the dream would pour. He could not stop it now.

He felt his muscles tightening behind his knees, in his calves. He knew he had to get dry, get into Voskov's pressure-suit while he could still move, before the paralysis that inevitably accompanied the images trapped him where he sat. He tried to get up, but his legs were a long, long way from his brain, and were rubbery and weak. He sagged back onto the seat. He punched at his thighs, as if punishing them for a rebellion—he struck himself across the thigh with the barrel of the gun, but he felt little. The hysterical paralysis had returned, taken over . . .

He was trapped, he knew. He could only hope that the dream, and the fit, would pass in time.

He could smell burning in his nostrils, and the noise of the shower crackled like wood on a fire. He could smell burning flesh . . .

There was a kind of grotesque, mocking courtesy about the way in which Baranovich, Kreshin, and Semelovsky were served with their coffee and sandwiches at the side of the aircraft itself. While the technicians, including the still-grinning, obsequious, ironical Grosch, left the hangar for the restaurant in the adjoining security building, the three suspected men were ordered to remain by the junior KGB officer in command of hangar security. Guards stood with apparent indifference ten yards from them.

Baranovich, as he sipped the hot, sweet liquid, was grateful that the KGB, as yet, seemed to have little idea of what to do with them. It would seem, he thought, that they had taken the easiest path, making sure that a number of eyes were upon them, at every moment. Baranovich smiled at Kreshin, whose lip trembled as he attempted to imitate the gesture.

Baranovich said: "I know, Ilya, that it looks very

much like a firing-squad, with the three of us with our backs to the plane, and the guards with their rifles at the ready." Kreshin nodded, and swallowed, still trying to smile. "Don't be afraid," Baranovich added softly.

"I—can't help it, Pyotr," Kreshin replied.

Baranovich nodded. "I gave up being afraid many years ago—but then, it was when the flesh no longer seemed to call so very strongly to me." He placed his hand on Kreshin's shoulder as the young man stood next to him. He felt Kreshin's frame trembling beneath his strong grip. Kreshin looked up at him, wanting to face the truth, and wanting to be told comfortable lies. Baranovich shook his head sadly. "You love her very much then?"

"Yes . . ." Kreshin's eyes were bright with moisture, and his tongue licked at his lower lip.

"I—am sorry for that," Baranovich murmured. "That will make it very hard for you."

Kreshin seemed to come to a decision. Baranovich's hand was still on his shoulder, and the older man could feel the muscular effort the man was making, to control the tremor.

"If—*you*, you can do this—then, so can I . . ." he said.

"Good. Drink your coffee now, and warm yourself. That guard over there thinks you are afraid. Don't give him the satisfaction." Unable to complete the heroic fiction, he added: "Even if such ideas are nonsense, to an intelligent man . . ."

"What do we do?" snapped Semelovsky, as if eager to complete the whole process, including his own demise. "We have little time left. Kreshin and I have slowed the work on the tail-assembly as much as possible—but it is nearly complete."

Baranovich nodded. "I understand. Grosch, my *bête noir*, my devil—he, too, will become suspicious if we do not finish within half-an-hour, or a little more." He sipped at his coffee, and then took a bite from a hefty ham sandwich that had been brought down to him. "Of course, you realize that our friends over there are indicating in no uncertain manner that—the game is up?" He looked at Semelovsky.

"Of course—we knew that. The weapons trials would be our deadline."

"And—you don't mind?"

"Do *you*?" Semelovsky asked pointedly.

Baranovich looked at the muttering guards for a moment—at each of the four faces turned to him. He wanted to answer in the affirmative, to explain that life becomes harder to throw away, the older one gets, not easier. That it is the young who make glad sacrifices, for good causes or for bad. He wanted to explain that the old are tenacious of life, on any terms. Instead, feeling a heaviness of responsibility, and of guilt, he gave the answer he knew they both needed, and wished to hear.

"No," he said.

Semelovsky nodded. "There you are, then," he said.

Baranovich swallowed the bile of guilt at the back of his throat. He, it was, who had led them here, to this place, and who would lead them, in time, to the cellars, and the questions, and the pain.

Baranovich was ruthless, with others, as with himself. He shrugged the guilt away and decided that he would, at least, grant them a quick death.

"It has to be the fire we talked about—over there. *No*, don't look about like that . . . by the second prototype. One of us has to be over there for some reason at the time we decide the operation will start. What do you think—what time shall we decide?"

"Six-thirty is the latest possible!" Semelovsky snapped in his habitual fussy, irritated manner. "I guessed it would come to that," he added.

"It is the only sensible place," Baranovich said. "Right in the area around the second prototype. As I said, it may damage the second plane, which will be to our American friend's advantage. Certainly, it

will mean that this aircraft . . ." He tapped his
hand on the cool metal of the fuselage at his side.
"This one will be ordered out of the hangar. If Gant
appears at the right moment and climbs into the
pilot's couch, no one will ask to see his papers, or
his face." He studied their reactions, saw the inevi-
tability of death looking out from their eyes.

Semelovsky nodded, his features softening. He
said: "I, for one, have no great relish at the thought
of Colonel Kontarsky taking out on my skin the anger and frustration of his ruined career."

"You understand what I'm saying, Ilya—also?" Baranovich asked.

The young man was silent for some moments, then
he said: "Yes, Pyotr Vassilyeivich—I understand."

"Good. You have your gun?" Kreshin nodded.
"Good. That means that you, Maxim Ilyich, will have
to start the fire. Besides," he added, smiling, "you
look the least dangerous."

"Mm. Very well. At—six-ten, I shall excuse myself, and make for the toilets. If a guard accompa-
nies me, so much the worse for him!" The little,
balding man seemed ridiculous as he puffed out his
narrow chest, and squared his stooping shoulders.
Yet Baranovich knew that Semelovsky was capable of killing, if necessary. In some ways, he was
the most desperate of the three of them, the newly-
converted zeal never having seemed to cool. He was
a crusader.

"Only if necessary are you to kill the guard,"
Baranovich warned. "We don't want you hurt."

"Not *before* I start the fire—eh?" Semelovsky's
eyes twinkled. Baranovich could sense the challenge
that the little man felt, the same kind of bravado,
though Baranovich did not know it, that he had revealed at the gate when Gant was in the trunk of his
car.

"No, not before." Baranovich relaxed into the
partial honesty of the moment. "When you come
out from the toilet, you will find the necessary ma-

terials stacked against the wall of the hangar, behind Prototype Two—some drums of fuel."

"I don't need to be told how to start a fire, Pyotr
Vassilyeivich," Semelovsky said, bridling.

"I agree. Just make it big, and bright."

"It will be done."

"At six-twelve," Baranovich said. "Then you and
I, Ilya, will have to cover the path to the second
aircraft until the blaze is sufficient to distract *all*
the security-guards—all of them. Understand?"

"Yes. We—are part of the distraction?"

Baranovich nodded. He looked beneath the fuselage of the aircraft as he heard the sound of returning voices in the echoing hangar. "Time to get back
to work," he said. He looked at his watch. "Start
counting the seconds now," he said. "It is five-twen-
ty-three now. Synchronize your watches when you
can do it without being observed."

He looked at his two companions. Suddenly his
eyes felt misty. "Good luck, my friends," he said,
and turned to the pilot's ladder and began to ascend.
Kreshin watched his back for a moment, and then
he followed Semelovsky towards the tail of the
Firefox. He glanced once in the direction of the
guards, now being relieved and reporting back to
their officer.

Concentrate your hate on them, he told himself.
Hate them, and what they represent, and what they
do. Hate them. . . .

Kontarsky looked at his watch. The time was seven
minutes past six. He had just received a directive
from the Center that the Tupolev TU-144 airliner
carrying the First Secretary, the Chairman of the
KGB, and the Marshal of the Soviet Air Force had
left Moscow, and was expected to land at Bilyarsk
at six-thirty. Kontarsky had been profoundly shak-
en by the news. The plane was not scheduled to arrive until after nine. He could do little but wonder
why the First Secretary should be precipitate in

his arrival. He suspected that it was some kind of
pressure put upon him, a calculated insult. The
Tower had been put on stand-by, to land the aircraft.
There was nothing else he could do, except what
he was engaged in at the moment, futile recriminations, coupled with the more practical step of
once more contacting Priabin and, through him, receiving a progress report on the foreign agent who
had penetrated Bilyarsk, and who was still at large.

A team of men sat at rickety tables in the bare
duty-room in the security building, each analyzing
the reports of the teams who had combed the project area thoroughly. The final search had just been
completed. Like the others, it had drawn a blank.

Below them, in a smaller room, with white walls
and powerful lights, Dherkov and his wife were being questioned. Each had been made to watch the
other's suffering—and neither of them had told
him what he wished to know. He was unable to
admit the possibility that they knew nothing of importance. There had been too many frustrations, too
many blind alleys. To him, and to the interroga-
tors, they were merely stubborn.

The doctor had used drugs. He had ruined the
man's mind almost immediately, sending him into
deep unconsciousness from which he had emerged
incoherent. The woman, despite the massive jolt to
her resistance that such damage to her husband must
have been, still refused to betray the whereabouts
of the agent, or his identity. Kontarsky had ordered the doctor to use the pentathol again, on her,
but the doctor had been unwilling. Kontarsky had
raged at him, but he suspected that the dosages
were too small.

Kontarsky's fingers drummed on the desk as he
waited for his connection to his office at the Center.
Priabin could not be found, for the moment. Kontarsky's call was being transferred to the computer-
room. As he waited, his eyes roved the team of men
bent at their tables, in shirt-sleeves for the most

part, intent, driven. No face turned up to him with an answer, with a possible line of inquiry. Kontarsky felt the bitter, selfish anger of a man who sees a fortune turn to ashes in his hands. He had felt, throughout the night, that he had only to reach out and he would grasp the answer. Each answer, each source of knowledge, had crumbled between his fingers. He felt trapped.

Priabin was out of breath when he answered his superior's call. Kontarsky heard his voice clearly, though there was some quality of distance about it that might have been elation. His own stomach jumped at the proximity of a solution.

"Colonel—we've got him. He's been identified!" he heard Priabin say. "Colonel, are you there?"

"Quickly, Priabin—tell me?" One or two of the nearest heads looked up, at the sound of Kontarsky's choked, quiet whisper. They sensed that the breakthrough had come.

"He's a pilot . . . Mitchell Gant, an American . . ."

"American?" Kontarsky repeated mechanically.

"Yes. A member of their Mig squadron, the one they built to train their pilots in combat with Russian machines, the Apache group, they call it, designated by the Red Air Force and ourselves as the Mirror-squadron."

"Go on, Priabin. Why him?"

"Obviously, sir, he knows our aircraft as well as anyone. He'd be a good choice for sabotage, or for analysis of information. Perhaps he intends a— close inspection of the Mig-31?" There was a silence at the other end of the line. The truth, huge and appalling, struck both men at the same moment. In the silence, Kontarsky's voice dropped like a feeble stone.

"He—he *can't* be here for that . . .?"

"No, sir, surely not. They couldn't hope to get away with it!"

Kontarsky's voice trembled, as he said: "Thank you, Dmitri—thank you. Well done." The receiver clanged clumsily into its rest as he replaced it. Kontarsky looked out over the team for a few moments, then he picked up the receiver again. He dialed the number of the guard-post at the hangar, and drummed his fingers as he waited.

"Tsernik—is that you? Arrest Baranovich and the others—now!"

"You've had news, sir?"

"Yes—dammit, yes! I want to know from them where this agent is—at once. And let no one near that aircraft—no one, understand?"

"Sir." Tsernik replaced his receiver. Kontarsky looked around the room again, at the men at their futile paperwork. Then he looked at his watch. Eleven minutes past six. "Some of you—all of you!" he shouted. "Get down to that hangar now—no, half of you there, the rest search this building—quickly!"

The room moved before him, as men gathered their coats, checked their weapons.

One voice, distant, said: "Who are we looking for, sir?"

"A pilot—dammit, a *pilot!*" Kontarsky's voice was high, piercing, almost hysterical.

Baranovich watched the slight figure of Semelovsky as he emerged from the lavatory at the end of the hangar. The little man stepped away from the door and began crossing the hangar, unconcernedly it appeared at that distance: Baranovich waited. A guard had followed Semelovsky to the lavatory. Baranovich wondered whether he would emerge.

Semelovsky reached the shadow of the PP Two, and the guard had still not appeared. Baranovich smiled, a smile of fierce success. Semelovsky, probably with a spanner or wrench, had killed the guard. He loosened the white coat which he wore on top of his overalls, not against the temperature, but to conceal the automatic thrust into the waistband of his trousers. Then he nodded, without looking in Kreshin's direction. He knew he would be watching for his signal.

The work on the aircraft had been completed a little after six. Grosch, suspecting that Baranovich was delaying completion of the work, but misconstruing the motive as simple fear, had returned to the restaurant, together with most of the other technicians and scientific team-leaders. One man, Pilac, an electronics expert like himself, had deliberately passed him as he left, nodding rather helplessly in his direction. Baranovich had been touched by the gesture, despite its futility.

He reached into the pocket of his coat, and flipped over the switch on a tiny transmitter. Inaudibly, it transmitted to the bleeper taped to Gant's arm, a one-to-the-second noise that would alert him to the fact that the diversion had begun. When Baranovich turned the switch over, the signal would become a continuous bleep, Gant's signal that he was to make his way to the hangar as quickly as possible. He turned his head to survey the distance between himself and the nearest guard. He estimated it at about twelve yards. The guards were still much in evidence—he counted four within twenty-five yards and, despite the hour of the morning, they did not seem tired, or inattentive. They had been changed too frequently to become thoroughly bored or fatigued.

He looked to the far end of the hangar. He thought, as his heart leapt in anticipation, he detected the flare of Semelovsky's lighter or matches. Almost immediately, burning across his gaze, a column of flame shot up. He could not any longer see Semelovsky's bending figure, and had no way of knowing whether the man had immolated himself in the sudden blaze.

He turned, drawing the gun from his waistband. Already, the moment before the column of flame had shot up, to roll out under the roof of the hangar,

there had been cries from the booth, away behind
him. Holding the gun across his stiffened forearm, he
shot the nearest guard through the stomach, and
then moved swiftly towards Kreshin and the other
end of the hangar. A bullet plucked at the fuselage
above his head as he ran in a ducking crouch, and
then someone screamed for the firing to stop, because it was endangering the Mig. He smiled to himself as he pushed at the immobile, frozen form of
Kreshin, caught as if in a spotlight, so that the two
of them were running towards the fire, together
with other forms.

The alarm bell began to clatter its hysterical note
and, despite the fire drills that had been endlessly
practiced, Baranovich got the impression of a surge
of people in the direction of the gouting flames.
He had a confused, jolting image of a small figure in
a white coat, burning like a torch, and he knew it
had to be Semelovsky. He thrust the automatic back
in his pocket and, shoulder to shoulder with Kreshin, he paused, in a shifting, purposeless group, the
heat from the flames like a desert wind striking his
face. He flipped over the switch on the transmitter
in his pocket, praying that his now continuous signal was reaching Gant. Pushed aside by an unseeing
guard tugging a hose behind him, then another, he
glanced down at his watch. Six-thirteen. He looked
over his shoulder. Over the heads of the crowd
pressing behind him, he could see the guard's body
near the Firefox and saw, too, the ring of security
men surrounding the aircraft. He knew they had discovered, or guessed, what was intended by the diversion, who the agent in Bilyarsk was, and what he
intended.

Somehow the distraction was understood for what
it was, and the Mig had not been left temporarily unguarded. He could see the squat form of Tsernik directing the formation of the ring of guards, and the
junior officer in charge of hangar-security detailing
men to fight the fire. A voice crackled over the loud-

speaker system, above the noise of the flames, which seemed to have made the watchers oblivious to their danger. Flame spilled across the hangar floor beneath the second aircraft, like swift lava, and the pall of smoke was beginning to engulf them, masking the most forward of the guards with their hoses and extinguishers.

The loudspeaker ordered them to clear the area, clamoring for their attention above the racket of the alarm and the new, added note of the fire-tender, rushing into the chaos of the hangar from its station near the development-hangar.

There was only one thing to do, he realized, the flames at his back now as he watched the fire-tender and the movements of a second group of hurrying guards, the off-duty squad hastily recalled. They were looking for him, and for Kreshin. There was only one thing to do—he had to show himself, draw their fire, draw away, if possible, the ring around the Mig. He began to move in the direction of the retreating tide of spectators as the bulk of the fire-tender edged its way through them. He glanced toward the door through which he knew Gant must enter the hangar. There was no sign of him.

At first, the signal from the bleeper was a muscular tic, not even a sound to Gant as he was consumed by the flames of his dream. He was still in the posture of defeat, sagging stiffly, immobile, on the lavatory seat, his body damp with sweat. Something pulsed in his arm, he was aware of it, but he could not move his hand to scratch it, to rub the spot. The dream was drawing toward an end, and he was patiently waiting for his release. There was no need to move, no need to fight. It had been bad, but it was ebbing now, the separate images flung off like frozen sparks, photographs of his past in a flickering album.

The noise ate down into his mind, the one-to-the-second bleeping of the receiver. A part of Gant's mind, the part that always coldly observed the progress of the dream, powerless to prevent or still, recognized that it was some kind of signal and fumbled, as with frozen fingers, to decipher its significance. Something to do with an alert—not an alert like others, not a scramble . . .

With sudden, frightening clarity he knew what it was, so that the image of the Firefox, in one of the photographs he had studied, was before him— then the memory of the cockpit simulator they had built for him, on which he had learned . . . He knew what it was. Baranovich. He saw the wise face, peering kindly, in Olympian pity, through the flames.

Tic and noise coordinated. The bleeper on his arm, taped there by Baranovich. The instructions filtered through, like pebbles dropped irregularly into dark water. The bleep was the alert—wait for the continuous sound, which is the summons.

He tried to move, felt that he was moving against a great wave, which pinned him where he was, struggled, tried again to raise himself—and did so.

The bathroom came into a kind of focus, and he shook his head, rubbed both stiff hands down his cheeks. It was like coming back from the dead, far worse than coming back from a narcotic trip, far worse than that. The water, still running, filtered through his mind as a distant sound, nothing to do with the crackling of flames. He had always been afraid of moving like this, before the dream had played itself out. Now he knew he had to.

He opened the bathroom door, his hand like a frozen claw gripping the door handle clumsily. He slammed the door behind him. He felt an ache, dull and distant, in his thigh. He looked down. There was a bruise across his muscle. He presumed it was some self-inflicted blow, performed an age before.

He walked stiffly, like a man on new limbs, across to the locker which he remembered contained Voskov's pressure-suit. He had to dress himself. . . .

The bleep is the alert; wait for the continuous

noise, which is the summons. Baranovich smiled
down on him, the memory of that moment in
Kreshin's bedroom, the white-haired man holding
the cup of sweet coffee. He saw the face from that
angle, as he had lain on the bed.

He spilled the suit onto the floor and bent wearily,
a long way down, to pick it up. He untaped the bleeper, then stuck it to the locker door. Then he began
to struggle into the legs, fitting his clumsy limbs
into the stiff, unyielding garment. He was running
freely with sweat.

Another sound clamored for the attention of his
fogged awareness—an alarm, a fire-alarm, he decided. He knew then what the diversion was, responding to stimuli as he was. He knew that it signaled an increase in the urgency of his efforts. It
marked another stage passed, a new tempo introduced. He began to struggle with the lacing, the all-
important lacing that was his only protection against
the disastrous effects of the G-forces he would encounter in the Firefox. It was a skilled job, it required more of him than he was able to give. Yet
it had to be right—it might kill him, as surely as
any mechanical malfunction in the aircraft, more
surely. He tried to concentrate.

It was not easy, but it was familiar. He knew what
he was doing. He forced himself to pay attention, his
own harsh breathing roaring in his ears.

The bleep is the alert; wait for the continuous
noise, which is the summons, Baranovich told him,
above the panic of the blood.

At last he had finished. The suit was hot, choking, sticky with his frantic efforts. He had no time to
put on dry underclothes. He picked the pilot's helmet from its shelf, glanced inside it, and could make
nothing of the contacts and sensors of the thought-
system. They had been checked by Baranovich the
previous day.

He tugged on the helmet, snapped down the visor,
and the image of flame roared up in his imagination,

the dying effort of the dream to swallow his consciousness.

Wait for the continuous noise, which is the summons, Baranovich whispered above the noise of the flames.

He realized that the bleep had vanished. There was a continuous, penetrating cry from the receiver on the locker. He reached into the locker, and picked from the shelf the innards of the transistor radio. He looked at the small black object, like a cigarette case now its disguise of transistors and batteries had gone. In the radio it had appeared nothing more sinister than a circuit-board.

The continuous noise is the summons.

He moved stiffly toward the door.

The crowd simply seemed, as if by a communal awareness and command, to disappear, to drift to either side of the two Jews. They were alone, and marked. There was nowhere to hide, no shelter for them. A group of guards in a semi-circle was advancing slowly toward them, through the smoke that was filling the hangar, rolling like a pall toward the open doors. Tsernik's head was hidden by the loud-hailer he had raised to his lips, and they heard his amplified, mechanical voice call to them.

"Put down your weapons—now, or I will order them to open fire! Put down your weapons—immediately!"

There seemed little else to do. The fire-tender had been joined, raucously, by its twin, and the fire-fighting units were soaking the aircraft and the hangar floor with foam, choking out Semelovsky's fire, Semelovsky's funeral pyre. There were people all around them now, backing away, as from something diseased or deformed—men in white coats, others in overalls, the technicians and scientists who had rushed toward the fire, then retreated from it like an ebbing wave. Baranovich and Kreshin were between the crescent of the approaching guards, and

the crescent of the fire-fighters behind them. Baranovich felt the drop in temperature as the foam
choked the life from the fire beneath the second
Mig. Around the first one, around Gant's plane, the
circle of guards had thinned, though they had not
disappeared, not all left their posts.

Where was Gant? He had turned over the switch.
The summons should have brought him by now. If
he did not appear within seconds at the door leading
to the security-building and the pilots' rest-
room, the guards would have arrested them, and re-
formed around the aircraft. The gleaming silver
flanks of the plane reflected the light of the dying
flames. The fuel tanks of the second Mig had not
caught fire as Baranovich had hoped. With luck, for
the Soviets, it would still fly.

There seemed noise like a wall behind him, pushing against him with an almost physical force. In
front of him, there was a cone of silence, with
Kreshin and himself at the point, and the semi-circle
of closing guards embraced within it as they moved
slowly forward. It was one of the most powerful
visual images of his life, the approaching guards
and then, beating at his ears, a palpable silence.

A gun roared at his side and its sound, too, seemed
to come from far away, as if muffled. He saw a guard
drop, and a second one lurch sideways. It was too
easy, he thought, they are too close together, as he
had once seen advancing Germans in the defense of
Stalingrad—too close . . . His mind did not tell him
to open fire. His own gun lay uselessly in his pocket.

"Drop your weapons, or I shall order them to
open fire!" he heard the distant, mechanical voice
say.

He did not hear the command, but he saw the
flames from the rifles, sensed, rather than saw,
Kreshin plucked away from his side. Then, with
growing agony and the terrible revulsion of the
awareness of death, he felt his own body plucked
by bullets, his coat ripped as if by small detonations.

He felt old. He staggered, no longer sure of his balance. He stumbled back a couple of paces, then sat untidily down on the ground, like a child failing a lesson in walking. Then it seemed as if the hangar lights had been turned off, he rolled sideways from the waist, like an insecure doll flopping onto its side. His eyes were tightly closed, squeezed shut, to avoid the terrible moment of death and, as his face slapped dully against the concrete floor, he didn't see Gant, a dim shadow in the dull green pressure-suit, standing at the entrance to the hangar from the security building. Baranovich died believing that Gant would not come.

Gant could see from where he stood something in a white coat on the ground, and the closing, cautious semi-circle of guards approaching it. He saw Kreshin's blond head, and his limbs flung in the careless attitude of violent death. The aircraft was thirty yards from him, no more.

There had been a fire at the other end of the hangar. He could see the two fire-tenders, and the foam-soaked frame of the second prototype now being rolled clear of the smouldering materials that had begun, and sustained, the fire. Already, he realized, the occupants of the hangar were in a position to begin to turn their attention back to the Firefox. He was almost too late—he might, in fact, be too late. The excuse for rolling the plane out of the hangar was almost over, the fire out. He saw a spurt of flame near the wall of the hangar, and an asbestos-suited fireman rear back from it. He heard the dull concussion of a fuel-drum explode. The second prototype was clear of the flame, but the men towing it with a small tractor hurried to get it further off. It was his chance.

His legs were still stiff, rebellious, from the hysterical paralysis of the dream, but he forced them to stride out, to cross the thirty yards of concrete to the Firefox.

The pilot's ladder that Baranovich had used for

his supervision of Grosch's work was still in place,
and he began to climb it. As he bent over the cockpit, a voice at the bottom of the ladder called up to
him.

"Colonel Voskov?"

He looked round, and nodded down at the young,
distraught, sweating face below him. The man was
in the uniform of a junior officer in the KGB. His
gun was in his hand.

"Yes?" he said.

"What are you doing, Colonel?"

"What the devil do you think I'm doing, you idiot? Do you want this plane to be damaged like the
other one? I'm taking it out of here, that's what I'm
doing." He swung his legs over the sill, and dropped
into the pilot's couch. While he still looked down at
the young KGB man, his hands sought for the para-
chute straps, and he buckled himself in, following
this by strapping himself to the couch itself.

The young man had stepped back a couple of
paces, so that he could still see Gant clearly. The
tinted face-mask of the helmet, combined with the
integral oxygen-mask, made it impossible for him
to tell that it wasn't Colonel Voskov in the pilot's
position. He was at a loss what action to take. He
glanced swiftly down the hangar. It was true that
the second Mig-31 was being towed towards him
from the far end of the hangar and, although it appeared under control, there was still smoke and
flame from the fire there. He had been told by
Tsernik that no one, on the express orders of Colonel Kontarsky, was to be allowed near the plane.
But did that apply to the pilot?

Gant ignored the KGB man and went through his
pre-start checks as swiftly as he could. He plugged
in his radio and communications equipment, finding
the location of the socket instinctively, as if he had
always flown that aircraft. The simulator which
had been built in Langley, Virginia, at CIA headquarters, from Baranovich's smuggled descriptions

and photographs and from computer projections, now proved its worth. Then, he plugged in the connection from his helmet to the weapons-system, a single jack-plug similar to the radio. He pushed the jack-plug home into the side of the ejector-seat itself. It was the final sophistication of the weapons system of the Mig: if he were forced to eject, then he could control the destruct mechanism of the system to prevent any part or fragment of the plane's weaponry and its control-system from falling into enemy hands.

He glanced down at the KGB man, swiftly, as if taking in the reading from one of his gauges. The junior officer still seemed perplexed, reluctant. Gant connected up his oxygen supply, then coupled in the emergency oxygen. Next, he switched in the anti-G device, a lead which plugged into the pressure-suit just below the left knee. It was this which would bleed air into the suit to counteract the effects of increased G-forces on his blood, forcing it round his system against the effect of sudden turns, dives or accelerations. Cautiously, he tested it, felt the air bleed in rapidly, and checked the gauges which confirmed his bodily reaction. It was working.

He knew he was stripping the pre-flight routine to the bone, but there weren't even seconds to spare. His eyes read the gauges; flaps, brakes and fuel. The fuel-tanks were full, and they would need to be since, as he sat there, he did not even know the nature or position of his refueling-point.

There was one more thing. He extracted the innards of the transistor radio from a pouch-pocket on the thigh of the suit, bared an adhesive strip, and then fixed the anonymous collection of circuits in their wafer-thin black case developed at Farnborough exclusively for his use to the corner of the instrument panel, with a silent prayer that it had not been damaged during the past three days. If it had been, he would never know.

He was ready. His routine had taken mere seconds

to complete. The second Firefox was only yards away as it trailed behind the small tractor. He had a single moment in which to convince the man below him. He leaned down, and waved his hand for him to move, yelling as he did so:

"You'll get your head knocked off if you stand there any longer!" He swept a finger across his throat, and pointed to the wing and engine-intake behind the Russian. The young man looked, understood, and self-preservation made him move clear, tugging the ladder obligingly after him.

Gant smiled, relaxed, and turned his attention to the aircraft. As he did so, his gaze swept across the door into the hangar through which he had entered perhaps a minute earlier. He saw Kontarsky, his face white, his arm extended, finger pointing in his direction. There were other men at his side, perhaps half-a-dozen, filling the doorway behind him. In a purely reflex action, he pressed the hood control, and automatically the hood swung down, locked electronically. Then he locked it manually as a standard double-check. He was isolated in the machine. A part of it.

The fogginess, the lethargy, the nausea of the dream, all had left him now. There was, curiously, no elation either. There was only the functioning of smooth machinery—a mechanism within a larger mechanism. Elation would come later perhaps.

He checked the cockpit air-pressure; then, reaching forward, he gang-loaded the ignition switches, switched on the starter-motors, turned on the high-pressure cock and, without hesitation, even for self-drama, pressed the starter-button.

Half-way down the fuselage, there was the sound of a double explosion, like the noise of a twelve-bore against his ears, as the cartridge start functioned. Two puffs of sooty smoke rolled away from the engines. There was a rapid, mounting whirring as the huge turbines built up; he checked gyro instruments erect. He saw the flashing light which indicated that he had forgotten the fuel-booster pump, switched it in, and the light disappeared on the panel. He eased open the throttles, and watched the rpm gauges as they mounted to twenty-seven percent, and he steadied them there. He glanced out of his side-window. Kontarsky and two of his men, as if galvanized by the explosions of the starter-cartridges, were moving forward but, by comparison with the speed of his actions and responses, as if they were moving underwater, slowly—too slowly to stop him now. He saw a gun raised, and something whined away off the cockpit, harmlessly.

With one eye on the JPT (jet-pipe temperature) gauge, he opened the throttles until the rpm gauges were at fifty-five percent and the whine had increased comfortingly. He released the brakes.

The Firefox had been tugging against the brakes' restraint and now that they were released, skipped rather than rolled forward, toward the hangar-doors through which Gant could see the dawn streaking and lighting the sky. He saw men rushing to the doors, in an attempt to close them against him— but they, too, moved with a painful, ludicrous slowness and they were too late, far too late. He checked the gauges and booster-pumps and then he was through the hangar doors and out onto the taxiway. In his mirror he could see running figures, left ridiculously behind him as the Firefox rolled toward the runway.

Using the rudder and differential braking, he turned onto the runway. As he straightened the airplane, he ran through the checks again.

He breathed deeply, once, then he opened the throttles to full. He pushed the throttles straight through the detent, and brought the reheat of the massive engines into play. He felt their power as a huge shove in the back, an almost sexual surge forward. There was a moment of elation, fierce, pure. The plane gathered speed. At 160 knots, it was skipping on the ridges in the runway-slabs. At 165 knots, he brought the elevator-controls into play, and the Firefox left the ground. There was a further stage of acceleration as the drag induced by contact with the runway vanished. He retracted the undercarriage.

The Firefox wobbled its wings as he over-controlled, unused to the quality and finesse of the power-control system. He was lifting away steeply now, within seconds.

In the rising sun he saw, off to the right of the nose, a glint of sun on metal. He pulled back, and hauled the stick to the right. He felt the pressure of the anti-G as he went into the turn, almost rolled the plane completely through his over-control, then leveled the wings. He looked out to his left, and below and behind him. A Tupolev Tu-144, carrying, he knew, the First Secretary, was turning to make its final approach to the runway at Bilyarsk. He looked at his altimeter. He was already at almost eight thousand feet.

It was fifteen seconds since the undercarriage had left contact with the runway. He was a thousand miles from the Russian border—any Russian border. As the sweat of reaction from his near-collision ran down his sides, beneath his arms, he grinned to himself. He had done it. He had stolen the Firefox.

THE FLIGHT

6
COUNTER MEASURES

By the time Kontarsky came aboard the First Secretary's Tupolev Tu-144, the moment after the giant supersonic airliner had rolled to a halt on the runway at Bilyarsk, dashing up the mobile passenger-gangway in which he had ridden from the hangar, the First Secretary of the Soviet Communist Party had already been told of the theft of the Mig-31 over the flight-deck UHF. As he was ushered into the military command section of the aircraft, aft of the passenger accommodation, the equivalent of the war command office on board the U.S. President's aircraft, he was confronted by what was, in fact, a council of war. The room was already filled with heavy cigar smoke.

Kontarsky saluted rigidly, and kept his eyes straight ahead. Only the back of a radio-operator's head at the far end of the cigar-shaped room filled his vision. Yet he knew that the eyes of the room's principal occupants were on him. An awareness that seemed to seep through the skin like damp told him where each of those powerful men sat. He knew that each was regarding him intently. He understood the details of the expression on each face. Directly in front of him, round the command table, circular in shape and fitted with projection equipment which would throw onto the table a relief map of any part of the Soviet Union, any part of the world, sat the First Secretary himself; on his right sat Kutuzov, Marshal of the Soviet Air Force, a world war ace, and a hardline Communist of the Stalinist school; to the left of the Soviet First Secretary sat Andropov, Chairman of the KGB and his ultimate superior. It was that trinity which so frightened him, which made the moments since he had stepped through the guarded door into this sanctum seem like minutes, hours . . . endless.

It was the First Secretary who spoke. Kontarsky, still rigidly to attention, and not requested to be at ease or to sit, saw from the corner of his eye the restraining hand of the First Secretary fall on the sleeve of Andropov's suit, and he caught the glint of an overhead strip-light reflected from the gold-rimmed spectacles worn by the Chairman of the KGB.

"Colonel Kontarsky—you will explain what has happened," the First Secretary said, his voice soft, authoritative. He seemed unhurried. There was no other sound in the room except the steady hiss from a radio. It was nearly three minutes since Gant had taken off in the Mig, yet nothing seemed to have been done.

Now that he had failed, Kontarsky was almost hysterically eager to encourage and exhort the efforts to reclaim—or destroy, he presumed—the stolen aircraft.

He swallowed. "An American . . ." he began, and coughed. He kept his eyes looking directly ahead, at the scrubbed neck of the radio-operator. "An American pilot called Gant is responsible for the theft of the Mig-31, sir."

"On the contrary, Colonel, it is you who are responsible," the First Secretary replied, in a voice bereft of menace, bereft of humanity. "Proceed."

"He infiltrated the compound here with the aid of various dissident Jews, who are now all dead."

"Mm. But not before they told you what you wished to know, I presume?"

Kontarsky looked down into the broad, lined face. It was a strong face. He had always thought so. The eyes were like chips of gray stone.

"We—learned nothing . . ." he managed to say.

There was a silence. He noticed that the radio-operator was sitting more upright in his chair, as if tense. When his eyes returned to the circular table, he could see the First Secretary's strong, veined hand tapping at the sleeve of the Chairman's dark, sober business suit, as if restraining him.

"You—do not know what the destination of the Mig-31 will be?" he heard the First Secretary ask.

"You know nothing?" Kutuzov interposed, shocked. Kontarsky saw the First Secretary glance swiftly at the aging Marshal who was in full uniform, the somber blue tinseled with insignia and overlapping decorations. The old pilot fell silent.

"No," Kontarsky said, and his voice was small and flat, as if the room were deadened, without reverberation.

"Very well," the First Secretary intoned after a moment of heavy, oppressive silence. At that moment, Kontarsky saw his ruin. For the First Secretary, and for the others, military personnel and KGB, gathered round the circular table, he had ceased to exist. "You will place yourself under close guard, Colonel." Kontarsky's lip trembled, and he looked once into the First Secretary's eyes. It was like looking in a mirror that refused to reflect his physical presence. "You are dismissed."

When Kontarsky had left the room, the door closing behind him softly, the First Secretary glanced in the direction of the Marshal. He nodded, once, and then turned his head to look at Andropov. He said:

"There is no time now for recriminations. That will come later. It appears obvious to me that this is a CIA venture, a desperate attempt to cancel the huge advantage in air superiority that the aircraft would have given to the Soviet Union. We know nothing else than the man's name, and his official file. It would tell us nothing of use. As each moment passes now, the Mig-31 moves further and further away from us, toward . . . where, Mihail Ilyich?"

The Marshal of the Soviet Air Force glanced over his shoulder at the back of an operator at a small console.

"Give us the 'Wolfpack' map of the U.S.S.R., quickly!" he said.

The operator punched buttons in instant obedience and, as the men seated at the table withdrew their hands, and packets of cigarettes and cigar-cases, the surface of the table registered a projection-map of the Soviet Union, clustered with tiny dots of varying colors. There before them on the screen of the table lay the diagram of the immense outer defenses of the Soviet Union. The First Secretary leaned forward across the table, and tapped at the map.

"Bilyarsk," he said. His finger traced a circle round the area he had indicated. "Now, in which direction has he gone?"

"We do not know, First Secretary," Kutozov said, his voice gruff. He had had an operation for cancer of the throat two years earlier, and it had left his voice a tired, dry whisper.

He looked across the table, across the glowing projection of the map, at Vladimirov, the tall, lean-faced officer with gray hair and watery blue eyes who sat opposite him. The ruthlessness, the confidence, of that face helped him to regain a little of his calm, after the blow of the theft of the Mig. He had been winded, temporarily paralyzed, by what had happened. It had been even more of a body blow than Belenko's defection in a Foxbat four years before. He could still see, in his mind, the bright, swift glint of the fuselage as the aircraft had pulled away from the Tupolev, climbing swiftly. A glimpse, that had been all he had.

Over the UHF, then, had come the information that an unauthorized aircraft had taken off from the single main runway below them in the strengthening light. He had known, with a sudden, sick realization, what aircraft it had been; before confirmation had flowed in, even as they touched down and the big plane had skipped once and then settled on the runway. Someone, an American, had stolen the greatest aircraft the Soviet Union had ever produced—*stolen* it.

"What do you think, Vladimirov?" he said.

The tall, lean-faced man glanced down at the map, then looked up, addressing his remarks to the First Secretary. General Med Vladimirov, commandant of the tactical strike arm of the Soviet Air Force, the "Wolfpack," as it was designated, was worried. He, too, understood the problem—how to trace an untraceable aircraft—but he did not intend to allow the First Secretary to see his doubts. Then, as lethargy seemed to have left him, he spoke.

"I suggest a staggered sector scramble, First Secretary," he said directly, "in two areas. We must put up as many planes as we can, along our southern and northern borders."

"Why there?"

"Because, First Secretary," he said, looking down at the map, "this lunatic must refuel if he is to fly the aircraft to a place of complete safety. He will not refuel in the air—we would know if some mother-plane were waiting for him over neutral or hostile sky."

"What is the range of this aircraft?" General

Leonid Borov asked, seated next to Vladimirov.
Borov was commandant of the ECM (Electronic
Counter-Measures) section of the Soviet Air Force.
He, it would be, in the event of a pre-emptive strike
by the West, who would coordinate the radar and
missile defenses with the air defenses.

"It would be fully fueled," Kutuzov said. "Almost
three thousand miles maximum, depending on what
this American knows, and how he handles the aircraft."

"Which would put him here—or here," Vladimirov said, his hand sweeping the Arctic Ocean, then
drifting across the expanse of the table to indicate
the Iranian border, and then the Mediterranean.

"Why would he go either north or south, Vladimirov?" the First Secretary asked. His voice had
become impatient now, and his body seemed eager
for activity, as if the blood were tinglingly returning
to his limbs after cramp.

"Because, First Secretary, any pilot who ran the
risk of the Moscow defenses would be committing
suicide—even in a plane that allows no radar trace!"

There was a brief silence. All of them there, the
five men round the circular table, and the team of
guards, ciphermen, radio-operators and aides to the
ranking officers, all of them understood that the un-
voiceable had been uttered. Now that the American
had stolen the Mig he had turned that unique fact
to his advantage, the fact that the airplane's defenses
incorporated an anti-radar system.

"It works too well!" Kutuzov growled in his characteristic whisper. "It works too damn well!"

"The American knows of it?" Andropov said,
speaking for the first time. Heads turned in the direction of the bland, urbane Chairman of the KGB.
He seemed unabashed by the failure sustained by
one of his officers, the monumental failure. Vladimirov smiled thinly. Perhaps, he thought, with a
hardline pro-Stalinist First Secretary, the Chairman

considered himself untouchable. He continued looking at the man across the table from him, who looked like nothing so much as a prosperous, efficient Western businessman, rather than the head of the most powerful police and intelligence force in the world.

"He must know," Vladimirov said, ice in his voice. "Your man's security must have been *full* of holes, Chairman, for the CIA to have got him this far."

The First Secretary's hand slapped the table once, the projection-map jiggling momentarily under the impact.

"No recriminations! None. I want action, Vladimirov—and quickly! How much time do we have?"

Vladimirov looked at his watch. The time was six-twenty-two. The Mig had been airborne for seven minutes.

"He has more than a thousand miles to go before he crosses any Soviet border, First Secretary. He will travel at sub-sonic speed for the most part, because he will want to conserve fuel, and because he will not want to betray his flight-path with a supersonic footprint—we have more than an hour, even should he fly directly. . . ."

"One hour?" The First Secretary realized he was in a foreign element, that Vladimirov and the other military experts would possess a time-scale where minutes stretched, were elastic—in which all things could be accomplished. He added: "It is enough. What do you propose—Kutuzov?"

"As 'Wolfpack' Commandant suggests, First Secretary, a staggered sector scramble. We must institute a search for this aircraft, a visual search. We must put in the air a *blanket* of aircraft, a *net* in which he will be caught. All our 'Wolfpack' and 'Bearhunt' squadrons know this sequence clearly. It leaves no holes, no gaps. We merely have to institute it in reverse order. 'Bearhunt' will begin, seeking the American within the area three hundred miles within our borders—'Wolfpack' can be scrambled at the same time, patrolling the borders themselves."

"I see." The First Secretary was thoughtful, silent for a moment, then he said: "I agree."

There was a relaxation of suspense in the War Command Center of the Tupolev. It was from that room that the First Secretary, if ever the need arose, would order Armageddon to commence—a replica, except for its size, of the War Command Center in the heart of the Kremlin. For the Soviet leader, and those members of the High Command who were present, it was the only stroke of fortune that early morning, that they possessed, in portable form, the nerve-center of the Soviet defense system. The suspense that vanished was replaced by the heady whiff of tension, the tension of the runner on his blocks, the tension that precedes violent activity.

"Thank you, First Secretary," Vladimirov said. He got to his feet, his thin figure stooping over the table, studying the colored zones overlying the topography of the map, picking out the spots of color that indicated his squadron bases, and their linked missile bases.

"Bleed in the 'Bearhunt' status map," he ordered. As he watched, the numbers of colored dots increased, filling the inland spaces of the map at regular intervals. He brushed his hand across the table, smiled grimly to himself, and said: "Scramble, with Seek-briefing, and in SSS sequence, squadrons in White through Red sectors, and Green through Brown sectors. Put up 'Bearhunt' squadrons, same briefing, G through N." He rubbed his chin, and listened to the chatter of the cipher machines, waited for the transmissions of the coded signals to the Communications Officer, a young colonel seated before a console behind him, with his team of three ranged beside him.

When the high-speed transmission had begun,

Vladimirov looked at the First Secretary, and said: "What do you wish done when they sight the Mig?"

The First Secretary glared at him, and replied: "I wish to talk to this American who has stolen the Soviet Air Force's latest toy—obtain the frequency —if he will not land the aircraft as directed, then it must be destroyed—completely!"

The inertial navigator that had been fitted into the Firefox was represented on the control panel by a small display similar to the face of a pocket calculator. It also possessed a series of buttons marked, for example, "Track," "Heading," "Ground Speed," and "Coordinates." He could feed into it known navigational information and the on-board computer would calculate and display such information as distance to travel, time for distance. By starting the programs in the computer at a known time and position, the computer could measure changes in speed and direction, and keep track of the aircraft's position. Standard procedure required the data displayed to be confirmed by more conventional means —such as visual sightings of landmarks.

Gant had an appointment to keep in the airspace north-west of Volgograd, with the early morning civilian flight from Moscow, a rendezvous which would establish him as traveling toward the southern border of the Soviet Union—a fact he very much wanted to establish in the minds of those who would be controlling the search for him.

He throttled back slightly, keeping his speed at little more than six hundred and fifty knots. He had not pushed the Firefox to its supersonic speeds because, traveling at his present height of almost 15,-000 feet, the supersonic footprint he would leave behind him would act like a giant arrow as to his direction for those with eyes to see and ears to hear. There were another twenty-three minutes to his rendezvous.

He had made a minute inspection of the equipment

packed into the Firefox. Most of it, communications and radar especially, had been built into the simulator at Langley, and was of a type which closely paralleled U.S. developments in the same fields. They weren't the reason why he was stealing the Firefox. One reason lay in the two mighty Turmansky turbojets which produced in excess of 50,000 lbs. of thrust each, giving the plane its incredible speed in excess of Mach 5. Another reason was in the magic of its anti-radar system which, as dead Baranovich had suggested, was non-mechanical, but rather some kind of treatment of, or application to, the skin of the aircraft, and a further reason lay in the thought-guided missiles and cannon the Firefox carried.

The sky ahead of him was clear, pale blue, the rising sun to port of him dazzling off the perspex, the glare diffused and deadened by the tinted mask of the flying helmet. There was nothing to see.

Gant had no interest in the stretching, endless steppe below him. His eyes hardly left the instrument panel, especially the radar which would warn him of the approach of aircraft, or of missiles. One of his ECM devices, which Baranovich had explained in his final briefing, was a constant monitor of the radar-emissions from the terrain over which he passed. Effectively, the "Nose," as Baranovich had called it, sniffed out radar signals directed at him. The "Nose" seemed unnecessary to Gant, since he could not be picked up on any radar screen on the ground or in the air but, Baranovich explained and he had seen, a visual sighting of him would lead to intense radar activity on the ground, using the sighting plane as the guide to his whereabouts. In addition, as long as he went on monitoring the readout on the tiny screen of the "Nose," he would know where, and in what pattern, missile-radars on the ground below him were.

Gant knew what form the search for him would take. The Russians would guess he would head either

direct north or direct south—that to the east was
only, eventually, and long after he ran out of fuel,
the People's Republic of China, while to the west,
between himself and a friendly country, lay the massive defenses that surrounded Moscow. He knew
that "Bearhunt" squadrons would be up looking
for him, and he also suspected the Russians would
be using their sound-detection system—NATO-
designated, with inappropriate levity, "Big Ears"—
which in the unpopulated interior of the Russian
heartland was designed to detect low-flying aircraft
that might have eluded the radar net. Gant had no
idea of how numerous might be such installations,
nor how efficient they were in obtaining accurate
bearings on machines moving at more than six hundred miles an hour—nor did he know at what
altitude the system ceased to be effective.

One other thing, he reminded himself. Satellite
photography, high-speed and infra-red. He didn't
know whether it would be effective within the tiny
time-scale of his flight. But it was something else
to worry about. He was fighting an electronic war.
He was like an asthmatic man with heavy, creaking
boots trying to move through a room of insomniacs
without disturbing them.

Gant had no idea of the nature, or precise location, of his refueling point. In his memory were a
sequence of different coordinates which he was to
feed into the inertial navigator.

He had left the UHF channel open, knowing that
they would attempt to contact him from Bilyarsk.
In fact, he hoped and expected that they would do
so. As soon as he spoke, anybody within a range of
two hundred miles of him using UDF equipment
would not only pick up the broadcast, but would be
able to obtain, with the assistance of two other fix
lines, an almost instant fix on his position. In his
case, it would only help to confirm the decoy of his
journey south.

He suspected that the silence since his take-off

was caused by the take-over of command by the War Command Center on board the First Secretary's Tupolev. He waited with impatience, a surge of vanity in him wanting, above the desire of being assumed to be heading toward the southern borders of the U.S.S.R., to hear from the First Secretary, or the Marshal of the Soviet Air Force, at the least. He wanted to feed upon their anger, their threats.

The radio crackled into life. The voice was one he recognized from newsreels, from interviews—that of the First Secretary of the Soviet Communist Party. Involuntarily, his eyes flicked to the instruments, checking his heading and speed, checking the conformity of the dials and read-outs.

"I am speaking to the individual who has stolen the property of the U.S.S.R.," the voice said, levelly, without inflection, almost as if on purpose to disappoint him. "Can you hear me, Mr. Gant? I presume you have discarded your military rank since you became employed by—shall we say, *other persons?*" Gant smiled at the man's emphasis, and his caution.

Ever since the U-2 incident, he thought. Softly, softly. It was not to be admitted, not yet, that he was working for the CIA, even that he was an American.

He said: "Go ahead—I'm listening."

"Are you enjoying your ride, Mr. Gant—you like our new toy?"

"It could be improved," Gant said laconically.

"Ah—your expert opinion, Mr. Gant."

Gant could almost see the big man, with the strong, square face, sitting before the transmitter in the War Command Center, while the frenzy of activity around him went almost unnoticed. Already, no doubt, someone had pushed beneath his gaze the details of the fix they had obtained on him. At that moment, however, it was between the two of them, between one man in an airplane, and another man with the powers of a god at his disposal. Yet Gant held all the cards, the voice seemed to say. Gant remained unfooled. He understood the fury of the search for him. He was being played like a fish, lulled, until they found him.

"You could say that," he said. "Don't you want to threaten me, or something?"

"I will do so, if that is what you wish," was the level reply. "But first, I will merely ask you to bring back what does not belong to you."

"And then you'll forget the whole thing, uh?"

There was what sounded like soft laughter at the other end of the UHF. Then: "I don't think you would believe that, Mr. Gant—would you? No, of course not. The CIA will have filled your head with nonsense about the Lubyanka, and the security services of the Soviet Union. No. All I will say is that you will live, if you return immediately. It is calculated that no more than forty flying minutes would be required before we would be able to sight you back over Bilyarsk. It has been a nice try, Mr. Gant, as you would say—but now, the game is most definitely over!"

Gant waited before replying, then said: "And the alternatives . . . ?"

"You will be obliterated, Mr. Gant—simply that. You will not be allowed to hand over the Mig-31 to the security services of your country. We could not allow that to happen."

"I understand. Well, let me tell you, sir—I *like* this plane. It fits me. I think I'll just keep it, for the moment. . . ."

"I see. Mr. Gant, as you will be aware, I am not interested in the life of one rogue pilot with a poor health record—I was hoping to save the millions of rubles that have been poured into the development of this project. I see that you won't allow that to happen. Very well. You will not, of course, make it to wherever you are heading. Goodbye, Mr. Gant."

Gant flicked off the UHF and smiled to himself behind the anonymity of the flying mask. All he really had to worry about, he told himself—the one

factor in the game which could cancel out all his
advantages—was burning in the hangar at Bilyarsk:
the second Firefox. If they could continue to trace
him, and put that up against him . . . He shrugged.

The civilian flight from Moscow to Volgograd
took him by surprise. Suddenly, there was a glint of
sunlight off duralumin, and he was on top of it. The
vapor trail, at that hour of the morning in those
air conditions, had become visible very late. He had
intended to cross the nose of the Tupolev, but there
was the short contrail away to port. He switched
off the auto-pilot.

He rolled the Firefox onto a wingtip, felt the
pressure-suit perform its anti-G function, tightening then loosening round his thighs and upper body,
and he pulled the aircraft round. The bright, hard
glint of the Tupolev Tu-144 was almost directly
ahead of him now. He had to give its flight-crew the
opportunity to make a positive visual identification,
and he had to be heading south as he crossed the
nose.

He banked away to port, accelerating into a dive.
He moved away from the airliner, losing sight of it.
It registered as a bright green blip near the center
of the radar screen. When he had decided that he
had slid across and behind it, and accelerated sufficiently to overtake it again, he straightened onto
his original course, watching the blip attempt to regain its position to one side of the screen's center
line. He steadied the Firefox like an eager horse as
the airliner moved into visual range to starboard,
and he could see the contrail and the tiny glint of
sunlight. He eased open the throttles, and the Firefox
surged forward on what would appear a collision
course to the pilot of the airliner.

There was never a moment when he considered
he might have misjudged the distance, the heading.
He rolled the plane onto a wingtip, and dived away
from the oncoming Tupolev, now filling his starboard window. They would have seen him, and pan-

icked, since their radar screens would be stupefyingly empty. The slim fuselage, and the huge engines of an unknown aircraft, suddenly appearing, would be imprinted on their minds by fear. He rolled the plane into a Mach descent, a thousand feet below the airliner, and listened to the chatter of the pilot over the Russian airline frequency, smiling in satisfaction.

The ground rushed at the Firefox as he screamed down from 15,000 feet. He trimmed slightly nose-up, then pulled out of the suicidal dive, leveling at little more than two hundred feet above the flat terrain of the steppes. The pressure on the G-suit was evident, uncomfortable, as he was thrust back into the pilot's couch. His vision blurred, reddened, and then cleared, and he read off the instruments before him.

He switched in the auto-pilot and fed in the next coordinates that he had memorized so exactly, and the inertial navigator took over, settling the Firefox onto its new course. He had been seen, and the sighting would confirm the UDF fix they must have. They would have confirmed the fact that he was heading south, beyond Volgograd, toward perhaps the border with Iran, and some kind of rendezvous in Israel, or over the Mediterranean. The search would fatten in that sector of the Soviet defense system. Now he had need of at least some fair proportion of the Firefox's speed capability. He opened the throttles and watched the rpm gauges swing over, and the Mach-counter which was his only intimation, other than his ground speed read-out, that he was traveling faster than the speed of sound. He was heading east, toward the mountain chain of the Urals, seeking the shelter, he hoped, of their eastern slopes before turning due north. He could not employ the real cruising capability of the plane. Nevertheless, it was with satisfaction that he watched the numbers slipping through the Mach-counter . . . Mach 1, 1.1, 1.2, 1.3, 1.4, 1.5 . . .

Just below him, the flat, empty, silent expanse of the steppes fled past, receded. The buoyancy he had felt, the clearness and pleasure of the first moments of the flight, returned to him. He was flying the greatest warplane ever built. It was a meeting of that aircraft, and the only human being good enough to fly it. His egotism, cold, unruffled, calculating, was fulfilled. A visual sighting at the height he was traveling became less and less likely. The supersonic footprint of his passage was narrow at two hundred feet, and there was little below him of human manufacture or human residence to record it. All he needed to avoid was the "Big Ears" sound-detection network. He had no idea of its capability, or location. In the Urals, however, the echoes set up by his passage would confuse any such equipment.

Suddenly, in a violent alteration of mood, he felt naked and his equilibrium seemed threatened. He was running for cover. Despite his better judgment, he pushed the throttles forward and watched, with satisfaction, as the Mach-counter reeled off the mounting numbers. Mach 1.8, 1.9, Mach 2, 2.1, 2.2 . . .

He knew he was wasting fuel, precious fuel, yet he did not pull back the throttles. He watched the numbers mount until he had reached Mach 2.6, and then he steadied the speed. Now, the terrain below him was merely a blur. He was in a soundless cocoon, removed from the world. He began to feel safe as he switched in the TFR (Terrain Following Radar) which was his eyes and his reactions, operating as it did via the auto-pilot. He had not expected to need it until he entered the foothills of the Urals, but at his present speed of almost two thousand mph, he had to switch them in. He was no longer flying the aircraft. The Urals were only minutes away now and there, safe, he would regain control of the Firefox. His sense of well-being began to return. The sheer speed of the aircraft deadened the ends of nerves. The steadied figures of Mach 2.6

on the Mach-counter was brilliantly clear in his
vision. At this speed, despite the draining-away of
the irreplaceable kerosene, a visual sighting was as
good as impossible. He was safe, running and
safe. . . .

"Give the alert to the contingency refueling loca-
tions at once, would you?" Aubrey said blandly.
He was speaking via a scrambler to Air Commodore
Latchford at Strike Command, High Wycombe. He
had, that moment, received a report from Latchford
which indicated a definite lift-off by Gant from Bilyarsk. The AEWR (Airborne Early Warning Radar) had recorded signs of a staggered sector scramble amongst border squadrons of the Red Air Force
and this, in conjunction with radio- and code-moni-
toring which had shown signs of furious code-com-
munication between sections of the Red Air Force,
and between the First Secretary and the Admiral
of the Red Banner Northern Fleet, as well as Russian ships in the Mediterranean—all of this evidence
amounted to a sighting of Gant lifting clear of the
runway at Bilyarsk.

Latchford affirmed an immediate alert for both
contingency refueling points to begin transmission
of the homing-signal which operated on the very
special frequency of Gant's transistor-innards which
would lead him home.

"Mother Two and Mother Three will go on alert
now," the Air Commodore said. "You'll take care of
Mother One yourself—at least, I presume you will,
since I have no idea where to find her?" There
was a chuckle at the other end of the line. Latchford had had to know about the two contingency refueling points, but had been kept in the dark concerning the one Gant was expected to use. Aubrey
sensed a communion of tension, of suppressed excitement.

"Yes, Captain Curtin will take care of Mother
One," Aubrey assured him, and then added: "Thank

you, Air Commodore—your news comes, if I may
say, like a ray of pure sunshine. Many thanks." He
listened to Latchford's throaty chuckle for a moment, seeming to draw comfort from the sound, and
then replaced the receiver.

Buckholz, elbows on his desk, was watching him
intently as he looked up. "They confirm? All that
activity isn't just because they caught our boy?" he
inquired.

Aubrey shook his head. "No, my dear Buckholz,"
Aubrey said blandly. "AEW Radar confirms the predicted air activity on the part of the Red Air Force,
northern and southern borders—Gant is in the air."

Buckholz breathed deeply, his breath exhaling
loudly. He turned to Anders, almost asleep next to
him, and grinned with the pure self-satisfaction of a
child.

"Thank God," he whispered.

There was a silence, broken by Curtin's creaking
descent from the step-ladder. When he regained the
floor, he said to Aubrey: "I didn't reckon on doing
the office-boy's job when I volunteered for this!"
He grinned as he said it. "You want me to tell Washington to alert Mother One, Mr. Aubrey?"

Aubrey nodded. "Yes, my boy—do that now,
would you? If the weather's still holding, that is."

Curtin walked back to the map, picked up a point-
er and tapped at a satellite weather-photograph
pinned high on the wall. "That's the latest—two
a.m., your time. All clear."

"And the track of Mother One?"

"Constant—moving slowly south, in an area of
loosened pack. Temperature low enough. She's holding."

"Good. Then put through your call, Captain.
Mother One it is."

Before Curtin could place the call, they were
startled by the chatter of a teletype from the Code
Room. Aubrey watched Shelley as the younger man
ripped the sheet of flimsy from the machine.

"Communications picked this up only minutes ago," he said, a slight smile on his tired face. "Plain language. Picked up by the operator listening in on the Soviet airline frequency."

"Ah," Aubrey remarked. "And . . . ?"

"He was spotted north-west of Volgograd—almost tore the nose off the airliner, before they lost sight of him. The pilot was screaming his head off, before someone told him to keep quiet!"

"Good."

Aubrey inspected the sheet of paper, and then offered it to Buckholz who had crossed to perch on the table.

Buckholz stared at it, as if needing to be convinced, and then said: "Good. Damn good." He looked into Aubrey's face, and added: "So far, so good?"

"I agree, my dear Buckholz. Hopefully, the Russians are now scrambling everything, including the mess bar, to the south of Gant." He rubbed his chin, and said: "I still worry about 'Big Ears', you know. Gant must be making a frightful amount of noise, heading east to the Urals."

"It is not, my dear Kutuzov, a war situation," the First Secretary said, seated in his chair before the round table. His eyes disregarded the map of European Russia, from the Polish border to the Urals, from the Arctic Ocean to the Black Sea, despite its glowing squares of color, despite the winking strings of tiny lights that signaled the interceptor stations with fighters in the air, despite the other lights forming links in the glowing chain which signaled the missile sites on full war alert. Kutuzov seemed, on the other side of the table, unable to remove his fixed stare from the hypnotic projection before him. Reluctantly, it seemed, he lifted his eyes, and gazed at the First Secretary.

"You have considered that this might be some kind of supreme bluff by the Americans, First Secretary. To distract us from looking northward, while this single aircraft attempts to escape to the south." It was not a question. Marshal Kutuzov was evidently serious in his supposition.

The First Secretary sighed and said: "No, Kutuzov. This is a CIA venture—with the backing of the office of the President, and the Pentagon, no doubt." His palms were raised from the desk to prevent interruption. "But it is no more than a wildcat affair. Elaborate, yes. Far-sighted, yes. Well-planned and executed, yes. All of those things. But it is not war! No. The CIA will have arranged a refueling point for this madman, somewhere—our computers will, no doubt, tell us the most likely places. But, if we shoot down the Mig-31, and even if we destroy the refueling-vehicle, the Americans will act dumb, as they say. They will do nothing. And that—all of you . . ." His voice was suddenly raised, so that the background chatter of the Command Center stilled, and all eyes turned to him. "All of you understand this. If we can destroy, or recover, the aircraft, then we will hear no more of the matter."

"You are sure?" Kutuzov said. His face expressed a desire to be convinced. He had been staring at the edge of a void from the moment the idea had occurred to him, that he was witnessing the opening move in the end-game for the world.

"I am—certain. The Americans, and the British, both want this aircraft, because they are aware of its potential. They both have made massive cuts in their defense budgets during the past few years, especially in the area of development and research. Therefore, despite the *free gift* of the Mig-25 some years ago, they have, as we know, nothing on the drawing-board remotely capable of matching the Mig-31."

He turned a suddenly baleful glare upon Andropov, standing at his shoulder. "Chairman Andropov —the security for this project was—unforgiveable!"

Andropov nodded slowly. The strip-lighting of the room glinted from his spectacles. Vladimirov, standing near Kutuzov, sensed the man's anger. Also, he understood the suppressed anger of the First Secretary which had prompted the icy remark.

"Yes—unfortunately, First Secretary." He looked across at the two military men on the other side of the table. "I remember that Marshal Kutuzov and General Vladimirov both wished the security to be strengthened, after the initial trials." He smiled, coldly. "It would appear they were right."

"The Americans knew far too much," Kutuzov growled, in a voice hardly more than a throaty whisper.

The First Secretary raised his hand. He realized that he had initiated yet another internecine squabble between the military and the KGB.

"Leave it at that," he said levelly. "It will be examined thoroughly. It would appear, from the Chairman's initial inquiries, that Colonel Kontarsky gambled—and failed." Behind the First Secretary, Andropov nodded slowly, then looked across the table.

Neither Kutuzov nor Vladimirov said anything. Kontarsky had played a lone hand. He had attempted to use the security of the Bilyarsk project to enhance his promotion, and his reputation. It had happened before. The KGB officer at the head of KGB observation-security in the Middle East, in 1967, had held back information vital to the Kremlin and to the Kremlin's satellite, Egypt, concerning the Israeli preparations for war, until they had taken him by surprise. Department V of the KGB, the assassination department, had liquidated him soon afterwards. Kontarsky would not survive his failure.

There was a knock at the door. The First Secretary's KGB bodyguard opened it and accepted the sheaf of papers that were handed to him by someone in a white coat. Then the door was closed.

"Thank you," the First Secretary said. He studied the papers for a moment, then looked up, and passed them to Kutuzov. "Tell me what they mean."

The old Marshal studied them intently, after plucking a pair of battered, wire-rimmed spectacles from the breast-pocket of his tunic. The background chatter of the code and communications operators was hardly sufficient to drown the noise of the papers as he shuffled through them. When he had finished, he pulled his glasses from his face, and handed the papers to Vladimirov.

Coughing, he said: "It is a damage report on the second Mig, First Secretary, as you are aware. It would appear that the dissidents failed to put the aircraft out of commission."

It suddenly became clear to Vladimirov, looking across the table to the First Secretary and Andropov, that the War Command Center was a venue of desperation. To those two preeminently powerful men, who did not understand the air or aircraft, this was some kind of panacea; this was what they were hoping for, what they had been anticipating with an almost virginal excitement. They truly believed that, if they could only put up the second prototype, they would be able to bring down the running American. He dismissed the beginnings of a smile from his face.

"How soon—how soon can it be ready to fly—armed?" the First Secretary asked, his voice unsettled with excitement.

"Perhaps an hour, perhaps less," Vladimirov put in, consulting the papers in his hand. "It was, of course, in a condition of flight readiness as a back-up to the PP1, but it has to be cleared of foam, preflighted and armed, First Secretary."

"But we need to know where he is, *exactly!*" growled Kutuzov in his familiar whisper. Vladimirov realized that his superior was less alive to the political niceties of the atmosphere in the War Command Center. All that the First Secretary wanted was to get the second plane airborne. He would not welcome reminders of the practical difficulties of a seek and destroy mission for the aircraft.

"I *know* that, Kutuzov!" the First Secretary snapped, silencing the old Marshal. He looked round the walls of the room, as if the bent backs of the operators would inspire him, supply him with the answer he required.

Vladimirov sensed his desperation beneath the icy calm, beneath the strength of the man's personality. For him, the staggered sector scramble provided the only hope, slim though it was. Something nagged at the back of his mind, something he had first thought of in the early years of the Mig-31 project, something that he had raised as a possible objection to the anti-radar system that had been developed, and thrust upon the Bilyarsk development. It had been a cool voice, a sprinkling of water on a burning enthusiasm.

Vladimirov was, by nature, a cool, rational man, a strategist. As O.C. "Wolfpack," commandant of the Russian interceptor force, he had found his fulfilment as a military man. He, with Kutuzov, had pressed for the delay in defense spending that would insure the rapid production of hundreds of Mig-31s, to replace the Foxbats that at present formed the strongest card in the Russian suit. The thought-guided weapons-system developed for the aircraft was, he recognized, its real trump, together with its huge range and frightening speed. It would put the Red Air Force into a different league, beyond the present or immediately future capabilities of the RAF and the USAF.

He wandered away from the tense, electric atmosphere surrounding the circular table in the middle of the War Command Center, and listened with half an ear to the flow of decoded reports issuing from the teams of operators. Everything was being re-

corded, ready for instant playback if there was need
to consult the reports.

The sighting north-west of Volgograd filled him
with suspicion. A former ace, he suspected the obvious. He had been forced to respect Gant, the
American pilot. Studying the KGB file on him,
transmitted by wire-print from the Center in Moscow, he appreciated the selection of the man by the
CIA. Gant was a rogue pilot, a Vietnam ace. Vladimirov hoped that, had the roles been reversed, he
would have had the foresight and the daring to select such a man.

He felt he knew Gant, felt the *need* of the man to
steal the Mig, to prove it could be done. Gant would
want to complete the mission. He would be determined to take the Mig home.

From the pilot's report, it had been made to appear that the American had been surprised by the
sudden appearance of the airliner to starboard of
him, right on a collision course. Vladimirov knew
that Gant's radar would have warned him of the
airliner's presence in plenty of time to avoid such a
sighting. And Gant was a fine pilot, perhaps the best
if his record told no lies. Even in an unfamiliar
aircraft, he would not have made such an error of
airmanship. Vladimirov was sure that a simulator
had been built at Langley, Virginia, to assist Gant in
his training. He mentally cursed Kontarsky who, in
the harsh glare of failure, appeared a gross fool. A
great deal of information must have passed to the
Americans over the past years, a great deal.

He dismissed Gant from his mind. To think of
him was to dwell on the unchangeable past. No,
there was something more important, something
that might circumvent Gant's supreme advantage
of the radar immunity of the Mig-31. What the devil
was it?

He rubbed at his chin as he walked, a continuous,
harsh motion of the hand. The voice of an operator
repeating a communication struck him clearly. The

words slid across his consciousness, without resonating.

"Positive sound-trace, installation at Orsk . . ." the voice at his side was saying. He was unaware of the stillness suddenly around him, unaware that the operator had turned to look up at him. No, he thought, it had nothing to do with sound. It was— was . . . Then he had it, elusive, yet brilliantly clear, even as his mind registered the silence around him and he saw the expectant face of the radio-operator from the corner of his eye.

He had said clearly, a lone voice amid the atmosphere of military and political euphoria, that radar-immunity by and of itself did not render any aircraft, however advanced, completely safe from detection. Infra-red detection equipment, designed not to bounce a signal off a solid object but to detect heat-sources on the ground or in the air, might be used to detect the presence of an aircraft immune to radar. The heat emission from a jet engine would show up on any infra-red screen as an orange blip. It would be a poor substitute in tracking and fixing a target, but it would, even within its limitations, cancel some of the total advantage of the Mig-31's anti-radar system. It might prove sufficiently accurate for heat-seeking missiles to be launched in the direction of the prospective target. They would then, with their own sensors, seek out the heat-source that would have shown up on the infra-red screens on the ground. That was it! He looked at his hand in front of his face, and saw that it was quivering.

It was the answer. His staggered sector scramble did not have to rely upon the faint possibility of a clear visual sighting. Every fighter could train its infra-red weapons-aiming system ahead of the plane, in a cone. Anything with a jet engine passing through that cone, in whatever atmospheric conditions, at whatever altitude, would show up as a bright orange heat-spot on the pilot's infra-red detection screen.

He saw the face of the operator, holding one hand to his head like a man with toothache, saw the smile of puzzlement on the face.

"Yes?" he said. "What did you say?"

"General—there has been an unidentified sound trace from a low-flying aircraft traveling at more than Mach 2, picked up on the mobile unit west of Orsk."

"Where is Orsk?" Vladimirov snapped, the excitement in the young face in front of him seeming to become infectious. Without waiting for an answer, the General turned to the man at the map-console, who computed the patterns and details to be fed onto the projection on the table. "Orsk! Blow up that region for me." He remembered. "It's at the southern tip of the Urals ..."

He slapped his hand against his forehead, not noticing the silence of the entire War Command Center as the truth of his suspicions came home to him. Gant had *deliberately* been sighted traveling south!

"What is the matter, General Vladimirov?" he waved his hand dismissively in the direction of the voice.

"Get me a confirmation of that report—quickly!" he snapped. "Call it out to me."

Swiftly, he crossed to the map beneath the screen of the table, oblivious to the rising anger displayed on the face of the First Secretary. Eagerly, he studied the enlargement of the southern tip of the Urals mountain chain, realized that the area was too small and said: "Replace this—give me a projection of the Urals, and of as much to the north and south as you can—now."

His fingers tapped at the table edges as he waited. The map dissolved, and then re-formed. The Urals spread like a livid scar down the center of the projection. To the south was the brown, dusty-colored expanse of Iran, and to the north the deepening blue of the Barents Sea and the Arctic Ocean. Still ignoring the First Secretary, who sat at the table like a carved figure, Vladimirov traced his finger across the map, first southwards, toward the Middle East and the Mediterranean; then, more slowly and thoughtfully, the slender, long-nailed finger tracked northward across the map, up the chain of the Urals. It paused over Novaya Zemlya, then pushed on north, then curved in an arc to the north-west into the Arctic Ocean.

When he looked up, it was only to hear the radio-operator who had informed him of the sound trace, saying: "Trace confirmed, sir. Aircraft, which refused to answer a demand for identification, heading north-east into the mountains. They lost the trace within thirty seconds, but they confirm heading and speed."

Vladimirov realized that Gant had made his first mistake, had made what might be promoted into a fatal error. He had ignored the demand for identification, and that made him suspicious. Also, he was traveling far too fast, running for shelter . . . his fuel could not last as long as he must have hoped at first, at that speed. He studied the map again, realizing that Gant was seeking the shelter, from visual and sound detection, of the eastern foothills of the Urals.

Which could only mean . . . yes, he realized with a mounting excitement, could only mean that his refueling point lay to the north of the Soviet Union, in the Barents Sea, or above it. He looked up.

The First Secretary had not moved. "Well?" he said softly.

"If you will look at the map, First Secretary," Vladimirov said, sensing Kutuzov at his shoulder, "I will try to explain my deductions." Swiftly, he outlined Gant's probable course. When he had finished, he added: "We can track him, despite his radar-immunity, First Secretary."

There was a silence and then Andropov, arms folded across his chest and standing behind the First Secretary, said in a soft, ironical voice: "How?"

Vladimirov explained, as simply as he could, the manner in which the infra-red weapons-aiming system could be used as a directional search-beam. Kutuzov clapped him on the shoulder, and Vladimirov sensed the quiver of excitement in the old man's frame. More distantly, he sensed that he had somehow sealed the succession, that he would be the next Marshal of the Air Force. The prospect did not affect him. At that moment, he was concerned only with the elimination of Gant as a military threat.

"Good—that is good, General Vladimirov," the First Secretary said. "You agree, Mihail Ilyich?" Kutuzov nodded. "This needs no mechanical adjustment?" Vladimirov shook his head.

"No—merely a coded instruction to that effect from you, or from Marshal Kutuzov."

The First Secretary nodded. "What, then, do you suggest, Vladimirov?"

"You must alert units of the Red Banner Northern Fleet, First Secretary. They must begin looking for a surface, or subsurface . . ." He paused. No, it had to be a surface craft, and even that was unlikely. "More probably, an aircraft, waiting to refuel the Mig in mid-air, First Secretary." The Soviet leader nodded. "Then, we must put up 'Wolfpack' squadrons nearest to our northern coastline, to seek out the mother-plane." He glanced round into Kutuzov's keen eyes. The old man nodded. "And, we alert *all* missile sites along the First Firechain to expect Gant. They, too, must use their infra-red aiming-systems to search for him, in concert with the 'Wolfpack' units."

Suddenly, his finger stabbed at the map, almost immediately in front of the First Secretary. "There," he said. "Just there. If he follows the Urals to their northernmost point, then he will use the Gulf of Ob, or the gulf to the west of the Yamal Peninsula as a visual sighting, before altering course for his rendezvous with the mother-aircraft. As you can see,

First Secretary, there are two fixed units in the First Firechain within range, as well as the mobile link between them, and our 'Wolfpack' squadrons based on the peninsula." He looked up, and there was a smile on his face. "It will take only minutes to organize, First Secretary—and the American will walk into the most powerful trap ever sprung." He was still smiling when he said: "Will you give permission for any Soviet aircraft who gains a visual sighting to act as a target for the missiles—if it becomes necessary?"

Vladimirov heard Kutuzov's indrawn breath, but kept his eyes on the First Secretary. In the man's gray, flinty eyes he could see the succession confirmed. This time, it moved him with a distinct, though momentary, pleasure. The First Secretary merely nodded.

"Of course," he said.

"Very well, First Secretary—then Gant is dead."

The journey through the Urals had taken Gant little more than two hours, since in covering the sixteen or more hundred miles from Orsk to Vorkuta through the eastern foothills, he had never exceeded six hundred knots, keeping his speed sub-sonic in order to conserve the fuel he now wished he had not burned in his panic-dash to the cover of the mountains. The lower speed would also stop his presence being betrayed by a supersonic footprint across the sparsely-populated ground below. The foothills had been wreathed in mist, which made visual detection almost impossible, either from the ground or from the air.

Knowledge concerning military installations in the Urals chain was sketchy. Buckholz and Aubrey had been able to provide him with very little in the way of fact. It had been assumed, dubiously, that the eastern slopes of the mountain chain would be the less heavily armed and surveyed. Once he had taken a visual sighting on Orsk, to obtain a bearing, he had fed the coordinates of his northward flight into the inertial navigator, and slotted the aircraft into its flight-path. Then he had again switched in the TFR and the auto-pilot, and passed like a ghost into a gray world of terrain-hugging mist, chill to the eye, featureless as the moon, or the landscape of his memory.

He had feared a return of the dream or, at least, of some of the physical symptoms of the hysterical paralysis—even the nausea. Yet, it had not happened. It was as though he had passed from shadow into light, as if the person he had been before the take-off had been shed like a skin. He spent no time in marveling at his new, recovered integrity of mind, calmness of thought. It wasn't unfamiliar to him. Even in Vietnam, toward the end, he had been able to fly almost perfectly, leaving behind him, like the uniform in his locker, the wreck of an individual sliding toward the edge.

His ECM instrument for picking up radar-emissions from the terrain below had recorded nothing since the beginning of his flight through the mountains. He had moved in a world cut off, entirely separate, the kind of isolation he had heard NASA men talk about after orbiting the earth in one of the Skylabs, or returning from testing the newest re-entry vehicles. Once he had met Collins, one of the lunar astronauts. He had said the same. In his own way, Gant had always felt that removed when his aircraft was on auto-pilot. There was nothing, except a cabin, pressurized, stable, warm—and the human multitude and their planet fled by formlessly as the mist through which he had travelled. That utter isolation was something he had never rid himself of on the ground, not even in violent drinking-jags, or in the relief of Saigon prostitutes. And the reason he sought that lonely superiority of the skies was because the ground had never offered him more than an inferior copy of the same empty isolation.

It was just after nine, and the mist was clearing at his height, shredding away from the cockpit, so that sunlight glanced from the perspex, and the faded blue of the morning sky was revealed. On his present heading, he knew he would pass over the Gulf of Kara, that sharp intrusion of the Kara Sea to the west of the Yamal Peninsula within minutes, at this present speed. With the cross-check of a visual bearing on the neck of the gulf, he would be able to feed in the next set of coordinates to the inertial navigator.

He looked ahead. Visibility was not good. There was no sign of water, only the hazy, gray absence of a horizon. He knew he would have to drop down as low as he could, risking visual sighting from the ground, risking the gauntlet of the Firechain which looped across this northern coast. Nevertheless, he had to do it.

The last northern strand of the mountains, limping towards the sea, neared again as he changed altitude, sliding down toward the pockets of mist not yet dispersed by the strengthening sun. He saw the small town of Vorkuta away to port, and knew that his heading was correct and that the sea lay only minutes ahead of him.

Suddenly then, the edge of his radar screen showed the presence of an aircraft, higher and away to starboard; big, probably a Badger long-range reconnaissance plane no doubt returning from a routine patrol out over the Kara Sea and the Arctic Ocean.

Moments passed in which he seemed content just with the knowledge that he was closing on the Badger, judging he would pass well behind it. He assumed that, with a minimum of luck, most of the electronic detection equipment on board the Badger would be shut down that close to its home base. Then, almost with disbelief, three bright orange spots registered on the screen, glowing, climbing, nearing. An infra-red source. Someone on the ground had loosed a bracket of missiles from a Firechain station.

They knew where he was. He realized this, his mind crying out at the jolt its apparent immunity from attack and detection had been given, the sudden draining of confidence.

He could not believe it. The missiles had to be heat-seeking, homing on the exhaust gases of the sky's hottest point. Somehow he was visible to them. And he knew how. The Firechain station had to be using its infra-red equipment to search for the imprint of his exhaust. He was invisible on radar; on an infra-red screen, he would be revealed as a point of orange light. Radar immunity of something which yet gave off hot exhaust gases—it would have to be him. They would have been told that much on the ground. The removing of his immunity stunned him. He watched in paralyzed fascination as the cluster of three glowing orange spots on his own screen enlarged as the missiles closed on the Firefox.

7
SEARCH AND DESTROY

Contact time, seven seconds. The moment of Gant's stunned failure to respond passed. He pulled his gaze from the three orange spots on the screen. Also registering on the screen was the bright green blip of the Badger, now no more than a few short miles away and moving away below him now and to port. The single screen which constituted the detection "eye" of the Firefox's electronics was built to register infra-red emissions of heat as orange spots, while radar images appeared as green blips. The missiles behind him were in the lower half of the screen, while the Badger ahead was in the upper half. He was still heading toward it, and it lay along the central ranging bar of the screen.

The Badger was the key to his safety, he realized. Here was a way he could misdirect the seeking missiles. He had to create a hotter spot than his own engines in the sky on to which they would home. He had to destroy the Badger, let it burn like a bonfire.

He pulled the Firefox onto a collision course with

the Russian plane. He ignored, with every effort his
mind could make, the three orange blips closing toward the center of the screen. Contact time, five
seconds. He pushed open the throttles; he had to be
closer to the Badger before he loosed one of his own
missiles. The anti-G suit tightened round him, then
relaxed as it countered the increased pressure of his
speed and dive. The three orange blips slipped across
his screen, then centered again as they followed
him. The green spot of the Badger enlarged. Gant
flicked the "Weapon Arming" switch on the console to his left. His thumb then flicked the switches
to activate the thought-trigger and -guidance systems. These switches safeguarded against the inad-
vertent firing and guiding of the weapons-system at
any time. Gant could guide his missiles visually by
direct observations of missile and target, or on the
screen. What he saw with his eyes, and required the
missile to perform, was converted in the brain into
electrical impulses, detected by the electrodes in
his helmet, and fed into the weapons-system which
transmitted a steering signal to the missile. As the
distance-to-target read-out indicated the optimum
moment for a hit, the thought-guided system automatically launched one of the missiles under the
wing. The missile left its bracket, then pulled up and
away from the track he had been following. For a
moment, light flicked at the corner of his eye as he
caught the firing of its motor.

Three seconds to contact time. He began to hope.
He saw the outline of the Badger clearly for a moment, directly ahead of him, an enlarging, slim gray
shape. He pulled the Firefox into a sudden turn to
the right, away as acutely as possible from the Badger. Two seconds. On the screen the orange spot almost seemed to be merging with, overflying, the
single green blip.

The Badger was in the center of the screen: it
was like a flower opening, a huge flower, orange,
the hottest part of the sky as his own missile deto-

nated. Contact time, zero seconds. The flower
bloomed even brighter, just below the center of the
screen as he left the maelstrom behind—full bloom
as the missiles detonated amid the inferno of the
Badger's destruction.

He realized he was sweating freely inside the pressure-suit, and he felt a wave of relief, sharp as
nausea, pass through him. Below him on the ground,
the infra-red screens which had picked him up
would now be confused, filled with light from the
massive detonation. When it cleared, he would be
out of range. He hoped they would draw the conclusion that he had himself perished in the explosion.

He checked his speed. Just below seven hundred
mph. He could not go supersonic as he neared the
coast. Too many trained ears, listening for the supersonic wake of his passage.

Now that he had survived, he began to take stock
of the Firefox. The thought-guided weapons-system
worked, as he had been certain it would. It had been
Baranovich's project and, despite the fact that it was
difficult to recall his face and the sound of his
voice, as though a gulf of time separated them, there
had been an unconscious, deep assurance that had
been associated with the Russian Jew. He had seen
only the tip of the iceberg. He had not needed to
react at the speed of thought, but had had to make a
conscious decision. But, when he had formed the
thought, regarding the port wingtip missile, the advanced Anab-type of AAM, it had fired. All he had
felt was the slight roll as the missile had detached
itself.

He glanced again at the TFR. He was crossing the
coastal strip. The mist that had clung to the coastal mountains had now become what he guessed must
be a sea-fog—light, threatening to dissipate, but con-
cealing. Best of all, it provided a sound-muffler,
dispersing the noise of his engines so that a sound-
trace such as the Russians were known to possess
would be confused by echoes.

Then he saw the coast as an uneven line across the TFR screen. The narrow neck of sea formed the furthest inland penetration of the Gulf of Kara. His memory supplied the next set of coordinates as the Firefox passed out over the water, even as he pushed the nose down and lost more height, keeping within the slim belt of fog which slipped past the cabin, gray and formless, removing him from the world. The read-out supplied him with the required heading, and he obeyed the inertial navigator, turning onto the heading that would take him toward the twin islands of Novaya Zemlya, north-west of his present position.

He registered that the altimeter stated two hundred feet, checked the TFR and eased back the throttles. The engine revolutions dropped, and he saw it register on the airspeed indicator. He leveled the aircraft, keeping it at a steady height of two hundred feet, and still eased back the throttles. While in the fog, he had the opportunity to conserve fuel, and thus make less engine noise. If he was heard, he wanted to sound as little like a fleeing thief as possible, and as much like an authorized search-plane as he could. At 250 mph, he steadied.

He reached up and his hand closed upon the transistor radio's innards, the special device developed for him at Farnborough, solely for the task which he now hoped it would perform. It was a homer pick-up, working on an incredibly complex pre-set pattern, searching for a beacon set on the same alternating pattern of signal frequencies. The signal remained on one frequency only long enough to be dismissed by anyone picking it up as static, or as unimportant. Gant could not tell, but the machine could, at what point it entered the sequence when switched on. The device had to be as complicated as it was because voice communication of any kind, however brief or cryptic, was open to being monitored by the Russians. He flicked the switch on the face of the apparently purposeless piece of hardware. Nothing, but at that moment he was unsurprised.

He knew the machine was searching the frequency band for a signal, and that there was a limit to its range when operational—yet he began to worry at the moment his hand flipped the switch. Only when the machine was functioning did he become truly aware of how much he depended upon it. Unless he picked up the signal transmitted by the refueling craft, and unless his receiver coordinated with the transmitter to make the homing signal a continuous directional impulse, then he was lost, and he would run out of fuel somewhere over the Arctic Ocean and die.

The "Deaf Aid," as Aubrey had called it with one of the bastard's sardonic smiles, was required because no one, not even Buckholz, with Baranovich's inside knowledge, could be certain that the Russians might not be able to jam every transmitter and receiver aboard the Firefox when it was in the air —in which case Gant would never find the fuel he needed. Even if the Soviets could only track every transmitter and receiver, then Gant would lead them straight to "Mother."

And, Gant thought, noticing that the sea fog was thinning, and that the oppressive grayness, the uniformity, of his visual world was lightening, they had not told him where to find "Mother," just in case he got caught. What he himself did not know, lunatic though the logic was, he could not tell anyone, whatever they did to him.

He looked at the fuel-gauges. Less than a quarter full. He had no idea how far he had to go. If, and when, he picked up the signal, he would know he was no more than three hundred miles away from the refuel point. The Farnborough gimmick remained silent.

He had switched in the auto-pilot, coupled with the TFR. The longest part of his journey was beginning, the part of the journey to stretch the

nerves, to test him as no other part of his mission
had done—flying by faith, and a single box of tricks
never operationally tested before. Guinea-pig. Pi-
geon. That was what he was.

Gant was an electronic pilot. He had relied on instruments all his flying life. Yet he had never depended on just one, one totally detached from his
flying skill, one totally unaffected by anything he
could do as the plane's pilot.

The featureless contours of the sea flowed across
the TFR screen, endless, empty of vessels. He
pushed up the plane's nose, rising above the still
thinning fog, into the brief glare of sunlight and an
impression of blue sky at four hundred feet. Nothing. He ducked the Firefox back into the mist. All
his instruments told him that Novaya Zemlya was
too far ahead to register—yet, he had wanted the
comfort of a visual check, as if his contemplation of
his dependence upon a single piece of electronic
hardware had made him revert to an earlier age of
flying.

He looked again at the fuel-gauges. The refueling
point would be hundreds of miles beyond the Russian coastline, had to be, for safety. Less than a quarter full, the huge wing tanks, the skin of the fuselage
itself that acted as a fuel tank.

Gant had no relish for the equation of fuel
against distance, and again cursed his panic-dash for
the Urals. What had given him a sense of escape
then, of life, might well have killed him.

"What is the matter, General Vladimirov?" the
First Secretary asked conversationally. Vladimirov
stopped in mid-stride and turned to face the Soviet
leader. "You must learn to accept success with more
aplomb, my dear Vladimirov!" The First Secretary
laughed.

Vladimirov smiled a wintry smile, and said: "I
wish I could be certain, First Secretary—much as

I fear my mood must displease you, I am *not* certain. . . ."

"You're not happy that we have lost the Mig-31?"

"No. I'm not happy that we *have* lost it—I wonder whether we could kill this man Gant quite so easily."

"But it was your plan we followed, Vladimirov —you have doubts about it now?" Andropov asked from behind the First Secretary, a thin smile on his lips.

"I never was certain of its success, Chairman," Vladimirov replied.

"Come," the First Secretary said softly. "What would make you happy, Vladimirov. I am in a generous mood." The man smiled, broadly, beatifically.

"To continue, and intensify, the search for Gant." Vladimirov's tone was blunt, direct.

"Why?"

"Because—*if* he's still alive, our self-congratulation might be just the help he needs. Find the refueling aircraft, or ship, or whatever it is, that must be waiting for him."

The First Secretary seemed to be looking into Vladimirov's mind as he debated the argument. After a long silence, he looked not at Vladimirov with his refocused gaze, but at Kutuzov.

"Well, Mihail Ilyich—what do you say?"

Kutuzov, his throat apparently rusty with disuse, said: "I would agree to every precaution being taken, First Secretary."

"Very well." The First Secretary's bonhomie had disappeared, and he seemed displeased that the euphoric mood of the room that had existed since the report from Firechain One-24 had been dispelled. He was brusque, efficient, cold. "What do you need, apart from the *massive* forces you have already called upon . . . ?" There was an almost sinister em-

phasis on the word, and he left the sentence hanging
uncomfortably in the air.

"Give me the Barents Sea map, and bleed in current naval dispositions in the area, together with
trawler activity and Elint vessels," Vladimirov called
over his shoulder, standing himself squarely in front
of the circular table, his hand plucking at his chin
thoughtfully. The projection of the northern coastline of the U.S.S.R. faded, taking with it the pricks
of light that had been the Firechain stations and the
"Wolfpack" bases, and was replaced by a projection
of the Barents Sea.

Vladimirov waited, as the map operator punched
out his demands on the computer-console. Slowly,
one by one, like stars winking in as dusk fell, lights
began to appear on the map, the stations of ships
in the Barents Sea and the southern Arctic Ocean.
Vladimirov stared at them for a long time in silence.

"Where is the print-out?" he asked after a while.
The map operator detached himself from his console,
and handed Vladimirov a printed sheet of flimsy
which registered the identification and exact last reported position and course of each of the dots on the
projection glowing on the table. Vladimirov studied
the sheet, glancing occasionally at the map.

North of Koluyev Island and west of Novaya
Zemlya, the clustered dots of a trawler-fleet registered in white. The neutral color signified their non-
military purpose. They were a large and genuine
fishing fleet. However, slightly apart from the close
cluster were two deep-blue dots, which signified
Elint vessels, spy trawlers, overfitted with the latest
and most powerful aerial, surface and sub-surface
detection equipment. They flanked the fishing fleet
like sheepdogs but, as Vladimirov knew, their interest lay elsewhere. At that moment, they would be
sweeping the skies with infra-red detectors, checking traces with the search-pattern they would have
received from the "Wolfpack" sector commander
the coast of whose area they were sailing. It was

early in the year for Elint vessels to be operating in
the Barents Sea, but Deputy Defense Minister, Admiral of the Soviet Fleet Gorshkov, liked his spy
ships in action as soon in the Arctic year as was
feasible. Because of the southward drift of the ice
in the Arctic spring, at the moment they did little
more than supplement the coastal radars.

Vladimirov's eye wandered north across the projection of the Barents Sea, picking up the scarlet dot
of a naval vessel. From the list in front of him, he
knew it was the helicopter and missile cruiser,
"Moskva" class, the *Riga,* and the pride of the Red
Banner Northern Fleet: 18,000 tons displacement,
armed with two surface-to-air missile-launchers, and
two surface or anti-submarine launchers, four sixty-
millimeter guns, mortars, four torpedo-tubes, and
four hunter-killer helicopters of the Kamov Ka-25
type. She was proceeding at that moment on an
easterly course, at the express command of the First
Secretary, through Gorshkov in Leningrad, which
would, within little more than an hour, bring her
close to Novaya Zemlya.

Elsewhere on the living map, Vladimirov registered the presence of two missile-destroyers, smaller,
less powerfully armed replicas of the missile-
cruiser, without that ship's complement of helicopters. One of them was well to the north of Novaya
Zemlya, near Franz Josef Land on the edge of
the permanent ice-sheet, and the other was steaming
rapidly south and east from the Spitzbergen area.
The majority of the Red Banner Fleet's surface vessels were in Kronstadt, the huge island naval base
in the estuary of the Neva, near Leningrad; it was
too early for operations, too early for exercises, in
the Barents Sea.

There were, however, Vladimirov saw with some
relief, a number of yellow dots glowing on the surface of the map, signifying the presence of Soviet
submarines. He glanced down at the list, identifying
the types available to him, mentally recalling their

armament and their search-capability. Soviet naval
policy in the Barents Sea was to keep the surface
vessels in dock during the bitter winter months and
during the early spring onslaught of the southward
drift of the impermanent pack-ice, and to use a single weapon in the arsenal of the Red Banner Fleet
for patrol duties—the huge submarine fleet at the
disposal of the Kremlin and the Admiral of the
Soviet Fleet. The policy explained why the Soviet
Union had concentrated for so long, and so successfully, on the development of the Soviet submarine
fleet, and why they had even returned to the com-
missioning of new, cheaper, conventional diesel-
powered submarines, instead of an exclusive con-
centration, as had been U.S. policy, on the hideously
expensive nuclear subs.

He ignored, for the moment, the three nuclear-
powered "V" type anti-submarine subs, and the
two ballistic-missile subs returning to Kronstadt after their routine strike-patrol along the eastern sea-
board of the United States. They would be of no use
to him. What he required were submarines with the
requisite search-capability for spotting an aircraft,
and for bringing it down.

"What are the reports of the search for wreckage
of the plane?" he asked aloud at last, tired suddenly
of the lights on the map. It was impossible for Gant
to escape, and yet . . . he should already be dead.

"Nothing so far, sir—air-reconnaissance reports no
indications of wreckage other than that of the Badger . . . the ground search parties have not yet arrived at the site of the crash."

"Give me a report on the search for the refueling-
craft," Vladimirov said in the wake of the report.

A second voice sang out: "Negative, sir. No unidentified surface vessels or aircraft in the area the
computer predicts to be the limit of the Mig's flight."

Vladimirov looked angry, and puzzled. It was
what he wanted to hear, from one point of view. No
planes or ships of the West anywhere near the area.

It was, frankly, impossible. There *had* to be a refueling-point. But the nearest neutral or friendly territory had to be somewhere in Scandinavia. It was, of course, possible to suppose that Gant was scheduled to make another alteration of course, to head west and follow the Russian coastline to North Cape, or Finnish Lapland ...

He did not believe it, even though he had taken the necessary precautions already. He believed that the CIA and the British SIS would not have been able to persuade any of the Scandinavian government to risk what the landing of the Mig on their territory would mean, in their delicate relations with the Soviet Union on their doorsteps. No, the refueling had to be out at sea, or at low altitude somehow. It could not be a carrier, there wasn't one in the area, not remotely in the area. Apart from which, the Mig-31 was not equipped for a deck landing. But could the base be an American weather-station on the permanent ice-sheet of the Pole?

Vladimirov disliked having to confront the problem of the refueling. Until final confirmation that Gant had crossed the coast, and the evidence that there was no refueling-station apparent, he had concentrated on stopping him over Soviet territory. But, now ...

"Where is it?" he said aloud.

"Where is what?" the First Secretary asked. His face was creased with thought, with his approaching decision.

"The refueling ship . . . or aircraft, whatever it is!" Vladimirov snapped in reply, without looking up from the map.

"Why?"

A thought struck Vladimirov. Without replying to the First Secretary, he said, over his shoulder. "Any trace on infra-red or sound-detectors further west, either from Firechain bases, or from coastal patrols?"

There was a silence for a moment, and then the

noncommittal voice replied: "Negative, sir. Nothing, except the staggered sector scramble in operation."

"Nothing at all?" Vladimirov said with a kind of desperation in his voice.

"No, sir. Completely negative."

Vladimirov was at a loss. It was like staring at a jigsaw puzzle that didn't make sense, or a game of chess where unauthorized moves had been suddenly introduced, to leave him baffled and losing. He realized he had operated too rigidly as a tactician, and that the people who had planned the theft of the Mig had been experts in the unexpected—security men like Andropov. He glanced quickly in the Chairman's direction. He decided not to involve him. Realizing that he was perhaps committing Kontarsky's crime, he decided to handle it himself.

There had to be an answer, but he could not see it. The more he thought about the problem of Gant's refueling, the more he became convinced that it was the key to the problem.

But, how?

He glared at the map as though commanding it to give up its secrets. On it, every single light represented a Soviet vessel, except for a British trawler-fleet on the very edge of the map, in the Greenland Sea, west of Bear Island.

He wondered, and decided that it was too far. Gant would not have sufficient fuel to make it—and how did the British navy expect to conceal an aircraft carrier inside a trawler-fleet? The idea was ludicrous.

No. The map didn't hold the answer. It told him nothing.

His hand thumped the map, and the lights jiggled, faded and then strengthened. "Where is he?" he said aloud.

After a moment, the First Secretary said: "You are *convinced* that he is still alive?"

Vladimirov looked up, and nodded.

"Yes, First Secretary. I am."

There it was, Aubrey thought, a single orange pin-
head on the huge wall map. Mother One. An unarmed submarine, hiding beneath an ice-floe which
was drifting slowly south in its normal spring peram-
bulation, its torpedo room and forward crew's quarters flooded with precious kerosene to feed the
greedy and empty tanks of Gant's plane.

He coughed. Curtin turned slowly round, then the
spell that had seemed to hold them rigidly in front
of the map was broken by the entry of Shelley,
preceded by a food trolley. Aubrey smelt the aroma
of coffee. With a start, he realized that he was hungry. Despite being envious of Shelley who was
shaved and washed and had changed his shirt, Aubrey was not displeased by the sight of the covered
dishes on the trolley.

"Breakfast, sir!" the younger man called out, his
smile broadening as he watched his chief's surprise
grow, and then become replaced by obvious pleasure. "Bacon and eggs, I'm afraid," he added to the
Americans. "I couldn't find anyone in the canteen
who could make flapjacks or waffles!"

Curtin grinned at him, and said: "Mr. Shelley—
a real English breakfast is the first thing we Americans order when we book into one of your hotels!"
Shelley, absurdly pleased with himself, Aubrey
thought, was unable to grasp the irony of Curtin's
remark. Not that it mattered.

"Thanks," Buckholz said, lifting one of the covers. Aubrey deeply inhaled the aroma of fried bacon, left his chair and joined them at the trolley.

They ate in silence for a little time, then Aubrey
said, his knife scraping butter onto a thin slice of
toast, his voice full of a satisfied bonhomie: "Tell me,
Captain Curtin, what is the present *condition* of
the ice-floe beneath which our fuel tanker is hiding?"

Curtin, eating with his fork alone in the American
style, leaned an elbow on the table around which
they sat, and replied: "The latest report on the

depth of the ice, and its surface condition, indicates all systems go for the landing, sir."

Aubrey smiled at his excessive politeness, and said: "You are *sure* of this?"

"Sir." As he explained, his fork jabbed the air in emphasis. "As you know, sir, all signals from Mother One come via the closest permanent weather-station, and are disguised to sound, if anyone picked them up, just like ordinary weather reports or ice-soundings. So we don't know what Frank Seerbacker in his ship really thinks, only what he sends. But the conditions are good, sir. The ice surface hasn't been changed or distorted by wind, and the floe still hasn't really begun to diminish in size—take it perhaps another three or four days to get south enough to begin melting."

"And—it's thick enough?" Aubrey persisted. Shelley smiled behind another mouthful of bacon and egg poised on his fork. He recognized the signs. Whenever Aubrey was at a loss in the matter of expertise, as he plainly was in the area of polar ice and its nature and behavior, he repeated questions, sought firmer and firmer assurances from those who posed as experts.

"Sir," Curtin nodded with unfailing courtesy. "And it's long enough and wide enough," he added, with the hint of a smile on his lips. "Gant, if he's anything of a pilot, can land that bird on it."

"And the weather?" Aubrey continued.

Buckholz looked up, grinned and said: "What's the matter, Aubrey? Indigestion, or something?"

"And the weather?" Aubrey persisted, not looking at Buckholz.

"The weather is, at the moment, fine—sir," Curtin informed him. He was silent for a moment, then he said: "It's abnormally fine for the time of year, in that sort of latitude ..."

"Abnormal?"

"Yes, sir. It could change—like that." Curtin snapped the fingers of his disengaged hand.

"Will it?" Aubrey asked, his eyes narrowing, as if he suspected some massive joke at his expense. "Will it?"

"I can't say, sir. Nothing large is showing up, not on the last batch of satellite pictures."

"What of the reports from the submarine itself?"

"Nothing yet, sir. The weather's perfect. The sensors are being thrust up through the floe from the submarine's sail every hour, on the hour. The local weather's fine, sir—just fine." Curtin ended with a visible shrug, as if to indicate that Aubrey had bled him dry, both of information and reassurance.

Aubrey seemed dissatisfied. He turned his attention to Buckholz.

"It's a lunatic scheme—you must admit that, Buckholz, eh?"

Buckholz glowered at him across his empty plate. He said: "I'm admitting no such thing, Aubrey. It's my end of the business, this refueling. You got him there, I admit that—a great piece of work, if that's what you want me to say—but I have to get him home, and you just better trust me, Aubrey, because I'm not about to change my plans because of your second thoughts."

"My dear chap," he said, spreading his hands on the table in front of him, "nothing was further from my thoughts, I assure you." He smiled disarmingly. "I just—like to be in the picture, so to speak, just like to be in the picture. Nothing more."

Buckholz seemed mollified. "Sure, it's a crazy scheme, landing a plane on a floating ice-floe, refueling it from a submarine—I admit that. But it'll work, Aubrey. There's just no trace of that sub, not at the moment, because it's under the floe, and showing up on no sonar screen anywhere, except as part of the floe. It comes up out of the water, fills up the tanks, and our boy's away." He smiled at Aubrey. "We can't use disguises, not like you, Aubrey. Out there, on the sea, you can't disguise a ship to look like a pregnant seal!"

There was a moment of silence, and then Aubrey said: "Very well, Buckholz. I accept your rationale for using this submarine. However, I shall be a great deal happier when the refueling is over and done with."

"Amen to that," Buckholz said, pouring himself a cup of coffee from the percolator. "Amen to that."

Almost as soon as the last of the coastal fog vanished and the bitter gray surface of the Barents Sea was sliding beneath him, strangely unreflective of the pale blueness of the sky, Gant was on top of the trawler. He was traveling at a fraction more than 200 mph, idling by the standards of the Firefox, heading for the twin islands of Novaya Zemlya, his next visual coordinate checkpoint, and the trawler was suddenly almost directly beneath him. As he flashed over the deck, at a height of less than a hundred feet, he saw, in the briefest glimpse, a white upturned face. A man had been emptying slops over the side. Then the trawler was gone, become a point of green light on the radar screen and he cursed the fact that he had confidently switched off his forward-looking radar when he crossed the coast. Now, too late, he switched it on again. In the moment of success against the Badger, he had been careless, excited. In the moment he had glimpsed the white, upturned face, he had seen something else, something much more deadly. As if to confirm his sighting, the ECM register of radar activity indicated powerful emissions from a source directly behind him, and close. What he had the vicious bad luck to pass over was an Elint ship, a spy trawler. Even now, they could be following his flight-path on infra-red.

He pushed the stick forward and the nose of the Firefox dipped, and the gray, wrinkled sea lifted up at him, threateningly. He leveled off at fifty feet, knowing that, with luck, he was already out of electronic view, at his present height. The Elint ship's

infra-red operators would have seen him disappear
from their screens, even as they informed the captain of their trace, even as the man with the empty
slop-bucket raced toward the bridge, mouth agape
at what he had seen. They would have some kind
of fix on him, a direction in which he had been
traveling. He was heading for Novaya Zemlya—a
blind man could pass that information back to whoever was coordinating the search for him.

He glanced at the fuel-gauge, and once more
cursed the panic that had made him run for the
Urals after visual sighting by the Soviet airliner
north-west of Volgograd. If only . . .

He had no time, he realized, to concern himself
with the futile. He could, he decided, do nothing except follow the course outlined, and to make the
next, and final, course adjustment when he reached
Novaya Zemlya.

His hand closed over the throttles. There were
missile sites on Novaya Zemlya, abandoned as a
testing-ground for Russia's nuclear weapons and
now serving as the most northerly extension of the
Russian DEW-line, and its first Firechain links. The
Firefox was capable, he had proven, of Mach 2.6 at
sea-level. How fast it could really travel he had no
idea; he suspected at height its speed might well
touch Mach 6, not the Mach 5 he had been briefed
to expect. In excess of four-and-a-half thousand
miles per hour. And perhaps two-point-two thousand miles per hour at sea-level. The Firefox was a
staggering warplane.

He pushed the throttles open. He *had* to use precious, diminishing fuel. Almost with anguish, he
watched the Mach-counter slide upwards, clocking
off the figures . . . Mach 1.3, 1.4, 1.5 . . . The Firefox
was a pelican, devouring itself.

The Firefox was nothing more than a blur towing
a hideous booming noise in its wake to the spotters
above the missile site at Matochkin Shar, at the
south-eastern end of the narrow channel between

the two long islands of Novaya Zemlya. On the infra-
red screens, he was a sudden blur of heat, nearing,
then just as suddenly, a receding trace as he
flashed through the channel at less than two hundred feet. Gant was flying by the auto-pilot and the
TFR—if a ship was in the narrow channel, he would
have no time to avoid it in the split-second between
his sighting it and his collision with it; but the TFR
would cope. His eyes were glued to his own screen,
waiting for the glow that would tell him of a mis-
sile-launch. None came.

As the cliffs of the channel, a gray curtain of unsubstantial rock, vanished and the sea opened out
again, he felt a huge, shaking relief, and punched
in the coordinates the Firefox was to fly. Automatically, the aircraft swung onto its new course and,
slowly, he eased off the throttles, claiming manual
control of the aircraft again, desperate to halt the
madness of his fuel consumption.

As the aircraft slowed to a sub-sonic speed, like
the return of sanity after a fever, Gant realized why
no missiles had been launched in his wake. Any
missile launched at a target at his height might well
have simply driven itself into the opposite cliff,
without ever aligning itself on a course to pursue
him.

Now he was flying on a north-westerly course, a
course which would eventually, long after his fuel
ran out, take him into the polar ice-pack at a point
between Spitzbergen and Franz Josef Land. Long
before he reached it, he would be dead. The bitter
gray sea flowed beneath him like a carpet, looking
almost solid. The sky above him was pale blue, de-
ceptively empty.

The loneliness ate at him, ravenous. He shivered.
The "Deaf Aid" gave him no comfort. It remained
silent. He began to wonder whether it worked. He
began to wonder whether there was something,
somebody, up ahead of him, waiting to refuel the
Firefox. The screen was empty, the sky above emp-

ty, the sea devoid of vessels. The Firefox moved on, over a flowing, gray desert, eating the last reserves of its fuel.

The report from the Elint ship, followed by the confirmatory information from Matochkin Shar had angered the First Secretary. It was suddenly as if he had accepted Vladimirov's doubts and precautions purely in the nature of an academic exercise; now he knew that they had been necessary, that Gant had not been destroyed in the explosion of the Badger.

It was perhaps the fact that he had been taken in that caused him to be so furiously angry that he turned on Vladimirov, and berated him, in a voice high, gasping with anger, for not having destroyed the Mig-31.

When his anger had subsided, and he had returned shaking and silent to his chair before the Arctic map on the circular table, Vladimirov at last spoke. His voice was subdued, chastened. He had been badly frightened by the outbursts of the First Secretary. Vladimirov now knew he was playing with his own future, professional and personal. Gant had to die. It was as simple, and as difficult, as that.

He moved swiftly now, without fuss, without consultation with the First Secretary or with Marshal Kutuzov; the former appeared to have relapsed into silence, and the latter, the old airman, appeared embarrassed and shaken by the politician's outburst against a military man trying to attain the near-impossible.

Vladimirov briefly studied the map on the table's glowing surface. If Gant's course had been accurately charted after he left Novaya Zemlya, then he was heading, though he could not yet know it, directly toward the missile-cruiser, the *Riga*, and her two attendant hunter-killer submarines. Out of that fact, if it was a fact, he could manufacture another trap.

Swiftly, he ordered search planes into the area of permanent pack toward which Gant was heading to make a possible landfall. It was possible to stop Gant. His finger unconsciously tapped the map at the point which registered as the present location of the *Riga*. At that moment, her two attendant protectors, the missile-carrying, diesel-powered "F" class anti-submarine submarines, were still submerged. Because of the importance of their role in protecting the missile-cruiser, they had been adapted to carry sub-surface-to-air missiles, to supplement the hideous fire-power of the *Riga* against aerial attack.

"Instruct the *Riga* to hold her present position," he called out, "and inform her two escorts to surface immediately."

"Sir," the code-operator replied, confirming the order.

"Send a general alert to all ships of the Red Banner Fleet," he said. "Prepare them for an alteration of Gant's suspected course. Give them that course."

"Sir."

"What is the prediction on Gant's fuel supply?" he said.

Another voice answered him promptly. "The computer predicts less than two hundred miles left, sir."

"How accurate is that forecast?"

"An error factor of thirty percent, sir—no more."

This meant that Gant might have fuel for another hundred and forty miles, or for nearly three hundred. Vladimirov rubbed his chin. Even the most generous estimate would leave him well short of the polar-pack. He ignored the inference, behaving as Buckholz's advisers had predicted. Vladimirov, since the days of his flying, had become a cautious man, unimaginative: daring by the standards of the Soviet high command, in reality safe, unimaginative. He could not make the mental jump required. If Gant's fuel would not last him to the pack, then the inference was that he would crash into the sea. There could not be another answer. He checked.

"Any unidentified aerial activity in the area?"

"None, sir. Still clear."

"Very well." He returned to his contemplation of the map. Gant would not take the aircraft up, not now, without fuel to make use of its speed. Therefore, as he had been doing when sighted, he would be traveling as close to the surface of the sea as he could. That meant, with luck, visual fire-control from the cruiser, at close range. Otherwise, there would be need to depend on infra-red weapons-aiming, which was not the most efficient of the fire-control systems aboard the *Riga*. However, it would do. It would have to do. . . .

A voice interrupted his train of thought. "Report from the Tower, Sir—Major Tsernik. PP2 is ready for take-off, sir."

Vladimirov's head turned in the direction of the voice, then, as his gaze returned to the map, he saw the First Secretary staring at him. He realized that something was expected of him, but he could not immediately understand what it was. There was no need to dispatch the second Mig, not now, with Gant more than three thousand miles away, and running out of fuel. He was not going to be able to refuel now, therefore the intercept role designed for the second plane was irrelevant.

"Who is the pilot?" the First Secretary asked bluntly.

"I—I don't believe I know his . . ." Vladimirov said, surprised at the question.

"Tretsov," Kutuzov whispered. "Major Alexander Tretsov."

"Good. I realize there is little time, but I will speak with him before he takes off." The First Secretary appeared to be on the point of rising.

Vladimirov realized, with a flash, that the First Secretary expected him to order the second proto-

type to take off and to pursue, at maximum speed,
the wake of the first.

Vladimirov knew it would take Tretsov less than
an hour to reach Novaya Zemlya on Gant's trail.
As far as he was concerned, it was a waste of time.
He looked at the First Secretary.

"Of course, First Secretary," he said politically,
judging the man's mood correctly. The First Secretary nodded in satisfaction. With an inward relief,
Vladimirov called over his shoulder: "Summon Major Tretsov at once. And tell the Tower and inform
all forces to stand by for take-off of the second Mig
within the next few minutes."

The refueling planes would need to be alerted.
At a point somewhere on the coast west of Gant's
crossing point, the Mig-31 would be refueled in the
air from a tanker. He ordered the alert. He realized
that he had to play the farce to its conclusion. It
would be impolitic, more than that, to voice his
feeling that Gant was not going to reach his fuel
supply, or that he was confident that the *Riga*
would bring him down.

The latter, he knew, would be a very unwise thing
to say, at this juncture.

He looked down at the map again. There was
nothing more to do. Now, it was up to the *Riga*,
and her attendant submarines. It was most certainly
not, he thought, up to Tretsov haring off into the
blue in pursuit.

There was still no signal from the "Deaf Aid." Gant's
fuel-gauge registered in the red, and he was flying on what he presumed was the last of the reserve
supply. He had switched in the reserve tanks minutes before. He had no idea of their capacity, but he
knew he was dead anyway unless he heard the signal from his fuel supply within the next couple of
minutes, and unless that signal was being transmitted from close at hand.

The sea was empty. The radar told him the sky

was empty of aircraft. He was dead, merely moving through the stages of decomposition while still breathing. That was all.

It occurred to Gant that Buckholz's refueling point had been an aircraft, one that had attempted to sneak in under the DEW-line—one that had been picked up, challenged, and destroyed. There *had* been a refueling tanker, but it no longer existed.

He did not think of death, not in its probable actuality, drowning, freezing to death, at the same time as the plane slid beneath the wrinkled waves. Despite what one of Buckholz's experts had described as a tenuous hold on life, Gant was reluctant to die. It was not, he discovered, necessary to have a great deal to live for to be utterly opposed to dying. Death was still a word, not a reality—but the word was growing in his mind, in letters of fire.

The radar screen registered the presence ahead of a surface vessel of large proportions. Even as he moved automatically to take evasive action, and his mind moved more slowly than his arm to question the necessity of such action, the screen revealed two more blips, one on either side of the surface vessel. He knew what he was looking at. Nothing less than a missile cruiser would merit an escort of two submarines. He was moving directly on a contact-course toward them.

The read-off gave him a time of one minute at his present speed to the target. He grinned behind his face-mask at the word that formed in his mind. Target. A missile cruiser. He, Gant, was the target. No doubt, the ship's infra-red had already spotted him, closed his height and range, tracked his course and fed the information into the fire-control computer. There was, already, no effective evasive action he could take.

If he was to die, he thought, then he wanted to see what the Firefox could really do. He made no conscious decision to commit suicide by remaining on his present course. He would have been incapa-

ble of understanding what he was doing in the light
of self-immolation. He was a flyer, and the enemy
target was ahead of him—a minute ahead.

It was then that the "Deaf Aid" shrieked at him.
He was frozen in his couch. He could not look at the
visual read-out on the face of the "Deaf Aid." He
did not want to know by how little he had missed,
how little the time was between living and dying.
The missile cruiser and the submarines closed on the
radar screen even as he watched them. Distance to
target read-out was thirty seconds. Because of his
near zero height, he had been on top of them before
he knew. Now it was too late.

The "Deaf Aid" signal was a continuous, maddening noise in his headset, like a frantic cry, a blinding
light. He stared ahead of him, waiting for the visual
contact with the missile cruiser, waiting to die.

8
MOTHER ONE

It could have been no more than a fraction of a second, that pause between fear and activity, that tiny void of time before the training that had become instinct flooded in to occupy the blank depth of his defeat, his numb, stunned emptiness. Nevertheless, in that fraction of time, Gant might have broken—the resolution of despair, suddenly shattered by the clamor of the homing signal, and the read-out which told him that the distance was less than one hundred and forty-six miles to his refueling point, to fuel and life—but he did not break. The huge blow to his system was somehow absorbed by some quality of personality that Buckholz or his psychologists at Langley must have recognized in his dossier, must have assumed to be still present in him. Perhaps it had only been the assumption by Buckholz that an empty man cannot break.

There was a fierce thrill that ran through him. A cold anger. A restrained, violent delight. He was going against the Russian missile cruiser. He clung to that idea.

Swiftly, coolly, he analyzed the situation. The homing device indicated that the source of the signal-emission, whatever it was, lay in an almost-direct line beyond the cruiser. His fuel-guage told him he could not take avoiding action. The shortest distance between two points . . . and he was looking for the shortest distance. He had to. He had to commit himself. Even if he wanted to live—and he realized, with a cold surprise, as if suddenly finding something he had lost for years, that he *did* want to live—he still had to go against the missile cruiser and its horrendous firepower. Now that there was no alternative, it was the path to life and not to death, and the thought gave him a grim satisfaction.

Radar analysis indicated that the two submarines were approximately three miles to port and starboard of the cruiser, providing a sonar and weapons screen for the big ship. Now they had surfaced, and would be training their own infra-red systems in his direction. If he remained at zero feet, they would be on his horizon, making an accurate fix by their fire-control difficult—with luck, he would have only the cruiser to worry about. The submarine closest to him, depending on which side he passed the cruiser, would not dare to loose off infra-red missiles in close proximity to the cruiser and its huge turbines.

Swiftly he analyzed the capability of the cruiser's weapons against the Firefox. At his speed, any visual weapon control was out of the question. The torpedo-tubes were for submarines only, as were the mortars, four in twin mountings. The hunter-killer helicopters might be in the air, but they might not have yet been armed with air-to-air weapons to do him any damage—though they were there, he acknowledged, and their fire control was linked into the central ECM control aboard the cruiser. The guns, 60 mm mounted forward of the bridge, would be controlled by the same electronic computerized fire-control system, linked to the search radar, which operated also in infra-red. Yet they were not important. At speed, at zero feet, they could, in all probability, not be sufficiently depressed to bear on him if he flew close enough to the ship.

He stripped the cruiser of its armaments, one by one. There was only one left—the four surface-to-air missile launchers of the advanced SA-N-3 type. Neither the surface-to-surface, nor the anti-sub missiles, had any terrors for him. But the SA missiles would be infra-red, heat-seeking, armed and ready to go.

He remembered the Rearward Defense Pod and prayed that it would work. The SA missile twin-launchers were located forward of the bridge super-structure, leaving the fattened, widened aft quarter of the ship for the four Kamov helicopters. Hoping to present the smallest target possible to him, the ship would be directly head-on to his course. There was no time now for any attack on the cruiser itself. Gant abandoned the idea without regret of any kind. He was part of the machine he flew, now; cold, cal-culating, printing-out the information recovered from his memory of his briefing.

He wondered how good the cruiser captain's brief-ing had been. Had he been told of the tail-unit, of the armament of the Firefox, or its speed? He as-sumed not. The Soviet passion for secrecy, for op-erating the most compartmentalized security ser-vice in the world, would operate like a vast inertia, the inertia of sheer habit, against the Red Navy officer being told more than was necessary. He would have received an order—stop the unidentified air-craft, by any means possible.

The read-out gave the time-to-target as twenty-one seconds, distance to target as two point two miles. Soon, within seconds, he would see the low shape ahead of him. It was the Firefox against the . . . He wished he knew the name of the cruiser.

A long, low ice-floe slipped beneath the belly of the Firefox, dazzlingly white against the bitter, unreflecting gray of the Barents Sea. He had passed

over other floes during the past few minutes, the
southernmost harbingers of the spring drift of the
impermanent pack. Then he saw the cruiser, a low
shape on the edge of the horizon which neared
with frightening rapidity. He felt that moment of
tension, as the adrenalin pumped into his system,
and the heart hammered at the blood, the precursor
of action.

He wondered whether the cruiser would wait like
a complacent animal, to swallow him in its fire, or
whether it would launch a brace of missiles while
he was still more than a mile away. Infra-red was
imprecise—technology had been unable to narrow
the inevitable spread of a heat-source as it registered
on the screen. It was not a good way to obtain an
accurate fix. Nevertheless, fire-control aboard the
cruiser, using infra-red missiles, did not need to be
precise.

He knew he was now visible to the men on the
bridge, a gray petrel seemingly suspended just above
the surface of the icy water. He watched the screen,
waiting for the sudden bloom of missile-exhausts to
emerge from the bulk of the cruiser. At the moment
of launch, any SA missile would show up as a bright
orange pinprick.

On the radar screen, he picked up what he guessed
was one of the cruiser's Kamov helicopters, and his
ECM read-out calculated height and range. He decided to launch one of his own AA missiles, as a
diversion, let the electronic adrenalin of the information flood the cruiser's fire-control computer, let
the physical diversion of a hit on the chopper add
another dimension to the chessboard across which he
moved towards the cruiser.

He launched. The missile pulled away, and
whisked up and out of his view. He watched it tracking across the screen, homing on the helicopter
which, he knew, would have picked up the missile,
and would be scuttling to take avoiding action. Gant

bared his teeth behind his facemask. The electronic war that was all he had ever known thrilled him to the bone, every nerve and muscle fulfilled. War was reduced to a game of chess, to an elaboration upon elaboration of move and counter-move. And he was the best.

The deck of the cruiser bloomed with pale fire, brighter spots on the screen. They had waited, anticipating that he would pull away from the threat of the submarines and the helicopters. Yet he had maintained the same course, heading directly towards them. The fire-control on the bridge, as he had hoped, had been triggered by his own attack upon the Kamov—the helicopter burst into flames in the sky above him, but he saw it only peripherally as a sudden orange flower, petals falling . . .

They had wanted to drive him between the cruiser and one of the submarines, expected him to pull up and away from them. But he had kept coming at them. Whatever the Soviet captain knew or did not know, he would have been told of the perilous estimate of the Firefox's fuel supply. That would have driven him to action. The Soviet captain had jumped the gun, triggered by Gant into a reflex action.

The ship was only hundreds of yards ahead of him as the SA missiles leapt from the twin-launcher forward of the bridge. Gant pulled away, sliding with exposed underbelly to port, to pass the cruiser. On the screen in front of him, he saw the missiles deviate from their original track, to close on him with frightening speed. Then, at his silent command as he reached the optimum moment, the thought-guided weapons-system triggered the tail-unit. Behind him, suddenly, there was an incandescent flare that paled the sun. He shoved the throttles forward, and the Firefox leapt across the water like a spun stone, skipping the tops of the wrinkled waves, the bows of the cruiser looming above the cockpit in one brief,

momentary glance, and then he could see nothing
but the gray water as he passed no more than fifty
yards from the ship's plates.

Behind him, the tail-unit, releasing a heat-source
which, for four seconds burned far hotter than his
two Turmansky turbojets at low speed, attracted the
pair of heat-seeking missiles, and the ball of fire on
the screen brightened until it seemed to hurt his
eyes, even behind his tinted facemask. Then the
bloom died suddenly. On the screen, the cruiser was
more than a mile behind him as he went supersonic.

His fuel-gauge registered empty. The Mach-counter showed him steadied at Mach 1.6. The altimeter
showed him skipping over the sea at less than fifty
feet, still, he hoped, out of sight of the submarines
and their infra-red, though by now they would have
a transmitted bearing and range from the cruiser.

He watched the screen, saw the two patches of
dull orange from the exhausts of a second pair of
SA infra-red missiles overhauling him. The Soviet
captain had been premature. He had been waiting
for the better target, the optimum moment, but the
trick of the tail-unit must have taken him by surprise. However, he had responded by ordering the
release of two more missiles—and . . .

Gant saw the patch of light at the port edge of the
screen as another two remotely launched SA missiles from the submarine nearest to him began to
converge on his exhaust.

He checked the read-out on the "Deaf Aid." The
bearing of the transmitter remained dead ahead of
his present course, right on the last course he had
fed into the aircraft after leaving the Novaya Zemlya
channel. The distance was still one hundred and
sixteen miles to its location. The homing signal began to clamor at his brain in the silent aftermath
of the split seconds of violent action. He knew it
was imperative to slow down.

Easing the throttles back he slowed, so that on

the screen the four distant dots of dull orange
seemed to draw swiftly nearer. The tail-unit had
worked. Gant knew he was gambling, but this time
he had an alternative, whereas before he had had
none. He could attempt to outrun the pursuing missiles until his fuel ran out.

It was a curious sensation of helplessness, with
not even a button to press, as his only link with
reality seemed to be the four closing points of orange
light. He felt, since he was not looking up from the
screen, as if he were a still, helpless point, a kind of
sacrifice. He could feel the sweat beneath his arms,
running down his sides, chill inside the pressure-
suit. He knew that under the weight of the grip he
was exerting on the throttles, his hand was shaking
fiercely. He waited . . .

He threw the throttles forward, and the Firefox
leapt like a startled animal, flew like a terrified
bird. The tail-unit released again and the explosion
was almost instantaneous, huge and audible; then
the shock-wave rocked the Firefox and he fought
to steady the plane. It was like an extra thrust of
engine-power. Quickly, he eased back the throttles
and the speed dropped to below 170 knots once
more.

He ignored the fuel-gauge. His eyes turned to the
"Deaf Aid" his whole attention being to the noise
of the homing signal. Less than a hundred miles. In
the sudden, almost sexual release after his escape
from the coordinated missiles from cruiser and submarine, he didn't see how he could make it.

Ice-floes, larger, more frequent now, passed beneath the belly of the Firefox as he headed north.

The First Secretary's conversation was brief, and
to the point. He wasted no time on an appeal to Major Alexander Tretsov's loyalty as a Russian and as
a member of the party, or on specious inspiration.
Rather, he used the other weapon which had become synonymous with his name—fear. He told

Tretsov what was at stake, and he impressed upon him the price of failure. Tretsov was to head northwards, at top speed, using the phenomenal power of the Mig-31, and to rendezvous with a tanker-aircraft over the northern coastline of Russia. From there, he would head for the current position of the *Riga*, from which vessel there had, as yet, been no report; here another tanker would be waiting in the event that he required a further refueling. The tankers were already en route to their contact coordinates.

Tretsov had been visibly nervous of the weight being thrust upon his shoulders. For a senior test pilot in the Red Air Force, he was young, in his early thirties, and he looked younger than that. Vladimirov had felt for him as the whole crushing weight of the First Secretary's personality acted upon him, and the silent presence of Andropov struck coldly. Yet he was good, his record was a fine one, Vladimirov was forced to admit. Whether, in the unlikely event of his being able to locate Gant, he was good enough to destroy the American, was another matter. Vladimirov was almost sorry for Tretsov that he was to be put to the test. He was technically the junior test pilot on the Bilyarsk project, and had flown fewer hours than his senior, Voskov—but Voskov was dead, killed by Gant. The KGB had found his body in the locker. Rather grotesquely, it had fallen comically out of the locker like a mummy from a sarcophagus.

The atmosphere in the War Command Center after the departure of the chastened, grim-mouthed Tretsov was, for the First Secretary, more congenial. The exercise of power, and the gratifying obedience tinged with fear that had shown itself in the pilot's eyes, soothed him, reinforced his sense of the overwhelming odds ranged against Gant, the American who had dared . . . The First Secretary felt his anger rising again, and fought to calm himself. The second Mig-31, cleansed of the foam sprayed on it following the attempted sabotage, and armed to the

teeth with AA missiles and cannon-shells, sat at the
end of the main runway, waiting for the final clear-
ance from the Tower. In moments, it would pass
close to the First Secretary's Tupolev. The Soviet
leader positioned himself at one of the small port-
holes let into the room to observe the take-off.

For Vladimirov, the situation was neither so simple, nor so gratifying. For the Commandant of
"Wolfpack," the period of the conversation of the
First Secretary with the almost silent Tretsov had
been a period of anxiety. The First Secretary appeared to wish to ignore the minutes ticking away,
the time approaching of Gant's expected interception with the course of the missile cruiser and her
two subs. The Soviet leader listened, perhaps, to
other voices, in other rooms. But Vladimirov knew
that the cruiser *had* to stop Gant, that it was the
last chance; last, because he still didn't know how
Gant expected to refuel, but knew that he must.
He churned the possibilities in his mind, in an attempt of his own to ignore the clock with its red
second-hand sliding round the face.

Carrier . . . carrier-sub . . . polar-pack . . . aircraft
. . . ditch, to be collected by sub?

None of them made any sense. It was almost impossible for a sub to hide itself in the Barents Sea
and he had nothing but a wild theory that the Americans could have produced a carrier-sub, especially
since the Mig was not adapted for a carrier-landing
of any kind. No, it had to be an aircraft. And there
wasn't one. Unpalatable though it was, it was the
truth. There was no unidentified aircraft in the
area, nor likely to be at the time one would be required by Gant.

He considered the possibility of Gant ditching the
Mig at sea, hoping for collection by a submarine. The
plane would be submerged, and could then be towed
behind the submarine back to wherever the CIA
had arranged. It was fantastic, but it might be made
to work. The plane would be damaged by sea water,

but the Americans would learn sufficient from it to remove the Mig-31 completely as a threat to air superiority.

Yet there was no submarine in the area either, and no surface vessel capable of reaching Gant's last position for hours.

Which meant it had to be the polar-pack. Gant must be hoping to use the last of his fuel in as steep a climb as he could muster, and to glide the remainder of the way. It was a desperate idea, but no more desperate than sending one man in the first place to take on the KGB, in order to get out of Moscow and arrive at Bilyarsk. And Gant had done that at the bidding of his masters—why not this? The theory was that an aircraft like the Mig could gain perhaps as much as two miles in a glide for every thousand feet it climbed. Gant could climb high enough, if he had the fuel, to glide to the edge of the permanent pack.

He was on the point of requesting the puzzle be fed to the computer for analysis when he heard the voice of the code-operator. The computer-conceived code in which the message had been transmitted from the *Riga* had been broken down and it was this that the operator read from his print-out.

"Sir," he said. "Message from the *Riga* . . ." It was as if the operator were unwilling to proceed with it, feeling the attention of the room drawn to him in an instant.

"What is it?" Vladimirov snapped.

"Contact made with unidentified aircraft. Missiles fired, infra-red type, from cruiser in two groups of two, and from submarine escort in one group of two . . ."

"Well?"

"The aircraft appeared to be carrying some kind of drone tail-unit which detached and ignited." There was a pause, then: "The Mig-31, sir, wasn't destroyed as far as they can tell. It was already over all radar horizons before the contact time of the mis-

siles, but the captain is not prepared to verify positive contact." The code-operator looked directly at
Vladimirov. "He would like clarification of the type
and capability of the aircraft that he attempted to
destroy, sir."

Vladimirov's head spun round, so that his eyes
stared into the gray, slaty surfaces of those of the
Soviet leader. The words of challenge and contempt
which were rising to his lips died in his mind. He
said nothing. The face that confronted him was im-
placable, and all the righteous indignation that O.C.
"Wolfpack" felt was squashed, buried. He could not
throw his career away, not so lightly as that, in heap-
ing his recriminations upon the First Secretary. Instead, he snapped at the code-operator.

"Secrecy must be maintained. Thank him for
the job he—*attempted* to do, and order him to stand
by for further instructions."

"Sir!"

The keys of the encoding-console clicked almost
at once. The disguised mimicry of the First Secretary's maxim concerning security was the furthest
Vladimirov felt he could allow himself to go. The
recognition made him ashamed. Then he dismissed
the feeling.

"What do you intend to do now, Vladimirov?" the
First Secretary asked him, his mouth a straight line,
his eyes completely without expression. In that face,
in that moment, Vladimirov saw the truth of power
in the Soviet Union, saw the heart of the cadres
and coteries that were contained within the Kremlin. Because the First Secretary was able to put the
blame for failure upon others, then the failure itself
was no longer important. If Vladimirov were dismissed, disgraced for the loss of Mig-31, that would
be all that would matter. This man before him cared
nothing for the realities of the situation, only for the
personal politics of his own survival.

Vladimirov was sickened, rather than frightened.
With selflessness in extremity taught as one of the

virtues of the military caste to which his family had belonged for generations, he gave no thought to his own survival or success. Yet the Mig-31 must not be lost to the Americans, thrown away.

"I—I shall order all available units into the area of the *Riga,* First Secretary," he managed to say in a level voice, from which he carefully excluded any trace of anger, or bitterness.

"And—what will *they* do?" Andropov asked with contempt.

Kutuzov came to his rescue. Perhaps he, too, had been sickened by what he had silently witnessed in the War Command Center, or perhaps he sensed the tension in Vladimirov and intended to help save his career for him. Whatever, the old man's bravery as he spoke with contempt to the Chairman of the Committee for State Security made Vladimirov warm towards him.

"*They,* as you put it, Chairman, will make every effort to recover the Mig-31 that your poor security in Moscow and at Bilyarsk allowed to be successfully stolen by one man—one single American!" The whisper from the ruined throat carried clearly to every ear in the room, the tone of the voice imprinting itself on every consciousness. The Chairman of the KGB flushed, two points of color on the parchment-toned skin over the cheek bones. The smile, cynical and aloof, disappeared from his face.

Vladimirov transferred his gaze to the First Secretary's face. The Soviet leader appeared disconcerted, as if reminded of painful realities. He said, as if somehow to make amends without actual apology:

"Mihail Ilyich—I know that you will do all you can. But—what is it that you propose to do, with the whole of the Red Banner Northern Fleet and most of 'Wolfpack,' northern sector, at your disposal?" The voice was calm, almost gentle—mollifying.

Kutuzov turned his gaze to Vladimirov, nodded, as if at some secret understanding, and then Vladimirov said: "The first priority, First Secretary, is to order the take-off of the Mig." The First Secretary turned back to the small window, as if prompted by the calculated priority the O.C. "Wolfpack" had placed on his own pet surmise.

"Of course," he said. "Pass the order to the Tower." The order was transmitted by one of the radio-operators. Still keeping his gaze on the runway through the window, he said: "And—next?"

Vladimirov looked down at the map in front of him, revealing the bright, isolated points of light in the wastes of the Barents Sea, north to the permanent pack.

"Order the *Riga* and her submarine escorts to alter course, and head north in the wake of the Mig at all possible speed."

Over the clicks of the encoding-console, Vladimirov heard the First Secretary mutter: "Good." Already, it appeared, the man's huge complacency was returning. Vladimirov had noted it often before, in his dealings with those who governed his country, the anodyne that could be found in action.

He looked down at the map, ignoring the broad back of the First Secretary in the gray suit, the fabric stretched across the powerful shoulders. Were he a less elevated individual, he thought, it might be possible to draw comfort from that rigid stance, that overbearing impression of strength.

"Scramble the Polar Search squadrons immediately," he ordered. He watched the leonine head nod in approval, saw the shoulders settle comfortably. Surface craft, he thought. "Order the missile destroyers *Otlitnyi* and *Slavny* to proceed with all possible speed to the predicted landfall of the Mig on the permanent pack."

"Sir."

"The three 'V'-type submarines to proceed at once on courses to the same landfall reference."

"Sir."

Vladimirov paused. Faintly through the fuselage

of the Tupolev, he heard the whine of engines running up. The Mig, cleared from the Tower, was preparing for take-off. He did not cross to the tiny window as he heard the engines increase in volume as
the Mig raced down the runway. Instead, he watched
the shoulders of the First Secretary and the slight,
hopeful tilt of the head. There was a blur from the
runway beyond the window, and then the unmis-
takable sound of a jet aircraft pulling away from the
field in a steep climb. For a moment, the First Secretary remained at the window, as if deep in contemplation, then he turned back into the room, and
Vladimirov noticed the slight smile on his face.

The distance to the transmitter of the homing-signal
still crying from the "Deaf Aid" registered as ninety-
two miles. The fuel-gauges registered empty. Gant
was flying on little more than fresh air, and he knew
it. It was time—and it might already be too late—
to go into a zoom climb and begin the long glide to
the contact-point with the refueling-tanker.

The more he considered the problem, the more
Gant became convinced that such a glide was his
only chance. He had to go as high as possible, and
then hope that he would leave himself enough fuel
for the tricky and delicate task of matching speeds
with the tanker-aircraft, and coupling to the fuel-
umbilical trailing behind the tanker. Not once had
he considered that the tanker might be some kind of
surface craft. It could not be a carrier—the USN
would not dare put a huge and vulnerable target
like that into the Barents Sea. Unlike Vladimirov,
he knew that the Americans had developed no carrier-sub.

Therefore, he was going to have to refuel in the
air. He knew the Firefox's predecessor, the Mig-25
Foxbat, had established an absolute altitude record
of almost 119,000 feet, and that the Firefox was intended as being capable of a greater performance.
And, in the present atmospheric conditions, at two-

and-a-half miles for every thousand feet of height, he could easily reach the tanker, if he could only pull the Firefox up to an altitude of perhaps forty or more thousand feet.

Yet he had to take a terrible risk. He still had to have plenty of height when he made the rendezvous, and sufficient fuel left for the final maneuvers.

The fuel-tanks of the Firefox had to be almost empty—had to be, he told himself. It was one aspect of the aircraft with which he was not familiar. Though he had asked Baranovich, the electronics engineer had been unable to help him.

The engines, at his crawling speed across the gray, ice-littered sea, still operated without hesitation. Yet he could take no further risk. The automatic emergency tanks must have cut in by that time, and he had no idea of the extra range they would give him but he suspected it wouldn't be sufficient to take him to the contact-point.

He pushed the throttles forward, and pulled back on the column. The nose of the Firefox lifted and he accelerated, watching the altimeter begin to climb, steadily at first, and then more and more rapidly as he increased the thrust of the two huge turbojets. He seemed not to breathe, not once during the minute-and-a-half of climb. The pale, spring blue of the sky began to deepen as he climbed.

He leveled out at sixty-two thousand feet, throttling back the engines until there was just sufficient power to maintain the function of the generators. At that height, he would be at about twenty-seven thousand feet when he arrived at the tanker's location. It would be enough. He checked the screen. Nothing.

There was only one thing to hope—that it remained as clean of activity as it was at that moment.

The bearing of the signal remained dead ahead of him. The distance read-out gave him eighty-eight miles to target. He still wondered how much fuel remained, and the thought nagged at him. He began to think that he might have overplayed the safety margin, with regard to his zoom climb. It must have drained the emergency tanks.

Ahead of him, far ahead, he saw the gray heaviness of cloud building up. The screen remained empty of activity. The Firefox glided silently through an empty sky, the dark blue canopy of the thin upper layers of the atmosphere above, the tiny, silent grayness of the northern limits of the Barents Sea below. Ahead of him, far ahead, beyond where the cloud seemed to be building, there was an edge of whiteness in sight—the polar-pack.

United States Navy Captain Frank Delano Seerbacker lay on his cramped bunk in his cramped quarters aboard the USS *Pequod,* a nuclear-powered "Sturgeon" class submarine, as it drifted beneath the ice-floe whose southward path it had imitated for the past five days. Seerbacker's submarine had passed beneath the polar-pack near the western coast of Greenland and, rigged for silent running, had slithered out into the Barents Sea after fourteen days at sea.

The journey had possessed three distinct phases for the captain, his officers and the crew. There had been the top-speed dash from the submarine's concealed base on the Connecticut coast, then the claustrophobic passage beneath the polar ice—and since then, the captain thought again with irritation, they had been drifting without engines, averaging three-point-one miles a day beneath the floe.

The *Pequod* was unarmed, another fact which Seerbacker bitterly resented. The submarine's torpedo room and forward crew's quarters were flooded with high-octane kerosene, fuel for the super-plane that the CIA was stealing for the good old US of A.

Seerbacker's craggy, lined face creased in a frown of contempt. His long nose flared. He disliked, he decided, the CIA—especially when that crud organization told him to sit under a damn ice-floe and wait for a superjet to land on it!

He stirred on his cot, raising his knees merely for the sake of altering the position of his limbs. His hands were behind his head, and he was staring sightlessly at the ceiling. He and his men were sick, he decided, of the whole monotonous routine of the mission; sick to death, following the ice-floe's unvarying, snail-like course southward.

It wasn't, he thought grimly, as if they'd even had the change of routine involved in looking for a suitable floe. The floe—the so-called runway, he thought with contempt—had been selected from the study of hundreds of satellite photographs, in the first instance, the findings of which had been checked and confirmed by a Lockheed Orion which had collected both photographs and visual findings. Proven statistical data from oceanographic surveys allowed experts at Langley to make a firm prediction about the floe's ability to take the weight of the Firefox. Seerbacker had merely been told where to find it. He realized he was being merely bloody-minded in cursing the domination of machinery, but he went on doing so anyway. There was after all, he told himself, damn all else to do except to curse the temporal powers and their crazy ideas, who had got him into this mess, who had messed up his boat with their kerosene!

There was a soft knock at his door.

"What?" he said, irritated rather than thankful at being roused from his fruitless reverie. A crewman handed him a sheaf of flimsy. On it, in the hand of his Exec, who was acting as weather-officer, he read the information that he had been expecting, but which was doubly unwelcome when it came. The temperature of the air above the floe was dropping much too rapidly. Cloud was building up in the area, cloud that would mask from Gant the position and dimensions of the floe.

Seerbacker tossed his head at the information. It was his bloody luck, just his godawful luck! He dismissed the crewman. He needed no further information. If there was anything else, then the Exec. would send it to him. He had no need to go to the control room, not yet. He cursed again the constant trimming of the tanks, the regular, futile checks to be made on the kerosene that flooded the tubes and the forward quarters, and on the weather, the surface temperature of the floe, the condition of the ice surface. . . . It was, he decided, no job for a man with twenty years in the service, and with one of the best crews in the Navy.

He considered the information concerning the air temperature. It was dropping rapidly, which could, and probably would, mean a change in the weather conditions which had been unusually settled and mild for those latitudes and the time of year. The change, when it came, could so easily become freezing fog, localized in their area, spreading perhaps as little as a few square miles. In freezing fog, Seerbacker did not have to know anything about aircraft and pilots to know that there was no way Gant could land on the floe. They had no navigational aids aboard that could help him, allow him to make an automatic landing—nothing except the transmitter that would tell Gant where they were. Already, as the message had told him, there was a local build-up of cloud. Perhaps Gant might not be able to get down, even in that. . . .

The introduction of doubt prompted his mind to review the emergency procedures. In the final event, he was to avoid capture at all costs. It could never be admitted by Washington that a submarine of the U.S. Navy had been a part of the scheme to steal the Firefox—he was to destroy the *Pequod,* if necessary, to prevent its capture by the Russians.

His mind winced away from the secret orders he had opened at sea; if Gant failed to land on the floe, or if he crashed onto the ice, or into the sea in the vicinity of the *Pequod*, then he was to make every effort to rescue the pilot—and an even greater effort to capture the plane, and tow it home beneath the ice-pack. The havoc that would cause with his crew, and his navigation, he was not prepared to consider. It was, he knew, theoretically feasible, but he hoped that none of this would be necessary and that Gant was good enough to set the Firefox down like a feather.

The trouble was, Seerbacker admitted to himself finally—Gant was late. He had been briefed as to the performance and range of the Firefox, and the ETA for the plane over the floe had already passed—was minutes past. And with that plane, he knew, minutes were really huge gaps of time—a big enough gap for a man's death. He would not know whether Gant had even stolen the plane until it appeared, or failed to appear, on the submarine's infra-red. Up through the ice was thrust a single metal spike, camouflaged in white, carrying the transmitter of the homing-signal tuned to Gant's "Deaf Aid," the complex, changing signal that he should be picking up. It was his one and only link with the American pilot.

Seerbacker cursed the British designer for not including a facility, built-in, so that Gant could identify himself—but it was strictly one-way. The *Pequod* transmitted, and the Firefox received—at least, until the aircraft was close enough for the transponder in the homing device to emit an identification signal, and that distance was within visual range anyway. As his Exec. had commented—if General Dynamics had fitted it as standard equipment in "Sturgeon" class subs, it would dispense Coca-Cola, along with doing the laundry and playing canned music. Seerbacker's lips twisted in a reflective smile.

When Gant appeared over the floe, the frequency of the signal he received would change, and he would hear the equivalent of an instantaneous echo, as on sonar. Then, no doubt, to his appalled mind it

would become clear that he would have to land on
an ice-floe—in cloud, Seerbacker added vitrioli-
cally, perhaps in freezing fog. This would probably
mean scraping the pilot off the ice, sinking the remains of the plane, and towing it thousands of miles
back to Connecticut. It didn't bear thinking about.

Gant was late. The thought nagged at him. Minutes only—but late. His fuel must be shot to hell
by now, Seerbacker thought savagely. Must be. He
thought about going down to the control-room, almost swung his long, thin legs off the cot, and then
decided against it. After five days, he couldn't start
showing a yellow flag as soon as the guy was a
couple of minutes overdue. He reflected that there
was very little aerial activity in the area—even if
that lack of activity included Gant.

There was no comfort to be found, he decided.
None at all. . . .

Surprisingly, it was Buckholz, massive, self-confi-
dent, almost silent Buckholz, who cracked first. Aubrey had been aware of the tension rising in the
room as the morning wore on, after Shelley had
cleared the breakfast remains, and they had finished with the coffee. Then, suddenly, there had
been nothing to do. The tension in the room had
been palpable, lifting the hair at the nape of the
neck like static electricity. A profound silence had
descended on the five occupants, broken only by
the creaking of the stepladder whenever Curtin as-
cended or descended, pinning his satellite weather
photographs to the wall, or altering and supplement-
ing the colored pins in the map of the Barents Sea.

Buckholz had ceased to take notice of the map.
For more than half an hour he had not looked once
in its direction. It was as if he were listening to some
inner voice, seeing some mental image, and did not
need the confirmation of pictures and pins.

Aubrey knew why he was silent, grim-faced,

tense. He shared that tension because he, too, understood how perilous Gant's fuel state must be. The last report from the *Pequod*, from Mother One and Seerbacker, was a routine weather report which contained no coded reference to sighting Gant by infra-red and contained, moreover, some discouraging news concerning the weather in the area of the floe, news that would make it difficult for Gant to land. Aubrey did not want his neat, carefully conceived, methodically executed operation to end with the humiliation of a crash-landing on the floe, and the ignominy of a Firefox damaged and affected by the corrosive sea-water from being towed home behind the *Pequod*.

But, it was the fuel state that worried him, more than the weather. To Buckholz, Aubrey guessed, it signified that Gant had already failed. Aubrey glanced up at the clock, and then again at Buckholz. It was the wrong thing to do, he realized, to remind Buckholz of what he had evidently forgotten but nevertheless, he said, his voice carefully deferential:

"Is it not time we released the decoy submarine into the arena, Buckholz?"

There was a moment of silence, then Buckholz, his lips working, snapped: "What in hell's name for?" His eyes glared at Aubrey, as if the latter had interrupted some kind of ritual, solemn and awful, proceeding within the American.

Aubrey spread his arms. "It is time, by the clock," he said blandly.

"Why waste it?" Buckholz asked.

"What?"

"The decoy—decoy for what, man?" Buckholz seemed to half-rise from his seat, as if to browbeat the small, rotund Aubrey.

"We don't *know* he's lost . . ." Aubrey began.

"What in the hell was all that coded stuff we picked up, between Bilyarsk and the *Riga*, then?"

Buckholz snapped. "They got him, Aubrey—blew the ass from under him!"

Aubrey tried to retain a smile of encouragement on his face, and said: "I don't know—it could have meant they *didn't* get him."

There was a silence. Buckholz seemed to sink back into his chair. Anders, standing behind him, a plastic cup clutched in his big hand, looked down at Buckholz's cropped head, then looked across the room at Aubrey. His gaze seemed quizzical. Aubrey nodded, and mouthed the single word: "Decoy." Anders crossed to a telephone in the corner, dialed a number, and spoke. Hearing his voice, Buckholz turned incuriously to watch him, then glanced across at Aubrey, and shook his head.

Buckholz had returned to his sightless contemplation of the papers in front of him. By that time Anders had completed his telephone call to an operations room in the M.O.D. which would alert the decoy submarine at that moment lying to the west of Spitzbergen and the decoy aircraft waiting to take off from Greenland, or already in the air to the east of that frozen land-mass.

Aubrey nodded to Anders in acknowledgment of his call, then proceeded to gaze across the room at the map. The decoy planes would be picked up by Russian landborne and seaborne radar within minutes, and be seen to be heading towards the vicinity of North Cape, while the submarine would entice Russian surface vessels and submarines to investigate, drawing them away from the *Pequod* while she was on the surface, refueling the Firefox.

A doubt suddenly struck him, cold in the pit of his stomach, clutching with a hot, burning sensation in his chest, like indigestion or a heart murmur. Would the *Pequod* ever need to surface? Looking again at Buckholz, it was evident that he didn't think so. Aubrey rubbed his smooth, cherubic cheeks, and wondered.

At twenty-two thousand feet, the Firefox dropped
into the top of the cloud-stack that Gant had
watched inexorably approaching. The silent, gliding
aircraft slid through the ruffled, innocuous edges of
the cloud, into the gray silence, with the helplessness of a stone. He had been unable to estimate the
depth of the stack—it could, he knew, reach down to
the surface of the pewter-colored sea. He was four
minutes to target, descending at a steady rate of
three-and-a-half thousand feet per minute, moving
ahead at 180 knots, three miles a minute. When he
reached the target location, he would still be eight
thousand feet above sea-level. It would have to be
enough. There was nothing on the screen. Only the
TFR reflected the monotonous pattern of ice-floes
slipping past him, below the cloud. There was nothing that looked remotely like a ship, anywhere within the limits of the target area. There was no aircraft. There was merely the incessant, monotonous
signal, emanating from some unknown source, beck-
oning.

In the cloud, Gant felt cold. The signal was his
only contact with reality, and yet it seemed to possess no other reality than that of sound. He was unable to believe in its physical source. Gant had always been an electronic pilot, always relied on
instruments. Stories older men told him, of flying
bombers over Germany in the last days of the last
war, were tales that might have come from ancient Greece—mythological. Therefore, he did not
panic, was not really afraid. The signal did have a
source, however distant, however ghostly. It was no
illusion. He trusted it.

Nevertheless, it began, subtly but certainly, to feel
cold in the cabin of the Firefox, a chill, arctic cold,
salt like the sea.

Seerbacker was swinging his legs off the bunk even
as his Exec.—who in his excitement had come in

person—peered round the door to his quarters and said, almost breathless with sudden, renewed tension: "Aircraft contact, sir—heading this way."

"Range?" Seerbacker snapped, tugging his cap on his head, and pressing past the younger man, who followed his captain's rapid progress towards the control-room.

"Less than four miles, sir—height about twelve thousand—she's on the bearing, sir. And there's no radar contact, only a very faint infra-red. She's either on lowest power or not using her engines at all."

Without looking behind him, Seerbacker said: "Then it's him." Then he added: "What's the surface temperature of the floe?"

"Still dropping, sir. Dewpoint's still a couple of degrees away."

Seerbacker suddenly stopped, and turned on his Exec. "A couple of degrees?" he repeated.

"Yes, sir."

"Wind?"

"Five to ten knots, variable."

"Insufficient turbulence, then?" he said mysteriously, and the younger man, Lt. Commander Dick Fleischer, nodded, understanding his drift. "But, what about *his* turbulence, when he comes in to land—uh? What happens then?"

"It shouldn't . . ." the younger man began.

"With this old tub's luck, Dick—what d'you think'll happen? He'll put the wheels down, stick back—and phut! The lights'll go out!" He tried to smile, but the effect was unconvincing. Both he and Fleischer knew that, however he said it, the content of his statement was deadly serious. Two degrees drop in the temperature would mean that the air above the surface of the floe would achieve dewpoint, that point on the scale where freezing fog would begin to form. The effect of the turbulence of the Firefox attempting to land could trigger the drop in temperature.

Seerbacker, as if prompted by his own lurid imaginings, clattered off down the companion-way. As soon as he thrust his thin, lanky form into the control-room of the sub, he said:

"Where is he?"

"Three miles—a little over eleven thousand feet, sir!" the radar-operator sang out.

"Is he still on the same bearing?"

"Sir."

"Can he see the floe?"

"Yes, sir. Cloudbase is thirteen-and-one-half thousand."

"Then let's surprise him, gentlemen," Seerbacker said with a grim smile. "Blow all tanks—hit it!"

The floe was the only thing down there that Gant really saw. He had dropped out of the cloud at thirteen thousand feet, only three minutes or a little more away from the target—and there it was. Big, perhaps two miles north-south, and almost the same across. It lay directly in his path. On the radar-screen, there was no craft of any kind. Yet the target lay less than six miles ahead of him. That floe was the right distance away. Only its distance from him had made him regard it at all.

He knew it had to be the floe. For a long time, he had suspected that he had never been intended to reach the polar-pack, nor had he ever been intended to rendezvous with a tanker-aircraft—that would have been too risky, too dangerous by half. It had to be the floe—and a landing. His eyes searched ahead, saw nothing. For a moment, then, he felt close to panic. A fat floe, like a dirty white water-lily on the surface of the bitter arctic water. It was surrounded by others, smaller for the most part. There was no sign of life! He felt the bile of fear at the back of his throat, and his mind refused to function, analyze the information—then it happened. The signal changed, the homing-signal began to emit a broken, bleeping call, two to the second. He recognized its similarity to a sonar-contact, instantaneous echo. Even as the seconds passed, the bleep became more and more insistent, urgent. He *was* closing on the target. He studied the condition of the sea, estimating the windspeed again—yes, five to ten knots, no more. Even before his questions had been answered, even before the shock of the changing signal had dispersed, he began the routines required if he were to land on the floe. The last of the ice-crystals starred on the windscreen dispersed under the effects of the de-mister. Again, more urgently now, he studied the surface of the floe, but only a small part of him was looking for signs of life. Principally he looked at the flatness, the length of possible runways, looked for markings, judged the direction of the wind . . .

When it came, it came with the sudden shock of freezing water, or a physical blow. At the western edge of the floe, away to port, and still ahead of him, the ice buckled, curled at the edge before cracking. The reinforced sail of a nuclear submarine came into view, and Gant saw the bulk of the ship beneath; ice spun away from it, sliding from its hull.

A bright orange balloon was released from the sail, and then an orange streamer of smoke which spurted vertically before the wind tugged it flat downwind of the submarine. Gant knew as soon as he saw the emerging sail that he was looking at an American submarine.

Automatically, he checked the radar. Negative. He eased on power, felt the aircraft shove forward, and dropped the nose. As he touched on the air-brakes, and stabilized his speed at 260 knots, the smoke was passing beneath his wingtip. He noticed, with almost idle curiosity, that the sonar-like pinging of the homing-device had changed to a continuous signal—instantaneous echo. The target was below him, a submarine full of kerosene; it would be a matter

of less than an hour before he was refueled, and
ready to take off. He hauled the aircraft to the left,
in a rate one turn that would line him up in the
direction of the wind-flattened smoke from the sail.

The wind direction was such that he would land
along the north-south axis of the floe, which gave
him almost two miles of snow-covered ice in which
to stop. He knew the snow, unless it was utterly
frozen, would act as an efficient braking-system—it
would be, he told himself with a grim smile, the
relief at finding the sub still warming him, like landing on a carrier—something else he had learned
to do in Vietnam.

He dropped the undercarriage, and the lights
glowed, registered the wheels "locked." He slowed
his speed to 220 knots, and leveled the wings. The
floe was ahead, with the dark cigar of the submarine
embedded in it, a lizard half-emerged from its shell,
its streamer of orange smoke in line with his course.

He checked back on the stick, and read his altitude as one thousand feet. He dropped his speed to
180 knots, and stabilized there. His rate of descent
was now 350 feet per minute. The grey, wrinkled
waves seemed to speed up, to reach up at him hun-
grily. He eased back the throttle, and the speed
dropped to 175 knots. He was almost dazzled now
by the glare of the ice-floe, yet through the dazzle,
the surface still looked good.

He chopped the throttle, and the Firefox suddenly seemed to sag tiredly in the air, began to sink.
He checked back on the stick into the flare-out position. On full flap, the Firefox seemed to drop for a
moment, then the plane jolted viciously as the
wheels bit into the surface snow, and the nose-wheel
slammed down. Visibility disappeared for a moment
as the snow spewed around the nose, and it was a
second or more before the de-mister coped. The forward screen cleared.

Even as Gant wondered whether the engine would

flame out because of snow in the air-intakes, he saw that his visibility had disappeared. He was rushing across a surface of ice and snow, enveloped in a thick, rolling gray fog.

9
PRESSURE

Gant understood what had happened—dewpoint; the formation of a thick, rolling blanket of fog along his rushing track had been almost instantaneous. The knowledge did not lessen the rising unease he felt, could not counteract the explosion of adrenalin in his system. The engines had not flamed out, and the snow flung up around the cockpit by the nose-wheel had slid from the screen—yet he could see nothing. He was helpless—the snow on the surface of the floe was slowing the aircraft as swiftly as any reverse thrust from the engines and yet he was slipping across an ice surface, down the north-south axis of a floe, toward the icy gray waters of the Barents Sea. If the size of the floe were too small, inadequate, if he had miscalculated, if . . .

The Firefox slowed to walking pace, trundling more unevenly now, jolted by the indentations and scabs of the surface ice beneath the thin blanket of snow. And the fog was already thinning, as the turbulence of his passage became less; it was spreading, thinning to a grey, damp mist. He looked over his

shoulder, shifting in the couch for perhaps the first
time in an hour. He could not see the orange balloon, nor could he see the line of the streamer of
smoke, which would give him some indication of the
direction of the sub. He turned the aircraft to port,
through one hundred and eighty degrees, and taxied
back up the line of his landing, crawling forward,
his eyes searching for figures moving in the mist,
lights or signals which might direct him. He felt
the unease and the adrenalin drain from him. He
was down.

He thought he saw a lumping, shapeless figure
moving to port of him, but could not be sure. The
mist seemed to have thickened again. The figure
had not been carrying a light. He pressed the button,
and raised the cockpit cover. The sudden change of
temperature as the heated air of the cabin rushed out
and was replaced by the arctic air above the floe
seemed to knife through the protection of the anti-
G suit as if it had been made of thin summerweight
cotton. He was chilled to the bone in a moment, his
teeth chattering uncontrollably behind the tinted
facemask of his flying helmet. His hands on the controls seemed to tremble, as if registering the ground-
shock of an explosion. He unlocked the helmet and
tugged it up and away from his head. His cropped
head seemed to prickle with a cold fire. Ignoring
the noise of his teeth, he craned his head, listening
and looking in the direction from which he had
glimpsed the figure in the mist.

He thought, twice, in swift succession, that he
heard voices away to his left, that he was paralleling the path of men searching for him—but he
couldn't be certain. The voices, like the cries of alien
birds, seemed to distort in the thick mist, and he
couldn't be sure of the direction from which they
came. Then he realized that the men would be heading to what they would have assumed was the point
of his halt, behind him now—they would not, per-

haps, have expected him automatically to make a
180 degree turn, and cover his tracks.

Then he saw a dull glow, lighting a misshapen,
lumbering figure, a lamp held low in a swinging
hand. He heard his own name being called, loudly,
yet seeming faint, unsubstantial. He did not reply,
and the figure called again. Gant felt a curious reluctance to speak, despite the cold, despite the sudden, rushing sense of loneliness, of the interminable
time of his journey from Bilyarsk—and before that,
from London. The voice was American. He smiled,
in spite of his detachment—that was it, he recognized, it was detachment he felt, a sense of *removal*
from this figure cautiously approaching. It was so, so
ordinary, a lumping shadow with a New York accent—nothing really to do with him, and the Firefox, and what he had done.

He shrugged off the feeling. The wind gusted to
perhaps twelve knots, and the blast of it struck him
in the face, reviving him to the present, to his physical cold and discomfort. He raised his hand to his
face, cupped it and yelled. His own voice sounded
thin, almost unreal. "Over here—the plane's over
here, man!"

"That you, Gant?" the voice replied. Gant realized
only as he began to cast about that his own eyesight
was vastly superior to that of the figure to his
left. He turned the Firefox in the mist, very slowly,
and saw the figure straighten, and become certain
of his whereabouts. "Jesus—I must need glasses,
for Chrissake," the figure said.

Gant had no need to apply the brakes; slowed by
the surface snow, the aircraft rolled to a halt. The
great turbojets made only an impatient murmur behind him. He could hear the figure, which now
seemed tall and thin, only given a tent-like shape by
the parka it was wearing, talking into an R/T handset.

"O.K., you men—I found him. Get over here, on

the double!" Then the figure moved forward. A mit-
tened hand slapped against the fuselage and Gant,
leaning out of the cockpit, stared down into an ascetic, lined face. He could see the gold leafing on the
peak of a Navy cap beneath the fur trimming of the
parka hood. Gant smiled, foolishly, feeling there was
nothing to say. A great wave of relief surged in him,
almost nauseous, and he began to shiver with emotion rather than the cold.

"Hi, fella," Seerbacker said.

"Hi," Gant said, in a choking voice. He saw other
figures moving in the mist, and the round globes,
furred and dim, of lamps.

"Hey, skipper—you want us to line up now?" a
voice called.

Seerbacker, seemingly distracted from a perusal of
Gant's features, turned his head, and yelled over his
shoulder. "Yeah—let's get this bird over to its mother—it's dying of thirst!" He turned back to Gant, and
added, in a low voice: "You don't look like anything
special, mister—but I guess you must be—uh?"

"Right now—you're pretty special yourself, Captain!" Gant said.

Seerbacker nodded, and lifted the handset to his
face. He said:

"O.K., this is the captain. Call it for me."

He listened intently as men began to call in, as
at a roll-call. When there was silence once more, he
looked up at Gant, and said: "I've got half of
my crew standing on this goddam ice, mister, in
two nice straight lines, all the way to the ship. Think
you can ride down the middle?"

"Like the freeway," Gant said.

Seerbacker raised his hand, gripped the spring-
loaded hand and toe holds and hoisted himself clear
of the ground.

"Mind if I hitch a ride?"

"They're pretty rough on freeloaders on this rail-
road."

"I'll take my chances," Seerbacker said with a grin. "O.K., let's roll."

Gant eased off the brakes, and the Firefox slid forward. He saw the first two men, their lights haloed, bright, and then other lights, a tunnel in the mist. He straightened the nose down the center of the tunnel, and the lights began to roll slowly past on either side, only just visible in the mist. He heard Seerbacker giving an order.

"O.K., you guys, move in, dammit! This bird won't bite—it's one of ours, for Chrissake!"

The lights ahead wobbled, narrowed, became brighter, more helpful to him.

"Thanks," he said to the invisible Seerbacker below him.

"O.K., mister. They're only here to help—even if they don't like it." There was an edge to his voice as he ended his sentence. Gant sensed, beneath the surface, the resentment that had emerged along with relief at his arrival—the resentment of men stuck in the middle of an enemy sea for day after day, tracking the drifting floe.

"I'm sorry," he said, involuntarily.

"What?" Seerbacker began, then added: "Oh, yeah. It's just orders mister—don't give a mind to it." Gant saw a long low shape, sail atop, ahead of him through the mist. "There she is," Seerbacker said unnecessarily, and Gant felt the pride in his voice. It was the pride of a commanding officer in his ship.

"Yeah—I see it," he said.

"Pull up alongside," Seerbacker said. "You want to eat in the car, or come on inside?" Gant swung the Firefox parallel with the fattened cigar of the ship, half-buried in ice, like something reptilian emerging from a white shell. He cut the motors, and the plane died. In the absolute silence of the next moment, Gant felt a fierce affection for the aircraft. It was not something he had stolen, a *freight* for the CIA—it was what had brought him from the heart of Russia, helped *him* to escape, taken on a missile-cruiser, taken on . . . Seerbacker interrupted the flood of his fierce, cold, mechanical love for another machine.

"Welcome to 'Joe's Diner'. The cabaret isn't much good, but the hamburgers are a delight to the weary traveler! Step down, Mister Gant—step down, and welcome."

Gant unstrapped himself from the webbing of the couch. As he stood up, his muscles and joints protested as he moved. The wind seemed to gust at him, the freezing cold from the Pole search through his suit, eat at him. He shuddered.

"Thanks," he said. "Thanks." He stepped out of the cockpit, no longer reluctant, down onto the ice.

"Call them out," Vladimirov said. "A report from every Polar Search Squadron now!"

It took four minutes for the report to be completed, time which the First Secretary seemed not to consider wasted, wherever Gant was, and whatever he was doing. Vladimirov loathed the political game that was being played and in which he had joined, his silence giving assent, his cowardice dictating his silence. When the last search-plane had reported on its findings in its designated area, it was clear that there had been no attempt by the Americans to establish any kind of fuel-dump on the ice, no attempt to mark out or clear any kind of runway. Vladimirov, his belief shaken but not destroyed, felt his bemusement hum in his head like a maddening insect. He *had* the answer, somewhere at the back of his mind, he was sure of it . . . !

The cold eyes of the First Secretary, and the glint of the strip-light on Andropov's glasses, made him bury his reflections.

"Now," the Soviet leader said, "order all available units into the North Cape area—everything you have."

Vladimirov nodded.

"Scramble 'Wolfpack' squadrons in the North Cape sector through to Archangelsk sector," he snapped. "Staggered Sector Scramble for *all* units." He did not glance at the map-table, did not ask for the map to be changed. He was oblivious to it, seeing in his mind with absolute clarity, the dispositions of all surface, sub-surface and aerial units that might be employed.

"Order the *Otlitnyi* and the *Slavny* to alter course at once for North Cape—order them to proceed at utmost speed."

"Sir!"

"Order all submarines on the Barents Sea map to alter course, and to proceed to the Cape area at top speed."

"Sir!"

"Order the *Riga* to alter course, together with her escorts, and to put up her helicopters at once—they are to proceed at top speed to the Cape."

"Sir!"

It was futile, he knew—the bellowing challenge of a coward after the bully is out of earshot, the simulated fury of the defeated. Yet he became caught up in its frenetic, useless energy. He was intoxicated by the power he possessed.

Like a child he had once seen building on the sands at Odessa a long time ago, he made himself oblivious to the sea of truth creeping up behind him, and threw all his energies into the task of making his fragile, impermanent structure of sand. He flung everything into the air, changed the course of every surface and sub-surface vessel in the Barents Sea.

The map on the table was now showing the western sector of the Barents Sea—its operator had bled in the map reflecting Vladimirov's countless orders. Vladimirov realized he was sweating. His legs suddenly weak, unable to support him any longer. He lowered himself into a chair, looked up and found the First Secretary smiling complacently at him.

"Well, my dear Vladimirov—that wasn't so bad, after all—eh?" He laughed. Behind him, like an echo, Andropov smiled thinly. Vladimirov shook his head, smiled foolishly, like a rewarded child. "You seem to enjoy it—eh? Power . . . you understand, eh?" The man was leaning towards him. Vladimirov could do nothing but continue grinning foolishly, and nod his head.

A voice cut into his vacuous confrontation with the Soviet leader. "Tretsov reports the Mig-31 crossing the coast on the line of longitude 50 degrees, near Indiga."

It was like a single stone dropping into the flat silence of a pond. All of them around that table were suddenly reminded of the awesome potentiality, the enormous power, of the thing that had been stolen. It was little more than twenty-five minutes since Tretsov had taken off. The coast was approximately 1250 miles due north from Bilyarsk, and the Mig-31 had already reached it, passed over it, heading for its rendezvous over the Barents sea with a tanker aircraft.

Vladimirov looked at the first Secretary, saw the momentary hesitation in the eyes.

"Shall I order Tretsov to alter course, First Secretary?" he asked tiredly.

The big man shook his head, still smiling. "Not for the moment—let Tretsov make his rendezvous with the tanker first. When we have a sighting, we will point him like an arrow at the American—eh, like an arrow, Vladimirov?"

The First Secretary laughed. Vladimirov derived no comfort from the sound, from the over-confidence it betrayed.

Twenty minutes after he had landed, Gant was back on the surface of the floe, checking the progress of the refueling. Despite the bitter, freezing cold, the raw wind that swirled the thick mist around him, whipped the smoking breath away from his numbed lips, Gant stood on the ice near the Firefox, as if unwilling to surrender the aircraft entirely to the attentions of Seerbacker's crew. The frost had already begun to rime the fur of his borrowed parka, which did not seem to warm him, and he stood, a hunched figure, his hands thrust into his pockets, staring into the gray, formless world of the floe, seeing shadowy, labouring figures on the ice. The two hoses, each four inches in diameter, snaked across the floe toward the plane. The crew worked like men at the scene of some desperate, frozen fire. A trolley-pump had been wheeled out across the ice, having been lowered from the forward hatch by a winch, and then a smaller hatch in the forward deck had been opened. Gant's nostrils had been assailed by the sudden, bitter-sweet smell of the kerosene. A heavy-duty hose disappeared into the hatch above the forward crew's quarters.

It would take, Gant knew, perhaps another twenty minutes to refuel. Unlike the huge pressure-pumps available at an airbase in the front line, which could transfer as much as three thousand gallons of kerosene a minute to the thirsty tanks of a warplane, this trolley-pump was an aged, short-breathed thing.

There had been a delay, while Gant devoured a plate of chili in Seerbacker's quarters, before the pump had begun to operate. The bonding wire running from the sub, which was required to earth the Firefox to prevent the danger of a spark from the static electricity in the fuselage igniting any spillage, had been too short. The sub's crew had spliced in another length of wire, and the huge crocodile clip had been fastened to the nose-wheel strut. Only then had the refueling begun.

When the two civilians carried by the *Pequod*— an engineer and an electronics expert—had begun working on the plane, Gant agreed to return to Seerbacker's cabin.

Once there, he sat in silence except when, after

looking at his watch, he murmured, "Ten minutes."

A minute or two later, there was a knock at the door.

"Yeah?"

The Exec., Fleischer, stuck his head into the room. "Weather report, sir," he said.

Gant suddenly seemed to come awake. His eyes fixed on Fleischer's face, the intensity of the gaze making the young man falter.

"What is it?" Gant said.

"The wind's getting up, sir—gusting to fifteen knots at times." Fleischer spoke to Seerbacker, quite deliberately. "The fog seems to be lifting."

Seerbacker nodded. Gant had relaxed. Fifteen-knot gusts were no real threat to take-off.

"What about the shore-party?"

"Almost through, sir—another seven or eight minutes, by Peck's reckoning." Seerbacker nodded. Peck, the *Pequod*'s chief engineer, would not be much out in his reckoning. He would have bullied the men into utmost effort, whatever his private considerations concerning Gant and the safety of the ship.

Fleischer withdrew his head, and Gant made to rise from his chair. The next thing he knew was the huge jolt of the deck moving beneath him, and he was flung head-first across the table. He had a brief glimpse of Seerbacker catapulting off his bunk, and then his left shoulder struck the bulkhead with a jarring blow. The ship's lights winked out, and then returned, glowing brightly again. He felt the numbness of his shoulder and side, and the weight of Seerbacker's body lying winded across his chest. He heard a clatter from the companion-way, presumably Fleischer's body being thrown to the ground. He shifted his body, and saw Seerbacker's stunned, frightened face staring up at him.

"What in hell's name . . . ?" he said, his voice small, choking.

"What was it?" Gant said.

Seerbacker struggled to his feet, ungainly, bruised.
Blood seeped from the corner of his mouth. He had
bitten his tongue. He wiped the blood from his face,
and stared at his reddened fingers for a moment.
Then he seemed galvanized into action by the sound
of running feet outside. He heaved open the door.

"What the hell's going on, sailor?" he bawled.

Gant picked himself off the floor, rubbing his
shoulder. Feeling was returning to it, and he
reckoned that nothing was dislocated or broken.

"Sir—we don't know."

"What? Then what the hell are you doing here,
sailor? Find out!"

"Sir!" The man's footsteps retreated down the
companionway.

"The Firefox!" Gant said.

"The hell with that!" Seerbacker exploded. "What
about my boat?"

Gant followed him out of the cabin. Fleischer was
leaning against the bulkhead, blood oozing from a
deep, livid gash on his forehead. Seerbacker ignored
him, dazed as he was, and pressed past him towards
the control room. Gant stopped briefly to examine
the wound, then he patted the young man on the
shoulder, and followed in the captain's wake.

The control room gave a confused impression of
men picking themselves up, of furniture overturned. Gant headed towards the hatch-ladder up
to the bridge.

"Get me a damage-report—and quick!" barked the
captain.

The freezing air bit through Gant's parka, and the
wind plucked his first raw breath away from him.
From the top of the sail, he could see the Firefox
in the improved visibility, apparently undamaged.
The men who had been working on the ice were
scattered, one or two still prone, obviously injured,
other men bending over them, others spreading
out over the ice.

Gant yelled down to a sailor near the submarine:

"What happened?"

The man looked up, saw the captain standing alongside Gant.

"Don't know, sir. We—heard this cracking sound, like a scream, and then I was trying to push my face into the floe. I thought it was a fish homing on the boat, sir!"

"It was no torpedo. Where's Mr. Peck?"

"He headed off that way, sir," the sailor replied, pointing due north across the floe.

Gant strained his eyes, but the mist still clung to the floe in patches, and visibility was no more than a hundred yards at best. He stared in the direction of Peck's disappearance, and there was an unstable yet formless apprehension watery in his stomach. As the minutes passed, the wind, stronger now it seemed gusted occasionally into his face, making his eyes water. And he began to be afraid.

Then he saw Peck's figure emerging from the mist. As if prompted by something in his mind, or as if Peck's appearance heralded an answer, he began to run towards the Chief Engineer.

"What is it?" he asked breathlessly, reaching the big man. "What's wrong?"

Peck looked down at him, and said simply: "Pressure ridge."

"What?" Gant's face was open with shock. "How big?"

"Three, maybe four feet—right across the floe, if my guess is right."

"Where, man—where? Show me!" He dragged at Peck's sleeve, and the big man turned round, following him. Gant's white, desperate face disturbed him, especially the way he kept moving ahead in obvious impatience and then looking round, like a dog hurrying its master. Seerbacker, puzzled, followed in their wake.

The pressure ridge was almost four feet high and it had emerged from the ice like a low wall stretch-

ing right across the floe, as far as Gant could see in
either direction.

"You said it—goes all the way?"

"All the way—I walked a fair piece of it, in both
directions. I guess it goes right across."

Gant looked as though he disbelieved Peck for a
moment but he knew that the engineer would
have understood the significance of the ridge, and
would have checked its extent for the right reason.

"How—did it happen?" he said stupidly.

"Only one way," the big man said grimly. "Gusting wind drove one of the smaller floes behind us
right up our ass—like an automobile smash. Result,
one pressure-ridge."

Gant turned on Peck, grabbing the sleeves of his
parka in both hands. "You realize what this means?"
he said. "I can't damn well get out of here. I can't
take off!"

The result of his deliberations, of his self-recrimina-
tions and the growing certainty that he was right
and the First Secretary was disastrously wrong was,
Vladimirov reflected bitterly, nothing more than a
hesitation, a glance in the direction of the most powerful man in the Soviet Union. When the bulky figure merely nodded, emphasizing his last order, Vladimirov turned back to the console in front of him
and spoke.

"Tretsov—Vladimirov." Though he had ignored
code, he would not identify the aircraft with which
he was communicating, other than by the pilot's
name. In that lay a degree of anonymity.

At that moment, Tretsov, the second test-pilot on
the Mig-31 project was at fifty thousand feet, his
nose-probe buried in the udder of a refueling plane,
with which the Mig had made rendezvous minutes
before.

Static crackled through the console speaker.
"Tretsov—over," came the faint voice.

"Vladimirov to Tretsov. Proceed to the North Cape area as soon as refueling is completed."

"North Cape—repeat your message, please."

Vladimirov's voice betrayed his anger. Of course the pilot wondered at the change of plan!

"I said North Cape—make radio contact with the following units—missile-cruiser *Riga*, 'Wolfpack' ground control Murmansk—do you copy?"

After a silence: "Tretsov—I copy. Proceed to North Cape, contact *Riga* and ground control Murmansk—over."

"Good. Await further instructions—over and out."

Vladimirov flicked the switch, and turned away from the transmitter. It did not matter, he thought, that the Americans would undoubtedly pick up the signal, transmitted in clear voice as it had been. It was merely another unit being directed towards the decoy area. He looked once more at the First Secretary but the Soviet leader was in whispered conversation with Andropov. He turned his gaze towards Kutuzov. The old man's rheumy eyes met his, and he shook his head slightly. Vladimirov's eyes thanked him for the gesture of sympathy, of understanding.

Then the thoughts began to nag at him again. If only he could be *sure* in some way . . . He knew how it had been done, what the search-units ought to be looking for. But he was afraid, afraid to risk the shred of his credibility, the remains of his career, on such a wild idea. He swallowed. He knew the answer—and he knew the First Secretary would not listen.

He despised himself. He was throwing away the Mig-31, handing it to the Americans on a platter! Yet he could do nothing—they would not believe him.

They had checked the floe. As Peck had surmised, the ridge ran the whole east-west axis. It was a little more than half-way down the length of the floe, down the runway for the aircraft. Gant could not possibly, by any mechanical or physical means, take off along the length of snow-covered ice available to him while the ridge remained.

"It will work, sir," Peck was saying, leaning forward, standing taller than the thin figure of Seerbacker. Fleischer, his training and experience inadequate for these particular circumstances, remained silent. Peck's second engineer, Haynes, contributed his assessments of time and effort in support of his chief. With Gant, there were now five of them, standing stiffly in the raw air, wrapped in the mist that still clung to the floe. The wind was still gusting, but less strongly now as if, having achieved its purpose, it had become satisfied, quiescent.

"Hell, Jack—have we enough axes and shovels on board to do the job?" Seerbacker said. His eyes slid for a moment towards Gant, who seemed to be studying the floe intently, taking no notice of the discussion. Seerbacker was irritated by the man's apparent detachment, then dismissed it from his mind.

"Sir, we've got enough—crowbars, heavy screwdrivers, axes—anything!" Peck seemed to take Seerbacker's caution as a personal affront. "And we could place a couple of small charges, maybe?" he added.

"Damn that, Jack!"

"No, sir. You place 'em properly, small ones—you won't damage the ice!"

Seerbacker was silent for a moment, then he said, addressing Gant:

"How wide is the wheel-track on that bird, Gant?"

"Twenty-two feet," Gant replied mechanically.

"You certain?"

Gant merely nodded, without shifting his gaze from the ridge. He kicked at it aimlessly with a boot. Some loose snow flicked away, spattered on the toe —he had not marked the surface of the ridge.

"How much d'you need—how much of this wall you want to come down?" Peck said.

Gant turned his head, recognizing the challenge in the big man's voice. He smiled humorlessly, thought for a moment, and then said: "Thirty feet."

There was a leaden silence for a moment, then Seerbacker said:

"Don't bullshit, Gant. You're not going to waste my time and wreck that bird just to prove something to my chief engineer!" His eyes flickered between the two men, sensing the challenge and response, its origins in Gant's earlier momentary panic in front of Peck.

"Thirty feet," Gant said. "That's all I'll need."

"Then it's thirty fuckin' feet you'll get, mister!" Seerbacker spat back. "Now you pick out the spot, man—and Mr. Peck and his team will get to work for you!"

Gant strolled away from them, and the four men tagged wearily behind him, as if unwilling. Seerbacker regretted the way he had handled Gant, bridling him, making him say something which he would obviously regret. Yet there was no sign of doubt on Gant's face, no fear that a margin for error of four feet on either side of the main undercart in the visibility now available to him was almost like cutting his throat with a blunt knife.

Damn him to hell! Seerbacker thought. He gets right under my skin!

Gant stopped, waited for them, and said: "Here."

He kicked a boot hard into the ice at the crest of the ridge at stomach height, and chipped the crest slightly. Peck reached into the pocket of his parka, pulled out an aerosol can, and sprayed it on the ice. Part of the chipped portion of crest sagged under the impact of the alcohol-based de-icing fluid. Gant paced out thirty feet, and waited for Peck to mark the ice. Then he nodded. Seerbacker sensed they were almost in the center of the ridge, near the center of the floe. Gant had picked the longest north-south axis for his take-off.

"How long to clear thirty feet, Mr. Peck?" Seerbacker asked.

"An hour, sir—if you include the spraying-down."

Gant wanted to tell them it was too long—but
there was no point in futile protest.

"An hour?"

Peck nodded. Seerbacker was silent for a moment,
then tugged his handset from his pocket. He pressed
the button, and said: "Waterson—hook me up to the
ship's address system, huh?" He waited until his request was accomplished, and then he said: "This is
the captain—hear this. It will take one hour for
the pressure-ridge to be cleared, and that means we
have to stay on the surface for that length of time. I
want utmost vigilance at all time; air, surface, and
subsurface searches to be thorough. If any of you
guys misses something, you kill all of us—understand that. You won't just be shitting on yourself or
your service record! And you stay rigged for silent
running—we're going to be making enough noise
up here for all of you, so keep it quiet. You guys on
the plane—just keep it de-iced and ready to roll the
minute you get the word. Mr. Peck is in charge of
the shore-party to work on the ridge, and I'll let
him tell you who's volunteered, and what equipment he wants out here. Just a minute—Doc?"
There was a pause, then:

"Yes, skipper?"

"What about our casualties?"

"Harper's concussed—hit that hard head of his on
the deck-plates. Smith lost a couple of teeth fighting the ice, and I'm putting four stitches in the back
of Riley's skull. Anything else is less dramatic than
that."

"Thanks Doc. Tell Riley it should improve his
brain—and Smith's looks will definitely have improved! O.K., here's Mr. Peck, you guys. Hear him
good."

He switched off and pocketed his own handset, and

left Peck calling out his list of names, the catalogue
of brawn that the *Pequod* was able to muster.

Seerbacker joined Gant. He stared at him for a
moment, then said: "You are sure?"

Gant nodded.

"Don't worry—Peck doesn't get to me. I can get
out through thirty feet of clear ice."

"In visibility like this?"

"In worse."

"Hell, man—O.K., but it's your funeral."

There was a silence, then Gant said: "Thanks,
Seerbacker—for the hour."

Seerbacker felt awkward. Gant, he sensed, was
making a real effort, meant what he was saying.

"Yeah—sure. I wouldn't do it for just anybody,
though," he said, and grinned.

"I—I'll go take a look at the plane."

"Sure—you do that."

Gant nodded, and walked away. Near the *Pequod*,
he could see figures hurrying through the gray curtain of the mist, wrapped in the white breath of
their effort. Peck, he thought without rancor, was a
taskmaster, and when he said jump, they jumped.
It wasn't his business. Peck knew what he was doing.

It had been his suggestion, from the beginning.
The crude hacking out of a section of the ridge, then
the smoothing process to follow, the former accomplished by brute force and axes, the latter by spraying the broken section of the ridge with the
superheated steam that drove the turbines of the
submarine, directed onto the ice by pressure hoses.

The Firefox was clear of ice. Alongside, looking
as if it had strayed from some gigantic toolshed, was
a ten-foot piece of equipment resembling nothing so
much as a garden-spray. This was linked by a hose
to a fluid tank in the sail of the *Pequod*, and from
it, pumped by a small electric motor, gushed a
stream of alcohol-based anti-icing fluid—the "booze"
as Seerbacker's crew referred to it. This kept the

wings and fuselage free of ice. Four men operated
the sprayer—two men pushed it on its undercarriage, and two others directed the fine, pressurized
spray from two small hoses tucked beneath their
arms. They went about their task with a mechanical,
unthinking precision, and Gant could see the light
indentations of the wheels beneath the sprayer
where they had ceaselessly circumnavigated the
plane.

Gant stood and watched the Firefox for a long
time, as if drawn to the machine, as if feeding
through his eyes. He had had no time until now, no
moment of being *outside* the plane with time to ab-
sorb its lines, its design, its functional wickedness
of appearance. The first time—there had only been
the confused impression of noise, and light, and the
fire at the far end of the hangar, and Baranovich's
white-coated figure lumped on the concrete . . .
Now he watched in silence, taking in the slim fuselage, the bulging air-intakes in front of the massive
engines, larger than anything Turmansky had ever
thought of fitting to an interceptor-attack plane, the
seemingly impossible stubbiness of the wings, with
the advanced Anab missiles slung in position beneath them. He saw the scorch marks where he
had fired two of them—one to bring down the
Badger, the other to goad the captain of the *Riga*
into premature action. He walked closer. The two
missiles had been replaced, making up his complement of four.

This didn't really surprise him. A Mig-25 had been
captured from the Syrians in the dummy-run for this
operation. Presumably, it had been armed and its
missiles, Anabs, had been assigned to Seerbacker,
for delivery. Buckholz, Gant realized, missed nothing.

The refueling had been completed even while he,
Seerbacker and Peck had discussed the ridge. The
hoses had been withdrawn, the bonding wire removed from the nose-wheel strut. Presumably, the

refueling crew were now taking their turn at the ridge.

He walked away with reluctance, then, as the distance increased, and the Firefox became a shadowy, insubstantial bulk in the mist, he lengthened his stride.

It took him almost half-an-hour to walk from the Firefox to the southerly end of the floe and then to traverse the floe from south to north, along the line of his visualized runway. The collision of the floes had not damaged the runway, other than by the ridge. He was returning from the northern edge of the floe when the handset that Fleischer had issued him bleeped in his pocket.

"Yes?"

"Gant?" Seerbacker's voice sounded labored, out of breath. "Listen to me, mister. We've got three sonar contacts to the south of us, along your flight-path."

Gant was silent for a moment, then he said: "Yes —it has to be the cruiser and her two escorts—hunter-killer subs."

"Jesus—you know how to make trouble for me, Gant—you really, really do!"

"How long before they get here?"

"Forty—maybe forty-five minutes."

"Then that's enough time."

"Fuck you, mister! Enough time for you to get the hell out of here—what about my ship? What about its gallant crew who are at this moment working their tails off to get you a runway you can use?"

"I—I'm sorry, Seerbacker—I didn't think . . ."

Almost as if he were winning a point, Seerbacker replied: "Anyway—it'll take longer than we thought. It seems Mr. Peck was a little optimistic in his estimates. We'll need almost the same time to get you out of here as they'll need to catch up on us!"

Gant was silent. Eventually, Seerbacker said: "You still there, Gant?"

"Uh—yeah. You sure they're heading this way?"

"Maybe, maybe not. They *weren't*, that's for sure."

"Weren't?"

"They were steaming west, across the track of the floe, but sure as hell is hot, Gant, if we can see them, then they can damn well see us!"

10
THE DUEL

Vladimirov confronted the First Secretary, a renewed sense of purpose doing little to contradict or overcome the tension he felt. He knew, with a sickening certainty, that he did not want to throw his career away, that he wanted Kutuzov's rank and post when the old man was put out to grass. Yet he was contained within a dilemma. Even if he managed to quell the rising doubts and proceed as ordered, there was still the chance that, if Gant succeeded in escaping with the Mig-31 intact, he himself would be blamed for the Soviet failure to recapture or destroy. It was that knowledge finally that persuaded him to demand that action be taken with regard to the sonar-contact reported by the *Riga* a minute before.

"In my estimation, First Secretary," he began, keeping his voice neutral, level, with a vast effort of will, "this contact, though confused by the presence of ice-floes, is worth investigation."

His words seemed to be swallowed in the silence of the War Command Center. Vladimirov was aware that everybody, from Andropov down to the most junior radio-operator, understood that the room had polarized around the First Secretary and the O.C. "Wolfpack." They were spectators in a power game being played out between the two men. They seemed to the General, tense with anticipation, almost to appreciate the fact that he was at last making his move—his final move.

"In your estimation," the Soviet leader said softly after a while, his voice seeming to blame Vladimirov for speaking.

Vladimirov nodded. Then he said: "I—I am sure that I understand now how they intended to refuel the Mig at sea . . ." He chose the cryptic words with care. He had to play the First Secretary like a recalcitrant, dangerous fish, a shark. Yet he had committed himself. If his assumption proved to be correct, and they still failed, it would be tantamount to professional suicide to have voiced his ideas. The wild idea had grown in him slowly; he had tried to deny it, rid himself of it and the personal perspectives it evoked. Now, however, it possessed him, and he could no longer avoid its communication to the First Secretary. Damnation, he thought, almost grinding his teeth as he envisaged the consequences of his ensuing conflict with the Soviet leader—but it was their last and only chance to prevent the Mig from falling into American hands, delivered by Gant.

His hatred of Gant burnt at the back of his throat like nausea.

"Yes—they have used—*are using*—a large ice-floe as a runway, and the refueling vessel is undoubtedly a submarine. That is the sonar-contact that the *Riga* has made!" In bald, hurried words, the idea seemed ridiculous, unconvincing. Yet, in his mind, he could visualize the scene so clearly! The parka-clothed figures, the fuel-lines, the aircraft sitting on the ice . . . there were a thousand floes the Americans could have chosen from!

"The aircraft has *landed*, Vladimirov?"

Vladimirov knew he had lost. The voice, dry and calm, told him he had failed to convince. He looked around him. Faces turned away, stares directed aside, or downwards, not meeting his eyes. Even Kutuzov turned away, the eyes of a spectator at a road accident.

"Yes." His voice was too high, he knew it. Damn, he could not even control his voice any more! How was it, he wondered, that the man was able to frighten him from the other side of the map-table, on the surface of which the colored lights scuttled towards the North Cape? They had accepted Aubrey's decoys —Vladimirov *knew* they were decoys, aircraft and a submarine, bustling to no purpose but to trick them —and the total available Soviet air and sea forces had been ordered to dash for the North Cape. The man in front of him now possessed power that could ruin him, drop him, crush him, imprison him—say that he was mad. And Vladimirov did not want to end up like Grigorenko, in an asylum.

He tried once more.

"The contact is on the flight-path last registered by the *Riga* and her escorts—just before the trace was lost."

Then he subsided into silence. He watched, almost like a spectator himself, as the large, square, gray-suited man stared, apparently idly, at the map-table. The *Riga* and the two escorting submarines were rapidly becoming solitary lights as the scene of Soviet surface and air activity moved further west. Then he looked up into Vladimirov's eyes. The incredulous General saw, from an instant before the eyes became hooded again, naked, stark fear. He could not assimilate the information, until the First Secretary said:

"It would take too long to recall the helicopters, and order them to make a search of the area. Instead, my dear general, because you seem to have this— obsessive concern with ice-floes and tanker-submarines . . ." He paused and Andropov, seated now next to him, smiled thinly. He supplied the expected reaction, even as his humorless eyes behind the steel-framed spectacles indicated that he understood the motives of the Soviet leader. "As I said—to give you peace of mind, my dear Vladimirov—we will dispatch *one* of the escorting submarines to investigate this highly dubious sonar-contact that the cruiser claims to have made." He smiled blandly, recovering from the moment of naked understanding he had seen in the Chairman's eyes.

"But, if it is . . ." Vladimirov began.

The First Secretary held up his huge hand. *"One* of the escorts, Vladimirov—how long will it take?"

"Forty minutes, no more."

"Then—if there is anything to report, if the contact turns out to be interesting—the second Mig-31 will be ordered to return from its rendezvous off the North Cape—at top speed."

It was over. Vladimirov felt the tension drain away, leaving him physically weak, exhausted. At least it was something. Yet he could not sense a victory. He was unable to do more than continue to despise himself.

Swiftly, as if to hide the feelings that must show on his face, he turned to the encoding-console to issue orders to the captain of the *Riga.*

Gant had watched the green sonar-screen and the sweep of its tireless arm until his eyes ached. The endless revolution of the arm, dragging the wash of whiteness behind it that left three crystalized points of light in its wake, unnerved him. After silent, tense minutes in the control room of the *Pequod,* leaning over the sailor wearing headphones, listening to the amplified pinging of the contact, it became apparent what was occurring. One of the blips on the screen, one of the escort submarines, had detached itself from its westward course, and was moving along the line of a bearing that would bring it homing on the *Pequod*. The other two blips continued on their westward course.

As yet the blips appeared only on the long-range sonar-screen, the extent of whose survey carried for a thirty-mile radius around the submarine. They were at the top of the screen—and the sonar had been working in a directional sweep, when the three vessels had been picked up. Now, the blip of the escort submarine homing on them was little more than twenty miles away.

After a huge silence filled only with the quick human breathing of the crew and the reiterated pinging of the contact-echo, Seerbacker, at Gant's elbow, said, "How long before it gets here?"

The operator didn't look up, but said: "Can't say, sir. You know what this long-range sonar is like—distortion factor of twenty percent, sometimes. I can't be sure, sir."

"Hell!"

"How fast can those Russian subs move?" Gant said.

"How the hell do I know?" Seerbacker stormed, turning on him, his long face white with anger, and fear. "I don't even know what *kind* of submarine it is, man! Until it transfers from the long-range screen into close-up, we can't get a 3-D image of it from the computer that'll identify it."

"Contact bearing Red Three-Niner, and closing," the operator called out, apparently undisturbed by the emotions of Seerbacker snarled in his ear.

"What—will you do?" Gant asked.

Seerbacker looked at him for a moment, and then said:

"I have a sealed packet for you—your route, I guess. That's the first thing. Second, I have to get our disguise out of the wardrobe, and dust it off!"

Gant looked at him, puzzled.

"Contact still bearing Red Three-Niner and closing."

Seerbacker looked at the operator's neck, as if he wished the man dead, or dumb at least, then he said: "Give me the blower." Fleischer thrust the microphone into his hand, and pressed the alert button at the side of the transmitter, signaling the crew to prepare for a message from the captain.

Seerbacker nodded, and then said into the microphone: "Hear this—this is the captain. It's operate 'Harmless' procedure, on the double. We have about thirty minutes, maybe less, I doubt more. Get the lead out of your asses, and move—move as fast as you've ever moved before."

Having relieved his tension by way of bullying his crew, Seerbacker turned to Gant with a more even countenance. Smiling, he nodded towards the watertight door leading to his cabin, and Gant followed in his wake.

"What is 'Harmless'?" he asked as the footsteps clicked along the companionway.

Seerbacker was silent until he turned into his cabin, Gant still behind him, and had locked the door. Then he went to a wall-safe, cranked the dial, and pulled the small door open. He handed Gant a package inside a cellophane wrapper. Gant nodded, as Seerbacker's two-fingered grip revealed the presence of an acid capsule within the clear plastic, the "auto-destruct" for the sealed orders.

Gant unfolded the single sheet of flimsy within the envelope, studying it carefully.

"What is 'Harmless'?" he repeated.

Seerbacker grinned. "Just our little joke—only it may save our lives," he said. "We'll go up top in a while—you can see for yourself."

Gant nodded, as if the answer to his question did not really interest him. His orders were simple. There was a list of map coordinates, and times, which he knew would take him at first low across the Finnish coast, east of the North Cape decoy area, across the lake-strewn landscape of Finland, towards Stockholm. Once there, where the Gulf of

Bothnia encountered the Baltic, he was instructed to rendezvous with the late afternoon British Airways commercial flight from Stockholm to London. He knew why. If he tucked in behind the plane, and below it, not only would he be out of sight of the crew, but all that would show up on an infra-red screen would be the single image of the airliner's heat-source. And the airliner would be expected across the North Sea, on route and on schedule. And he was immune to any sort of detection other than visual—an unlikely possibility. No Elint ship in the North Sea warned to watch for him would guess where he was. When he arrived at a specified coordinate off the English coast, he was to call R.A.F. Scampton in Lincolnshire on a frequency within the general aviation band, assuming the identity of a test-flight for a commercial passenger plane receiving its Certificate of Airworthiness check-up. With luck, if it worked, the Russians would lose him, if they had ever found him, off the eastern coast of Sweden, when he linked infra-red images with the British Airways flight.

He read the coordinates once more, committing them firmly to memory. Then he replaced the sheet in its buff envelope, and the envelope in its wrapper. Seerbacker had already placed a large steel ashtray on the table. Gant placed the packet in the ashtray, then ground the heel of his hand on it. Almost immediately, the fumes of the released acid rose pungently and the packet began to dissolve. Gant watched it until it consisted of no more than a few blackened, treacly specks.

Then he nodded, as if to himself, and said: "O.K.— let's get urgent, Captain. I want to see what progress has been made on my runway." His eyes, surprisingly to Seerbacker, almost twinkled for a moment, and he added: "And I want to see 'Harmless'."

Of course, Aubrey reflected, he could not be certain —no, not by a very long way, not just at present.

Nevertheless, he was unable quite to extinguish the small flame of hope that warmed his stomach like good brandy; the heat of success. The code activity from the Russians, combined with the success of the decoy-missions around the North Cape area, and the signal from Seerbacker aboard the *Pequod* that the Firefox was safely down, and refueled—all added to his barely suppressed sense of satisfaction.

Shelley, too, he could see, could hardly keep a schoolboyish grin from his smooth features. The Americans, having swung down with the graph of Buckholz's doubts, been infected by indecision, now lifted in a rising curve again. Curtin was on the steps, adjusting the positions of Russian planes and vessels as they moved further and further into the decoy area. Aubrey glanced up at the huge map, and saw only the position of the floe, and the colored pin representing the Firefox alongside it.

Had Seerbacker risked getting off another signal, to confirm the sonar-contact with the approaching Russian submarine, or had Aubrey been aware of Vladimirov's intuition, and partial success in Bilyarsk, his mood might have been less equable, his ego-temperature somewhat lower. But he was still blinded by the brilliance of his own design, and Seerbacker had not informed him of the suspicious escort submarine in his vicinity. For Aubrey, the design had become now only a mechanical matter—as long as Gant followed instructions, it was in the bag.

Aubrey maintained that he was a man who never, absolutely on no occasion, counted his chickens —but now he did. The magnitude of what he had achieved, from inception, through planning, to execution, stunned him, shone like a fierce sun on his vanity, causing it to bloom.

"Hm—gentlemen," he said, clearing his throat. "I realize that perhaps this may be a little premature . . ." He smiled deprecatingly, knowing that they shared his mood. "Nevertheless—perhaps we might permit ourselves a little—a modicum of celebratory alcohol?"

Buckholz grinned openly. "You sure put it tortuously, Aubrey—but yes, I reckon we could open a bottle," he said.

"Good."

Aubrey moved to the drinks trolley that had stood throughout their vigil in the corner of the operations room. Suddenly, the place seemed to be without the stale, almost rancid, smell of old cigar smoke and unchanged clothing. The faces were no longer strained with tension. It was merely that they were a little tired—tired with the satisfying tiredness of a job well done, of something completed.

He broke the seal on the malt whisky, and poured the pale gold liquid into four tumblers in generous measures. Then, deferentially, he handed the drinks round on a small silver tray, brought from his own flat, in readiness.

Aubrey raised his glass, smiled benignly, and said: "Gentlemen—to the Firefox . . . and, of course, to Gant."

"Gant—and the Firefox," the four men chanted in a rough unison. Aubrey watched, with mild distaste, as Buckholz threw his drink into the back of his throat, swallowed the precious liquid in one. Really, he thought, the man has absolutely no *taste* —none at all.

As he sipped at his own drink, it seemed more than ever merely a matter of time. He glanced at the telephone. In a few minutes, no more, it would be time to order the car to transport them to R.A.F. Scampton—if Gant were not to arrive before themselves, which would not do at all.

He smiled at the thought.

Peck was standing in front of Gant and Seerbacker, looming over them both. Sweat rimed the fur of his hood in crystals of ice, and ice stood out stiffly on his moustache. His face was pale, drained by effort.

"Well?" Seerbacker said, his hand still on the sail-ladder of the *Pequod*.

"It's done, sir," Peck said. Then he looked at Gant, and his voice hardened. "We've cleared your damn runway, Mr. Gant!"

"Peck!" Seerbacker warned.

For a moment, Gant thought the huge Chief Engineer was intending to strike him, and he flinched physically. Then he said: "I'm sorry, Peck."

Peck seemed nonplussed by his reply. He scrutinized Gant's face, as if suspecting some trick, nodded as he appeared satisfied, and then seemed to feel that some explanation was required of him. He said: "Sorry—Major . . ." Gant's eyes opened in surprise. It was the first time anyone had used his old rank. Peck meant it as a mark of respect. "We—it's just the feeling, sir. Working out there on that damn pressure-ridge, the men and me—well, we just kept thinking how we could have been getting out of this place, instead of breaking our backs." The big man's voice tailed off, and he looked steadily down at his feet.

Gant said: "It's O.K., Peck—and thanks. Now, tell me where we are, what stage have you reached."

Peck became business-like, immediately formal. "We've got a thirty-feet gap hacked out of the ridge. Now we run the hoses from the turbine on a direct-feed—we need a lot of pipe, Major—it'll take time."

Gant nodded.

"Get to it, Peck—the sooner you've done, the sooner you can get going. When you've finished smoothing down the surface of the floe—and make it as smooth as possible, 'cos I don't want to hit a bump at a hundred-and-fifty knots—I want you to spray steam on the ice, down the length of the runway, starting as near the northern edge of the floe as you can, running down to the Firefox—if you have the time."

Peck looked puzzled. "Why, Major?"

"Clear the surface snow, Peck—that's what it'll

do. I don't need to be held back by the surface-re-
sistance . . ."

"Get to it, Peck," Seerbacker said. "I've just got
to check on the decoy procedure, and then I'm coming to take a look at your night-school efforts!"

Peck grinned, nodded, and moved away down the
length of the *Pequod,* forward to the hatch above
the turbines, where two members of the engineering
crew were feeding down great serpent-loops of hose
into the belly of the submarine.

"You want to see 'Harmless?' " Seerbacker said.
"Come take a look."

"Harmless" was hurried, crude, and brilliant, Gant
was forced to admit. The feverish activity of those
members of the sub's crew not working on the pressure-ridge at first seemed to obey no overall strat-
egy, tend toward no definable object. Then he realized what was happening.

The submarine was being transformed into the
headquarters of an arctic weather-station. Over the
transmitter in his pocket, Seerbacker snapped out
orders that the torpedo-tubes and forward crew-
quarters were to be flushed out with sea water, the
evidence of the kerosene to be removed. This would
be followed by faked evidence of hull damage to
explain the presence of residual water in both com-
partments. On the ice, a hut had been assembled
from its components, and crude wooden furniture
carried inside. Maps and charts covered the newly
erected walls, Gant saw as he peered through one
of the windows. Impressive lists of figures filled note-
pads and sheets attached to clipboards. Two masts
had been erected, one twenty feet high, the other
reaching to thirty feet. The taller of the pair was a
radio mast, while an anemometer revolved on the
top of the other one, and below this a vane swung,
indicating direction of the measured wind.

A white chest, a Stephenson Screen, containing
thermometers and hygrometers, stood beneath the
smaller mast, and the disguising of the floe as a

weather-station was completed by holes drilled into
the ice, in some cases through to the sea beneath,
into which thermometers had been lowered.

As Gant watched Peck and his men unroll the
lengths of hose, clip the sections together, he saw a
bright orange weather-balloon float up into the sky.
Still clinging to the surface of the floe were shredding, rolling embers of mist, but above it, the cloud
base began at thirteen thousand feet. A second balloon hovered a hundred feet above the *Pequod,* attached by a nylon line. The balloons would explain
the earlier release of a signal balloon when he
landed.

It took a little more than fifteen minutes to trans-
form the surface of the floe into the appearance of a
U.S. weather-station studying the movements and
characteristics of a large ice-floe in its southward
path to immolation. The fact that the *Pequod* was
operating in the northern Barents Sea, rather than
east of Greenland, was the only weakness as far as
Gant could see.

As Seerbacker said, as he joined Gant near the
bridge-ladder of the submarine: "They can't prove a
thing, Gant—as long as you're long gone from here
before that Russian boat climbs all over us!"

Gant glanced reflectively down at the ice, and
then said: "What about the exhaust—they'll be
keeping infra-red watch on this floe. They must have
tumbled something?"

"Hell, Gant—I don't give a cuss for your heat-
trail. Just get that bird out of here, and leave me to
do the worrying, will you?"

Gant smiled at the mock ferocity of Seerbacker's
answer. The man was frightened, knew he was
treading a fine edge of ground steel. He nodded.
"Sure. I'll get out of here, just as soon as I can."

"Good." Seerbacker plucked the radio-trans-
mitter from the pocket of his parka, pressed it to his
cheek, and flicked the switch. "This is the Captain—
you there, Fleischer?"

"Sir." From the radio, Fleischer's voice had a quality of unreality, one that impressed upon Gant the whole situation—the tiny floe, the bitter wastes of the Barents Sea, the approach of the Russian hunter-killer submarine.

"What's the news on our friend?"

There was a pause, then the Exec. said: "We're getting a computer-prediction now, sir. Subject to a seven-per-cent error in the sonar-contact . . ."

"Yeah. Tell me the bad news."

"The ETA for the sub is seventeen minutes."

"Jesus!"

"Course and speed appear to be exactly the same, sir. She's coming straight for us."

Seerbacker wore a strained look on his face for a moment, then he grinned at Gant. "You hear that?" Gant nodded. "O.K. Fleischer—I'm leaving this set on receive from now on—I want you to call it to me every minute, understand?"

"Sir."

"When the sub comes up on close-range sonar, call me the exact speed and distance every thirty seconds."

"Sir."

Seerbacker clipped the handset to the breast pocket of his parka, tugged at it to insure that it wouldn't come adrift, nodded to Gant, and headed away from the submarine in the direction indicated by the two hoses which trailed like endless black snakes away into the mist. Following him, the ridge still out of sight, the violent hiss of steam hardly audible, Gant was once more possessed by a sense of the precariousness of his position. The hunched, loping figure of Seerbacker seemed slight, almost unsubstantial, certainly not a presence capable of supporting the weight of his escape. The firm ice beneath his feet, the glimpse of the Firefox in the mist as he turned his head to glance at it—they did not reassure him. The Russian submarine was homing on the floe and the *Pequod*. They had sixteen minutes, give or take a little.

Two men manned each nozzle, directing a jet of superheated steam onto the ugly, unfinished plasterwork of the hole in the ridge. It was supposed to be thirty feet across. Gant's brain measured it—to his imagination it looked small, too small. The steam played over the rough surface of the floe, over the hacked, torn edges of the gap—smoothing it out. It took them only a couple of minutes to give the gap smooth edges, a smooth, gleaming floor.

Peck had turned once, acknowledged the presence of Gant and the captain, and then ignored them. As soon as the gap was smoothed to his satisfaction, he bawled at his team: "All right, you guys—get this runway smoothed off!"

"What for, chief?"

"Because I'm telling you to do it—you'll enjoy it, Clemens!"

The hoses snaked away into the mist, unwillingly following the men dragging at them. They snaked past Gant's feet, slowly, far too slowly. He looked at his watch, just as Fleischer's voice squawked from near Seerbacker's shoulder.

"The sub's transferred to close-range screen, sir."

Seerbacker leaned his head like a bird attending to ruffled feathers, and said, "Tell me the worst."

"Computer-identification: Russian, type hunter-killer submarine, range four-point-six miles, ETA nine minutes. . . ."

"What?" Seerbacker bawled.

"Sorry, sir—the sonar-error must have been larger than we thought . . ."

"Now you tell me!" Seerbacker was silent for an instant, then he said: "Get off the air—Peck!"

"Sir?"

"You heard that, Chief?"

"Yes, sir—we'll never get this runway cleared, not a thirty-yard width all the way down the floe."

Seerbacker looked at Gant. "What the hell do you want?" he said.

"I—a hundred yards this side of the floe," Gant replied, pointing beyond the gap in the ridge, to the north. "Just give me that, and a clear runway this side of the gap." He waved his hand towards the Firefox.

Seerbacker repeated his instructions. Peck sounded dubious that he could complete the work, but affirmed that he would try. Gant stared into the mist, saw the huddled, squat shapes of men moving closer, straining as they dragged the unwilling hoses back on their tracks. He heard the recommencement of the spraying, smoothing out his runway, blasting the loose, powdery surface snow clear. If he was to reach the take-off speed he required, it *had* to be done. And he had to wait until it was done.

Seerbacker was speaking again. "Give me a status report on 'Harmless'—and this is the last time anyone refers to anything except the weather—understand?" He listened intently, almost leaning forward on the balls of his feet. When the voice at the other end had finished, he nodded in apparent satisfaction. Then he looked at Gant. "It's O.K.—we're covered, as long as we get you airborne."

"ETA seven minutes." Fleischer's voice was infected by something that sounded dangerously like panic.

"When he contacts you—give him the low-down, like on the script—O.K., Dick?" Seerbacker's voice was soothing.

"Sir."

Gant watched the steam skid across the snow. Blasts of powder lifted into the misty air. The hoses snaked nearer, the men straining at them, joined now by other, anonymous figures who passed Gant, summoned by Peck's call over the handset. Around the men, the self-inflicted blizzard raged, until Gant himself was enveloped in the blinding white smoke.

"ETA six minutes . . . still no radio contact, sir."

Gant heard Fleischer's voice coming squeakily from
the settling storm, saw the thin figure of Seerbacker
outlined once more as the hoses passed away down
the floe towards the plane. He wiped the snow from
his stubbled face with the back of a mitten.

Seerbacker remained silent for a long time, his
back to Gant as he watched Peck's party clearing the
runway. To him, they appeared to be moving slowly, far too slowly. Unable to bear the tension or the
silence any longer, he turned to Gant, and said:

"Are they going to make it?"

Gant nodded. "A minute to spare," he said.

"Can you get out of here in that time?"

"So far away, you wouldn't believe!" Gant said,
with a grim smile.

"You better be right, mister—you just better be!"

"The contact is confirmed, First Secretary!" Vladimirov said, his hand slamming down on the map-
table, so that the lights joggled and blurred for a
moment.

The man in front of him seemed unmoved, perhaps
still even contemptuous of the military man's urgency. Vladimirov knew that he was risking everything now, that there was no time for the niceties of
career, and politics. He had *known* that it was an
American submarine, and he had known its purpose.
The silence had told on him. He was white and
strained, and there was sweat on his forehead. He
sensed that, alone in the room, only the old man,
Kutuzov, supported him. Even he was silent.

"Vladimirov, calm yourself!" the First Secretary
growled.

"Calm—calm myself?" Vladimirov's voice was
high-pitched, out of control. He had committed
himself now, he knew. Yet he could not stand by,
even though he had schooled himself to do so, tried
to quell the pendular motion of self-interest and
duty that had plagued him throughout the morning. He had been unable to eat lunch, there had been

such tightness in his stomach, such a knot of fear.
Perhaps, he sensed, it was that he was afraid, the
appalling knowledge that he was a coward, that had
driven him to do his duty.

"Yes—calm yourself!"

"How can I be calm—when your stupidity—*stupidity,* is losing that aircraft to the Americans? You
have read the file—you know what this man Gant is.
He could land that aircraft on an ice-floe, and take
off again. Listen to me—before it's too late!"

Like a frozen hare, Vladimirov watched the emotions chase each other across the face of the First
Secretary. The initial hot rage at the insult was
controlled in an instant, becoming once more the
cold contempt of habit; a sense of sadistic pleasure
seemed present to Vladimirov—lastly, however, he
saw the emotion for which he searched . . . doubt.

Vladimirov pressed on, knowing that, even as he
ruined himself, that the First Secretary was afraid
to ignore him any longer. The Soviet leader was unable to hold Vladimirov's gaze, and turned to look
over his shoulder at Andropov. The Chairman's
face was inscrutable.

"You *must* act, First Secretary—it is too *late* for
politics."

The big man seemed as if poised to spring at the
O.C. "Wolfpack," then he summoned a smile to his
face, lightness to his voice: "Very well, Vladimirov,
very well, if it means that much to you . . ." The
voice hardened. "If you are so ready to—*spoil*
things by your behavior—I can do no more than
humor you." He waved his hand in a generous gesture. "What is it you require?"

"The immediate recall of the second Mig from
the North Cape rendezvous."

Vladimirov felt his voice tighten in his throat. His
energy drained away. Now there was nothing left
but fear, the sense of lost honors, of power thrown
away. His victory was a bitter, icy moment in time.

The First Secretary nodded, once. It did not matter about the remainder of the massive forces misdirected to the Cape. Not now. Only the second Mig-31 and Tretsov could affect the outcome this late. And, as if in recompense for his career sacrifice, he wanted Gant dead now, wanted Tretsov to finish him.

As he crossed to the console to issue orders to Tretsov, he glanced in the direction of Kutuzov. He thought for a moment, that he saw a kindly, even admiring, wisdom in the rheumy eyes, coupled with a profound compassion. Then he received the impression that the old man was detached, unaware of what was going on. He felt very alone, unable to decide which impression was the truth.

He snapped out his orders—possibly the last orders he would issue as O.C. "Wolfpack," he reflected grimly—in a calm, level voice, aware of the eyes behind him, watching him. The room was still with tension.

As Tretsov acknowledged, and the second Mig altered course for the ice-floe using its top speed of over four thousand miles an hour, Vladimirov grasped at this last chance that Tretsov would kill Gant.

"They're calling, sir—want identification immediately, sir," Fleischer's voice creaked out of the handset still clipped to Seerbacker's top pocket.

"The hell they do. You know the routine, it's written down. Do it."

"The Russian wants to speak to you, sir."

"Tell him I'll be along—I'm engaged in goddamn experiments at the other end of the floe! Tell him I'll be along."

"Sir. ETA three minutes and fourteen seconds."

The conversation had gone on somewhere outside Gant, at a great distance. He and Seerbacker, waiting now by the aircraft, watching the snail-like approach of the men and the hoses, were miles apart in reality. Gant knew, almost to the second, how much time was left, and how much time they needed. They had precisely one minute to spare.

Seerbacker was visibly on edge. The voice of Fleischer acted on his lanky form like a twitch of the puppeteer's strings, pulling him taut. He could not as the Russian closed on the *Pequod*, any longer believe that the crude hut, the bogus charts, and the thermometers and the masts, would save him. Gant, however, was like a passenger whose train has arrived, calmly collecting the luggage of his thoughts prior to departure. He was no longer what Seerbacker had privately thought him, a man without a past on his way to no discernible future. He was in transit, and the figures on the landscape of mist and ice had little or nothing to do with him.

"Hell—they'll never make it!" Seerbacker snapped, unable to bear the tension.

"They will," Gant said calmly, his voice so level, almost a whisper, that Seerbacker looked at him curiously.

"Man, but you're cool . . ."

Gant smiled. "Somebody once told me I was dead—the flying corpse they called me in Vietnam," Gant said.

"You minded?"

"No," Gant replied, shaking his head slightly. "Most of the guys who used the name were dead before they pulled us out . . . missiles, AA guns, enemy planes."

"Yes," Seerbacker said softly. "Hell of a war . . ."

Peck, sweating, pale, angry and weary, came toward them. There remained only a hundred yards of runway left to clear. He said, towering over Gant: "We won't make it, mister—if you don't get that bird out of here before the Reds arrive, we're all bound for Lubyanka!"

Gant shook his head. "You have a minute in hand, Chief," he said. Peck stared at him, his mouth opening and closing, his eyes reflecting baffled incomprehension which changed slowly to conviction.

"If you say so," he muttered and turned away, back toward the hoses, exhorting his men blasphemously.

"You sure impress the hell out of the chief," Seerbacker said with a thin smile. "I just hope you don't have to do it to the Russians."

"ETA two minutes and thirty seconds," Fleischer said. "He keeps asking for you, sir. He wants convincing—I don't think I've done a very good job."

"To hell with that, Dick. Keep stalling him—does he look like surfacing? Has he asked any awkward questions?"

"No, sir. He seems just naturally suspicious—not as if he's looking for anything special."

Powdery snow blew into Gant's face. For a moment, distracted by the voices, he glanced up at the cloudy sky half-hidden by the shreds of mist. Then he realized that it was the vanguard of Peck's blizzard. The hose-men were still on schedule. He smiled to himself, and pulled off the parka. Peck's men were forty yards away from the Firefox. The de-icing team trundled past him, and stopped to look inquiringly in his direction. He nodded at them, at which they seemed vastly relieved, and the giant garden-spray was wheeled speedily toward the *Pequod,* to be hauled aboard and stowed before the arrival of the Russians.

Gant waited, like a guest anxious to be gone, until Seerbacker had finished his conversation with his Exec.

Seerbacker seemed surprised that he was stripped to his anti-G suit once more. He smiled awkwardly. "I—er, of course . . ." he said.

"So long, Seerbacker—and thanks."

"Get out of here, you bum!" Seerbacker said with mock severity.

Gant nodded, and swung his foot to the lowest rung

of the pilot's ladder set in the fuselage. He climbed
up, and slid feet first into the cockpit. There, he
tugged on the integral helmet, plugged in the oxygen, the weapons-control jackplug, and the communications equipment. He needed first of all to taxi
gently back to the southern extremity of the floe,
where the snow had not, as yet, been cleared—it
would be slowing, he knew, but he needed the maximum distance to the ridge. He went through the
pre-start checks swiftly. He plugged in the anti-G
suit automatically, even as he read off the dials and
gauges that informed him of the condition of flaps,
brakes and fuel. The fuel-tanks, he saw, smiling
grimly, were satisfyingly full. It seemed eons since
there had been so much fuel in his universe. He
pressed the hood control and it swung down, locked
automatically, then he locked it manually. The handset issued him by Seerbacker was in the breast-pocket of the pressure-suit. He heard Fleischer's voice,
from a great distance, saying:

"ETA one minute and thirty seconds."

"You hear that, Gant?" Seerbacker's voice chimed
in. He continued, without waiting for a reply:
"Good luck, fella. Got to get Mr. Peck's suspicious
hoses stowed now, so get out of here!"

Gant gang-loaded the ignition, switched on the
starter motors, turned on the high-pressure cock,
and pressed the button. He heard, with relief, the
sound of a double explosion as the cartridge start
functioned. There was the same rapid, mounting
whirring that he had heard in the hangar at Bilyarsk, as the huge turbines began to build. He
switched in the fuel-booster, and eased open the
throttles, until the rpm gauges were steady at twenty-seven percent. He paused for only a second, then
pushed the throttles open, until he reached the fifty-
five percent rpm, then he released the brakes.

The Firefox did not move.

He hauled back the throttles, and applied the
brakes again. Even though he knew instantly what

it was, and knew that it could be cured, his own failure to anticipate it made him weak and chill with sweat.

He opened the hood, tugged open the face-mask, and yelled into the handset: "Seerbacker—get those hoses over here—on the double!"

"What in the hell is it, Gant—can't you leave us ..."

"Get over here! The wheels, they've frozen in!"

"You're stuck—with those engines, man?"

Already, even as Seerbacker apparently argued with him, he saw Peck and the others tugging the hoses toward the aircraft.

"If I try and pull myself out, I'll end up on my belly!"

Looking over the side of the cockpit, he saw Seerbacker's face looking up at him. Seerbacker was openly grinning. Steam billowed around him, snow flew up around the cockpit of the Firefox as the superheated steam was played carefully over the embedded wheels. Gant had not needed to warn Peck that if he played too much steam onto the tires, at too high a pressure, he would, literally, melt them.

Peck had understood. He emerged from beneath the fuselage, looked up at Gant, and said into his handset: "O.K., Major Gant—now, for God's sake, get out of here!"

Gant signaled him with the thumbs-up, closed the hood once more, checked the gauges, and opened the throttles, until the rpm gauge once more showed fifty-five percent. He released the brakes, the aircraft jolted out of the pits which the wheels and the applied steam had made, and rolled forward. Peck, Seerbacker and the others were moving away swiftly, tugging the thick, snaking hoses after them. Already, men were emerging from the *Pequod*, dressed in civilian parkas, the decoy scientists and technicians who should, by virtue of Seerbacker's ploy, occupy the floe when the Russians arrived.

Gant turned the aircraft, and headed down the floe, directly in the line of the runway. He kept the Firefox completely straight on course. He would need his own tracks on his return.

The gray sea was ahead of him. He searched for any sign of the Russian submarine. There was nothing. Probably, the captain had decided not to surface until he arrived and stopped engines at the *Pequod*'s position, something to do with psychological surprise. Whatever it was, Gant was grateful on behalf of Seerbacker and his crew. No one would visually sight the Firefox.

He turned the plane in a semi-circle, lined up on his own tire tracks in the surface snow, and opened the throttles. Almost immediately, he felt the restraint of the surface snow, the inability of the aircraft with normal take-off power to accelerate sufficiently. He could not use too much power. It would have the effect of digging in the nose, changing the relative airflow over the surfaces of the plane. He would, in fact, slow the plane if he used more power. There was little impression of speed until he passed over the spot on the ice where he had parked, and joined the smoothed, polished surface of the ice-runway blasted out for him by Peck and his men. Only now could he see the ridge, a tiny hump ahead of him. He could not see, in the poor visibility, the gap of thirty feet that had been carved in its face. The undercarriage shook free of the restraining snow, and he felt the plane lurch forward as if freed from glue or treacle. Now he was able to open the throttles, push up the rpm, and gather speed. The only impression of speed was from the crinkled, roughened edge of the runway as it flowed past him at an increasing rate. He had to be right in the center of the crude runway because he couldn't use the brakes to steer on the ice. They would have no effect. The rudder would not operate effectively until he reached a speed of eighty-five knots. At that moment he was at a little more than fifty.

As his eyes strained into the shredding mist, he heard, coming from a great distance, but with utter clarity, Seerbacker's voice.

"Good luck, man. Can't stop to talk, we've got visitors!" The voice had come from the handset.

His body was chilled, but he sweated. The second it took for him to pass into that region of speed which returned the power of steering to him seemed like an age. Then his speed topped ninety knots, and he centered the Firefox smoothly on the runway. He eased open the throttles, and the rpm needle seemed to leap with a jerk across the face of the dial. He saw the gap rushing at him; now that his eyes had a point of focus in the diffused whiteness of the floe, he was suddenly aware of his speed, transferred from his dials to the landscape. In cold air, he recited to himself, he needed less distance for take off. He did not believe it, not for a split-second.

The gap leaped at him, the distance it had been from him eaten by the huge engines. He was through the gap at 150 knots, and 170 was his take-off speed. He shoved the throttles into reheat, and pulled back on the stick. He dare not now plough back into the soft surface snow where Peck had had no time to clear the runway.

He could see the snow—he swore that he could see it, the point where the runway of ice ended. It was impossible. It passed under the plane's belly as he hauled back on the stick. He knew the undercarriage was clear of the floe, yet there was no impression of climbing.

In the rear-view mirror, Gant saw a cloud of snow belly out behind him, caused by the sudden down-thrust of the jets. The Firefox squatted, it seemed for an instant, nose-high, then, like a limb tearing itself free of restraining, glutinous mud, the aircraft pulled away from the floe. Gant trimmed flaps up, and retracted the undercarriage. The airspeed indicator flicked over, and he pushed the throttles forward. The plane kicked him in the back, and he felt the anti-G suit compensate for the sudden surge of acceleration. He checked the fuel flow, saw that all the needles were in the green, and hauled the aircraft into a vertical climb.

The climb toward the cloud took no more than a few seconds. As he entered the cloud, the Mach-meter crossed the figure 1—then 1.1, 1.2, 1.3, 1.4 . . .

The Firefox burst out of the cloud at 22,000 feet, into dazzling sunlight, cloudless, vast blue.

He had taken off heading due north. Now he set his course, punching out the coordinates for his crossing-point on the Finnish coast. He banked the plane round to a heading of 210 degrees, still climbing. The maximum altitude of which the Firefox was reputedly capable was in excess of 120,000 feet —more than twenty-five miles high. Gant intended to use as much of that staggering height as he could. It was unlikely, he knew, that he would be able to avoid infra-red detection, even at that height. However, moving as fast as the aircraft was capable, in a vast leap over the Barents Sea, it would be impossible for any interception to take place. A little before he crossed the coast, he would descend to sea level, and begin his complicated, top-speed dash across Finland to the Gulf of Bothnia, and Stockholm.

There was no aircraft that could touch him, no missile that could home on him, at that height, that speed. He smiled to himself as the altimeter indicated 50,000 feet and still climbing. Now, he thought, now he could put the Firefox through its paces, really *fly* the great plane. . . .

There was a fierce, cold joy in him, his closest approximation to an ecstatic emotion. There was nothing to compare, he knew, not with this.

He had read the army psychiatrist's report in Saigon—he had broken into the records office, late at night. An emotional cripple, that's what they had called him, though not in those words—an emotional cripple scarred for life by his early experiences. That Clarkville crap that he had fed the head-shrinker, he'd based his judgment on that, his judgment of a man who had flown more than fifty combat missions, who was the best, the judgment of a fat-assed head-shrinker hundreds of miles from the nearest 'Cong soldier, or missile-launcher.

He calmed the adrenalin that was beginning to course through his system. There was no point, he told himself, no point at all. He was the best. Buckholz knew it, knew it when he picked him. The Firefox climbed through 60,000 feet.

There was no thought for Upenskoy, for Baranovich, and Kreshin, and Semelovsky, and all the others. Since he had left Bilyarsk, they had dropped from his mind, gone more completely than faded, sepia photographs of the dead on wall and mantel.

Tretsov saw him punching through 60,000 feet, the vapor-trail ahead and below him was clear against the gray sea across a gap in the cloud. He knew it was Gant. There was infra-red, but no radar image on his screen. It had to be the stolen Mig-31.

Tretsov's mind worked like surgical steel. He knew what he had to do. He knew Gant's file, knew his experience in combat. His own combat experience, in the old Mig-21, was limited to engagements with Israeli Phantoms in the Middle East as a very young pilot seconded to the Egyptian Air Force, one of a select few reinforcing the inadequate pilots the Red Air Force had trained. Gant was better than he was . . .

On paper.

Gant had flown the Mig-31 for perhaps five hours —less. Tretsov had flown the aircraft for upwards of two hundred hours. Gant wanted to complete his

mission. Tretsov had Voskov to avenge. And fear
—always, the fear. He would kill Gant. He had to.

He had to get into the tail-cone of the other Mig,
so that the missiles would have the best chance of
homing on the heat-source of the huge engines—
and because Gant's infra-red would only pick him
up when it was too late to do anything about it. At
that moment, watching the Mig still climbing steadily, he knew that Gant was not aware of him, that
crossing his path and being on Gant's starboard flank,
the infra-red's blind spot hid him temporarily. He
would have to slot in swiftly behind the American,
and then . . .

The Mig moved above him now, through his own
cruising height of 70,000 feet, still climbing. He
changed course, still holding a visual sighting on
the contrail, confirming the information of his
screen. He eased the Firefox PP 2 in behind the
American until the bright orange blip on the screen
was directly ahead of him, along the central ranging
bar. The thought-guided weapons system launched
two of the Anab missiles and he watched them slide
up the ranging bars, homing on the brighter blip of
the American's heat-source.

The ECM equipment bleeped horrendously in Gant's
earphones, tearing at his memory. He saw the two
missiles, sliding up the ranging bars toward him.
Impossible, but there . . . The mind deliberated, refused to comprehend, sought the source of the heat-
seeking missiles—even as the body responded, seized
the electronic means of survival, reaching back into
old patterns and grabbing at an old technique.

There was one, he knew, of avoiding infra-red
missiles—only one chance. It had been used by Israeli pilots in the Six-Day War, and by Americans
in Vietnam. If he could change direction with sufficient suddenness, then the heat-source from his
engines would be lost to the tracking sensors in the

nose of the missiles and they would be unable to maintain or regain contact with the Firefox.

He chopped the throttles, pulled the stick back and over into a zoom climb, seeking to bend the plane's course at an acute angle to his former course, removing the heat-source of his engines from the sensors of the closing missiles. He rolled the aircraft to the right at the same time, and allowed the nose to drop, following a curve which brought him under the line of the missile's path. His vision tunnelled with the G-effect. He stared at the G-meter, and saw that he was pulling plus 8-G. If his vision narrowed any more, he knew it would be the direct precursor of a black-out. Ten G, and he would black out for certain, and the plane could go out of control. All his vision now showed him was the ominous G-meter, the pressure suit a distant sensation as it clamped on his legs and stomach. He cursed the fact of finding himself with a lower G-tolerance at that critical moment in time.

The missiles, suddenly and violently altered in position on the screen, slid past him on their original course, past the point in space and time of expected impact. They had lost the scent and would continue, vainly, until their fuel ran out and they dropped into the sea.

He eased back on the stick, and his vision opened, like blinds being drawn in a room. His speed was beginning to fall off, and he found himself sweating desperately. He had almost been taken; like an inexperienced boy. There was nothing on the screen. Tretsov, though Gant did not know it, was still directly behind him and in the blind spot of the infra-red detection. A sense of panic mounted in him. He had to find the enemy visually, or not at all. He was blind, a blind man in the same room as a psychopath. The cold fear trickled down his body, inside the pressure-suit. He suspected the nature of the enemy, but would not admit it yet.

The pilot of the other plane—aircraft it had to be —had obviously climbed to follow him, angry no doubt at his failure to press home the surprise, make the quick kill.

In the rear-view mirror, Gant caught a glint of sunlight off a metal surface. Still nothing on the radar. Now he knew for certain. Baranovich and Semelovsky had not immobilized the second Firefox by means of the hangar fire. Somehow, whatever damage had been done had been repaired, and they had sent it after him.

Now he felt very cold. The rivulets of sweat beneath his arms chilled his sides, his waist. Beneath the pressure-suit, he could sense the clammy coldness of his vest. The other plane was the equal of his, the mirror-image—and the pilot was vastly more experienced . . .

The mind proceeded, its infection of imagination unabated, raging in his system while the body calculated that if they continued on their climb turn, the Russian would intercept him. The eyes picked up the glint of light again in the mirror, the hands pushed open the throttles savagely, and the body was comforted by the release of energy from the huge turbines. The body was pressed back into the couch.

The body stopped the climb and pulled the Firefox even more sharply to the left. The Russian kept with him, coming inside him to the left, closing the range. Gant pulled even tighter to the left, then straightened out with a suddenness that caused the inertia of the head to bang the helmet against the cockpit. His hand operated the lever, and the couch dropped into its "battle position," flattening the body almost to the horizontal.

In the mirror, the Russian stayed with him, and the body was only able to hold off the hunter behind from an optimum firing position which the Russian pilot would now be seeking, now that he had wasted two of his four missiles. He might even

be closing for a cannon burst, to cripple and slow
his quarry.

The man was good, the mind admitted, overheat-
ing with its own fever. It was unable to free itself
from past and future, the moments before, the moments to come. He had been taken—whatever he
did, the Russian would stay with him, behind him,
closing the range.

The body registered the appearance of the second Firefox on the screen as an orange blip. It was
old information, useless to the body. He already
knew what plane it was tucked behind him.

The body tried another stratagem, because the
Russian's plane was coming into the "up-sun" position. Gant flicked the aircraft to the left, then continued into a barrel-roll. At the same time, he saw
in the mirror the series of ragged puffs of mist from
the wings of the Russian plane, the burst of cannon fire they signified. Orange globules drifted with
apparent slowness toward him, accelerating as under a great depth of water to overtake him. Tretsov
had fired because he, too, was on edge, anxious to
end the developing drama, make the fictitious quick
kill. The power of his aircraft lulled him into precipitate action.

The Russian, now that Gant was in the roll and
realizing that the cannon burst had gone wide,
would expect him to turn into the line of the sun.
Instead, he held the roll another ninety degrees,
checked and pulled on the stick—the Firefox shuddered through its length, and Gant's stomach muscles cramped up, the vision narrowing again to the
long tunnel. He screamed into the face-mask to reduce the effects of the mounting, stunning G-force.
The G-meter registered plus 9, he saw with his
severely limited vision of the control panel.

As he came out of the roll, he saw the Russian
plane ahead of him. The mind shouted with relief,
the sudden prospect of an optimal firing position
as his vision cleared and he saw the Russian plane

emerging from the expanding diaphragm of the lens
his vision had become. He was in the Russian's tail
cone, at a range of six hundred yards. He thought,
and two Anab missiles were launched. The aircraft
shuddered again, straightened, and he watched the
missiles slide home. He had aimed via the aiming
system, a reflective panel in front of the windscreen,
since he had no guidance just as the Russian had
possessed none. The thought-guidance system was
linked to the radar, not infra-red.

Tretsov had been unable to direct the missiles
once he had fired, without the radar image, and
Gant now saw, with a stunned sense of defeat, that
he was unable to do so either. He saw the Russian
pilot use his own trick, chopping the throttles and
pulling the aircraft into a climb and roll to the right.
The Anabs drove harmlessly past, seeking the heat-
source the Russian had whisked away from them.

Gant realized that the mind had interfered with
the body, infected it. It was like the last days in Vietnam, before the hospital. A sense of the failure of
the past, and a present inadequacy, crushed him for
a moment. He was flying badly now, as then—on
raw nerves and a draining supply of mental energy.
He was afraid again. He could be dead—already
the matrix of circumstances which had made his
death inevitable might have been established. It
might already be too late to initiate an action that
would save him.

The body, functioning a split second below its
unimpaired best, wrenched the plane to the right.
Again, the G-forces momentarily stupefied body
and mind. Vision closed in. He followed the Russian.
He had been too quick, too eager, squeezing the
thought like a firing-button, loosing the missiles.

It was too late to calm himself. He was committed now. He was the electronic chessmaster who had
lifted his hand from the piece he had elected to
move. There was no going back, no reappraisal.
He had to fly as he was, the system buckling under

the flow of emotion, the adrenalin pumping through him, memory flickering on a screen as if lit by flames.

He eased the controls, and the gray Arctic Ocean swung slowly across his head as his eyes quartered the airspace. The search was frantic because he had lost the Russian again. The sea slid down behind his shoulder. Then his eyes caught a reflection of light in the mirror. He had found the Russian, who had used Gant's own trick of the barrel-roll. He was now behind him, closing the range rapidly, coming for the kill—and making certain that Gant would have no time, no room, in which to wriggle away; small fish from hungry predator. The body recognized that the Russian was good—the mind gibbered that he was dead already.

Gant trod the left rudder, and smacked the stick hard over, pulling the Firefox to the left, seeing as he did so a missile flick away from the Russian plane, bright, mesmeric orange. He wrenched the column back, feeling the G-forces sagging him deep into the couch, the awful pressure for a moment on legs and stomach and the mask pulling at the flesh of his face, his head pinned to his chest . . .

The mind retreated from the sudden pain, leaving the clarity of the body that he needed. Then the plane kicked in response to his hand on the column and there was a wild shuddering through its length.

He was in a flat spin, the nose of the plane pitching fifteen degrees and more above and below the horizon. There was a moment of relief as the Anab was left targetless high above him—then alarm spread as the G-pressure mounted on the meter, through 8½, toward 9-G. His airspeed plummeted toward the 100 knot marker.

There was a clicking in his headphones as the automatic igniters worked madly to prevent a flame-out in the huge turbines behind him. The disturbed airflow of the spin was dousing the engines like a liquid, and they were being relit every half second. His eyes flicked to the rpm gauges, and saw that they were down to sixty percent and the needles flickering. Before he realized it, he had tumbled through eight thousand feet, the altimeter unwinding madly.

He lost all sight of the Russian aircraft, but Tretsov had watched him, and thrust his own aircraft into a dive. The American was a sitting target.

Gant went through the SOP for a flat spin, applying opposite rudder and shoving forward on the stick. The Firefox did not respond. Now, the Russian above him and no doubt following him down had no existence or reality. Now he was fighting the plane itself as it plunged out of control toward the sea. He moved the column back and forth, jockeyed the throttles to get the nose down and to give him better airflow over the elevators. He was trying to put the plane into a more nose-down attitude in order to pick up speed and regain control.

For perhaps two seconds, nothing happened, except the continued chatter of the auto-ignition and the unwinding of the altimeter. Already he was down to thirty thousand feet, and still falling like a leaden leaf. In desperation, he reached his hand for the controls, and dumped the undercarriage to provide a sudden shock of drag on the plane—something the body remembered from a conversation, a story long before. The tail lifted with a twitch, and the nose dipped suddenly and the spin steepened. He applied opposite rudder, and opened the throttles. He was twenty thousand feet up, the altimeter still unwinding but he was back in control. He exerted pressure on the column to level out, and retracted the undercarriage. He pulled the column steadily toward him, and eased the throttles further open. The plane began to level out. The body breathed, its first dragging inhalation since the spin had begun.

Then he saw with an icy shock that the Russian

was a bright glow on the screen. The pilot had followed him down, battening on him as he recovered from the spin. The speed of his approach, Gant calculated, was in excess of Mach 1.6. The Russian knew he could kill, that he could get close enough to finish Gant. There was to be no margin for error, no slight gap through which brilliance or luck might slip.

Gant saw him in the mirror, an image leaping at him. The mind cracked open, gibbering in the moment of its death. The orange globules that sprang out of the puffs of mist at the wing edges chased him at a frightening speed, overhauling him. He flung the plane aside, as if trying to avoid some charging animal, and saw in the mirror the Russian turning to follow him, turning inside Gant's heat-cone, jockeying for the optimum position with one missile left.

There was a false relief that he knew was vapid and unreal even as he felt it; to have escaped the cannon fire was meaningless, a prolongation of seconds.

The body, struggling to master the crying mind, fought to regain control. His hand opened the throttles and he eased the column back and to the right. The mind cried out for something to fire at the tailing Russian, something that would operate on an enemy behind.

The mind's imperative overrode the body. It was a command the body would never have considered. The mind screamed the order to the thought-guidance system, and the last of the decoys in the Rearward Defense Pod was jettisoned. There was a blinding light in the rear mirror that burned eyesight as the decoy heat-source, the incandescent ball, detached itself and hung for a moment in the air. Then the mirror erupted in burning light, brighter than the ball. The body, stunned by its own apparent inactivity, sensed the shock-wave.

Gant held the Firefox in the tight turn. As he steadied the aircraft, there was nothing within the

circle he was describing in the air except a pall of
black, oily smoke, lit from within by livid, orange
flame. Glistening fragments of metal tumbled down
from the smoke-pall, like metal leaves turning in
the sunlight.

He understood what had happened. While the
mind spewed its relief, its incoherent sense of escape and victory, it realized that the incandescent
ball of fire released from the tail of the Firefox had
been greedily swallowed by one of the huge intakes
of the Russian Firefox and it had exploded instan-
taneously.

Gant wanted to throw up. He choked on his
vomit, preventing it from filling the face-mask and
suffocating him. The mind invaded the body, and
he realized that he was shaking all over.

While he remained capable of effort, he switched
in the auto-pilot and then punched in, hesitantly
and with a vast effort of memory, the coordinates
of his course. The Firefox banked round, steadied,
and headed for Finland, while he lay back in the
couch, weak, empty, shaking.

Eventually, he knew he would recover. Then he
would take over the manual control of the plane.
But not yet, not just yet . . .

The Mig-31, NATO codenamed Firefox, and the
single, priceless example of its type, cruised at 80,-
000 feet, at a speed of Mach 3.7, toward the hidden
coast of Finland.

*Pick up the pulse-pounding action where
FIREFOX left off . . .*

FIREFOX DOWN

Craig Thomas

Bestselling author of FIREFOX

FIREFOX IS MISSING . . .
EVERYONE WANTS IT BACK . . .
THE RACE IS *ON* TO RECOVER THE FIREFOX!

FIREFOX: the NATO codename for a supersonic Soviet warplane so
deadly it can wipe the West out of the skies.

Stolen for the West by ace U.S. pilot Mitchell Gant, the Firefox is shot
down in a hair-raising dogfight. Now the plane lies submerged
beneath the icy waters of a frozen Finnish lake, waiting to be salvaged
by British Intelligence. And Mitchell Gant is running for his life, from
the tracker dogs and helicopter patrols of the KGB border guard. As
international tension mounts, East and West wage a desperate
offstage battle – a frantic race to FIND THE FIREFOX!

ADVENTURE/THRILLER   0 7221 8449 2   £2.25

Also by Craig Thomas and in Sphere paperback:

FIREFOX   SEA LEOPARD   RAT TRAP
SNOW FALCON   WOLFSBANE   JADE TIGER

A selection of bestsellers from SPHERE

FICTION

TOUGH GUYS DON'T DANCE	Norman Mailer	£2.50 ☐
FIRE IN THE ICE	Alan Scholefield	£2.25 ☐
SOUVENIR	David Kaufelt	£2.50 ☐
WHAT NIALL SAW	Brian Cullen	£1.25 ☐
POSSESSIONS	Judith Michael	£2.95 ☐

FILM & TV TIE-INS

MOG	Peter Tinniswood	£1.95 ☐
LADY JANE	A. C. H. Smith	£1.95 ☐
IF I WERE KING OF THE UNIVERSE	Danny Abelson	£1.50 ☐
BEST FRIENDS	Jocelyn Stevenson	£1.50 ☐

NON-FICTION

WEEK ENDING: THE CABINET LEAKS	Ian Brown and James Hendrie	£2.95 ☐
THE POLITICS OF CONSENT	Francis Pym	£2.95 ☐
THE SPHERE ILLUSTRATED HISTORY OF BRITAIN VOLUMES 1, 2 AND 3	Ed. Kenneth O. Morgan	£3.95 each ☐

All Sphere books are available at your local bookshop or newsagent, or can be ordered direct from the publisher. Just tick the titles you want and fill in the form below.

Name _____

Address _____

_____

Write to Sphere Books, Cash Sales Department, P.O. Box 11, Falmouth, Cornwall TR10 9EN.

Please enclose a cheque or postal order to the value of the cover price plus:

UK: 55p for the first book, 22p for the second book and 14p for each additional book ordered to a maximum charge of £1.75.

OVERSEAS: £1.00 for the first book plus 25p per copy for each additional book.

BFPO & EIRE: 55p for the first book, 22p for the second book plus 14p per copy for the next 7 books, thereafter 8p per book.

Sphere Books reserve the right to show new retail prices on covers which may differ from those previously advertised in the text or elsewhere, and to increase postal rates in accordance with the PO.